Another

# SAILING
# Dangerous
# WATERS

## D. Andrew McChesney

**outskirts**press

DENVER, COLORADO

Sailing Dangerous Waters
Another Stone Island Sea Story
All Rights Reserved.
Copyright © 2014 D. Andrew McChesney
v2.0

Cover Image created and provided by D. Andrew McChesney.

Outskirts Press, Inc.
http://www.outskirtspress.com

ISBN: 978-1-4787-2189-5

Library of Congress Control Number: 2013917663

Outskirts Press and the "OP" logo are trademarks belonging to Outskirts Press, Inc.

PRINTED IN THE UNITED STATES OF AMERICA

*Chapter One*

# The Long Wait

A rivulet of perspiration trickled down Edward Pierce's forehead and threatened to flow into his left eye. He squinted, changing the contours of his face so the sweat dripped off the tip of his nose. As the drop fell free, the persistent fly that had harried him for the past half hour landed on his right cheek. He swatted at it, ineffectively.

"We should rest. Tom grows weary." Pierce was one of four men moving easily through the glade, balancing the desire to keep moving with the need to rest. Towering evergreens blocked the February sun's brightness but did not ease the heat felt at their roots. No breeze cooled those moving through the undergrowth. Other creatures had sense enough to wait for the evening's relative coolness.

"I'm quite all right," Tom Morgan panted from the rear.

"Edward is right." In the lead, the Original Vespican's diction and accent strongly contrasted with his appearance. Darker than the others, he wore a breechcloth, linen leggings, and deerskin moccasins. His uncovered hair fell loosely about his shoulders. Two nondescript feathers were woven amongst its strands.

"If we are in no haste," asked Isaac Hotchkiss, "why do we push so?"

"I must say, you learn quickly. I've seen those raised on the edge of the wilderness not master life here as quickly. That you are seamen amazes me that much more."

Seafarers or not, the three seemed accustomed to life in the forest. Baltican in appearance, they dressed more completely but similarly to their guide. In the afternoon's heat, none wore more than buckskin trousers and homespun linen shirts. Pierce and Hotchkiss sported old misshapen round-brimmed hats. Tom Morgan wore a fur cap, complete with the striped tail of the creature. He walked with a noticeable limp and worked harder to maintain their leisurely pace.

"We have an excellent teacher," replied Pierce. "And Isaac is right to wonder about our haste." He swiped half-heartedly at the fly.

Tom sank gratefully to the ground in spite of insisting he wasn't winded. The three carefully leaned their muskets against a nearby stump. The leader's rifle, a fine precision-made firearm was also within quick reach. They weren't hunting, nor did they fear any immediate danger. Still they remained alert, not knowing what threat might materialize out of the deep forested groves.

"The only haste is on Tom's part, I believe," said Isaac. "Were I en route to see someone as dear as she, a little afternoon heat would not stop me."

"Nor would a missing leg, Mr. Hotchkiss." Tom twisted and stretched, the wooden end of his right leg clattering against an exposed root.

"Does it pain you, lad?"

"Not at all, Doctor. I believe it has healed completely over the past months. A bit of fatigue from continual movement is all it is."

"Do I examine it and be assured? Perhaps the stump is not callused enough for such a prolonged journey."

"If you choose to, sir. But any aches I feel are due the awkwardness of movement and not any tenderness."

"Then I will forego a look, Tom. But you must promise to notify me of any additional discomfort."

"Of course, Doctor."

"Edward," said Isaac, addressing the second individual. "Is this similar to your search for the herbs needed to treat Tom's leg?"

"Yes, but we were mounted and did not roam so far away from the settlements. I'm sure Lord Sutherland was more troubled then because I was out of his immediate control."

"With your behavior over the past months, and my own minute

influence, I believe he is more at ease with your current absence," said Dr. Robertson.

The four drank moderately from the water bags they carried. Silence ensued as each became lost in his own thoughts.

Edward Pierce took his rest stretched out on the soft carpet of the forest floor, his eyes closed and his breathing slowed. But he was not asleep; his active mind and the ever-present fly would not allow it.

Several months ago, Pierce had been quite despondent, depressed by the capture of HMS *Island Expedition* and its internment by the Tritonish Consulate in Brunswick, New Guernsey. He had also been very worried about Tom Morgan's health. The schooner's senior midshipman, wounded in the battle with HRMS *Hawke*, had his leg amputated. Healing had proceeded normally until a deadly infection set in. The schooner's surgeon, Dr. Matheson, and one called in by the consulate, a Dr. Blackburn, had been unable to halt Tom's deterioration. Then Dr. Robertson had arrived, and with a combination of modern Baltican and ancient Kalish medicines, reversed the trend toward the midshipman's ultimate demise. With Tom Morgan on the mend, and with Dr. Robertson's assurances that as a Vespican Unity Congress delegate, he would work to obtain the release of the schooner and her crew, Pierce had found himself in a much cheerier state of mind. But that had been in September of 1803.

Now, near the end of February, 1804, Pierce knew that the Baltican-educated, half-Rig'nie doctor was making his best effort, but progress was slow. *Island Expedition* was still tied up at the pier in Brunswick's harbor, guarded by marines from the Tritonish Consulate and Vespican militia. While he and his crew were treated most cordially by the consul and his staff, and indeed by the local Vespicans, they were restricted in their activities. Pierce and Hotchkiss his first lieutenant were not permitted aboard the schooner at the same time. Only a third of the crew was permitted aboard on any given day, as a way of ensuring the vessel did not put to sea. That, of course, would have been a foolhardy venture, as the schooner was moored deep within the harbor, and would have had to pass by many Tritonish-flagged merchantmen, which upon word from the consulate could easily prevent an escape to the open sea. At times there were also various Tritonish warships in the harbor, the presence of which further prohibited any rash attempt to leave.

As the months slowly passed with no resolution to their predicament, Pierce slowly lost the optimism that Dr. Robertson's initial appearance had brought. It should have been easy to see that the crew of *Island Expedition* was not a band of Galway Rebels and pirates. Perhaps the sticking point was in convincing the Tritonish that they had come from a different world to locate a lost and legendary island. Had he not experienced it himself, Pierce could see that such a tale would be unbelievable to those hearing it. Now he wanted most of all to sail from the Vespican port where they were held, return to the island, see to the colonists' well-being, and eventually return to England.

Pierce had grown more morose, and as his spirits had declined, his shortness with consulate's staff and schooner's crewmembers had increased. Finally, when word was received that HRMS *Furious* would arrive to take on supplies and effect repairs, Dr. Robertson suggested some time in the wilderness. Following their capture by the Tritonish Navy's Flying Squadron, *Furious* had served to transport Pierce and Hotchkiss to Brunswick. It had also escorted and guarded *Island Expedition* as it sailed to the same port under a prize crew. Pierce particularly detested Lowell Jackson, captain of the frigate, an exceedingly rigid disciplinarian. He routinely meted out the severest and cruelest punishments to his crew. If in Jackson's presence again, would Pierce be able to control the rage within, and refrain from bodily attacking him?

He had agreed wholeheartedly with the doctor's suggestion of a small wilderness expedition, cumulating in a visit to the doctor's Kalish people. He would not have to face the hated Jackson, nor see

Leona with him. Pierce did not love her, but the situation would have been awkward. Both Jacksons, husband and wife, were known for their lustful wanderings. While she complained privately of his, he jealously suspected, and perhaps rightly so, every man who might be even innocently in her company. If he did not directly challenge any such individual, he often worked in the background to bring the unfortunate person to personal, financial, or professional grief. The frontier journey was the best solution for Pierce's safety.

Dr. Robertson stirred, stood up, shouldered his bag, and picked up his rifle. "We should push on a bit more. We are near the river and will camp there for the night. If fortunate, we find a canoe in which we might continue our journey to Shostolamie's village."

The four reached the river in the early evening and encamped for the night. The next morning they searched for, and after a short time found a serviceable canoe a few hundred yards upstream.

Pierce was concerned that taking the craft might be theft. "No," replied Dr. Robertson. "It is unmarked. Those who left it do not intend immediate reuse. Kalish custom is that such equipage is for all. Should one require its subsequent use, he would place his personal totem on it. Then we would know the canoe is reserved."

"An amazing display of trust, Doctor."

"Indeed, Isaac. Many values and beliefs of the Original People differ from those of Balticans, or in your case, Europeans. Traditionally we are not so concerned with individual possessions. Most things belong to all. We will use this canoe to reach my father's place. Someone else will then use it for another journey and leave it for yet another party."

That day they paddled upstream against the gentle current. The river was broad and flowed easily so they did not need to overly exert themselves. Nevertheless, when they rested along the river at night, they were sore from bringing unused muscles into play.

Early the next afternoon they spotted smoke from several cooking fires blanketing the treetops beyond the next river bend. Dr. Robertson guided the canoe to a smooth beach upstream of the large Original People's village. On the open water they were spotted immediately, and their guide mentioned that they had no doubt been observed and their progress followed since early that morning. As the sharp prow of the canoe grated on the sand, Pierce and Hotchkiss jumped out. Lighter now, it floated free, and the two remaining aboard gave a final tremendous stroke with their paddles. Pierce and Hotchkiss grabbed the gunwales and hauled the craft farther up the beach. The doctor got out and helped steady it so that Morgan could climb out.

A large crowd of children, many of them naked in the afternoon heat, gathered around. They pressed close to Dr. Robertson and shouted with good-natured joy. The children did not fear the Englishmen, but having never met them, avoided getting too close. The youngsters' noise set the dogs to barking, and soon the entire village was awash in the canine din. At the racket's crescendo, the older children and adults abandoned their normal routines and headed for the beach and the recently arrived party.

While Pierce could not fathom the words, he could tell by the expressions that this was a joyous occasion, and that as guests of the doctor, they were welcome. Many greetings and well- wishes were exchanged by the doctor and the village inhabitants. Then the crowd quieted, and a small party of important villagers made their way forward. Pierce had met some before and easily recognized them.

The old man, his hair turning gray, the lines and wrinkles beginning to dominate his features, still moved with dignity and bearing, even though he was attired only in a breech cloth, moccasins, and woven grass cape. Feathers dangled seemingly at random from his hair, and leather bands encircled his upper arms. Dr. Robertson approached him, made a small gesture of respect, and the two formally embraced. The old man said something that brought a smattering of laughter from the crowd.

The old man cleared his throat, a habit Pierce remembered, smiled broadly, and said, "Now here smart man. Ha! Ha! Drink coffee like Dream Chief. Him plenty smart! Bring coffee, Edward Pierce?"

"Of course, Revered Shostolamie, Dream Chief of the Kalish People."

"Son teach you good, Edward Pierce." The old man shook Pierce's hand vigorously. "Shostolamie happy see Hotchkiss!" he said and shook his hand as well.

"Happy see Morgan. You still alive! Son good doctor!" Shostolamie laughed, shook Morgan's hand and clapped him on the shoulders.

An older white woman stood close by the Dream Chief's side.

"Mother!" said Doctor Robertson. They embraced, first in the manner of the Kalish, and then in a more Baltican fashion. "It gives me joy to see you again."

"As it does me, my son," she said.

"Gentlemen, may I present my mother, Alice Madison, wife of Dream Chief Shostolamie. Mother, please say hello to Commander Pierce, Lieutenant Hotchkiss, and Midshipman Morgan?" begged the doctor.

"Your servant ma'am," said Pierce, followed closely by similar expressions of greetings from the other two.

"I have heard much about you from the good doctor, your son. I am honored to finally meet you."

"And I you, Edward. May I call you 'Edward'?"

"I would be honored, ma'am."

"But you must call me 'Alice.' Or 'Mama Alice,' if the first doesn't fit with your ideas of social decorum."

"Of course, ma'am," responded Pierce. He was about to correct himself and add "Mama Alice" when another group of villagers pressed gently into the circle. Of these, Pierce recognized Bessie and her daughter Cecilia. The younger was Dr. Robertson's protégée and assistant, and had nursed Morgan in his recovery.

Night Fisher--the doctor's cousin, Bessie's husband, and Cecilia's father--was with them. His Kentish was on a level with Shostolamie's and he greeted the Englishmen with sincere but abrupt warmth. He spent an extra minute sizing up Morgan, but soon gave the one-legged midshipman a grin and pumped his hand vigorously.

Bessie beamed at Dr. Robertson, greeted him in the Kalish fashion, and allowed herself a quick smile and a perfunctory handshake with Pierce and Hotchkiss. Then, as was her habit regarding younger men in the presence of her daughter, she scowled. But when she turned to Morgan, her smile was wider and it lasted longer. She warmly embraced him in the fashion of her people, and surprised, Pierce saw the midshipman return the gesture with practiced ease.

Cecilia said hello to her cousin in the traditional way, and then acknowledged the presence of Pierce and Hotchkiss. "I'm very glad to see you both again," she said in nearly perfect Kentish. "I hope you enjoy your stay."

"I am sure we shall," said Pierce.

Then the young lady knelt before Morgan, her face full of joy and her eyes filled with tears of happiness. She spoke in Kalish, and whether the midshipman understood or not, Pierce did not know. Morgan knelt as well, facing her with an equivalent look of happiness on his face, and spoke several lines of Kalish. There were murmurs of approval from the crowd, and a few good-natured chuckles, as Morgan stumbled over some of the words. She reached for him in a variation of the ritual she had used to greet her cousin. He responded to her movements, having been coached by the doctor, or perhaps by Cecilia herself those many weeks ago in Brunswick. Their movements, their gestures, were slow and stately, a well-choreographed, traditional means of greeting someone very special. The formal, proscribed part of the greeting ritual over, the young couple melted into a warm embrace.

"Everybody meet! Everybody happy!" shouted Shostolamie. "We eat! Edward Pierce, drink coffee. Shostolamie drink coffee!"

Pierce could not sleep that night in spite of the large and delicious meal they had been served. The bed, in the fashion of the Original People was comfortable, clean, and airy, and he should have fallen into a deep slumber the moment he lay down. Had he consumed too much coffee? He often drank that much or more and never had a problem sleeping. No, he decided after several hours of wakefulness, coffee was not the problem. He was thinking of things that kept him awake, things that he usually did not dwell on as he fell asleep.

When Dr. Robertson had suggested a wilderness excursion to keep him out of harm's way, he had invited Hotchkiss along as well. Pierce's childhood friend had always expressed an interest in the lives of American Natives, and Robertson understood the similarities of the Original Peoples and the Indians of North America. He thought Hotchkiss would benefit in spending time with them. All were aware of the deep relationship that had developed between Tom Morgan and Cecilia as she had nursed him back to health. It would have been a tremendous affront to both, not to have included the midshipman in the visiting party.

All this explanation was perfectly ordinary and straightforward in nature. At this level, everything was as it seemed, and as it was intended. He was happy to be in Shostolamie's village, away from Jackson and his possible rage should he suspect any improper relationship between Pierce and his wife. Hotchkiss was ecstatically happy to experience even a brief moment of a life he had read about since childhood. And Morgan, of course, was extremely happy and very lucky to be with Cecilia once again.

That was the problem, and it became clear to Pierce as he lay quietly, breathing slowly, his eyes closed, feigning the appearance of sleep, but in reality, wide awake. Morgan had the opportunity to be with the one in his heart. How Pierce wished to be in England at that very moment, wrapped with passionate joy in Evangeline's embrace! That he wasn't, and that he wanted so much to be with her, pained him greatly.

Perhaps Morgan's present happiness made his aloneness all that more acute! Did his friend's great joy magnify his loneliness and make it that much more unbearable?

With sleep unable to overtake him, Pierce's mind raced through the night. He fought not to think too much of Evangeline, and tried to focus on the present situation regarding his vessel and crew. Could they ever convince the Tritonish officials they were not Galway Rebels? At times, he thought they were close to believing him. At others he felt he might as well try to make a river to flow upstream. Their one hope lay with the Vespican Unity Congress and then the Vespican Joint Council. Dr. Robinson, a Unity Congress delegate, had been pressing the issue, and Pierce had been somewhat upset to find the doctor away from the Bostwick sessions. Earlier that evening he had somewhat bluntly brought forth his objections to the doctor.

"But we have other pressing matters as well," Robertson explained. "Try as I may, I cannot keep debate focused on your plight. With the coming of summer, the Congress and the Joint Council have both adjourned. Many delegates have obligations they must attend to at home. There are short sessions in the latter half of February, but they are largely ceremonial--the seating of new delegates and the like."

"It is disappointing, Doctor," Pierce replied, "to know that nothing is being done at the moment."

"I do understand, and believe me, Commander, were the Congress meeting today, I would not be in Shostolamie's village. Rather, I would be pressing for a resolution regarding your internment. However, neither the Congress nor the Joint Council does anything more than get acquainted in these current sessions. There are speeches, ritualistic events, and dinners, sir, but no actual work ever gets done during the summer sessions. When cooler weather arrives, perhaps in May or June, then the real work occurs. When it does, please rest assured that I'll be there on your behalf."

The pallet next to Pierce rustled. Hotchkiss stirred and sat up.

Then he stole quietly from the lodge and into the warm moonlit night. He returned a few moments later, crawled onto his bed, and tossed about momentarily. From the sound of his breathing, he was soon asleep again.

While he and his crew enjoyed a quite benevolent detention at the Tritonish Consulate, and the honest hospitality of the Vespicans, the fact that they were trapped more than a world away from home gnawed a small but growing hole in Pierce's stomach. He was, however, grateful that Dr. Robinson had established a precarious correspondence with Harold Smythe and the other Englishmen on the island. At least they had an idea of the predicament that Pierce and *Island Expedition's* crew found themselves in.

Thinking of that made Pierce wonder if it was proper for the most senior officers to be away on what could be described as a holiday. He did not doubt the abilities of O'Brien the master, Dial or Spencer, master's mates, or Andrews the second senior midshipman. But was he remiss in his own duties to have left them on their own?

No, it was better he avoided Jackson while *Furious* was in port. Should he regard Pierce's absence with suspicion, he would be told that Pierce and the others had accompanied the convalescing Morgan, who sought to regain his strength in the wilderness.

As the eastern sky lightened with the coming of the new day, Pierce finally fell asleep.

The three Englishmen remained in the Kalish village until the end of March. Then reluctantly they set out to journey back to civilization. Pierce missed the lazy idyllic days of hunting, fishing, and learning the ways of nature. Some days he had done absolutely nothing, other than drink coffee and talk with the Kalish Dream Chief. But Pierce was aware of his responsibilities and knew he must return to Brunswick, his crew, and the interned schooner.

Hotchkiss had filled two journals with notes as he had

enthusiastically experienced the day-to-day lives of the Original People. He too regretted leaving, but like his captain, he knew duty required him to return.

Leaving was hardest for Morgan. His weeks in Shostolamie's village had been as near paradise as he would probably ever be. There were tears in his eyes, and tears in Cecilia's eyes as the three seamen and Dr. Robertson paddled downriver.

A week later they were back in Brunswick. Pierce and Hotchkiss resumed their residence at the Tritonish Consulate, each in the very room he had occupied upon arriving the previous July. Morgan, at his insistence, now berthed with the other midshipmen and warrant officers. His stump had healed, and as he was pronounced fit by the doctor, he did not rate a private room.

Pierce was relieved that no serious problems had arisen during their absence. The visit by HRMS *Furious* had been anti-climatic. There had been words between Jackson and his wife, and the former had spent much of the port visit in the company a local woman of somewhat shady reputation. Yet, true to his nature, Jackson had questioned his wife's romantic activities prior to his arrival. To Pierce's immense relief, he had not come under suspicion, but a military aide at the neighboring Gallician Consulate had. The young Gallician had looked too long and lustfully at Mrs. Jackson, and the captain had accused him of being her latest paramour. It could not be proven true or false, and diplomatic considerations between two warring nations in a neutral country further complicated matters. While Jackson openly flouted his tryst with the Brunswick woman, he did not actively pursue satisfaction regarding his wife's suspected indiscretions.

Practically speaking, Pierce was thankful for the latest of Jackson's lustful interests. Had he not been so involved with her, his probing and suspicious mind might have deduced the connection between Pierce and his wife. He chided himself for ever having been involved with

Leona Jackson. Such a relationship, in spite of the physical pleasures, was not necessarily worth the attendant problems.

Another effect of Jackson's somewhat lengthy port visit was that all Brunswick was afforded a view of his stentorian disciplinary means. Unlike many Tritonish Navy captains, Jackson did not permit his crew liberty while in port. He was afraid of desertion, and having seen firsthand the rigid and brutal means by which he controlled his men, Pierce would not have blamed them. It would have served the bastard well if half the crew had run.

It took only a few days for Pierce to settle into what had been and what would once again become routine. He made his visit aboard *Island Expedition* every third day. He attended various dinner and supper parties, hosted by well-to-do Brunswick merchants, bankers, and officials, or those held by either the Tritonish or Gallician Consuls. He took no real pleasure in these affairs, other than the chance to ascertain the current level of hostility between the two nations. He also used these events to gauge the resentment held against both by the local Vespicans, whose own nation was insultingly trod upon at every instance.

He thought to break off the relationship with Leona Jackson, and for several weeks after his return, saw her only at the various dinners. But when she knocked at his door late one night, the temptation was too great, the physical needs too intense, and she remained with him until the early morning hours. After she left, and as he lay exhausted, he wondered if he should refuse her renewed advances. Would rejecting her wantonness cause her to become a vengeful, deadly foe, who sought to destroy the one who had so recently been her lover?

The weeks passed by slowly, but soon it was May and the first snows came. On that particular day, Pierce shivered as he left the schooner and walked through the half-melted snow. He had planned to return directly to his room at the consulate, but the thought of a warm cup of coffee or even a glass of rum entertained him. He made up his mind, reversed his steps, and headed for the Frosty Anchor. That establishment had become a second home to Pierce and indeed all the hands from the English schooner.

Humphrey the owner greeted him as he entered. "Coffee is fresh, Commander. A cup, do you think?"

Pierce stamped the snow off his feet. "No, not today, I've had more than enough. But do you have it; a brandy or rum would surely warm a body."

"Aye, it would. Now you look positively frozen. Sit here, close to the fire, and I'll fetch a glass for you."

Pierce sat at the table, soaking in the heat of the roaring fire and all the while feeling the brandy, which he sipped slowly, spread its own warmth within him. He was slipping back into his despondent angry mood, and the weather certainly did not help. He tried to bury the frustration and anger in the back of his mind and appreciate the niceties of his current situation. He was deep in somewhat meditative thought when the voice broke through.

"Commander! Commander!" said Dr. Robertson with some urgency. "I had waited for you at the consulate, believing you would return there. But I cannot say I blame you in stopping to warm up."

A workman at the end of the counter looked at the doctor with contempt but said nothing. Perhaps he felt that the doctor, despite his prestige and well-made Baltican clothing, did not belong in even such a place as the Frosty Anchor. Some Vespicans had very little tolerance for Rig'nies in their midst. The doctor caught the glance and ignored it. Humphrey saw it as well and glared at the man, who soon turned back to his mug of ale.

"It is a raw day, Doctor. The weather fits my disposition, and I sought to warm them both."

"In that case, Edward, I have news that may warm your spirits as well. I depart in the morning for Bostwick. The Unity Congress resumes session next week, and I will go once again to put forth your case."

"That indeed is good news, sir. Now, will you have a glass with me?"

"Indeed, sir!"

"Then I must return to the consulate. I'm expected at a late dinner and do not have the means of begging off."

"Obligations have their rewards, Commander, as well as their distractions."

"Aye."

Pierce finished his second glass of brandy and accompanied by Dr. Robertson, made his wet and snowy way back to the Tritonish Consulate.

## Chapter Two

# Good News

O n a bright sunny day, early in October 1804, Edward Pierce sat in the comfortably warm stern cabin of His Majesty's Schooner *Island Expedition*. She was still at the pier in Brunswick, New Guernsey, one of the Independent Lands of Vespica. She was prohibited from sailing by Lord Sutherland, the Tritonish Consul, whose staff continued to investigate the possibility that her crew were Galway Rebels. Now that the southern spring was here again, and with the overall commendable conduct of all assigned to the vessel, many restrictions had been eased. It was not Pierce's scheduled day to be aboard, but since the last snow in August, that stricture no longer applied. It was no secret that the learned and persuasive Dr. Robertson was working through Vespican channels for the schooner's release. So he would not be seen as too much the villain, Lord Sutherland had relaxed many of the restraints placed upon the British crew.

Pierce had moved the entire crew onboard. Each third of the crew spent an entire duty day aboard, worked the next day at various jobs about the harbor, and then had a day of liberty. Pierce remained aboard much of the time and looked to his duties on a regular basis. Now that he and Hotchkiss were permitted aboard together, they accomplished a great deal.

There was still a foreign presence aboard. Kentish marines maintained a small guard detachment, but now *Island Expedition's* own British marines bore arms and stood by their counterparts to guard the vessel. Pierce hoped that soon the only armed men aboard would be British.

The cabin grew overly warm and Pierce went on deck. He shook his head at Andrews, indicating that his presence was to be disregarded. He paced a bit, but soon settled at the rail, resting his arms on the newly strung hammock netting.

Across the harbor a Gallician frigate was anchored in close, taking on stores from barges and lighters clustered about her. She had arrived yesterday to join a sister frigate already there for the past week. A fine, well-built ship, she was bigger than most of the Kentish frigates he had seen. Were Gallician ships generally of better design and heavier armament than those of the Tritonish Navy? Did the Tritonish, like the British, counter with higher-quality construction and better-trained crews?

The truce between the Unified Kingdom of Triton and the Republic of Gallicia while in Vespican territory amazed Pierce. They prowled the seas, took and destroyed the other's shipping and naval forces, and yet appeared to strictly observe Vespican neutrality. Despite the calm that existed on the surface, a hotbed of intrigue and hidden conflict boiled away. Caught in the middle of the two great warring powers, Vespica both suffered and prospered.

The supplies being loaded aboard the Gallician frigate were gotten with cold hard cash. The merchants and bankers in this new nation fared well and collected monies from both sides for services rendered and products offered. Tomorrow those same barges might ferry supplies to a Kentish ship.

Other Vespicans chafed under the presence of their former colonial masters as well as their one-time ally. Vespica, ten weak and uncooperative Lands, could do nothing to rid herself of their bullying presences. She could not stand by one and oust the other from her shores. The nation driven out might extract a terrible vengeance upon the cities, towns, and commerce of the small, insignificant country.

Amongst the Vespicans, there was no clear consensus regarding which of the warring nations to support. In Brunswick, New Guernsey, the populace was quite evenly divided. Some favored stronger ties with the Kentish, some desired a bond with the Gallicians, and others wanted both to leave Vespica to her own affairs.

Quite possibly Pierce and *Island Expedition* figured into this high-stakes, high-keyed game of international intrigue. Why had the Gallician Consul offered to intercede for them? "Just mention the word, *mon capitaine*! We will offer you the protection, under which you may sail as you please."

Pierce had rejected the offer. They were too much like the French. Their offer had nothing to do with the goodness in their hearts, but rather with gaining an advantage over the Tritonish. The Gallicians could not care less whether he bettered his current situation or not.

Pierce chafed under the restraints (lax as they now were) imposed by the Tritonish. But they were a known quantity, and as a parallel to Britain, he more readily understood their concerns and motives. But it bothered him that they maintained such an imperious presence on foreign soil, and rode roughshod over the nation hosting them. He understood the resentment and loathing that many throughout Vespica had for the Tritonish. Did Great Britain invoke the same feelings among certain peoples of his own world? As a loyal British subject, he sincerely hoped not.

Like their foes, the Tritonish played his presence for all that it was worth, and surely sought some profit from it. Being suspected as a Galway Rebel was a cover for the real reason the detention continued. They wanted something from him, and in his current state of agitation he would be damned if they would get it, if indeed he ever discovered what it was.

Hotchkiss joined him at the rail. "Another fine day, sir," the first lieutenant remarked. "But we should experience it from the island, or perhaps England."

"That we should," said Pierce conversationally, having sorted through and rejected several angry retorts as his solitude was ended. "We might sail any day now, I'm thinking. That is, if the doctor can gain support at that Congress of his. The Joint Council will need persuading as well."

"We must hope, but I suspect he is having a tough go. All I have heard about the Joint Council is its inability to act in concert. But the good doctor's last report said the Unity Congress had agreed on a resolution. That they found accord may bode well for us with the Joint Council. They may actually act in our behalf."

"That, Isaac, is my fondest dream!"

The conversation drifted. Moments later they heard a voice from the pier and Andrews respond to it.

Then Andrews turned to his captain. "Sir," he said. "A message from the consulate, and Lord Sutherland would see the captain when most convenient. The first lieutenant as well, if possible, sir."

Pierce looked quizzically at his friend. Hotchkiss's return glance mirrored the same puzzlement, as never had the Tritonish consul ever sent for either or both of them--not when they were not physically present at the Consulate.

Pierce must have dwelled on this for some time, for Andrews spoke again. "Beg pardon, sir. But the messenger is awaiting a reply to Lord Sutherland."

"Quite right, Mr. Andrews. Tell him we will arrive within the hour!"

"Aye aye, sir!"

"Now we have some time--some short time--to be spent making ourselves presentable."

"No, it would not do, half a bucket of slush on my trousers. But I could never resist helping grease the carronade slides."

Fifteen minutes later Pierce and Hotchkiss appeared on deck in full dress uniform, polished, shined, and brushed clean and smooth. "Mr. Andrews, you have the deck, it would seem. Normal routine, if you please, for the remainder of the day!"

"Normal routine it is, sir. Shall you go ashore with ceremony, sir?"

"I think not, Mr. Andrews. We've the hands busy for once, and would be a shame to break them from it."

"Aye, sir!"

As they walked along the waterfront, Pierce had to check himself and continue past the Frosty Anchor. It had become a habit to stop there. Hotchkiss saw the slight change in pace as his captain recovered. "I too thought to stop."

"The place has been a refuge at times. When we do leave here, the Frosty Anchor is one place I will remember with some affection."

"As will I," answered Hotchkiss. "Would it be His Lordship summons us with news of that event?"

"Deep within my soul, friend, I do hope for that. But if I were a gambling man, I'd not wager it."

"Dr. Robertson's last communiqué was quite optimistic. Perhaps we can take heart from that."

"But he said progress was being made, not that any real results were forthcoming."

"Aye!" sighed Hotchkiss. "It is nice to think we may soon be away from this place. As much as we would welcome our departure, I would worry about Mr. Morgan's heart."

"I daresay the bond between them grows stronger each day. It is fortunate that she and her mother have joined him here."

"Indeed, sir," continued Hotchkiss. "I believe there is real caring between them. It's not the old 'girl in every port,' as said about sailors. I've enjoyed my time with Gisele, as I am sure you have enjoyed yours with...."

"With Leona Jackson?" Pierce finished the thought. "I catch your drift, Isaac. And yes, I have enjoyed my time with her."

"To be sure, sir. I mean, we both have something here which we don't see as permanent. What we choose to see as lasting waits for us in England. For Mr. Morgan, however, I believe he sees this as the one for all time."

"I hope leaving does not overly distress him. We left our 'permanents,' and have done well."

"Speaking for myself, Edward, many times I thought to swim back to her."

"As did I. Perhaps Sutherland will really permit us to leave."

They strode on in silence, each deep in thought. Pierce's heart leapt joyously at the thought of leaving. Still, reality checked that joy and kept him anchored to the idea of their departure being several weeks away.

The Unity Congress had debated their situation intensely, and Dr. Robertson, their most vocal advocate, was a man of persuasion. But even with his diplomatic skill, could he convince unknown men to aid total strangers? Could the Unity Congress sway the Vespican Joint Council, an organization noted for being totally inept? Members rarely agreed on anything, and when they did, they had not the power to enforce it. Would they be able to influence the Tritonish in regards to the English schooner? Far more than likely, the Tritonish would simply say, "Thank you, but these matters are not of your concern."

Hotchkiss broke the silence after a few minutes. "I find it hard to believe Lord Sutherland still believes us to be Galway Rebels."

"That tale has worn thin, indeed, Isaac. There is more to it. They want something from us. What, I cannot say," Pierce responded. "It must be a matter of some delicacy, or they would simply have asked."

"Yes, and we are held in hope they obtain it, and the Gallicians do not. I wonder what effect action by the Joint Council will have on that?" asked Hotchkiss.

"That we may soon learn, Mr. Hotchkiss!" They were at the consulate building and as they neared the gates, they saw several carriages lined up outside. "His Lordship has visitors, apparently of an official nature, and it would surprise me they do not deal with our situation."

"Aye, they might at that. They might at that!" reflected Hotchkiss.

They were passed through the gate with familiar ceremony, the

Tritonish marines on duty familiar with them, as they were with the marines. They made their way to the consul's office, where Stimpson, the secretary, bade them sit and wait. He was one of the few staff members they had come to despise. He concealed his arrogance and complete lack of civility behind an air of efficiency and duty.

The wait allowed them to recover their breath and cool after their walk in the warm afternoon.

Pierce grew impatient. They had been there for some while and Stimpson had made no move to inform Lord Sutherland of their presence. He heard voices, muffled and unintelligible beyond the door to the inner office. Stimpson carried on with his busy work, seemingly unaware of anyone on either side of the door.

At last, as Pierce thought to remark caustically to him, Stimpson got up and slowly and cautiously opened the door to the inner offices. "Milords! The British captain and first lieutenant have arrived. Should I bid them enter?"

Pierce heard a voice in reply but could not make out the words. Stimpson shut the door gently, turned around and said, "I'm afraid their lordships will be a while longer. Please retain your seats for the time." Then he sniffed arrogantly, lost all recognition of the two, and returned to his chair.

"Thank you, Mr. Stimpson," said Pierce in reply.

And as the man returned to his seat, Pierce whispered low to Hotchkiss. "I would use him to demonstrate the effects of flogging to new hands."

"He is not of much use for anything else," whispered Hotchkiss, surprised at his friend's statement. He knew well Pierce's abhorrence of the cat-of-nine-tails. "A person in his position should have some personality. Do you really loathe him that much?"

"No, but he does irritate me."

The brief conversation ended. Pierce sat deep in his thoughts and wondered at the delay. After a few minutes that to him were hours, a small bell ring-a-linged gently at the secretary's desk. Perhaps now they would have their answers.

Stimpson got up eventually, nodded condescendingly at Pierce and Hotchkiss, and opened the door wide. "My lords, Master and Commander Edward Pierce, and Lieutenant Isaac Hotchkiss!" With an impatient look and a twist of his head, he directed them to enter.

"Come in, gentlemen! Come in!" Lord Sutherland smiled politely, extended his hands and symbolically drew them into the room. "I am so sorry to have kept you waiting. Last-minute details, you know. Now, there are some gentlemen that you must meet. Lord Lancaster, His Regal Majesty's Ambassador to the Independent Lands of Vespica."

"Most honored to meet you, sir!" said Pierce, bowing and not really meaning one word. He did not dislike the man, but having just met him, had no real opinion. There was an air of aristocracy about him, and Pierce determined that he would not use it to color his future views of the man.

Lancaster was tall and thin, dressed in the best, and obviously comfortable with being in charge. Haughtily he responded to Pierce's salutation. "So you are the supposed rogue that has had us in a dither this past year. I must say, you seem somewhat civilized after all."

He turned slightly towards Hotchkiss, who had since mumbled his acknowledgement of the ambassador's presence. "And his number one cohort, I take it."

"Yes, milord!" responded Hotchkiss. He glanced quickly at Pierce, but that was enough to say he did not care for Lancaster's assessment.

Lord Sutherland continued with the introductions. "General Sir Vaughn Chesterfield, senior military aide to the ambassador."

"Sir!" said both Pierce and Hotchkiss with a slight nod of the head, enough that it could be considered a bow.

"Ah yes, very much pleased to finally meet both of you. Come, come now, milord. Let's be on with these greetings. These two haven't a drink, and I daresay they are thirsty. I understand you walked from your ship."

"Aye, we did, sir," answered Pierce. "But it is not far." Pierce did not know this individual either, but something told Pierce that he was of a more jovial nature than Lord Lancaster.

"May I present His Excellency, Mr. James Warren, Chairman of the Vespican Lands Joint Council; Council Secretary, Elias Johnson; Council Members Fox, Lee, and Jefferson. And the President of the Unity Congress, His Excellency, Joseph Braxton."

The remaining introductions, greetings, and salutations passed quickly. True to Chesterfield's suggestion, Pierce and Hotchkiss each found himself with a drink in hand. "And now, gentlemen, if we may be seated," directed Lord Sutherland. "I believe we have business that these two will be most interested in."

"Those seats at the far end of the table are for you."

Pierce looked at Hotchkiss questioningly. Hotchkiss's glance gave no answer, but merely returned his captain's puzzlement.

When everyone was seated, when everyone's glass or cup was reasonably full, and when members of the consulate staff had left and shut the doors, Lord Sutherland rose and began.

"As we all know, gentlemen, some sixteen months ago, the Tritonish Navy's Flying Squadron sighted several sail requiring investigation. Most of the ships lay in one direction and one lay in the opposite. Commodore Hargrove dispatched HRMS *Hawke* to deal with the lone sail, and with the remainder, went to deal with the other vessels.

"The several ships investigated by the Flying Squadron proved to be of no threat or potential profit. However, the vessel investigated by *Hawke* proved suspicious from the start. She flew colors opposite in color pattern to those of the Unified Kingdom, colors often used by Galway Rebels to insult and defy His Regal Majesty. Upon request they heave to, this vessel responded with a signal that is meant as an obscene insult to the person of His Regal Majesty.

"Thus, Commanding Master Horatio Newbury, captain of HRMS *Hawke*, fired a shot across her bows. When that was not obeyed, he fired a full broadside into the vessel.

"That vessel, a well-armed and maneuverable schooner of remarkable size and build, returned fire, and in no time, to Commander Newbury's chagrin, was soundly taking the measure of his ship.

"When Newbury realized further combat would result in death and injury to more Tritonish seamen and perhaps the loss of his ship, he reluctantly agreed to a cease fire.

"Master and Commander Edward Pierce, captain of the schooner that so badly mauled *Hawke* had, out of humanitarian concerns, originally proposed it. The scene went instantly from one of combat, death, and destruction to one of aid and succor, as both crews repaired damage, most of which had been inflicted upon *Hawke*.

"Newbury wisely did not inform Pierce of the Flying Squadron. Later, that unit approached from windward. The schooner departed, attempted to run eastward and escape. They soon found themselves between the Flying Squadron and the rocks and reefs off the Gregorian coast. Commander Pierce recognized the odds against him, and rather than see his men killed and his schooner destroyed, opted to surrender.

"At that time, the Flying Squadron believed they had caught one of those infamous Galway Rebels that have so tried our patience for the past decade. But Commander Pierce and his crew told an entirely different and incredible tale. Commodore Hargrove did not believe it, but open to possibilities, he sent the schooner under a prize crew, into port here. He sent along the schooner's captain and first lieutenant in the escorting frigate *Furious*, Captain Lowell Jackson commanding.

"Does that fit your remembrance of the events, Commander Pierce?"

"Certainly, milord," answered Pierce. "And I must thank his lordship that the account is remarkably unbiased."

"Indeed, Commander Pierce, we shall be as truthful in relating those events as can be," said Sutherland.

"Upon meeting Commander Pierce, Lieutenant Hotchkiss and others of the schooner, and having read the reports of both Commander Newbury and Commodore Hargrove, I believed as they did, that we had apprehended a Galway Rebel. Yet, I had some doubt and sought to investigate further. I resolved not to imprison or closely confine them, but rather to treat them as honored guests. There were, of course, certain restrictions set in place to prevent their departure before final determination was made regarding their case.

"Gentlemen, as you know, life in this small former colonial community can grow tedious, especially during the colder winter months. Commander Pierce's presence and the presence of his crew brightened those cold months, both here in the consulate, amongst local society, and in the city as a whole.

"By the end of this past July, it was established that these gentlemen and their vessel were not Galway Rebels or of any force hostile to the Crown. If their story was completely accurate, they could possibly be of immense help to Grand Triton in the war with Gallicia."

"That we could have been of aid was never discussed with us, milord," objected Pierce. "Nor would we have necessarily agreed to it, had it been."

"No sir, it was not. The entire explanation would take more time than we have today. But had we asked, the effect would have been nullified. You would have had to offer it freely for it to benefit us, and thusly benefit you."

"I don't see it," said Pierce. "It is truly a puzzlement that we could have offered it to you and yet have no idea of what it was."

"Mark it up to international intrigue, my boy!" interjected Sir Vaughn. "And the strangely powerful effects of Rig'nie tradition and superstition."

"Sir Vaughn! I caution you that too much said along those lines will let them know what we seek. Once they have been told, it is worthless, even that they do offer it freely," said Lord Lancaster, greatly irritated with his military advisor.

"Be assured, milord," said Pierce. "What we have and that you desire, but for which you cannot ask, is still a mystery to us."

"To continue," said Lord Sutherland. "Some weeks after their arrival, that most famous of Vespican statesmen and medicos, Dr. Robertson, arrived. He and his father, the Kalish Dream Chief Shostolamie, had evidently been in contact with Pierce's people on Stone Island, where they have established a colony. The commander and his schooner were missing, and the good doctor had heard tales of a vessel and group of strangers enjoying our *hospitality*. Beyond successfully treating a midshipman's infected amputation, Dr. Robertson agreed to work through Vespican channels to obtain their release."

Pierce's freedom, and that of his crew, might well be at hand. But the path they were on could turn the other way. Had the Tritonish tired of waiting for the offer of what they wanted, and in frustration decided to end the standoff?

Briefly Pierce wondered if this were really a trial, after which he and Hotchkiss would be hanged and the schooner's crew pressed into the Kentish Navy. With dread he waited for the proceedings to continue.

"Gentlemen, I now call upon His Excellency, Joseph Braxton, President of the Vespican Unity Congress."

"Thank you, Lord Sutherland," said Braxton, rising as the Tritonish Consul sat down and took a long sip of his wine.

"As you are aware, the Unity Congress feels a more unified government with stronger bonds between the Lands can only prove best for Vespica. A delegate, Dr. Robertson, came to us with a tale of detained seamen from a far-off unknown land. More important was that they were part of a colony established on Stone Island, and apparently welcomed by the Rig'nies. He pressed us for a resolution asking the

Vespican Joint Council to obtain their release. Dr. Robertson insisted that such action would do well to show the need for a more united and a stronger central bond between the Independent Lands.

"In our most recent session, and after several long days of debate, we arrived at a resolution, approved by the largest majority practical. That resolution was then forwarded to the Joint Council." Braxton was silent, and after a moment sat back in his chair.

"His Excellency, Mr. James Warren, Chairman of the Vespican Joint Council," announced Lord Sutherland from his seat.

"Thank you, milord. When this resolution was read, I believed it would result in another bill for which we would not find any agreement. I believed any attempt at legislation would divide us further, and it would die from lack of support.

"I was wrong. Perhaps because those concerned were not from any particular Land, the Joint Council rallied behind them. We determined to annex Stone Island as the eleventh Independent Land of Vespica and declare all there, or from there, Vespican citizens. That done, we approached the Tritonish and demanded that Vespican citizens held without charge or probable cause be released immediately."

"Thank you, Mr. Warren," said Lord Sutherland. "My lord?"

Lord Lancaster, Tritonish Ambassador to Vespica, stood. "The Unified Kingdom of Grand Triton and Galway has always taken what it has wanted or needed. For much of its history, the Unified Kingdom has maintained what it has by whatever means necessary. But, gentlemen, such things do not always last. A few decades ago we were forced to recognize the independence and sovereignty of our Vespican colonies.

"Now representatives of those former colonies come to us and claim we hold individuals they deem to be citizens of the Independent Lands of Vespica. It is clear the citizenship is bestowed in order to obtain their liberty. But we must follow international law and the accords established between the Unified Kingdom and the Independent Lands.

"While I feel that in some way these gentlemen, their schooner, and the others on Stone Island may one day prove a threat to the Realm of Geoffrey the Fifth, I cannot do less than is required of me. Having been presented a copy of the Joint Council's annexation of Stone Island as the eleventh and newest Independent Land of Vespica, and having been presented a copy of the Joint Council's resolution demanding complete restoration of freedom and liberty for all those now deemed Vespican citizens, I find that I can only accede to those demands.

"Were not the Regal Tritonish Navy, and indeed the Tritonish Army, presently hard- pressed in defense of the kingdom, I assure you the Unified Kingdom would bring pressure to bear, at whatever level required, to avoid this diplomatic capitulation. I have been informed by His Majesty's Government that despite all we could gain from these individuals, His Regal Majesty's Government is not prepared to forcibly press the situation.

"Therefore on behalf of His Regal Majesty Geoffrey the Fifth, his government, and as the senior Tritonish official in Vespica, I bow to the demands placed upon me by that government and grant the requests of the Independent Lands of Vespica. The Unified Kingdom of Grand Triton and Galway does hereby agree and declare that all those residing upon or all those who have journeyed from Stone Island are indeed full citizens of the Independent Lands of Vespica. As such, and having found no charge for which any of those citizens can be legally held by His Regal Majesty's Government, those individuals are declared fully free and at complete liberty.

"Lord Sutherland, you will see that any restrictions placed upon these new citizens of the Independent Lands of Vespica are removed at once!"

*Chapter Three*

# Farewells

For a long moment, Pierce did not react. He had just heard what he had hoped to hear for the past year. He held back any display, almost as if he expected to awaken and discover it was a dream. Had Dr. Robertson's cure of Morgan's leg and the lessening of restrictions upon the schooner's crew had been dreams as well?

"Yes, milord," Lord Sutherland replied to the Ambassador's order to set *Island Expedition* and her crew at liberty.

"Captain Pierce, I have already issued the necessary orders, although it may be tomorrow before all concerned have the word. I know you are anxious to leave and rejoin your countrymen on Stone Island. But, pray, don't depart without proper preparation."

"Milord," said Pierce, rising from his seat, "if we leave with the next tide or tarry for social amenities, it will not be a departure in haste. We were ready to leave the very day *Furious* escorted *Island Expedition* into the harbor. Certainly, we will leave as soon as is practical, but we will say our goodbyes to those whose hospitality we appreciate."

"And there must be a dinner, I would think!" Sir Vaughn joined in. "This might be a loss for Kentland, but certainly it is a fortunate occasion for Vespica and her newest citizens. They should celebrate their liberty and new citizenships."

Lord Lancaster glared at the general. He had been dead set against meeting the demands of the Vespican Joint Council, but had agreed only because of directives from his government and practical aspects of the war with Gallicia. He saw it as a defeat for the Unified Kingdom and a lessening of the prestige and power that Grand Triton held in its former colonies. To speak as Sir Vaughn had done was nearly treason, in Lancaster's view.

"We should have a celebration of some sort!" echoed Joint Council member Jefferson. "But where could we hold such a dinner?"

"Aye, we should. The Tritonish consulate certainly would have the space for it," added Joint Council member Lee.

"They have the space, and the staff to prepare, that it is certain. But would we not offend them, asking that they host a party for a situation that went against them?" asked Unity Congress President Braxton.

"Gentlemen, we have had the pleasure of hosting Commander Pierce and his men for several months. Despite suspicions that surrounded them at first, and the rewards we hoped to gain from them, they have been well-found company. I, for one," said Lord Sutherland, "would not be offended to honor their good fortune."

Lord Lancaster coughed and shot a reproachful glance at Sutherland.

"But perhaps under the circumstances, there are other arrangements more suitable." Lancaster nodded as Sutherland's last words acknowledged his disapproval.

"Surely, gentlemen, we can find some place that will accommodate a celebration," stated Councilman Fox. "But any fête should be the choice of those celebrated. What say you, Commander Pierce?"

"Gentlemen, I am overwhelmed. I thank you for your efforts on behalf of strangers from more than a world away. All in *Island Expedition* are deeply indebted to the Unity Congress and the Joint Council.

"I also thank Lord Lancaster and the Tritonish Government, that they did see reason in the situation. Being from a nation much like the Unified Kingdom, I understand the anguish of such a decision."

"But what of the dinner, sir?" asked Mr. Fox. "Surely you will let us provide a party to celebrate this momentous occasion. It would delay you only slightly."

"Indeed, Commander Pierce!" interjected James Warren, the Joint Council Chairman.

"Aye," seconded Johnson, the Council Secretary, silent until now, but attentive to every word. "This moment is of great importance to the Independent Lands of Vespica, and it should be well celebrated!"

"I am not opposed to the idea. You wish to celebrate a small but significant and bloodless diplomatic victory. We would celebrate our freedom and indeed the honor of our citizenship. But gentlemen, let us have it somewhere public and open. If we celebrate, let it not be only for the few. Have it where all our crew and anyone in Brunswick may attend, regardless of station."

"Then I know just the place, sir," said Hotchkiss.

"Pray tell, where would that be?" queried Sir Vaughn.

"Why, the Frosty Anchor, sir!"

"Indeed, the Frosty Anchor!" Pierce echoed. "I believe Humphrey would delight to put something together."

"We would not impose upon the consulate to host it," said Jefferson. "No doubt a relief for them."

"A judicious decision, gentlemen," said Lord Lancaster. "Sutherland, Chesterfield, come! Let these colonials gloat." With that stab of superiority, the Vespicans, including two very new citizens, were left alone.

In spite of his nation's loss of face, Lord Sutherland invited all present to stay for a late supper. Pierce would have returned to the schooner, but it would have been in bad taste to have left abruptly. In addition, he was fond of the roast pork that was served, especially as prepared by the consulate's cook.

As dinner ended, Pierce was full to bursting, and sleepy from the wine. The room was stuffy and warm and he urgently needed to be in a cooler location. He excused himself, walked out into the hall, and stepped into the garden behind the consulate. The sun was down far enough that the air was cooler, and a refreshing breeze swirled through the trees. The fresh air revived him as he wandered about the carefully tended growth.

He wanted a moment of solitude, to be alone with his thoughts, and to reflect upon the good fortune that had finally come his way. Not particularly religious, Pierce felt moved enough by the recent occurrences to wonder if a higher power had had a hand in it.

He wondered about the Vespican citizenship conferred upon him, his crew, and those on Stone Island. Was it a tool to obtain their release, or were they actually citizens? If so, did they have duties, responsibilities, or restrictions because of it? Would it conflict with their status as British subjects?

What would Smythe think of the Vespican Joint Council annexing the island? Communications over the past months from Dr. Robertson should have informed him of such a possibility. Such action would not set well with one desiring as little outside contact as possible. But as Pierce understood the legislation's wording, approval by every Land, including the Land being annexed, was required. Whether Stone Island became the eleventh Independent Land of Vespica would, in the end, be up to Smythe.

Were Shostolamie's words coming true? The Kalish Dream Chief had spoken of the English settlers bringing a new age to their ancient lands. Even the Joint Council acting in unison to release *Island Expedition* might be seen as a start. Would he, his crew, and the others on Stone Island be the catalyst of a new and vital Vespica?

He was not alone. "I haven't seen much of you, Edward, since you were permitted to stay aboard your ship." Leona spoke quietly. "I've missed you!"

"I have my duty," he replied. "But I have missed you. When we leave, I will remember, and will indeed miss you."

"But not so much that you will stay?"

"No."

"Of course. We have had what we wanted from each other. We are obligated, or think we are obligated, to others. It is best we return, if not in person, then in our hearts, to the 'other.'"

"I do look forward to that reunion. And are you anxious for yours again?"

"Of course! I am glad that you will be gone when it occurs. It eased the situation greatly that you were not here when last he visited." She was silent for a few moments, her eyes downcast. She spoke again. "And now, my love, one last kiss! One last embrace!"

Pierce kissed her tenderly. She clung to him, and her presence stirred the flames within. Strangely, he had no overriding desire to pursue and quench the fires. He felt something beyond the undiluted lust that had bonded them over the past year. Their former wantonness was replaced by friendship, and even respect.

No more was said between them that evening. When their embrace ended, a new and deeper understanding had been exactingly communicated.

Pierce returned to the table. He apologized for his abrupt departure, explaining his need for air. Then he claimed the person of Lieutenant Hotchkiss, by now well-eased in his thirst, and begged that they might be excused to return to their vessel. Lord Sutherland, always attentive, called for a carriage so they might return in style and with greater rapidity than afoot.

When he awoke and went on deck the next morning, Pierce noticed there were no Kentish Marines on board. The only sea-soldiers present were *Island Expedition's* own red-coated British Marines. The Vespican militiamen on the pier had withdrawn to points farther away, and their numbers had lessened.

He grabbed a cup of coffee from the galley stove and returned to the quarterdeck. Hotchkiss was there, but he did not speak to him. Pierce moved to windward, the seaward side, and began to pace. The others scattered to the lee quarterdeck and remained out of his way.

When he finished his coffee and felt a little more human, Pierce joined Hotchkiss. "If you did not send the watch below to the shipyards today, you will have made me a happy man."

"I sent only two, sir, to notify them we would no longer send anyone."

"Excellent, Mr. Hotchkiss! We have been so ready to sail all these months, but we have so much yet to be done. I fear it will be two or three days before we can depart."

"Aye, sir. And we must contact Humphrey about the celebration."

"I'll leave that in your hands."

"Aye aye, sir!"

Hotchkiss was silent for a moment. "And what of this citizenship, with which we are now blessed?"

"I'm not sure. But I will accept it, if only that it gets us away from here. Hopefully we will see Dr. Robertson before departure and he will explain it further. We may also have an opportunity to meet members of the Joint Council who could more fully explain it."

"We could have learned more yesterday. We had time alone with representatives of the Vespican Government. Surely we could have had our answers then," said Hotchkiss.

"If we had only thought to ask."

"Aye! I'm sure we will learn the full measure with time."

The next afternoon *Island Expedition* was nearly deserted. Only those who had volunteered and the usual few denied liberty for disciplinary reasons remained aboard. The rest were at the Frosty Anchor enjoying a feast. As befitted a waterfront public house, the supply of beer, ale, hard cider, rum, and various wines was deep and seemingly inexhaustible.

Many things were being celebrated. The Tritonish had released the English schooner and its crew, the Joint Council had for once acted in concert, and Vespica had gained another Land and new citizens.

It was, as Humphrey, owner of the Frosty Anchor put it, "a significant step for Vespican unity, sovereignty, and prosperity."

Pierce originally thought he would eat and drink sparingly. He would not gorge himself until bloated, nor drink until besotted. But with the gaiety of the occasion, the mountains of food provided, and the endless supply of wine, beer, and spirits, his adherence to such an ideal soon slipped away. They were no longer kept from leaving by the Tritonish, and that they would leave shortly was well worth celebrating. Even if he might awaken tomorrow with an aching head and a protesting, churning belly, that did not deter him. He piled his plate high and ate until only crumbs and traces of sauce remained. He filled his mug, often, to the brim, and drained every last drop.

With a half-eaten joint of beef in one hand, and a half-empty mug of beer in the other, Pierce happened upon Midshipman Steadman. "How do you find this little gathering, Mr. Steadman?" he asked.

"More than a little gathering, I'd say, sir," answered Steadman between bites of ham. "Never seen so many eating and drinking so much, all at one place."

"Be sure you get your share and more, Mr. Steadman." Pierce remembered his days as a young gentleman and the perpetual hunger many contended with. Stores were often scarce in midshipmen's berths, and added to that were the ravenous appetites of still-growing boys and the demands of their duties.

"If you would be kind enough to see that some is sent for those aboard to enjoy?"

"Certainly, sir! Aye aye, sir!"

Pierce drained his stein and refilled it. Hotchkiss happened by, a plate balanced in one hand and a glass of wine in the other.

"Quite the event!" he exclaimed. "We will remember this feast for some time!"

"That we will, Isaac. That we will! But one who should be honored as much as anyone is not here!"

"That is?"

"Dr. Robertson, to be sure. If not for him, this and the reason for it would not have been possible."

"But, Edward, if you look, you may find him. I have heard he arrived within the hour. With the informality of the occasion, I'm sure that you have simply missed each other."

"Let us hope so. I have several things I hope to discuss with him before we sail."

"You may yet have your chance." Hotchkiss took a bite of bread, chewed thoughtfully, and continued. "Have you ever wondered, Edward, whether the good doctor has a first name? We have known him only as Dr. Robertson for this past year, and even that we are considered friends, we do not know how to address him, should first names be apropos."

"I've not given it much thought, Isaac. Truth be told, I don't recall ever being told of his first name. I believe 'Robertson' is because his mother's family once called his father Robert."

"Logical, I would suppose," replied Hotchkiss, who paused momentarily to sip at his wine and take another bite of bread. "Look, I believe it is the good doctor now."

"Where, Isaac? I don't see him."

"Just beyond Humphrey there!"

"Ah, yes, I have him in sight. If you will pardon me, friend, I shall close and gain further insight into our current and future situation."

Pierce finished his beef bone and tossed it to one of the dogs running loose amongst the revelers, and refilled his mug once again. Then he headed for where he had last seen Dr. Robertson.

When Pierce found him, the man was with his cousin's wife, Bessie, her daughter Cecilia, and Midshipman Morgan. Young Tom was trying a new leg that the carpenter had made. The first, made several months ago, in a bit of bravado on Tom's part, had splintered. The new leg fit and felt differently, and demanded new skills and coordination. As Pierce approached, Morgan stumbled. Cecilia caught him and helped him stand easy.

Pierce smiled at the ease with which Tom and Cecilia interacted.

Bessie did not glare menacingly at the young British midshipman. At times she positively beamed at him. Tom Morgan had already won a big part of the courtship battle, having found favor with his young lady's mother.

Dr. Robertson and Cecilia moved and interacted with the crowd in a familiar and easy fashion. They had spent a great deal of time in Vespican society, even such as was at this celebration. Everyone from stable boys, housemaids, and ordinary seamen, to doctors, lawyers, sea officers, and government officials were present. They knew how to act and respond appropriately to all that came their way. That included obvious signs from a few Brunswick townspeople who thought that Rig'nies should not be allowed at such an occasion. The doctor and Cecilia fended off the occasional look and the occasional remark with aplomb and style. Tom Morgan was comfortable in their company, and more than once sent a withering glance at any questioning their presence.

Bessie had spent all her life in wilderness Kalish villages. This was only her second visit, the first a year ago, to a relatively large Vespican city. She was confused, startled by the boisterous laughter and riotous behavior. She was jostled, pushed, and shoved, and appeared not at all to enjoy herself. But she maintained her dignity and readily put up with the discomfort in order to be with her daughter, her daughter's beau, and her husband's cousin.

Pierce spotted Midshipman Andrews, alone and without drink or plate in hand. "Mr. Andrews, there!"

"Sir?"

"Be so kind as to provide an escort for Madame Bessie. You and Mr. Morgan would provide me a great service, should you provide for the ladies while I chat with the doctor."

"Certainly, sir. But I do have an engagement later."

"I shan't be long, and you must remind me if time runs short."

"Aye aye, sir."

"Ah, Captain Pierce," said Doctor Robinson. "I had hoped to see you today."

"And I you, sir!" Pierce continued. "Mr. Andrews has gallantly volunteered to look out for Madame Bessie. Mother and daughter will be well cared for. And then, sir, we can talk."

"Quite right. It is awkward for her, but she knows Tom and Cecilia have only a few more days. Perhaps only a few more hours. Yet she must do her duty and maintain a mother's watch over her child."

"A brave soul," commented Pierce. "But as the two are provided for, I do have questions of you."

"Come then, Captain. I'll fetch a mug of sweet cider and we'll sit at that small table there, and you may question me to your heart's delight."

Pierce and Dr. Robertson sat on the front step of the Frosty Anchor. The doctor sipped slowly at his cider. "And now, Captain, just what may I answer for you?"

"To begin, sir, I do not have a question, but rather I would extend my thanks for all you've done. You've treated Tom Morgan's leg, and he is well recovered. Your efforts within the Unity Congress and at the Joint Council have gained us our liberty. With that, we sail in two days' time. All those in *Island Expedition* surely owe you a great debt, sir."

"From my vantage point, Edward, I did what had to be done. I appreciate the kind words and thoughts. Perhaps it is best that I simply say, 'You're welcome, sir!'"

"But now, I must ask the questions that have preyed on my mind as of late."

"Of course."

"Firstly, I would know what obligations this new citizenship places upon us. I point out that if any conflict arises between Vespican citizenship and British loyalty, my native and natural status must take precedence."

"Quite understandable. Be assured the citizenship is real and binding, but it is also of an honorary nature. The Joint Council would not consider placing your citizenship in conflict with current allegiances. Perhaps, Edward, when you are here, consider yourself a Vespican. When you are in your world, consider yourself British."

"A commendable solution, Doctor," agreed Pierce. "But I do have another matter to ask about."

"And that is?"

"Some days prior to the events we celebrate today, I concluded the Tritonish wanted something from me--from us. Even as we were granted our release, certain statements confirmed that. But I am at a complete loss as to what they wanted. Would you have an inkling of what it might be?"

"Most assuredly, my friend. It is because you have not spent time, nor grown up here that you do not understand."

"I am still at a loss, good sir!"

"It is really quite simple. Your people have been granted access to Stone Island by the Ancient Ones through the Kalish Dream Chief. Now you have the right to decide who might be on the island. Occasional visitors, or persons in need or under threat are not of any concern. But you have the power to grant any person, any group, or any nation access to the island."

"That is what the Kentish wanted? Access to Stone Island?"

"Indeed! Because of certain actions over the centuries by Kalish and other Original Inhabitants of Vespica, most Balticans, and many Vespicans believe they cannot even suggest that you invite them. You must act entirely on your own, or the access to and use of the island's resources will come to naught."

"If the Kentish had access to Stone Island, it would give them an advantage over Gallicia?"

"Quite! Or had the Gallicians gained use of the island, they would have had the same advantage. Again, due to superstitions planted long ago by Original Vespicans, those not granted rights would face disaster, should an attempt be made on anyone, including an enemy, legitimately entrenched on Stone Island."

"So simple, and yet I never would have fathomed it. I am glad I didn't, for it would have been much harder not to have invited them."

"I am glad as well, Edward Pierce. I believe these recent events have set us on the path of change my father sees in his dreams."

"Perhaps."

"I know you will depart in a day or two and return straight away to Stone Island. Then you will sail for your own world and England. I am not a Dream Chief, but I believe you will return. You will be a very important person, both to the Kalish and the Vespicans."

"That I complete this voyage and return to England is certainty. Whether I will return here is not yet determined. Should it be, I will look forward to your friendship and guidance once again."

When the conversation ended, Pierce stood, stretched, and walked about. The entire block fronting the Frosty Anchor had been given over to the celebration. As he strolled through the throngs, he shook hands with well-wishers. He said "goodbye" and "farewell" to friends and acquaintances he had made in Brunswick.

Some of the Tritonish consulate staff were there, too. He readily accepted their best wishes and passed on to them his own. He was pleasantly surprised when Major Howard remembered that this particular day, the ninth of October, was his birthday.

As the afternoon wore on, Pierce sensed jubilation floating on the wind. He had eaten too much and drunk much too much, but he was contentedly happy. He finally had control of his destiny. In two days he would leave this place. Because of his presence, the Independent Lands of Vespica had taken its first steps toward becoming a truly united country. The Vespicans celebrated that, while he and his men celebrated their imminent departure.

Pierce sighed, sat down again and watched the celebration.

There was some sadness as well. Many crewmen had become friends with their fellow shipyard workers. Some had found sweethearts and lovers, and leaving was a very hard thing to do. Certain crewmembers, while saddened to leave their young ladies, were thankful to depart before the results of those relationships showed in swollen bellies, irate fathers, or by chance, very angry husbands.

A few of the relationships were real and would last if given the chance. In particular, there was the bond between *Island Expedition's* senior midshipman, Thomas Morgan, and Cecilia, Dr. Robertson's young assistant. Pierce sensed the strength of their closeness and knew Morgan found it unbearable to think of leaving her. He thought to let Morgan stay but rejected the idea. Fairness would require him to leave half the crew behind. He could only hope for Thomas Morgan's sake, and the sake of others with honest and true relationships, that someday they would be able to return.

But now they must leave. He would allow the hands and himself one day to recover from effects of the food and drink before sailing.

## Chapter Four

# A Star to Steer By

E dward Pierce was awake. The dawn's half-light seeped through his cabin window. He stirred, gently and gingerly, because his head throbbed and ached. His stomach churned, and he groaned quietly. With the duty that had been instilled over the years, he should rise and be about the day. Just before he painfully pulled himself out of his cot and went for that most desirable first cup of coffee, Pierce remembered that this day was set aside so he and the crew might recover from the previous day's festivities.

He pulled the blanket over his head to block the morning light, half-heartedly scolded himself for overindulging, and fell back asleep.

When he awoke again, the day was brighter and he felt a little better. Regardless of how he felt, it was time to get up. The need to use the head was too urgent, and the smell of freshly brewed coffee penetrated even to his cabin. Both cancelled further thought of sleep.

With the all-important mug of coffee in his hand, he noticed the unusual quietness about the schooner. The bell had not struck to mark the time, nor had he heard the normal sounds and activities of a crew going about its daily duties.

When he gained the upper deck, Midshipman Andrews was there. The final grains of sand fell through the glass, and Andrews noted it on the slate. He turned the glass but did not move to sound the bell, nor direct anyone else to do so.

"Morning, sir," Andrews said softly. "All quiet and as normal as to be expected."

"Good!" His own voice pounded in his ears. "I trust all hands are taking advantage of a day out of discipline."

"It would seem so, sir. I doubt we could roust more than half a dozen at the moment. Most are totally out. May I say, sir, a very wise move after yesterday's celebration?"

"Why thank you, Mr. Andrews. I did put it forward for my own benefit as well as that of the hands. They deserved the day. We deserved the day. One more before sailing will not be a waste."

"Indeed, sir."

"My thanks, Mr. Andrews, that you and a few others refrained. So good of you to take the duty for those not so controlled."

A pleasure, sir, to be sure. And often having felt as some surely do today, I would not wish them to be on watch at all."

"Aye." Pierce shuddered slightly, unnoticed by Andrews, as a mild wave of nausea flowed over him. He gulped at his coffee. "All the same, Mr. Andrews, I'll be glad when we sink this place."

"Aye, as will we all, sir. But I don't fully understand their change of heart."

"I didn't fully fathom it either, until I spoke with the good doctor yesterday."

"When I escorted Madame Bessie?"

"Yes."

"And? If I may be bold enough to ask, sir?"

"As he told it, it had to do with Tritonish and Gallician desire for access to the island. Because of superstitions planted by the Kalish and other Original Peoples, they could not ask us to invite them. They could not even hint at it. We would have had to have asked completely of our own free will."

"Why should we have a say in it, sir?"

"I gather that we have been granted control of the island by the Ancient Ones. Shostolamie thinks we are the ones destined to inhabit it."

"So the Galway Rebel charges were an excuse to keep us here until we should invite them?"

"I believe so, Mr. Andrews."

"Then our Vespican citizenship must have disrupted their plans?"

"Aye."

"I am then, truly grateful for the Unity Congress and Joint Council! It's hard to say how long we would have been kept here, had they not taken action."

"I agree. That they did, and that we sail tomorrow, are certainly reasons to celebrate. But now, do excuse me. I need another cup."

After two more cups of coffee, Pierce felt ready to get on with the day. He sat at his writing table, updating the schooner's log and his personal journal. That done, he took up a book recently purchased in a Brunswick shop and sat back to read it. To relax and read would be an excellent way to spend a very rare day off.

Before he became totally immersed in the story, Pierce detected sounds of more crewmen stirring. More recovered as the morning passed by. Four bells sounded aboard the Gallician frigate across the harbor. Ten o'clock. The day was still young. Come the same time tomorrow, he and the crew of *Island Expedition* would be underway.

They had spent the previous fifteen and a half months in Brunswick, New Guernsey, treated as celebrated guests, even while suspected of being rebels and pirates. All the while they had been kept from leaving. It had been a strange but pleasant ordeal, and had taken place in a world and amongst peoples and nations of whose existence they had not known two years ago.

Strangely, their primary oppressors were those most like their fellow Englishmen. The Unified Kingdom of Grand Triton was in many ways this world's equivalent of the United Kingdom of Great Britain. Kentland was a near copy of England. Perhaps the Kentish were a bit more aggressive, a bit more zealous as the most dominant force in this world. Still, many things, including language, a large and powerful navy, and a desperate fight against a determined foe were the same.

Pierce had also seen a love of liberty and a yearning for individual freedom, tempered with respect and reverence for social rank and distinction, much the same as he had experienced all his life.

While Great Britain was at war with France, Grand Triton was fighting the Gallician Empire, a close approximation of Napoleon's France. Triton also dealt with revolt in the homelands, where Galway Rebels sought their own independence and freedom from Kentish rule.

The rather small detail of different color arrangements between the British and Tritonish flags had caused the Tritonish to suspect that Pierce and his crew were Galway Rebels. Yet, their captors had had their doubts, and rather than sending them to Kentland for trial, had detained them at a Tritonish consulate in Vespica.

Pierce fell asleep despite his interest in the book. Perhaps he wasn't as recovered from the past day's indulgences as he thought. No matter, as that was precisely why he had excused himself and all hands from any sort of duty today.

His unplanned but pleasant nap was interrupted by a gentle rap at the cabin door. "Yes?"

"Mr. Dial's compliments, sir, and *Hawke* has just moored."

"Thank you, Mr. Steadman. Tell Mr. Dial I'll be on deck shortly."

"Aye aye, sir."

Pierce had slept a good while. Dial having the deck meant that noon had passed and that Andrews was no longer on duty. He hurried on deck.

"Good day, Mr. Dial. I understand an old friend has made an appearance."

"Indeed, sir. She's anchored just aft of the Gallician frigate."

"Ah yes! I have her." Pierce looked at the trim Tritonish sloop-of-war. The savage battle between her and his own *Island Expedition* had led to their capture and internment here, even though the British had actually won the ship-to-ship fight.

He should invite Commander Newbury to join him aboard the schooner for a late dinner. But it would be a near thing, to stir up enough life in a well-besotted and recovering crew to provide a truly hospitable meal. Perhaps Newbury would invite him to visit *Hawke?* Pierce thought on.

"Mr. Dial, I believe enough hands are active that we might conduct a signaling drill."

"Signaling drill, sir?"

"Aye. I'm sure we need practice, and I desire a message reach Commander Newbury quickly. You may have Mr. Steadman round up hands to man the signal lockers and halyards."

"Aye aye, sir."

When a sufficient number of semi-sober crewmen were assembled, Pierce said. "Now, lads, shall we send *Hawke's* number and ask Commander Newbury and any others desiring and permitted, to join us at the Frosty Anchor, perhaps beginning with the second dog watch?"

The signal took some time to get together. Pierce had to send Dial below for the list of Tritonish ship identity numbers. The signalmen had to spell out the majority of the message, and that required the use of a great many flags to complete the hoist.

*Hawke's* crew quickly sent along Newbury's affirmative reply. With an engagement scheduled for later, Pierce finally had some structure to his day. Now, he wondered, where was Isaac Hotchkiss, the schooner's first lieutenant?

As the day was a true day off, no one, other than duty volunteers and restricted men, were required to be aboard. Undoubtedly, Pierce's childhood friend had found company to keep him occupied for the night and hadn't yet returned. But he did wish for his friend's presence, if only to invite him along to the popular tavern later that evening.

In a rare fit of righteousness, Pierce mentally denounced Hotchkiss's supposed amorous activities. The fool had a girl waiting for him in England, a girl he had vowed to wed upon his return. But Pierce could not long maintain the condemnation, as he too had succumbed to the charms of a particular captain's wife, and he too had someone waiting.

Hotchkiss returned aboard at seven bells in the afternoon watch, and after being told of the evening's outing, shaved and shifted into his full dress uniform. Now he stood on the quarterdeck, along with Pierce and the sailing master, O'Brien. Three bells in the first dog watch sounded. Five-thirty.

Pierce, washed, shaven, and impeccably dressed, remarked, "I'm quite sure our friend has reported to Lord Sutherland this afternoon. I've not seen his gig return for him, so quite possibly he will go directly to our engagement."

"Possibly," replied Hotchkiss. Being on the quarterdeck and in the presence of the master, he did not assume the intimacy of using his friend's first name. But being friends, he omitted the "sir."

"Then we should be off, Mr. Hotchkiss. Having extended the invitation, our guests should not arrive before we do." Pierce gazed about the schooner's upper deck, studying it in detail.

"You are content to remain as officer of the watch, Mr. O'Brien? Should you desire to join us, I'm sure one of the young gentlemen could be persuaded."

"Oh no sir, I'll be fine. I've had my time at yon Frosty Anchor, and yesterday's doings were enough for me."

"Quite right, then! Remember, if you will, port watch aboard by the end of the evening watch, amidships watch and the starboards aboard at the end of the morning watch."

"Aye aye, sir."

Pierce and Hotchkiss saluted the colors, saluted the quarterdeck, both salutes being returned by the master, and hurried down the brow to the pier. They set off at a leisurely pace towards the Frosty Anchor.

Brunswick's waterfront streets were crowded as laborers and ship-yard workers made their way home for the evening. Liberty parties from the various men-of-war in the harbor jostled their way through the crowds and competed for food, drink, and amorous adventures with merchant seamen and fishermen. A good-natured din filled the air.

At the Frosty Anchor a capacity crowd overflowed the tables, booths, and chairs. Humphrey, the proprietor and his help dashed here and there to accommodate the thirsts and hungers of the many customers. Hotchkiss and Pierce heard the ongoing racket of the place before they turned the corner and saw the entrance.

"A lively place tonight!" remarked Hotchkiss.

"Aye. I would expect a fight or two before closing."

Nearly at the entrance, they stopped abruptly when the door flew open and a body cascaded onto the street. The ejected individual lay still for a moment and then rolled over and sat up, shaking his head. His head somewhat clearer, he stood shakily and headed back inside.

Pierce caught him by the collar before he could take his first step. "You would do well, Williams, to return aboard, now! I'll be asking Mr. O'Brien just what time you returned."

Williams swayed a bit and struggled to focus on his captain. He looked almost pleadingly at Hotchkiss. Hotchkiss nodded in agreement with Pierce, and the seaman slumped a little, nodded, and headed back towards *Island Expedition*. Leaving, he raised his knuckle to his brow in salute and murmured, "Aye aye, sir."

"As I said, a busy place tonight."

"Yes," answered Pierce. "I hope Newbury doesn't mind."

Inside, Humphrey greeted them warmly. "Can't stay away, can you?"

"Apparently not, Humphrey. But it appears no one else can either. I've never seen such a crowd here."

"To be expected, sir. We have two Gallician merchant ships, that one remaining frigate, a Tritonish sloop-of-war, and several newly arrived merchantmen in harbor. All, it seems, have captains or masters not afraid their hands will run."

"The ruckus a minute ago? My crewman?"

"A bit o' disagreement between some from *Hawke* and the Gallician frigate. Your man side with the Kentish lads, but got pitched out."

"I've sent him back aboard."

"As well, for I would have barred him from further entry. Not fair, I know, but it helps keep the peace. Now, gentlemen, if you would like quieter accommodations, Lisa can show you to one of the rooms."

"That would be excellent, sir. And there may be more to join us, including the *Hawke*'s captain and some of his officers."

"Old enemies met for a drink," said Humphrey. "They come around, I'll send them back."

"Our thanks."

They followed the serving girl to a smaller private room. Pierce unconsciously observed her form and wondered if he would take advantage, given the chance.

"Shall I bring you something now, sir?" she asked, "or would you wait for the others?"

"A mug of the best ale for us both, if you would. And perhaps a tray of anything left from yesterday."

Pierce had barely touched his beer and Hotchkiss had not, when Newbury and Jarvis arrived. Lisa came in with two more mugs and a pitcher of ale.

"Does this suit you, Captain Newbury, Mr. Jarvis?" asked Pierce. "Or would you prefer a wine?"

"This will do for the time, Captain Pierce. Are we to dine formally, or do we take advantage of what is already provided?"

"You must decide, of course. I would do well with what is here, but if you wish a set meal, we can arrange it."

"This should do. Does remind me of the salt pork and peas we shared after our set-to."

"Indeed! And how is your mizzen topmast holding up?"

"Well, Captain Pierce. Very well. A strong and robust spar, to say the least. I do hope you will not need it in the future. I do appreciate your gift of it."

"From observing *Hawke* today, it does seem somewhat out of proportion. A trifle long, I'd say."

"Aye," answered Newbury. "But it serves well, and I'll not replace it merely for aesthetics."

"Nor would I, sir, were it my choice to do so," said Jarvis. "It is reminder to all aboard of our battle and later accord. And may I say, sir, that in having temporary command of your schooner, I found her a true seaman's delight!"

"I am amazed, sir," said Hotchkiss, "that we have not seen much of the Flying Squadron in port since our arrival. I understood that the ships rotated in a regular basis for supplies."

"Normally we do. This should have been our second or third visit since your arrival. Because of current operations, we have been revictualing in Nassau."

"*Furious* called. A change in current plans?"

"Oh, I believe Jackson received word his wife was here. Have you met her?"

"Indeed! A charming woman," responded Pierce with an innocent tone. "I didn't see Jackson, as we were in the wilderness, attending to the healing of Mr. Morgan's leg."

"We've heard of his near fatality and subsequent recovery. Our operations recently shifted back to local waters, and we were next in rotation," continued Jarvis. "We were originally scheduled in the end of August, but were delayed further, due to requirements of the service."

"I see," said Pierce. "Here, gentlemen, you must try some of this beef. Most excellent, even cold." Having had nothing but coffee for most of the day, Pierce had an uncommon sharp appetite.

"Amazing that you didn't put in earlier for repairs. I dare say we did considerable damage."

"You did, sir. But you also effected significant repair. Others of the squadron were instrumental in restoring us to full capability. And Nassau has a Regal Navy yard."

"An advantage of being part of a greater unit, even when overseas."

"Aye!"

"And of having access to proper facilities, I believe."

"Quite true, Commander."

The pitcher emptied, and within minutes, Lisa appeared with a full one. Pierce topped everyone's glass.

"You must know," said Newbury, "I honestly thought we had caught a Galway Rebel. I am greatly relieved to learn we did not."

"What convinced you, sir?"

"Many things, to be sure. Perhaps after our initial conversations, my doubts surfaced. When Sir James realized what island you had colonized, what island you had sailed from, he knew the truth."

"And he passed that along to Lord Sutherland, I believe," commented Jarvis.

"Then the entire time we've been here has been because of the island."

"Indeed, Mr. Hotchkiss," said Newbury. "As a loyal subject of King Geoffrey, I had hoped that you would have granted Grand Triton access to Stone Island. But as a friend, I'm glad that you did not yield that point. Better you sail tomorrow with pride intact."

"Truth, Captain Newbury, we didn't know the full measure of it until recently. It was only yesterday that I learned the full details."

"I too confess a certain ignorance. It was not until *Furious* and *Island Expedition* departed the squadron that I learned of the implications of your presence. As I said, I really thought you to be Galway Rebels."

"Evidently," concluded Jarvis, "the full details of the superstitions and legends are not as well-known as one would think. Perhaps the

Vespicans are better-acquainted with them. It is understandable that you would not know of them. But that many of us do not, does seem odd."

"But they are superstitions, are they not?" asked Hotchkiss. "Surely someone will realize that. This is after all, is the modern age, and surely scientific truth and logic will prevail. We are of course grateful for the belief, but how long will it hold sway?"

"Your point is well taken, Isaac," said Pierce. "I have wondered that myself."

"Truly, I have as well." Newbury rose from the table and stepped to the tray of food on the sideboard. He reloaded his plate and sat down.

"For the moment, superstition or not, the balance of power is preserved. Nothing has changed between Gallicia and Triton. Stone Island's annexation does extend the Vespican Truce there as well."

"A blessing, I should suppose, Mr. Jarvis," said Hotchkiss.

"Indeed."

"But Captain Pierce, I must warn you, and indeed all of Vespica, that this truce may not hold," stated Newbury. "Already Gallicia presses the limits more and more. In response, so do we. I would not count indefinitely on the protection of the truce or of the old superstitions."

"Quite understandable."

"As well, once the truce is broken, Vespica is no longer protected. She then enters the world of nations, guarded only by her own strengths. As a new and weak nation, she would be vulnerable to advances from nearly any established power."

"Including Grand Triton?"

"I am reluctant to say so, but yes."

"Bluntly, sir," said Jarvis. "The Unified Kingdom will do what it takes to preserve itself. If that includes trampling upon the toes of a weaker nation to defeat an enemy, such will be done."

"Again, most understandable."

"I think our own Great Britain would act, perhaps has acted in much the same way. Would you not agree, Edward?"

"Most certainly, Isaac."

Newbury yawned. "I'm afraid the day is catching up with me. And on the morrow I have provisioning to attend to, so perhaps we should call an end to this gathering."

"But the evening is still quite young, sir! We have made only slight inroads into the provided refreshments. Still, I see your point. We too shall be busy tomorrow. Getting underway with a crew trapped ashore this past year will not be easy."

"Very true! But first, Captain, a toast to you, your crew, and *Island Expedition*."

"And in return, sir, to you, your crew and *Hawke*."

"Captain Pierce, as we depart this evening, may I state that I sincerely hope we never again meet in battle. But do we meet, bear in mind sir, I will be a much more determined foe, one who will have learned much from our first encounter."

"I would expect nothing less."

"But now Captain, I know you have a long, an impossibly long journey ahead of you. God grant that you have fair seas, steady winds, and a star to steer by."

Despite drinking and eating moderately the evening before, Pierce was not ready to awaken when four bells sounded in the morning watch. The time rang out loud and clear, followed by the shouts of Cartney the bo'sun and his mates, Davis and Campbell, as they roused out the crew. Their bellowed yells of "Out or down!" and "Lash and stow!" penetrated to Pierce's sleeping cabin.

Minutes later, dressed, and with a cup of coffee in hand, Pierce arrived on deck. Morgan, telescope under his arm, had the watch. Hotchkiss was there as well. Pierce shook his head slightly, ignored them, and proceeded aft to the taffrail. He gazed out at Brunswick harbor, at the myriad of commercial shipping and smattering of foreign men-of-war. From what he could see, his own schooner, HMS

*Island Expedition* might be the closest thing to a Vespican warship in port. That was due only to their new and somewhat honorary status as Vespican citizens. Most certainly they were the only British ship there, and with quite certain probability, the only British ship in this world.

Because of that honorary citizenship, he and his crew would be leaving today, once the tide turned and was favorable for their departure. With that thought he awoke a bit more and took another drink of his coffee.

"Good morning, Mr. Hotchkiss, Mr. Morgan," he said.

"Good morning, sir!"

"And to you," replied Hotchkiss. "A fine day, I think, for our departure."

"Aye, Mr. Hotchkiss," said Pierce. "I know you reference the weather. But regardless, our leaving makes it a fine day. Would it be the tide turned now?"

"Of course, sir," said Morgan the senior midshipman. He did not look happy.

Pierce noticed the despondency. "Mr. Morgan, you must hold your head up now and understand that this is how many of us felt upon leaving England. No doubt there are others aboard who will be leaving someone behind."

"Aye aye, sir. But I will miss her, sir--truly I will."

"I'm sure of it, Tom. I hope a way opens for you to return someday."

"Aye, sir. Thank you, sir!"

Hotchkiss spoke to fill the void in conversation. "All hands are back aboard. Three arrived past the stated times. I have their names should you wish to prescribe any punishment."

"I think, Mr. Hotchkiss, that the efforts of getting underway after a night of liberty would do most wondrous things in that line. But do pass me their names. It will certainly lessen their chances for leniency in the future."

"Aye aye!"

At six bells in the forenoon watch, *Island Expedition* cast off her lines. Because of her location in the inner harbor, the amount of shipping about, and the adverse direction of the wind, she could not immediately set sail. Instead, cables were carried out in the boats and secured to pilings. The hands manned the capstan, and through sheer physical effort, hauled the large schooner into the harbor's waters. When the cables were nearly all aboard, they moored temporarily to the adjacent piling and transferred the cables farther out.

By these means and the exhausting labor they entailed, they eventually reached a point where a minimum of sail could be set, and with judicious seamanship, they could proceed, short board by short board, out of the harbor.

The task called for intensive concentration by Pierce and the other officers. The schooner had lain idle in port for several months, and the crew had lost its highly trained edge. Perhaps the officers had lost theirs as well. He cautioned them to be particularly cautious with each step of the procedure.

As the first sails were hoisted, Pierce noted that they would pass close by HRMS *Hawke*. The sloop-of-war was dressing ship, running up a myriad of national flags, naval ensigns, and signal flags. Hands turned out in their best shore-going rigs to man the rails and the yards.

"Mr. Hotchkiss!" Pierce bellowed. "It appears Newbury is giving us a proper send-off. We must acknowledge, of course. All hands that can be spared, man the starboard rail!"

"Aye aye, sir. Shall we pipe?"

"Of course, providing Davis or Campbell can be spared."

As *Island Expedition* neared the anchored warship, those hands who were available lined the rail. As they drew even with the Tritonish man-of-war, Hotchkiss called the crew to attention and nodded at the bo'sun's mates. They began the call while Pierce and the others lifted their hats in salute. At the same time, drums rolled aboard *Hawke*, pipes squealed, and on the quarterdeck, Newbury, Jarvis, and others saluted. Then, as the two vessels were broadside to broadside, a rousing three cheers issued forth from *Hawke*.

"We shall return their cheers!" ordered Pierce, and the English seamen responded enthusiastically. He suspected that many hands from both vessels had spent the past evening taking in the town, drinking and carousing together.

Other ships and vessels in the harbor had caught the celebratory mood, and as *Island Expedition* passed, each offered their own salute, their own cheer, their own form of recognition. However, as the schooner passed the remaining Gallician frigate, the other had sailed the day before, there was near silence. Those on deck either observed the passing schooner casually, without reaction, or turned about and pointedly ignored the departing Englishmen.

"I should feel insulted, Isaac, were I not so damned happy to be underway at last. No doubt they are angry that we did not offer them use of Stone Island."

"But neither did we offer it to the Kentish."

"True! And note we have not seen Lancaster or Sutherland since. I'm sure *Hawke's* salute was between two vessels, captains, and crews, not a reflection of official policy."

"The merchant ships cheer us, because we emerged victorious from what seemed an impossible situation. And our small victory has added to Vespican integrity in this world."

"Most likely, Mr. Hotchkiss."

Pierce glanced about, checking their course, the wind's direction, and the location of other vessels. "Port your helm! Bring her about! Handsomely now!" It was time to be handling the schooner and not to be wondering about the varied reactions to their sailing.

*Chapter Five*

# The Chase

When they cleared the last buoy marking the channel into Brunswick's harbor, Pierce set course, north northwest by north. The island lay to the west, but first they had to clear Cape Stanislaus, a large body of land that ran north for nearly ninety miles. Then, and only then could they take a more direct course to the island. Even so, they would be forced to beat to windward. While he desired a speedy return to the island and knew the schooner could safely carry more sail, he refrained from ordering it set. They were still in the relatively confined and shallow waters of Graves Bay, and he didn't want to risk going aground or colliding with another vessel. He had new and updated charts, courtesy of a Brunswick-based shipping company, but he was not familiar with these waters. It was better to proceed at a moderate pace and be alert for danger.

But even now, the schooner was out of the congested waters of the harbor, and the intensity of navigation had eased considerably. Pierce climbed into the windward main shrouds, his preferred spot when addressing the crew.

"All hands! All hands! Lend an ear there!" he yelled. "Lads, we are on our way home! I commend your deportment during our enforced stay in Brunswick. You all represented His Majesty and His Majesty's Navy in a most impressive manner!"

That pronouncement brought forth a general roar of approval. "Well then," said Pierce. "If you are so damned proud of it, give yourselves three cheers!"

Pierce waited until the "huzzahs" were over, and continued. "When we sailed last, I insisted we drill. Now we have been in port so long that we have surely grown rusty and unsure of our skills. We must relearn our seamanship. When those basic skills come back, we will resume those drills that once honed us to such a fine edge.

"You might expect we would splice the main brace. Lads, we've been ashore for months, and none of you have thirsted. From what I see, a few days abstinence would do all some good.

"We should return to Stone Island in two weeks' time. There we will assess the state of the colonists and make further repairs and preparations for our return to England. When ready, we will sail again, bound for England and home!"

The last statement also brought cheers.

"Now lads, let's carry on in a shipshape manner. Mind your duties and keep an eye on your shipmates. Trust God that He bring all of us back to England!"


The next day *Island Expedition* cleared Cape Stanislaus as seven bells sounded in the forenoon watch. Pierce was still on deck. He had been there through the night, tired though he was. He did not want to lessen the sensation of being free and at sea again, even to go below for a rest. To avoid taxing the unused maritime skills of the crew, *Island Expedition* wore ship, rather than tacked as she came about. However, upon reaching the open sea, Pierce cracked on all sail the schooner could carry. But he did so slowly, one sail, one task at a time, allowing for the crew's lack of practice.

With a west northwest wind, *Island Expedition* thrashed along magnificently on a starboard tack, running two points large. Her lee rail was nearly submerged in the churning white foam as she drove forcefully into each mounting sea. Spray flew over the deck, refreshing those there.

Pierce had never before pushed the schooner as hard as he did now. He was usually conservative with what sail he set, maintaining a margin of safety to avoid damage to the top hamper. Now he felt such a strong urge to be away from Brunswick, New Guernsey, and to re-join those on the island, that he abandoned all caution.

He pushed *Island Expedition* to the limits, surprising all by setting more sail when most would take some in. Prudence and caution went by the boards as Pierce was driven to be away, far away from the place of their recent captivity. Or did he enjoy the freedom of being at sea again, and of having the option, and the ability, to sail the sticks right out of her, should he choose to do so?

On the fifth day at sea, Pierce sat below and worked the ship's posi-tion. They were making good daily runs, splendid indeed, in spite of sailing into the wind. Yet their projected course tended more southerly than he would have liked. Much more and they would sail south of the island and miss it. It was time to come about and assume a port tack for the remainder of the day. A few leagues to the northwest would place them in a better position to finally raise the island. He would also be able to see if the crew had regained their maritime abilities.

"Mr. Hadley!" he called to the officer of the watch.

"Aye, sir?"

"Call the watch below, if you would. We shall be going about!"

"Aye aye, sir!" Hadley replied and then turned to the bo'sun's mate.

Calls squealed from the pipes, and shouts rang down the hatches. "All hands! All hands! All hands 'bout ship!"

Stations were manned in decent time, but not with the lightning-quick speed in which Pierce knew it could be done. He refrained from commenting.

"We shall tack, Mr. Hotchkiss."

"Aye, sir."

"A day or so on the port tack will do us well, I believe."

"That it will."

"All hands! Stand by!" yelled Pierce. "Helm alee!" The wheel spun and the schooner nosed into the wind.

"Headsail sheets! Staysail sheets!" The bow was nearly into the wind. The schooner's momentum and the leverage of the headsails would carry her through to settle on the opposite tack.

Topsails and topgallants thundered as the wind no longer struck from aft. The huge canvas sheets thundered against the masts. "Lee braces!" shouted Pierce. "Bring them around!" The heavy yards had to be braced around to allow the wind to push once again against the sail's after sides.

But the hands weren't quick enough. Headsails were shifted too slowly. Yards weren't braced around as smartly as in the past. *Island Expedition* lost the impetus of the turn. The square sails remained aback, pressing against the masts, rather than pulling away from them. The headsails did not fill and pull the bows through the wind. The schooner was caught in irons.

"Damn!" said Pierce and nothing more, even though several profane, sarcastic, and biting oaths came to mind.

*Island Expedition* effectively came to a stop and began to gather stern way. "Starboard your helm!" ordered Pierce. That would swing the bows to starboard, and the final effect would be as desired. Yards could be braced to have the wind behind the sails again. The fore and aft sails would fill and allow the schooner to resume her forward progress.

"We need work at this, Isaac," said Pierce when they had settled on their new course.

"Quite so, Edward. A relief this performance was not witnessed."

"Aye. A rather lubberly showing. We'll drill this afternoon."

"Deck there! Sail on the starboard bow!" the mainmast lookout hailed.

"What do you make of her?" Pierce asked.

"Just visible, sir! Can't make much of it!"

"Keep your eye on her!"

"Aye aye, sir!"

Master's Mate Dial watched the sand fall into the bottom of the glass, turned it, and nodded to the seaman at the belfry. Six bells, eleven o'clock, and in an hour the forenoon watch would end.

"A harmless passing of two ships upon the sea, one would hope, sir," said Hotchkiss.

"I do hope that is true, Mr. Hotchkiss. I've no desire to lose time in conversation. We have learned all and more than I desired to know before we fell in with Newbury and *Hawke*."

"A meeting of that nature would be most unwelcome."

"Should such a storm appear to be brewing, my friend, I'll not hesitate putting wings to her and showing them our heels."

"Aye. A prudent choice, if I may say so."

After a few minutes passed by, Pierce unconsciously checked his watch. It was a quarter past the hour.

The lookout hailed again. "Ship rigged, sir! Looks to be intercepting us!"

"Any details yet?"

"Barely. Might be that Gallician frigate what sailed the day before us!"

"Are you sure?"

"No, sir! Too far, even with the glass!"

"Mr. Dial, you may run below for my best glass. Then to the crosstrees with you."

"Aye aye, sir."

"Hopefully mine will better define what can be seen, Isaac."

Moments later Dial was perched in the main topmast crosstrees, expertly matching the movements of the schooner with the large telescope. His movements cancelled the roll and pitch, felt with greater degree aloft, and allowed him to keep the glass directly on the object of interest.

"He's right, sir," Dial said. "It's almost certainly that Toad frigate!" At home he would have referred to the French as Frogs. Here he adopted the Tritonish euphemism commonly applied to the Gallicians.

"Her course, Mr. Dial? Can you ascertain her course?"

"Drawing closer, sir! Looks to be on the starboard tack! Close hauled and closing!"

"Very well!" Pierce was silent after that. He paced the deck, thinking. "I'm not sure what she's up to, but it can't be good. I never have trusted these Gallicians. Remind me too much of the French," he said a few moments later.

"Quite the same with me, sir," replied Hotchkiss.

Pierce wondered if he shouldn't alter course immediately, crowd on even more sail, and bear away from the approaching frigate. But would such flight bring on a hostile reaction from the nearing frigate? Perhaps the Gallician only wished to talk.

At the wheel, Mitchell deftly turned the glass. Dial was still aloft, and the helmsman timed his move to when he could momentarily leave but one hand on the spokes. He nodded, and forward the marine, Nesbit rang the bell seven times. Eleven-thirty. With "all hands" previously called, the entire crew crowded the deck. There was a growing rumble of chatter as they assessed the situation.

"Silence!" roared Pierce. "With a Toad frigate approaching, we may need excellent and rapid sail handling. No! We shall not fight should they desire it. We are no match, and I will not see us detained again!"

A disappointed rumble vibrated over the schooner's deck. Pierce glared and opened his mouth to speak. Out of the corner of his eye he saw O'Brien the master and Hotchkiss the first lieutenant glare as well. Evidently the looks were enough, for the muttering soon died down. Pierce knew that should he order it, this crew would lay the small schooner alongside a hostile first rate. He admired their bravado, but questioned their common sense.

Morgan, Andrews, Townsend, Hadley, and Spencer were now on the quarterdeck, each with his sextant for the noon sightings. An added complication, along with the consideration of dinner, thought Pierce. While he currently had little appetite, he prided himself on ensuring the hands ate as scheduled whenever possible. In a half hour, noon would be declared and hands would await the word to pipe all hands to dinner. But could they afford that when at that very moment he might need all hands to 'bout ship, set more sail, and bear away from the frigate?

The Gallician was visible from deck when *Island Expedition* rose to the swell. Using the officer of the watch's glass, Pierce observed the approaching vessel in on-again, off-again fashion. He could see well enough to determine that as Dial suggested, she was the one that had left Brunswick the day before they had. He wondered if the approaching ship had dispatches for them, but having sailed a day earlier, he knew that couldn't be the case. If the Gallician captain did have any messages for them, they could have been passed while both had been in port. This was another reason why he should consider the frigate as hostile.

Pierce took a bearing on the approaching ship, and a few moments later took a second bearing. "She's head-reaching on us, Mr. Hotchkiss. She'll cross our path well before we cross hers."

"Fast ship, sir. Well-handled, it seems."

"Aye."

Pierce looked at his watch, which showed ten minutes remaining until noon. He watched as the crowd of master's mates and midshipmen worked their way forward in order to gain a better view of the sun. Today, neither he, Hotchkiss, nor O'Brien would participate in the noon sightings. Their accuracy, and hence the determination of current noon and their daily fix, would depend upon the master's mates and midshipmen. Pierce was more concerned with the approaching ship.

He watched as the younger officers took their noon sightings. Stealing a second of observation away from the approaching frigate, he saw them nod their heads in agreement. Spencer separated from the group and made his way into Lieutenant Hotchkiss's presence. Hotchkiss nodded in reply to the quiet message.

Then he turned towards Pierce, raised his hat in salute, and said, "Indications are that it's noon, sir."

"Very well! Make it noon!" Pierce eyed the Gallician. "You may pipe to dinner, Mr. Hotchkiss. One watch at a time, and idlers to eat in rotation."

"Aye aye, sir! Sound eight bells! Pipe to dinner by watches!"

The starboards had eaten and were back at their duties. The port watch and remaining idlers were well into their midday meal. Pierce watched the ever-closer frigate, gauged its approaching speed, and compared that to the progress of the meal. It would be a close thing if all hands finished before action of some kind was required.

Only two thousand yards separated the two vessels, and that distance lessened fast. As determined earlier, the frigate would reach the intersection of their courses first, and would cross the schooner's bows. The range would be extreme, lessening the danger, but still *Island Expedition* would be at a disadvantage, facing into the frigate's murderous broadside. If he were captain of the other vessel, Pierce would let her fall off a bit and shorten the distance that would exist when courses crossed. He saw no sign of the Gallician coming off the wind.

Most of the port watch finished their dinner and returned, nervous and excited, to their duty stations. The last time a ship had approached them like this, they had fought a tremendous and terrible battle. Would another take place in a matter of moments? Pierce again gauged the approach of the frigate. He was glad that all hands had had their dinner. He would not hesitate to call them into action should it be warranted.

The distance between the two vessels lessened rapidly. Now only a thousand yards of water existed between them. They were in range, although the chance of a hit at this distance was slight. Pierce, if he were going to fight, would want the range much reduced. Were the Gallicians like the French, and prone to open fire at longer distances?

For some time now, Pierce had been able to observe the Gallician from deck. Her long black hull was unrelieved by any contrasting stripe along the gun ports. A keen eye now and memory of close observation in Brunswick told him that narrow stripes of dark red, each a single strake wide, ran along the hull, one above and one below the main deck gun ports. Behind the still-shuttered ports lurked eighteen-pounder long guns. Like the French, the Gallician weapons fired shot closer to twenty pounds in weight. A single broadside from them would devastate the schooner.

"Activity on her fo'c'sle, Edward!" said Hotchkiss quietly.

"I see it."

"Bow chasers?"

"Perhaps. Maybe a warning shot. Should we be forced to maneuver, pray we do better than this morning."

"Aye!"

His heart beat faster and Pierce felt a sudden need to use the head. It would be a useless trip if he succumbed to the urge, so he remained on deck. He finalized his plans, what he would do, based on what the Gallician did. He had no intention of trading broadsides with the much larger ship. Yet he would not flee or alter course until given a reason. *Island Expedition* had every right to be on her present course, and Pierce would not change it except to avoid collision or to avert damage from hostile action.

Smoke billowed from the Gallician's bows. The sound reached them as the shot raised a splash thirty yards ahead. Signals broke out on the frigate's leeward main yardarm.

"I understand the shot, Isaac! But the signal?"

"Perhaps what the shot is meant to reinforce? Can Mr. Spencer enlighten us?"

"Very well! And quickly, lad!" Pierce again needed to visit the head. With determination, the sensation passed.

Spencer approached with the Tritonish signal book in hand. Someone in Brunswick for whom Pierce had done a small favor had obtained it for him. "Standard Kentish naval code," said Spencer. "Simply says, 'surrender!' sir."

"Like bloody hell!" said one of the helmsmen who overheard.

Aboard the rapidly nearing frigate, Gallician mariners struggled to reload the bow chaser. The frigate rose to a swell and her leeward heel lessened. The nine-pounder boomed again. There was the buzzing sound of the shot punching through the air. A tear appeared in the mainsail, feet over Pierce's head.

Because the frigate heeled towards them, Pierce saw a flurry of activity about her deck. She was making ready to turn and bring her broadside to bear. But they would first need to run out the guns, and that would take some time. Unless, thought Pierce, the higher-positioned guns of the windward battery were already run out. Perhaps she would make more of a turn and bring her starboard battery, rather than the visible port battery to bear on her non-compliant victim.

"Now lads!" roared Pierce. "Helm alee!" He fervently hoped that they could pull off this episode of coming about better than they had earlier. "Headsail sheets! Staysail sheets!"

The bows faced squarely into the wind. This time things worked as they should; *Island Expedition's* head carried through the wind and she fell off on a starboard tack. Pierce let the turn continue.

The wind was on her beam and then on her quarter. "Hold her at that!" Pierce shouted at the helmsmen. "Mr. O'Brien, ringtail and windward studding sails!"

"Aye aye, sir!"

"Let's show these Toads just what she has for heels," Pierce said in a conspiratorial tone to Hotchkiss.

"We should be free of them come nightfall."

Pierce chanced a look at the frigate. She had swung her bows directly at and then past the schooner. True to his earlier realization, her starboard battery was ready and run out, and as her turn continued, the guns came to bear on the *Island Expedition*. "Port your helm!" Pierce shouted.

If the Gallician gunners were well-trained, they would aim slightly forward of the schooner. By turning back into the wind, Pierce hoped to upset that aim. A destructive broadside was coming, and he wanted to avoid as much of it as possible.

Savage flashes of light burst from the guns. Smoke billowed and cloaked the frigate's side. The rumbling thunder reached his ears, and at the same time shot screamed overhead, tearing several holes in the sails. Lines parted and the main topmast trembled. He waited for the crash of shot striking the hull, and the clouds of splinters that eighteen-pound shot would send up.

To port, several shots splashed harmlessly into the sea. Some fell where the schooner would have been, had she not turned back into the wind. But most fell well short of the mark, and damage would not have been that great, even had he not ordered the course change. As the frigate's guns had bore, she had been caught by a particularly large swell. With her guns pointed directly at the schooner's presumed position, the excess and unexpected movement had thrown off the gun captains' aims.

"Starboard helm! There! There! Hold her so!" The schooner was again on the starboard broad reach achieved after her first turn. The additional sails ordered set earlier were spread to the wind. Pierce ordered royals set as well, and *Island Expedition* thundered through the sea.

The frigate had ceased her port turn, and had come around to starboard until she was on the same course as the schooner. As Pierce watched, additional sails blossomed from the frigate's masts. Topgallants, royals, skysails--all made an appearance. Windward, her starboard side studding sails appeared, as did those on the foremast to leeward. The frigate's spirit sail and spirit topsail appeared under her bowsprit.

"She intends to run us down, I think!" remarked Hotchkiss.

"She does, but I doubt she will," Pierce answered. "I know of no vessel that will keep up with us."

"But she moves right along, sir," offered O'Brien the master. Flashes and smoke appeared briefly on the frigate's fo'c'sle. "Bow chasers, again," he remarked, and two splashes along the port side rained water on the deck. The schooner dug into a larger swell and water came over the port bow and rushed along the deck.

"I can move a gun aft, sir?" said Harris the gunner. "Chips and his mates can cut a port for it?"

"I think not, Mr. Harris. We will look to outdistancing her."

"Aye, sir." The gunner was disappointed. He had hoped to return even a token of fire at the pursuing Gallician, and if lucky, knock away a spar or important stay.

"I'm sure we will have times when such gunnery will be needed, Mr. Harris. Now, I see no need for it." Pierce said.

"And I say, gentlemen, it looks as if the chase is on!" commented Hotchkiss.

"Strange that we are pursued and not pursuing, sir," observed Andrews.

"But not for long, I would think," said Hadley.

"Gentlemen! This quarterdeck is a session of Parliament, what with the debates and discussions? Surely you have duties to attend to.

"Mr. Hotchkiss, you may dismiss the watch below. Pass along that all hands are to be alert for instant recall."

"Aye aye, sir."

The frigate's bow chasers thundered again. The twin splashes rose well astern.

*Island Expedition* thrashed through the seas. She rode over them, shouldered them aside, and on occasion seemed to dive right through them. Pierce scrutinized the set of the sails and felt with his very being the strains and twists placed upon the schooner. He would press hard, expose every scrap of canvas possible to outdistance the Gallician frigate. There was a limit that meant escape and safety if not exceeded. Go beyond, and the lofty powerful top hamper could come down in a shower of ripped sail cloth, parted lines, split spars, and more. Such destruction would be the same as being struck by enemy shot, slowing them up and allow their pursuers to close in.

"Mr. O'Brien," shouted Pierce. "Should you slack the mainsheet half a fathom, you will find she draws better."

"Aye aye, sir. A fathom off the mainsail sheet, there!"

"Helm, come up half a point!"

"Aye aye, sir! Up half a point!"

With the excitement of the encounter dying away and their flight well in hand, Pierce relaxed. Did he dare leave the deck to go below? He hadn't bothered to eat when the crew's dinner was served and now the pangs of hunger stabbed at him.

The Gallician's actions and apparent intentions puzzled him. *Island Expedition* sailed under the Vespican flag, indicating the recently granted citizenship of her crew. The Independent Lands of Vespica were neutral in the current war between Grand Triton and the Gallician Republic. That particular frigate had been in Brunswick when Pierce and the British seamen had been released by the Tritonish Consulate. It was hard to believe that the Gallician captain did not know what vessel he had tried to detain and now pursued. To Pierce it was a blatant disregard of the rules of neutrality and common courtesy of the sea. But the Gallicians were this world's equivalent of the French. From his few dealings with them, Pierce knew the Gallicians might be as treacherous.

Throughout the bright afternoon the two vessels flew over the water, sails spread to the skies as they sought to gain every measure of speed from the light but steady breeze. Occasionally fire and smoke bloomed from the frigate's bows, but rarely did the shots come close enough to cause comment aboard the schooner. At the start of the first dog watch, Morgan announced that while still hull up, the frigate was indeed much farther away. Slowly and steadily *Island Expedition* pulled away.

As the sun set, and as twilight pervaded the sky, the frigate was still visible from deck, her sails a brilliant man-made star, low on the horizon. Pierce relaxed a bit more. At this rate they would be well out of sight by morning. Then the only foreseen difficulty would be in reversing their course and slipping by the Gallician.

## Chapter Six

# Evasion

At the end of the second dog watch, the Gallician frigate was no longer visible from deck. From aloft, her cloud of canvas was just visible on the horizon, faintly illuminated in the southern spring's lingering twilight. Because she was so far away, and because each moment increased that distance, *Island Expedition* settled into a normal nighttime routine.

Pierce, along with Hotchkiss, Morgan, Andrews, and O'Brien, sat in the stern cabin. Remnants of a half-finished meal and half-finished glasses of brandy sat on the table.

"As I've always believed, sir," said Andrews. "These damn Gallicians are as bad as the French."

"Worse, in my opinion," said O'Brien.

"What could be their motive?"

"I surely wouldn't know, Mr. Morgan," answered Pierce.

"Captain Newbury did remark that the Toads are pushing the limits of Vespican neutrality. Perhaps this is an example of it," Hotchkiss joined in.

"But to attack a neutral flagged ship, sir! Would that not cause a neutral third party to seek alliance with one's enemy?"

"My first inclination, Mr. Andrews, is that that would be true. But did they act against any ship flying Vespican colors, or did they seek us out?"

"Aye, sir. They sailed a day before us, knowing we sailed the next day." O'Brien stretched, yawned, and took another sip of brandy. "They knew where we are bound."

"Perhaps, sir," offered Morgan, "they do not understand the

details of our release. Do they think we secretly offered access to the Tritonish? As I understand the superstitions, action against us would not gain them the island or an advantage. Surely any attack would be a pure act of vengeance."

"If these Gallicians are like the French, that would not be the case, Mr. Morgan." Hotchkiss continued. "They are too cunning, too devious to attack simply out of spite. No, they are up to something more insidious."

"Indeed, Mr. Hotchkiss! Pray we fathom it beforehand. Now gentlemen, the hour is late. Some of you have the duty later in the night. Let us get what rest we can, and in the morning we will figure a course past that frigate." Pierce drained the last of his brandy.

With a hostile vessel in pursuit, many captains would remain on deck and in full charge of the situation. Edward Pierce had the utmost confidence in his officers, and allowed them their duties. He went to sleep, assured that all minor difficulties would be handled, and that he would be called in event of any major development.

The next morning Pierce awoke, not to four bells in the morning watch, but to the shouts of the lookouts and the profane curses of those on deck. At first he was perturbed by this unusual disturbance of his rest. He had planned to sleep another thirty minutes, until four bells did indeed ring to bring the schooner to life. The noise's meaning sunk in, and he hurried on deck.

Pierce didn't bother to dress, refresh himself, or even go after his first cup of coffee. He arrived on deck, still in his night shirt, slippers on his feet, and his oldest undress uniform coat thrown haphazardly about his shoulders. He wiped the sleep from the corners of his eyes.

"There, sir! There, almost dead astern, sir! That damned Toad frigate!"

"I gathered that, Mr. Spencer. A little more quiet about the deck, if you please, sir! We are still awaiting four bells."

"Aye, sir. Sorry, sir. I was about to send Mr. Steadman to wake you."

Hotchkiss arrived, looking as disheveled as Pierce. The shouts had brought him out of his sleep as well. "What the...?"

"That Gallician frigate," said Pierce.

Hotchkiss squinted and peered at the white dot on the horizon. "It can't be! At the rate we were gaining at sundown, she should be well astern and of no concern by now."

"Aye," said Pierce. He contemplated the situation.

"She gained a little since first sighted, I think, sir," suggested Steadman. "Stands out clearer than before."

"Indeed, Mr. Steadman." Pierce continued. "There is surely some explanation for this." He crossed to the rough deck log to look over the entries made during the night. Perhaps there was some clue there. Had there been lulls in the steady but light wind, slowing the schooner and not affecting the frigate, allowing her to close the distance? Had there been such anomalies, he would have been summoned. There was nothing noted in the log to account for the Gallician's nearness, nor had he been notified of any unusual circumstance of wind or weather.

"Mr. Steadman, if you would, coffee for Mr. Hotchkiss and myself." Perhaps he would think more clearly if he had his first cup of the day.

"Most certainly, sir."

The coffee did not allow him the luxury of a solution. It confounded him to know they had pulled steadily away from the pursuing frigate as the sun set, but the dawn's light found it to be in sight once again. A second cup of steaming hot coffee did not help. After draining it, Pierce saw that the frigate was indeed a little closer.

"Deck there!" came the shout from the main topmast crosstrees.

"Aye!" acknowledged Spencer, officer of the watch.

"It's not the same frigate, sir!"

"Preposterous!" snorted O'Brien who had joined them.

"How so?" Pierce shouted aloft.

"Patch on the fore topgallant, sir. Had one yesterday, but not now."

"My God, sir!" exclaimed Morgan. "Were they lying in wait for us?"

"Possibly." Pierce thought for a moment. Such would explain the ship now in their wake, but it would not explain that even now, that vessel gained on them.

Andrews grabbed a glass and went aloft.

Pierce strode to the helm. He watched the compass in the binnacle as the helmsman held the schooner on course. The man at the wheel was an old hand, and the wake remained smooth and straight. "Does she handle all right?"

"Aye, sir. Near same as she always does."

Pierce checked the deck log again, paying particular attention to the wind conditions noted and the schooner's speed as recorded at half-hour intervals. Nothing seemed amiss. Yet with a quick glance aft, he could see that they were being overtaken.

Andrews hollered from the main topmast. "He's right, sir! It's a different frigate. Looks like one that was in port six weeks ago!"

Pierce digested the confirmation. The first frigate, the one they had fled yesterday, had left port a day ahead of them. Knowing the Englishmen's destination and probable route, it had lain in wait for them. During the time before the interception, it had chanced to rendezvous with the second frigate. That ship had stationed itself farther along the intended route, providing a second chance at accosting the schooner.

That much was clear and made sense. The reasons behind the aggression were not. As had been tentatively discussed the night before, he was sure it had to do with their release by the Tritonish, and the ongoing war between Triton and Gallicia. But these details were not important at the moment. What did matter was that they were losing the race to the second frigate, and in a matter of hours would be prisoners again, if they were not blown out of the water.

But how could they be losing? How could that Gallician frigate be steadily gaining on them? *Island Expedition* was by far the fastest vessel Pierce had ever sailed in. She should pull away from her pursuer with ease. Was her bottom fouled? She had been afloat for over two years, the last twelve months tied up along a pier in Brunswick, New Guernsey. That provided ample time for various marine growths to gain hold on her underwater surfaces.

"Beg pardon, sir," said Morgan, daring to break into Pierce's concentrated thought.

"Yes, Mr. Morgan?"

"I do not wish to intrude into your thoughts, sir, but something just came to mind."

"Regarding our predicament?"

"Quite possibly, sir."

"Well then, let's hear it."

"Aye, sir. I was remembering how in Brunswick, when I had first recovered enough to get around on crutches. Weak as I was, I fatigued myself more, trying to move my legs as if walking normally. Cecilia told me to relax and let the crutches and my good leg do the work. I got around much easier remembering that."

"And?"

"Perhaps we are pushing her too hard. Might we make better time with a little less canvas to the wind?"

"I don't see that as possible, sir," remarked O'Brien. "The more sail, the more speed. And in these light airs, we need all the sail we can spread."

"I would agree," said Pierce. "But I do see Mr. Morgan's point. We have never sailed under these exact conditions before, and very likely the press of sail could be overpowering her, forcing her deeper into the water."

Momentarily, O'Brien looked thoughtful, and then his expression indicated that he saw Morgan's point.

Pierce glanced astern and calculated the frigate's rate of closure. "It appears we have another hour or two before she is within range. All hands to have a good breakfast, and then we experiment."

"Aye, sir!"

"Mr. Hotchkiss, after breakfast, you may beat to quarters."

"Aye aye, sir."

Pierce suddenly needed to use the head.

When the crew had breakfasted, the marine drummer beat the rapid tattoo that called, "All hands to quarters." The galley fires were extinguished, bulkheads and partitions were struck below, and decks were sluiced and sanded. Harris the gunner donned his felt slippers and stepped into the magazine to fill cartridges. Guns were manned, cast off, and run in for loading.

Out of habit, Pierce checked his watch. It was not the quickest he had seen this crew do it, but they had not drilled lately and he thought the time taken to be most satisfactory. Hotchkiss reported to him that all stations were manned and that all hands were present and sober.

"Double shot the guns, Mr. Hotchkiss! Load and run out, if you please!" Pierce ordered.

"Aye aye, sir."

"Now, Mr. O'Brien, let us see if there is anything to Mr. Morgan's suggestion."

"Aye, sir."

"We will make any changes slowly. Hopefully the Toads won't notice and compensate. To begin, we need a cast of the log so we can judge if anything done is effective."

When that task was done, Hadley reported that they were making just over ten knots. While that was exceptionally rapid, Pierce was disappointed. He had hoped for something in the neighborhood of eleven to twelve.

"Easy now, helm," he said. "Slowly, lads, bring her three points into the wind. A point at a time and hold there momentarily." At the wheel, Jones and Hopkins eased the spokes through their fingers as the turn began. As soon as the gentle change of direction began, they reversed the wheel and held to the new course. They waited while *Island Expedition* surged over two large swells, and then again they eased her another point to starboard. Moments later they made the third and final part of the easy turn.

Pierce studied the frigate through his best glass. For the moment she appeared not to have noticed the subtle change in direction of her prey. He saw no evidence of her altering course in a similar fashion.

"Another cast of the log, if you would, Mr. Hadley!"

The results of that showed a very slight increase in their velocity.

"Another point into the wind!" ordered Pierce. Once accomplished, this slight adjustment to their course gave them near to eleven knots.

"We'll hold this awhile and see if it is enough that we pull away from her."

"Aye, sir."

"Mr. Hotchkiss, you may leave guns loaded. But do secure them and stand down! You may secure the watch below and relight the galley fires. We will have our dinner unless interrupted."

"Aye aye, sir."

There was a minimum of grumbling as the prospects of a fight faded. It always amazed Pierce that men who could so easily be wounded, killed, or maimed were always so eager for a fight. And it did not matter to them if they served aboard a first rate running down a gunboat, or in this very schooner going broadside to broadside with an enemy twice their size. He shook his head silently, satisfied and relieved that he would not be forced at the time to risk their lives.

The subtle change in course was only somewhat effective. Their speed increased enough that they stayed a set distance ahead of the

Gallician frigate. It neither gained on them, nor did they pull away from it. Perhaps now it was time to investigate Morgan's theory. Did they carry too much sail, that the excessive press of it drove them deeper into the water, rather than more swiftly over it?

He saw a certain logic to it, but Pierce did not want to visibly shorten sail. He wasn't sure what implications such an action would have when seen from the frigate. Better, he thought, that they make any changes in a less dramatic fashion than obviously shortening sail.

"Mr. O'Brien, if you would, slack off all sheets a half fathom. Let's spill a little of the wind. But easy now, so that the Toads don't see it."

"Aye aye, sir," the master answered, a minute skeptical tone in his voice.

Canvas, stretched taut and flat against the pressure of the wind, eased slightly in its strain and billowed into more rounded form. Pierce felt the constant port list ease a tiny amount, and the strain on the backstays lessen imperceptibly. He thought the schooner seemed to be sailing faster, but he wasn't sure.

"The log, Mr. Hadley!"

"Aye aye, sir."

When the log had been cast, Hadley reported. "Nigh on eleven, sir."

"Thank you. Now, Mr. O'Brien, ease mainsail and foresail sheets another half fathom!"

When that had been accomplished, Hadley again cast the log. This time he was able to report, "Eleven knots and two fathoms, sir!"

Pierce nodded acknowledgement and studied the frigate through his glass. Some time ago she had detected the schooner's slight shift in course and had compensated for it. But judging by her apparent size in the magnified view, she was no longer gaining. After some time, Pierce saw that *Island Expedition* appeared to be drawing slowly away from it.

Seven bells sounded. The forenoon watch was nearly over. Smells of the dinner boiling in the coppers wafted over the deck. Those officers not on watch headed below for sextants and paper, as it was approaching time for the noon sightings. Upon their return, they temporarily relieved those standing watch, so that they too could fetch their instruments for the sightings.

When it was determined that it was noon, and when Hotchkiss had ceremoniously informed Pierce of such, he replied. "Very well, make it so. Pipe hands to dinner. Then you may secure fully from quarters. Restore the bulkheads and partitions. Leave guns loaded for the time. We may drill later--or indeed, with our luck, we may need them."

"Aye aye, sir."

Pierce looked through the glass. From deck the frigate was now hull down, a sure sign that at last they were outdistancing it. He breathed a sigh of relief. Then he went below and joined the other officers for dinner.

Contrary to the practice and tradition of most Royal Navy vessels, the captain and officers of HMS *Island Expedition* ate at the same time as the hands. This had begun on the voyage from England, when the schooner had been packed with one-time convicts sentenced to transportation, now the pioneering members of Harold Smythe's freedom colony. It had been more practical then to mess officers, hands, and passengers at one time--and even now, with just the crew aboard, it was still found to be the most efficient. Then as now, Pierce and the schooner's officers ate from the same stores as did the crew, and as had the passengers.

Pierce felt that if meals were so unfit that he and his officers couldn't eat them, they were also unfit for anyone else. Whether this was in response to any particular aspect of his upbringing or earlier training was not clear. In earlier service, especially during his stint aboard HMS *Orion*, Pierce had followed the older more established ways of the service. Perhaps it was Granville Jackson, captain of

*Theadora,* whose sometimes radical and novel ideas concerning the relationship of officers and crew that had established his sense of fairness. He also found that unless prepared badly or from totally rotten stores, he preferred the simpler diet of the hands.

On an everyday basis, what he and the other officers had aft was, with small exception, the same as the crew had forward. True, the combination captain's table, wardroom, and gunroom might have had better utensils and tableware, as well as various bottled drinks, and the occasional reserved condiment, but the food all came from the same coppers boiling away on the camboose.

Following dinner, Pierce remained below. Seated at his miniscule writing desk, he updated the ship's logs and his personal journal. He studied the charts and their position as based on the latest noon sightings taken only an hour or so ago. Upon leaving the Vespican mainland and clearing Cape Stanislaus, he had hoped that a close-hauled starboard tack would bring them to the southeastern corner of Stone Island. Then it would simply be a matter of following the coast, one way or another, until they fetched up at the large bay on the northwestern shore, where Smythe's freedom colony had been established. Wind had been slightly contrary and they had tended too much to the south. Because of that, they had come about onto a port tack, which he had planned to maintain for the next day or so.

The sighting and obvious hostility of the first Gallician frigate had altered that plan, as they had fled, all sail set, running in general to the south on a starboard broad reach. His original plan in light of that development had been to sail out of sight of that frigate, head more and more into the wind until once again close-hauled on the starboard tack, come about onto the port tack, and hold that course for a couple of days.

Spotting the second frigate this morning, and the fact that they had reeled off many more miles to the south as they sought to gain some speed advantage over it, altered those plans as well. To regain a

position that would put them back on anything resembling their former plans would necessitate sailing nearly due north, either on a port
reach or slightly into the wind. With two and perhaps more unex-
plainably hostile Gallician men-of-war in that direction, that option
did not appeal to him. Perhaps it would be better to continue south,
gently change course into the wind, and end up working their way via
port and starboard tacks to the west. Far enough in that direction they
could come about, run free on a broad port reach, and come up on
Stone Island's western shore.

But would the pursing frigate guess at the same move? Once out
of sight, would she alter course into the wind and head to the southwest on a starboard tack? Would she seek to be the third side of the
triangle, with the schooner's southerly and then westerly course providing the first two?

Agitated at this prospect and unable to reach a fool-proof solution,
Pierce went back on deck. With his naked eye he could no longer see
the frigate. He hailed the masthead and was told that from aloft she
was hull down, a mere speck of white on the horizon.

Midshipman Morgan had the deck. "I believe you were correct,
Tom," said Pierce privately. "My thanks!"

"We should completely sink her by the end of the afternoon watch,
I would think, sir."

"Aye. But we'll hold this course through the night to make sure.
I doubt that there will be a third Gallician to surprise us tomorrow
morning."

"Aye, sir." Morgan moved to check the current course on the compass. The leather tip of his wooden leg thumped on the deck.

At the end of the first dog watch, the glass started to fall. The
wind rose in intensity, and the air chilled. Hotchkiss, on deck at the
time sent word to Pierce and asked that they might shorten sail. Pierce
came on deck immediately and inquired about the frigate.

"No sign of her since the watch began, sir!" was the answer shouted from above.

The schooner moved more violently with the increasing wind and heavier seas.

"By all means, Mr. Hotchkiss, let us get some sail off of her. Quickly now, the studding sails, royals, and ringtail!"

"Aye aye, sir!"

"And Mr. Hotchkiss, have whatever can be spared over the side. A spar or two, line, an old sail, and so on. If the frigate happens upon them, she might think we floundered and went down."

Hotchkiss nodded and grinned. "Aye, sir. That might buy a little time, at that."

The sky darkened, the air grew colder, and the wind blew even harder, altering its direction. Having come out of the west since their departure from Brunswick, it now came out of the south. Pierce changed course to compensate, steering further and further to the west, at first on a starboard tack and as the wind shifted, on a port tack. By the end of the second dog watch, they were headed due west on a port reach. Already they had reefed topsails and had gotten in the topgallants. The wind continued to increase in velocity and a cold driving rain began to fall.

"All hands, Mr. Hotchkiss. Another reef in the topsails, if you please! Double reef fore and main as well!"

"Aye aye, sir!"

With that done, the schooner rode easier and Pierce felt more at ease. The wind and rain were refreshing after the heat and light airs of the last several days. The change in weather would also serve them in evading the Gallician frigate.

Supper had been prepared and served before the weather had worsened. Now as the schooner pitched and rolled to the higher winds and heavier seas, the galley fires were put out. It was best they did not burn, lest a sudden movement cause them to spill about the deck and set afire the very hull that contained them. A small flame still burned in an isolated and guarded corner of the stove, serving to keep the coffee warm.

Pierce neared the galley, his mug stained and brown from many previous cups. He poured it full, sniffed, and found it to fresh and hot enough that he did not need to reprimand the cook or his mate.

Franklin, the cook's mate spoke. "Should be all right, sir. Was made just as the wind got up."

"It's fine, Franklin. You have a helper through the night watches?"

"Aye, sir."

"You would do well to see the pot remains full. In this weather, many will appreciate the warmth."

"Aye aye, sir."

Having taken a sip or two, Pierce topped it off and went on deck. There, on the lee side of the deck, somewhat sheltered by the higher windward side, the reefed mainsail, the mainmast itself, and other deck furnishings, it was relatively calm and quiet. Sheltered and dry due to the sou'wester and tarpaulin he wore, Pierce relaxed and assessed the day's events.

Although he tried to avoid it, he found himself thinking of home. He had a great need, a tremendous urge to be in England again, and to see, hold, and kiss Evangeline. Even as she entered his mind, he knew that this was likely to be a night of very little sleep for him.

But he was glad for the dirty weather. The change in wind worked to their advantage, placing them directly into the wind from the Gallician frigate. Now he could make his run to the west without tacking into the wind, and the frigate would be required to do so, should she desire to come as far south as the schooner. With the rain and clouds, visibility was a lot less than it had been that morning, and if the frigate drew near enough, it was possible they would escape her notice, even at distances far less than would have been required only hours earlier.

Pierce shivered slightly as the cold rain, driven by the shrieking wind, impinged upon his solitude. He sipped again at the still-hot coffee, and imagined his chilled body warmed by the fire of Evangeline's embrace.

With the coffee gone, he made a final check with the officer of the watch, and went below.

*Chapter Seven*

# First Homecoming

The lookouts sighted Stone Island early on October 31st. Pierce felt a joy nearly the same as if England had been sighted. It took them the rest of the day to sail along the coast and arrive at the large harbor where the colony was established. The sun was well down on that Wednesday Halloween when sails were furled and the schooner warped alongside the quay.

In the dark of the late evening, Pierce saw that many changes had occurred during their more than year-long absence. Lighted lanterns hung at regular intervals along the quay and up and down the adjacent streets. Brush was cut back, stone paving repaired, and many old buildings restored to usable condition. New structures had been built as well, and the entire place had a look of bustling prosperity about it.

Ahead of them, another vessel lay along the quay. She was a small ship, not much larger than the schooner. She was a typical merchantman, with a fat hull for cargo, and spars for easy sailing, rather than for driving her relentlessly through the sea. At her flag staff fluttered the horizontal red, white, and blue stripes of the Independent Lands of Vespica, the same flag that had flown over *Island Expedition* on her recent voyage from the Vespican Mainland.

Pierce wondered that there hadn't been a *colors* ceremony at sundown, with the flag being hauled down with respect and dignity. But then he saw that what billowed in the light breeze was a small ensign, apparently made to be flown in hours of darkness or inclement weather. Because it was the Vespican colors Pierce saw, it gave him comfort as to the nature of the vessel.

Under the Vespican stripes, a second smaller flag snapped in the light wind. This was dark blue, even black, depending upon the available light. On it was a single white four-pointed star or compass rose. It was the flag or sign that Shostolamie, their first visitor, had told them would mark any ship as a friend. Pierce had learned since that day long ago that the four-pointed white star was also the symbol of the Unity Congress.

A considerable crowd awaited as *Island Expedition* eased gently against the pier. Pierce recognized many of the faces, having sailed with them from England. There were several strangers among the crowd, but they also wore expressions of joy to mark the schooner's return. Lines were passed, made fast, and finally they were back amongst friends.

"Port watch!" Pierce bellowed. "Liberty until eight bells in the morning watch! Any man not aboard and ready for duty will lose his spirit ration!" Such a threat would better serve his needs than to promise a flogging. Pierce was reluctant to make such a promise, and even more loath to act upon it.

"Starboard watch! In port routine! Mr. Morgan, please detail the required in port duties.

"Aye aye, sir!"

On the quay, willing hands manhandled a well-built gangway across the small gap separating the vessel from the pier, finally positioning it at the entry port. As captain, Pierce stepped ashore first and back onto what was now known as Stone Island. Smythe was there, beaming, and in the joy of the schooner's return, exuberantly embraced Pierce. "It is really good that you are back, Edward!" he said joyfully.

"It is good to be back, sir," Pierce replied. As glad as he was at his return, Pierce could not close the formal gap and use his employer's first name. "It is really good!"

In the small but excited crowd, someone yelled, "Three cheers for *Island Expedition*!"

The "hip hips," the "huzzahs," and the "hurrahs" rang out, straining the voices of the celebrants, both ashore and aboard the schooner. Hotchkiss stepped ashore and was also enthusiastically greeted by Smythe.

Pierce turned and directed his voice back aboard. "Mr. Andrews, the port watch is now at liberty!" That half of the crew was soon ashore as well. They were warmly met and made welcome by the colonists, many of them friends from the long voyage so many months ago.

A stranger advanced towards Smythe, Hotchkiss, and Pierce. Smythe quickly announced, "Captain Pierce, Lieutenant Hotchkiss, please meet Randolph Cooper, master of *Evening Star*. Captain Cooper, may I present Master and Commander Edward Pierce, captain of *Island Expedition* and Isaac Hotchkiss, first lieutenant!"

"Most pleased to meet you, sir," said Cooper, as he shook hands with both Pierce and Hotchkiss. "I have heard a great deal of you and *Island Expedition*. At a glance, a most unusual but obviously serviceable vessel."

"Most serviceable indeed, sir. *Evening Star* appears well-suited to her purpose."

"Come along now, gentlemen," Smythe said. "We can continue in comfort at the Colonial Building! Captain Cooper brought our first shipment of supplies from Vespica."

"You have remained since?"

"Indeed not, Captain Pierce. Our third visit."

"I see."

Reference to the Colonial Building confused Pierce. When he had sailed a year and a half earlier, the colonists had been living in tents, although a few old dwellings were being prepared for habitation. Now the large headquarters tent and the nearly identical cook's tent were no longer in sight. "You've made remarkable progress, I must say!" he remarked to Smythe.

"We've only touched the surface. This was once a very large city. From the size of the island and the legends, there are other and perhaps larger cities awaiting discovery."

The Colony Building was a medium-sized and yet imposing stone edifice set back a couple of streets from the quay. Pierce vaguely remembered it from before. Then it had been overgrown with trees, shrubs, brush, and weeds, and so filled with debris as to be nearly unrecognizable as a building. Now it served as the focal point of the colony, its seat of government, and Smythe's residence.

Well into the night, the four sat, sipped their drinks, and discussed the months of adventure, captivity, wondering, and despair. Pierce told of the events that befell *Island Expedition* after leaving near the end of May 1803. He did not mention his involvement with Leona Jackson.

Smythe told them about the arrival of *Evening Star*, Dr. Robertson, and the welcome supplies promised by Shostolamie, the Kalish Dream Chief. While Smythe had thought the small colony well enough equipped to survive the Southern winter, the blankets, winter clothing, and cattle for meat and fresh milk had been most welcome. Despite his original desire that the erstwhile convicts be remotely located and isolated, Smythe had come to welcome the Vespicans' visits.

Over the past year they had welcomed additional colonists from the Independent Lands of Vespica. Like the English colonists, many had been falsely accused, or unfairly convicted of a crime. Some, like a few original colonists, were actually guilty, but circumstances surrounding their offenses allowed them to be accepted. Smythe announced that they would soon undertake a search for such disadvantaged persons in Baltica as well.

After a sip at his glass, and in response to a remark that Hotchkiss had made, Smythe said, "Indeed so, Isaac. But I would hear more, your thoughts on the processes that have set you at liberty? We have had word of the Joint Council's decision, but not of the details."

"A most welcome and judicious choice, if I might say so. It pleases me greatly that the Tritonish bowed to their demands."

"A bigger concern, sir," said Pierce, "is how you and the others react to the idea of annexation, particularly in light of your original determination that the colony be as isolated as possible."

"Circumstances being as they were, I believe it to have been the only road that the Joint Council could have taken. It did win you your freedom, did it not?"

"Indeed, sir," said Hotchkiss.

"Does this new citizenship pose a dilemma for you, Captain? Particularly, I mean, as you are a King's Officer. Any question of divided loyalties?" asked Smythe.

"I felt it might, and should they conflict, I would renounce this Vespican citizenship instantly."

"Then you now have no problem with it, sir?" asked Cooper.

"It was pointed out to me," said Pierce, "that England and Vespica lie in two different worlds, worlds that will never directly interact. When I am here, I will consider myself a Vespican. Upon traversing back to our world, I will once again be a British Subject and a King's Officer."

"A reasonable solution, Captain."

"I would agree," said Smythe. "Perhaps it is an idea the rest of us from our world can adopt as well."

"But to return to the original question, sir, do you favor Stone Island as the eleventh Independent Land of Vespica?" asked Hotchkiss.

"Surely it is not what I had wanted upon leaving England. With reality as we have found it, I would not be greatly opposed, but I shall closely study the details to be sure. Of course, it would not be my choice alone. Such a matter must be decided by all living upon the island."

"A fair choice, sir," said Cooper.

"Aye," echoed Hotchkiss.

"I have aboard, properly secured, official documents from the Joint Council that detail the annexation. Briefly, as I understand it, the choice is ours, and should we accept, the other ten Lands must also approve," Pierce said.

"Fair. Quite fair, I believe."

"I still find it strange that you are now so accommodating of ties with Vespica. I remember how strenuously you hoped we would avoid all outside contact!"

"Indeed, sir!" added Hotchkiss.

"That was once my hope, Edward, Isaac. In studying the old legends I did not see the possible existence of other lands and other peoples. I had always thought that the island was completely alone. I would have preferred it that way, and at times, I still wish it were so. But it is not. Now that we find ourselves with neighbors and friends, perhaps your prior arguments have a much greater validity."

"And we may also now have enemies!"

"Heaven forbid, sir! Who?"

"Surely not the Kentish?" interjected Gibbons, who had recently joined them. "While they may not agree with our aims, I can hardly see them opposed to a people so very much the same."

"Do remember, sir," said Pierce. "It is because of them that we were detained the past several months in Brunswick."

"But I understand that your departure was amiable."

"Apparently so, although some were not ecstatic about it. And I have not implied that they could not be an enemy. Their actions and pomposity left a bitter taste in my throat, such that I cannot regard them as friends."

"But who then, Edward?" Smythe had a worried look upon his face.

"We could have arrived a week ago, my dear sir, if not for two hostile and belligerent Gallician frigates. Their aggressive pursuits forced us farther southward than we intended. A gale and a shift in wind allowed us to make to the west. We finally determined that they had lost us, and approached the island from the west southwest."

"You did not seek to engage them as you did *Hawke?*" suggested Gibbons.

"Indeed not. Had I not been so pig-headed, that engagement would never have occurred. We were outgunned then, but not to the extent we would have been against either of the frigates. The odds did not favor us."

"I see, sir."

Pierce added. "There are acceptable odds, when one can cancel an enemy's superior weaponry with the skill of his men and the handiness of his vessel. But there are limits to that, and against either of the frigates, that limit would have been greatly exceeded."

"Perhaps the Toads are up to their old tricks, sir," suggested Cooper.

"Old tricks?"

"Aye. They think Vespica owes for their help during our Fight for Freedom. When the war between the Unified Kingdom and the Gallician Republic began, they stopped Vespican ships possibly trading with Kentland. They tried to hire the naval militias of the various Lands as letters-of-marque to prey upon Tritonish shipping."

"America and France a few years ago," remarked Pierce. "What some call the Quasi-war."

"We thought the matter was settled, but apparently it is not."

"Did they attack because we sailed under the Vespican flag or because of who we are?" Hotchkiss sipped at his drink, rum and water, the grog so prized by the hands. His was a most refreshing libation, made with pure fresh water, flavored with lemon juice, a little ginger, sugar, and chilled with a bit of ice.

"I would not be able to hazard a guess in that regard," said Cooper. "But when I am home, I will look into it."

"That would be most appreciated," replied Smythe.

"We appear involved in this world's affairs, even should we wish not to be," remarked Hotchkiss.

Smythe continued. "It seems so. But we must take time to decide this annexation, and plan the most proper course. But might this apparent Gallician hostility complicate the situation?"

"Truly, sir, it might."

"The hour grows late. I'm growing older and need my rest. And after your voyage, I'm sure you gentlemen are in need of yours as well."

Hotchkiss yawned, suddenly reminded of his fatigue. "Yes, I believe I could afford to turn in now."

Pierce nodded in agreement.

"Will you return aboard, or may I provide accommodations here for you?"

"I shall return aboard, sir. Isaac?"

"I as well, sir."

"Then Captain, I will say good night. And I hope that you and all officers that can be spared will join me for dinner tomorrow."

"Delighted, sir!"

Pierce slept very well that night. At the quay, *Island Expedition* was nearly still, but she did move a little, and that gentle motion lulled him into a deep and restful slumber. Dr. Robertson had also passed along a trick wherein Pierce imagined himself lecturing midshipmen on a particularly dry and boring subject. As he would have predicted the young gentlemen to be in a state of nodding heads and sagging eyelids, the imagined presentation soon put him to sleep as well.

The muffled sounding of three bells in the morning watch woke him. He lay for a moment, deciding whether to arise or wait for the harsher, more strident clanging that would come in thirty minutes' time. He had barely made his choice, turned over, and closed his eyes again when a clamor erupted on the quay. It spilled onto the deck above his head. Pierce reluctantly and somewhat angrily reversed his decision.

As he hurriedly pulled on his trousers and tucked his shirttails in, he heard the master, O'Brien roar, "Silence there! Stand down, all of you!"

The din faded, but did not die out completely. Pierce threw his uniform coat on, neglecting waistcoat and neckerchief. He hurried on deck.

Several crewmen, members of the liberty party milled about on deck, forward of the mainmast. They angrily glared at a group of colonists who stood irate on the quay. Duty marines and seamen kept that crowd from coming aboard. "Stand down, I say!" O'Brien shouted again.

"What is this, Mr. O'Brien?" Pierce asked. At the sound of his voice and the realization that he was there, the returning crewmembers quieted further. In contrast, the crowd on shore increased their din, painfully loud because everyone bellowed at once. Pierce could make no intelligible understanding of it.

"I couldn't say, sir," answered the master.

"Then let us find out."

"Aye aye, sir."

"Silence! Silence on deck!" Pierce shouted. The recent liberty party hushed completely, some looking a little sheepish as they stood swaying on deck. As to be expected, the majority of them were drunk. One, with a bit of a swagger, staggered and opened his mouth to speak.

"No, Folsum, you will be still!" Pierce said. "Do not speak, unless you are spoken to. I will have silence on deck!" Wisely the seamen clapped his mouth closed and remained, mute and swaying, with the rest of them. He glared defiantly until drunkenness caused his eyes to lose focus.

Pierce stepped to the head of the gangway. He stared hard at the riotous angry crowd on shore. "You will be silent!" he said loudly. When that had no real effect, he shouted, "Damn you all! Quiet!"

The noise subsided, although the mob on the quay still stared and gestured with malice. Pierce directed his gaze and his voice at one individual, an older man whom he did not recognize--one of the Vespicans lately settled on the island, perhaps? He was the most vehement in his shouts, and nearly trembled in his wrath. "Sir, what is the cause of this? Why do you disturb the peace at such an hour?" Pierce asked.

"Not me disturbing no peace, Captain!" the man shouted back. An angry buzz from the hostile crowd arose, threatening to overwhelm the beginning discussion.

"Be still, all of you!" Pierce was exasperated. The man on the pier quickly hushed his compatriots.

"We want that man of yours, Captain! We want his slimy water-logged hide!"

"Which man, and why?"

"The skinny one there! Blond hair, two missing teeth! By God, he'll make it right for what he's done!"

Pierce glance quickly at the returned members of the liberty party. Folsum, who minutes ago was ready to speak up in his captain's face, shrank back visibly. He tried to disappear into the mass of his shipmates. "And tell me, what has he done?"

"Caught the sot with my daughter, I did! Heard noises outside, looked, and there they were. Clothes half off, the both of 'em! I'll kill the bastard! Or he'll settle proper and marry the girl!"

"There will be no killing, sir!" said Pierce forcefully. "If he has wronged your girl, he will make proper amends."

"He'll marry her?" asked the Vespican.

"Perhaps. I'll need to hear the whole of it. And it will be his choice--her choice as well. Now, leave quietly, all of you! I'll investigate, and you may return peacefully tomorrow to learn of the disposition."

"He'll let 'im go, just you wait and see," said another on the quay. "Just wait and see if them foreign sots don't back their own!"

"The captain's a fair man, Jacob. He'll do you right." Pierce recognized this voice. He had been a passenger on the voyage from England and had volunteered as a crew member. A good hand, as Pierce remembered.

A murmur went through the crowd on the quay. They moved about nervously, eyeing the marines along the rail, muskets at the ready, and the grim and determined on-duty seamen. Did they contemplate storming aboard and seizing the man in question? Pierce hoped that they would not be so foolish. He would not want to see any of them--nor any of his crew--injured or killed.

"Sergeant Lincoln, your men will not discharge muskets unless I expressly order it!"

"Aye aye, sir!" responded the marine non-commissioned officer.

Both the order and the reply had been loud enough that the threatening crowd could hear them. More than a few took a second look at the armed and ready marines.

"Go along now, will you!" Pierce said again. "Mr.? Mr.?"

"Blondin, Jacob Blondin."

"Mr. Blondin, if you will return tomorrow, say at four bells in the forenoon watch, I will have your answer."

"When is that?"

The individual who had pointed out Pierce's fairness whispered in Blondin's ear. He nodded with understanding, stood silent for a moment, and then turned to his companions. "Let's go, lads. We can't do nothing this way. But," he said, looking back at Pierce. "I will be here, come ten o'clock tomorrow!"

"I will expect you."

When the crowd ashore had disbursed, Pierce turned to the men on deck. "Liberty people, get below and sobered up. For his sake, keep Folsum below, so they can't see him. Folsum, you will report to my cabin after eight bells!"

Pierce went below, grabbed his last remaining mug, and went forward for a cup of coffee. It was fresh and hot, and he sipped gratefully at it as he returned aft. Friction between the schooner's crew and the small colony was not what he needed, and damned if they hadn't been back only one night before it occurred.

When he had calmed himself somewhat, when his anger and apprehension had left, Pierce washed, shaved, and dressed, properly this time, remembering his stockings, waistcoat, and neckerchief. As was his habit and now tradition aboard *Island Expedition*, he did not have meals brought aft especially for him. Breakfast was one meal he very rarely ate, and if he did, he joined the other officers and midshipmen in the great cabin for the meal. As he finished dressing, the smell of the day's breakfast stirred his appetite and he joined them for eggs, bacon, and toast.

Seated at his writing table, Pierce heard the sounds of the schooner starting its first day in port. Divisions mustered, the names called and responses given drifted indistinctly to his ears. Hands were told off for particular duties. The pumps were manned, the deck sluiced down, and the past day's grime scrubbed away with holystones. Pierce also heard the remaining liberty personnel returning from their adventures ashore.

At eight bells, the former liberty men mustered and were assigned their work for the day. All hands would remain on duty until the end of the afternoon watch, at which time those who had had duty the previous night would be free to go ashore. Moments after the forenoon watch began, there was a knock upon the great cabin's door. "Come in, Folsum," said Pierce as he stepped out of his private quarters and into the larger, more communal compartment.

The door leading forward remained shut. Somewhat exasperated, Pierce again said, "Come in!"

At this, the door opened and Folsum stepped tentatively in. He or his mess mates had worked to ensure he was in presentable condition to report to the captain. He had washed thoroughly, and had changed out of his soiled and stained shore-going rig, exchanging it for worn but clean working clothes. He stood silently, expectantly, his hat in his hands.

"Able Seaman Tim Folsum, sir," he said.

"Very well. You may stand at ease, should you wish."

"Aye, sir. Thank you, sir." There was not that much difference in his stance. Pierce had not expected more; the extreme rigidity of a marine or soldier at attention was not expected of a seaman. Nautical discipline and skill lay in other areas besides military drill.

"You may sit, if you wish," offered Pierce. He wanted the man to be comfortable as he could be while in the presence of his captain. Short of sleep as he likely was, Folsum would no doubt think more clearly if seated and comfortable. He remained standing.

"As you wish," continued Pierce. "Now, about last night, what happened?"

"Have you seen 'em, sir, all the new folk on the island? And they got a tavern or two as well, you see. Me and Jones, and maybe Tucker, we was roaming about, looking for some life, and there was plenty o' that, sir. Island folks seemed really glad for us to be back.

"We found a little spot, one o' them taverns, sir, and chased a few pints. Rum too, I think. Didn't need to cough up for it. Like I said, sir, they were glad we are back.

"And the one serving wench, sir, a real looker. And I said, 'I don't remember you from afore.'

"And she said, 'I arrived after your ship sailed.' I should have told her it ain't no ship, but a schooner of sorts, but my thinking wasn't right. And she said, 'What's your name?' and I told her mine, seeing how I been brought up proper, sir. And it ain't right not to give your name what somebody gives hers. See, she'd told me her name when first she brought our ale."

"Nothing improper in that, Folsum."

"No, sir. Thank you, sir. Well, sir, we talked some, when she could between her duties. And when it got late, she said, sir, 'I'm off now, would you be a good lad and see me home? Pa don't like me on the streets late like this.'

"And so I says, 'With pleasure, milady,' as if I was gentry and her a duchess or what. And she was so fine-lookin' sir, what I couldn't help it. And I kissed her sir, just a quick one, and I thought she'd whack me a good one, sir. But she didn't, so I kissed her again.

"And the lass got into it, sir, and she said, 'We can go in here,' which was a cave along her house, and she says, 'I never knew, Tim,' that's me, sir, 'that you are the one I've waited for, for so long.' And I weren't gonna fight it sir, even did we just meet. Early in the evening, you remember, sir? And I weren't caring if she felt for me or not, not caring what she said, just knowing she was willing."

"You indeed found some excitement for the evening."

"Oh yes, sir! So I thought, sir! We was getting into it sir, and there must've been somethin' adrift in there, sir. Scared the tar and oakum outa me, sir, what when it gave out and fell. And a cat screeched and run off. Ever hear a cat run scared? Sounds like a horse! Then a light showed in the window, and a man showed against the light, and she said, 'Oh God, it's Pa, and he'll kill you, what he catches you!'

"By then sir, don't want to say it sir, but some of my rig; some of her rig had come off. And I'm trying to get my trousers on, and her pa, he's charging out the door under full sail, and he's like a first-rate with guns all run out, sir. And he's hollering and shouting, waking the dead. I get my trousers on, and she gets wrapped up near enough proper, and she says, 'Run, Tim! Run! I'll find you!'

"So I run, but the old man is there, and his neighbors too, mad on of account of the noise we made, but mostly on account of all his hallooing. And he's saying, 'Stop that damned man, lest he spoil another man's daughter.' And I run, sir, even as the old man beats her with a strop and sends her into the house.

"I wanted to go for her, sir, but figured it was like us and them two Toad frigates. Not a fair match at all, sir. Not me against him and all the others, sir.

"So I lit out, sir, what with the whole fleet of 'em after me, and as I come by the corner, there's three of my mates, and I holler, 'Them buggers what gonna kill me!'

"And one o' them says, "Not if ya get aboard, ya lout, else the captain will kill ya, himself, what you're caught fighting.' And he was right, so we all ran back, and more mates joined up with us. And when we got aboard, sir, Mr. O'Brien, sir, he starts yelling at us, and yelling at them. And...."

"Which brings us to my rather rude awakening and the stand-off on deck, I believe."

"Aye, sir."

"Would you marry the lass, if it takes that to save your hide and her honor?"

"Wouldn't be fair to her, sir, what with us going back to England. Never saw me a married man no how. And her honor is not destroyed on my account, sir. And believe it, sir, it would've been no more, other than all them goings on and all."

"Then nothing was completed?"

"No, sir. Ever tried to run, sir, with...."

"I understand. You will be aboard today and tonight, having the duty. But tomorrow you will restrict yourself to the vessel. And I will order it as punishment for disturbing the order of the colony and the peace on our deck."

"Aye, sir! Thank you, sir!"

"You may go now, Folsum"

"Aye aye, sir." He left the cabin.

The schooner had been back for less than a day, and already there was trouble. The little freedom colony was fast turning into a miniature version of the typical seaport town. Seamen, given their liberty, having a bit of their pay to spend, out searching for what they could find. And even here, in this miniscule community, it seemed that some were willing to offer just what those randy hot-blooded young mariners were after.

Pierce wondered if he shouldn't be angrier with Folsum, taking more personal and official affront at his behavior and actions. But he knew that under similar circumstances he well might have done the same. The memories of Leona Jackson and the nights with her in

Brunswick flooded his thoughts. No, it would not do to punish him for being a man. And as far as could be determined, he hadn't forced or tricked the girl into acting against her will.

The real question, realized Pierce, was the girl herself. Was she really the innocent who walked precariously along the edges of lascivious behavior? Was there really an instant bond between her and Folsum, one in which she was willing to do all because of an unexplainable attraction to him? Or was it an act on her part, one to play up to his lustful needs and then rob him of his infrequent riches?

He would have to find out about her before he made a final decision. He had work about the schooner for the rest of the morning, and in the afternoon, dinner at the Colonial Building. Perhaps the evening would see time to further his investigation. And certainly he could ask Smythe and other island residents their opinions as well.

*Chapter Eight*

# Dry Dock

Isaac Hotchkiss tapped lightly on the door to the great cabin. He did not wait for a response, but immediately opened the door and stepped in. "Excitement so soon, Edward?" he said.

"Indeed! More than I had planned for. For his own safety, we will keep Folsum aboard the next few days. I do want this resolved fairly and peacefully."

"Of course."

"My one concern is the character of the young lady. I do not question it per se, but without having met her, I do not know in what light I should regard her."

"Understandable. With the influx of new colonists, Vespicans, and others, let us pray this is the only trouble that occurs."

"I will say 'amen' to that, Isaac."

"Yes, and Mr. Townsend is aboard. He wonders do you wish to see him?"

"By all means! Have him come in."

Midshipman Townsend and four seamen had remained behind when *Island Expedition* sailed a year ago May. They had stayed, primarily to man the lookout site and signal tower atop the ridge of land that lay between the bay and the open sea. A few remarks the evening before by Harold Smythe had allowed Pierce to understand that the young gentleman had performed his duties with skill and aplomb. That he hadn't reported sooner resulted from his taking on extra duties the evening before, so those in his charge might be reunited with their shipmates.

"Commendable, Mr. Townsend," said Pierce. "Do you wish coffee?"

"Oh no, sir. Too much already, I believe."

"You and your hands will continue through today with the signal and lookout tasks. Tomorrow we will bring them back aboard and detail that chore from amongst the entire crew."

"Aye aye, sir."

"We are invited to dine with Mr. Smythe today. I will not insist, but surely you should be there."

"I certainly shall be, sir. Mrs. Packingham is a fine cook, sir." Seeing Pierce's slightly puzzled look, Townsend went on. "She's one of those who came from Vespica, sir, his cook and housekeeper. And some say there's more between them."

"I'm sure that is entirely their business, unless there is a Mr. Packingham?"

"Oh, indeed there isn't, sir. She's widowed."

Eight bells in the forenoon watch died away, and the afternoon watch began. With little going on aboard, most of the watch standers and other duty personnel remained idle about the deck. On a pleasant spring day they went about their minimum of work easily, although some still suffered from events and actions of the night before.

Within minutes of the bell, Pierce in his full dress uniform, followed by the other officers, each in his best attire, strode down the gangway and on to the quay. Smythe had invited all officers that could be spared, and Pierce was taking him at his word. Every officer, commissioned, warrant, or civil, was en route to dinner at the Colonial Building. In any other port, even in England--perhaps especially in England--Pierce would have wanted at least one commissioned or senior warrant officer on board. But here, even with the troubles of the early morning, he felt confident in leaving Campbell, the duty bo'sun's mate, in charge for the afternoon. Mr. Dial would return by the end of the afternoon watch and assume duties as officer of the watch.

Smythe met the group at the door. "Welcome, gentlemen! Please come in. It appears quite warm today, so unless personal decorum prohibits, you may remove your coats. Please allow yourselves to be comfortable." There was that comforting hospitality that Pierce remembered of Smythe from the first time he had met him.

"Very good to see all of you again," Smythe continued. "Mr. Morgan, I trust the leg has healed well, and that you have no trouble with it?"

"It has healed very well indeed, sir." The leather tip of Morgan's wooden substitute sounded in counterpoint to the footfalls of the others. "Dr. Robertson is an amazing physician, of which I can vouchsafe from personal experience."

"In more ways than that, I believe, gentlemen."

"Quite so, indeed."

"Mr. O'Brien, so good that you could be here. And Mr. Gray, as well. Truth said, this group hasn't been together at table since our first landing here."

"Indeed we haven't, sir," replied the purser.

"And Dr. Matheson," continued Smythe. "I hope praise of Dr. Robertson's success hasn't soured you as to your value to the crew, or indeed all of us on Stone Island."

"Dr. Robertson succeeded where I did not. There is no reason that I should be offended. Had he not, we well could be short one member of the party."

"True! True! If you'll follow me, we'll have some refreshment before dinner is served."

Smythe led them down a corridor, past several rooms that were still being cleaned and organized. Near the rear of the building he gestured them into a large, airy, and comfortable space. A large table was already set with plain but serviceable utensils and some of the dishes that they would soon indulge in. Along the outer edges stood smaller tables, each with several bottles and a myriad of glasses.

"You all know my penchant for practical hospitality, I believe. Do not hesitate to serve yourselves whatever you wish."

"Of course, sir," replied Pierce. "Mr. Hadley, Mr. Spencer, do observe that we are not here to drink the place dry. You will do well to moderate your intake, particularly before having eaten."

"Aye aye, sir," the two replied. Pierce glanced significantly at a couple of others as well, knowing their past inclinations to drink and drink, simply because it was available.

"We will have other guests as well," said Smythe. "They should arrive shortly."

As they waited, Pierce told Smythe about the morning's altercation. "What do you make of this Blondin fellow?" he asked. "I'm afraid he was not in temper suitable to my fostering an unbiased opinion."

"That would be him. Surely many men have a cooler head. But he is watchful and protective of his child. Some say too much so, and that he will drive her away."

"And the girl?"

"You wonder did she play young Folsum for a fool?"

"Quite."

"If there are fools, it would be both. She may think she's attracted to him. Too many other young men have made their play at her. Should you be here long enough, you may spot them from time to time. They usually sport a blackened eye, a swollen nose, or other noticeable contusions."

"Her father?"

"Indeed no! The lass herself."

"This does make my decision in the matter a little easier, I must say. But I cannot see that he allows her that sort of employment with such a watch over her."

"She insisted, primarily to be out of the home, I believe. And once she bloodied the first young swain's beak, he's been more at ease with it. And the tavern owner is a friend who tries to watch over her as well."

"I am near satisfied as to hearsay, but I will go for an ale later and judge her character myself," concluded Pierce.

Voices echoed in the hall leading from the door as the other promised guests arrived. Two of them were original colonists, men that Pierce remembered well from the long voyage. Three others had settled from Vespica, their alleged legal troubles within the parameters for settlement in the freedom colony. Smythe introduced the group as the island's council and his advisors. They had, as Smythe said, shown him their ability for clear thinking and a willingness to put the colony's interest ahead of, or at least on a level with, their own.

Pierce, long a proponent of equality and representative government, silently noted his approval. While he had utmost confidence in Smythe's sense of duty, justice, and fair play, he was relieved to see him bring others into the decision-making process.

Joining them again was Randolph Cooper, master of *Evening Star*.

Soon after these guests arrived, Smythe invited the gathered company to sit. Dinner was served, Mrs. Packingham herself bringing it to the table. Smythe introduced her to Pierce and the others lately returned to the island, and implied that as both chef and *de facto* mistress of the house, she was welcome to join them. She refused politely, mentioning that such a meal was really a meeting, and that she could not make any contribution to the proceedings. She added that since she had not planned to dine with them, she would take a portion of what remained to provide a meal for an elderly man a few doors away.

The meal was simple and hearty, consisting of a beef ragout, freshly baked bread, and cheese. There were no removes, no courses. All was set at once on the table, and Pierce was once again reminded of Smythe's somewhat peculiar but eminently practical hospitality.

Conversation of a most general nature followed the progress of the meal. Pierce found the food delicious, filling, and spicy enough to end up feeling quite flushed, although some of the heat may have been induced by repeated filling of his wine glass. No doubt his thirst resulted from the ragout's spiciness. The task of eating such an excellent repast was enjoyment enough, and he rarely entered the ongoing dialog. When the ragout was nearly gone, and when more platter than bread remained, and when all vehemently swore they could not eat another bite, a pitcher of iced gentlemen's grog made its appearance and was passed around. Pierce found the coolness refreshing and quickly drained his glass.

He glanced about, paying particular interest to the younger midshipmen and master's mates, wondering at their behavior, with all they could want to both eat and drink. He did not expect them to refrain from eating well, or from drinking comfortably. But he did watch that none went to excess, and was neither a glutton nor a drunkard. He was not disappointed in what he saw. But he was surprised to see Hotchkiss reach for the pitcher again. Having had a couple of glasses the evening before, his friend was fast developing a fondness for the iced drink.

At length Smythe announced, "Now that we are all well satiated, gentlemen, we should be to the matters at hand. I believe you are all aware that Captain Pierce and his crew owe their release and present freedom to the proposed annexation of Stone Island by Vespica. Here is a copy, verbatim, of that proposed annexation. I would know your feelings on the matter."

The document, which Pierce had brought with him from the schooner, made its slow way around the table. Pierce had read it, in fact had studied it quite closely, and most if those present from *Island Expedition*, had at the least discussed it in some detail. The only ones that really needed to read it were those who had been on the island for some time. As one after the other familiarized himself with the paper, a murmur of sound grew louder as more offered up their opinion of it.

"It seems that we would favor such a move," said Smythe. "But we do need to know the mood of everyone on this matter. Speak to your friends and your neighbors. Find out their take on this. We appear to prefer it, but the majority may not. If they do, we do. If they do not, then we do not."

"Be damned stupid not to!" offered Dial from the far end of the table. Perhaps he had had enough of the iced grog. With everyone looking at him for the moment, he reddened and stared hard at the table.

"May we have your opinion, Captain Pierce?" asked Mr. Mally, a recent arrival from Vespica. "You and your men were why the Joint Council proposed such a move."

"Indeed, sir. As it helped secure our return from Brunswick, it finds favor in my eyes. An association between this island and the Independent Lands would surely strengthen all of Vespica."

"Aye! Well said, Captain!" cheered Andrews, who like many of them, had lost a few inhibitions as he had consumed more drink.

"I believe so as well," said Mally. "And will you and *Island Expedition* remain? Or do you sail for that other world and the home you left behind?"

Pierce answered, "We were never intended to remain. I must report the voyage's success, and I have reports for the Organization, as well as for the Navy and His Majesty's Government."

"And when shall you leave, Captain?"

"I shall stay a short time. We will careen the schooner and have a go at cleaning the bottom. A couple of shots from *Hawke* struck below the waterline and we should ensure those are adequately repaired. Before beginning a long perilous journey I want the vessel in perfect condition."

"I see," said Talbot, one of the original English colonists.

"Depending upon finding a suitable beach, we would have it complete and be away late this month or early in December," said Pierce.

"But could you not be persuaded to stay into the new year, sir?" asked Cooper. "Perhaps into late February or early March?"

"I would not want to seem ungrateful of your company, gentlemen, but why should we tarry? It is understood that our portion of the mission is complete here. We now have only to return to England to finish it."

"Eventually, Captain," explained Cooper. "The decision for or against annexation will need to be delivered to the Joint Council. If in favor of annexation, one from here must go to Bostwick and take his seat in the Council."

"It says so, here, sir," said Townsend who had the document before him, and who amazingly hadn't yet fallen asleep from the food, the drink, or the dry diplomatic language of the paper.

"I know that!" said Pierce, a little vexed. "I've had three weeks to study the thing. Why does possible implementation affect *Island Expedition's* departure?"

"Why what better way for the new delegate to arrive, than aboard what might be seen as the official Stone Island vessel? True, the news and the councilman could gain passage on a merchant hull such as *Evening Star*, and if I am here at the time, I will gladly offer passage."

"For a fee, of course!" said someone down the table, quite obviously into his cups, but who evidently knew Cooper very well.

The merchant master ignored the remark and continued. "You are aware, Captain, that Vespica as a whole does not have an army or a navy. Each Land has what it can provide, usually a battalion of infantry or artillery, or one or two ships of their so-called naval militias. As it is, you and *Island Expedition* are Stone Island's naval militia. It would be most proper that you deliver word of acceptance and Stone Island's first delegate."

Pierce nodded, not so much in agreement, but in understanding. "But surely that can be done sooner? If winds are fair, and we are not waylaid, such a journey could be made, there and back, in less than a month!"

"If winds are fair! And indeed on your voyage here, you were nearly intercepted. It will take some time for a decision to be reached, and if needed, for a representative to be selected. Before the end of November, the Joint Council enters its annual summer recess. They will observe the Holidays with each member home in his own Land. They will not reconvene until late January or early February for a largely ceremonial session. Once any important matters are considered, and new delegates seated, they normally recess again until the fall. The real work of the Council takes place during the cold of winter."

"And Edward," said Smythe. "It would be most proper for you and your crew to personally thank the Joint Council."

"The Unity Congress as well, sir!" added Talbot, who had been silent for the past few minutes. "As well, they recess over the summer."

"You seem to have me, gentlemen. I do see your point, although I had really hoped to be well on our way much sooner. And I do see that I and these fine gentlemen of the sea, and *Island Expedition* herself, could be considered, dare I say, the Stone Island Navy."

"A nice ring to it, wouldn't you say?" asked Smythe. "Perhaps we should offer you post rank in this new service. As senior, you could have your flag, should you wish."

"But even as master and commander, I am senior naval officer here, and that is sufficient. As such, I shall carry out my original intention to careen the schooner. Perhaps the beach south of the quay, beyond where Shostolamie and the Kalish first landed, would serve?"

"Indeed it would, Captain," said Smythe. An amused twinkle radiated from his eye. Puzzled, Pierce looked at the others. There were knowing looks on the faces of those who had been on the island some time. Townsend glanced at his plate, perhaps searching for the last bite needed to fully satiate his hunger. The remainder of his officers, who like him had just returned to the island, also exhibited expressions of confusion.

"I'm not sure what is about," said Pierce.

"We are sorry, sir," said Townsend, slightly red-faced and struggling to control the grin threatening to steal across his face, "to see you planning to careen the barky when it may not be necessary."

"But I have determined that it is necessary." Pierce was mildly indignant.

"Would a dry dock serve instead, Captain?" asked Smythe.

"A dry dock! Here?" Pierce took a long deep swallow from his glass. "You could not have built...."

"Oh no, Captain," interrupted Talbot. "We found one what was left by them ancient ones."

"Not something left by colonizing Balticans?"

"Oh, it is definitely the work of the Ancient Ones. The stonework matches what we've found elsewhere, and the inscriptions are not at all European or Baltican," said Gibbons. As was usual for him, he had remained silent and unobtrusive throughout the meal, and had spoken only when what he had to say was of importance.

Smythe explained, "A crew was clearing a trail north from the central city, the area where we are now. Someone stepped into the bush for matters of necessity, and spotted a path leading towards the shore. Later two men followed and nearly fell into the dry dock. Thinking that it might be of use, we stopped work on the trail and set about clearing it instead."

"And is it clear? Usable? Large enough for *Island Expedition?*" Pierce asked.

"Oh, it's quite big enough, sir!" said Townsend. "Why, I believe it would take *Victory*, and *Orion*. *Temeraire* as well, and with room left for something such as us."

"That large, is it?" exclaimed O'Brien. "A waste to be so much larger than any one ship."

"But perhaps ships large enough to need such a basin existed at one time," countered Smythe. "It is said the Chinese once built ships over twice the length of what we regard as gigantic."

"Highly unlikely," snorted the master.

"It is nearly cleared out," offered Mally.

"And knowing your desire to keep the hands busy while in port, perhaps completion of that would provide suitable work."

"An idea," agreed Pierce. "Unless it requires more effort than to careen."

"I could not hazard a guess, sir," remarked Talbot. Perhaps we should look."

"Now?" said Hadley, half-asleep.

"Why, what better way to assure you're alert for duty tonight?" grinned Morgan. "My leg is game, and I pray the rest of you are as well."

"Aye, a stretch after such a meal is what we all need. A stroll in the country would serve Mr. Dial's readiness as well. Is it far?"

"A couple of miles or so, sir," said Townsend. "Not far at all."

But Midshipman Townsend had been ashore the past year and a half and had ranged far and wide around the settlement. He had not been confined to the limits of a relatively small vessel at sea, nor restricted in his movements while a prisoner in Brunswick. As they neared the end of the first whole mile, Pierce found that he was breathing heavily, and that sweat poured freely from him, soaking through his uniform. Looking around, he saw that the others recently aboard ship appeared as fatigued as he was.

Smythe turned off the route they had been following. "It's not much farther." He led them away from the cleared portion of the ancient trail. They moved through uncleared terrain, much the same as it all had been when they first arrived. The path grew narrower and rougher. They pushed brush and small limbs out of their way.

"Don't touch the nettles, sir!" said Townsend, pointing. "They blister and itch something awful, sir."

"Thank you, Mr. Townsend. I shall avoid them if possible."

Pierce and the rest followed Smythe around a clump of vine maple and past the fallen trunk of an ancient cedar. Over a small rise, the heavy forest growth died away. Ahead, down a gently sloping grade, lay a large cleared expanse. Some was the result of recent work, but Pierce saw that much openness existed from before. The extensive stone structure partially sunk into the ground adjacent to the water's edge caught his eye.

"A dry dock!" he exclaimed. "There truly is a dry dock!"

"Indeed, Edward!" said Smythe. "Now you should be able to do the work needed on the schooner without careening her."

"But one must crawl through the bush to reach it?"

"No. Look there to your right. That trail leads inland and meets the trail back to the settlement. We came this way as it is shorter, and I thought the effect more dramatic."

"It was, indeed!" concluded Pierce.

"But the work required to empty such a large basin might equate that needed to careen, sir," observed Hotchkiss.

"It might, at that. But still…." Pierce was politely interrupted by Gibbons.

"My apology, sir, but one should never underestimate the ingenuity of the original inhabitants. It appears that the basin can be divided and subdivided, allowing one to flood and drain only what is needed."

"And," continued Mally, "there is evidence of powered devices for removing the water."

"Powered?" asked O'Brien.

"Indeed, sir." Gibbons went on. "If you will notice, gentlemen, there, on the far side, a hundred yards or so beyond the obvious structure, there is the mouth of a moderately large stream. Follow it inland several hundred yards and there is evidence remaining of a substantial dam. Channels cut in the rock lead to where there were apparently several large water wheels. Their positioning and other indications show that they powered devices akin to Archimedes' screws."

"They could empty the entire basin or select portions of it at will, and all without any strenuous physical labor on the part of anyone."

"It needs a final clearing out, Captain, of a portion big enough at least for *Island Expedition*," said Cooper. "The waterwheels and screws need to be built. But with that done, it should be usable after so many, many centuries."

"Even do we delay as you have asked, do we have time to make it ready, and then actually use it?" Pierce asked.

"One can never be certain, Edward," said Smythe. "But with the help of your crew, particularly certain skilled artisans, and concentrated effort by the entire colony, it should be operational early in December."

Pierce thought for a moment. "Gentlemen, this is a most momentous discovery. I am tempted to make use of it, but I must have time to contemplate. I have other matters to attend to this evening, but within the next day or two, I will make my choice known.

"Now I would suggest that those of you scheduled for duty return aboard directly. The rest of us may return or pursue other interests as suits us."

While Pierce's remarks effectively ended the day's activities, the group made its way back to the settlement together. Faintly hearing *Island Expedition* sounding seven bells, Dial, Hadley, and Spencer stretched out smartly and gained a noticeable lead over the others. Amongst those, small groups formed and walked along together, conversing. Pierce, Hotchkiss, O'Brien, and Morgan ended up going at the same pace.

"The leg, Tom?" asked Pierce. "How does it hold up?"

"Without a problem, sir. A touch of soreness, but it isn't bad. Quite normal, I think, sir, on extended walks."

"Plans for the evening?"

"I thought to find a couple of glasses of ale, sir, and then back aboard to write more to Cecilia. I'm sure Captain Cooper would see it posted when he is next in Vespica."

"Then, gentlemen, shall we stop at a particular tavern and avail ourselves of their hospitality? We might also observe something of the character of Folsum's young lady."

"A plan, I would say, sir," responded Hotchkiss. "You can then better decide what to tell her father."

"Aye."

"And after a stroll such as this, I could stand a pint of good ale!" said O'Brien.

"I don't recall that it was promised to be good!" laughed Morgan. "Who's buying?"

Pierce awoke the next morning, having arrived at two decisions. After breakfasting lightly and enjoying several cups of moderately good coffee, he updated his logs and took up a book to await four bells in the forenoon watch.

Jacob Blondin was prompt, if he was anything at all. Pierce's watch said nine fifty-six when he heard the aggrieved father shout gruffly but politely from the quay that he had business aboard with the captain.

Moments later, the marine outside the great cabin knocked and announced the man's arrival. Blondin stepped in, his worn, torn, and soiled hat in his hands.

"Come in, Mr. Blondin," said Pierce. "Be seated, if you will. May I offer you coffee? Or would you prefer something else?"

"No. What have you decided?" The man was also blunt and to the point. He wasted no time with pleasantries. "Will you punish your man, or turn him over that we can see justice is done?"

Pierce chose to respond in a like manner. "It is my opinion, sir, that no offense was committed. I will not punish him, nor will I allow you and your companions to mete out any lower-deck version of justice."

"What I thought you'd say, Captain. 'No offense was committed.' Bloody hell, there would've been, but I heard 'em. Enough noise to rouse the dead, I tell ya! Always got to be keepin' them young fools what's got their thinkin' danglin' 'tween their legs away from her."

"I understand that she is most successful in thwarting unwanted advances. Perhaps she did not consider his attention unwanted?"

Blondin tensed and stepped nearer to Pierce. His face reddened and his frown deepened. "You don't be saying such about my girl. She's no sailor's whore! Ain't nobody's whore!"

Pierce felt a twinge deep in the pit of his stomach. His last re-mark had not come across as he had intended. "I never implied, nor meant any insult to her honor," he said. "But give the lass her due, Mr. Blondin. She is old enough to make her own choices, even should they be wrong."

"Never a chance of that, Captain. Let her choose? Do you think me mad? She'd be spoiled goods today. Had I not heard the ruckus, she'd be livin' with her choice now and ne'er a chance to be a wife to anyone worthy. Let her choose!"

"However, nothing did happen. I cannot consider charges against my crewman. But should he wish it, I may have charges brought against you."

"What sort of charges?" Blondin asked incredulously. "I'm the one what was wronged!"

"No, Mr. Blondin! You are the one who threatened a member of this crew with bodily harm, and acted with such ferocity that he feared for his safety."

"But Captain!"

"And witnessing you strike your daughter only added to his fear that your anger would soon turn on him, had he not fled."

"Damned coward!" Blondin sighed and sagged visibly. "Didn't fig-ure there'd be any justice. You so-called English are just like them damned Kentish! See if we put up with your shit for long!"

"My decision, sir, has naught to do with nationality. I could not find that any real crime was committed. Should you wish, I will order him to stay away from her."

"If I catch him within a hundred yards of her, I'll kill him! I'll kill him!"

"And you, Mr. Blondin, you will maintain your distance from him as well!"

The man's face reddened again, and his mouth moved as if to speak. No words came forth. Pierce once again felt his insides knot.

"You may leave now, Mr. Blondin."

Grumbling, swearing under his breath, the man stalked angrily from the cabin. Pierce heard his footsteps go across the deck and re-sound loudly as he stomped down the brow.

Perhaps there had been enough activity on Folsum's part to have charged him with indecent liberties. Yet the girl was of age and had apparently entered willingly into it. While he would not encourage such behavior on her or the seaman's part, he could not blame them. They were old enough to decide and live with the consequences.

As promised, he would order Folsum to stay away, but for a speci-fied amount of time. If there was an attraction or a beginning bond between them, orders to the contrary would not keep them apart. He did not want to punish Folsum for violating orders, should he eventu-ally see her again.

# Chapter Nine

# Trouble Escalates

For the rest of the day, Pierce remained in an irritable funk. *Island Expedition* was barely two days returned and already there was trouble between the crew and a few island residents. He had hoped to avoid such circumstances, knowing that they could lead to more trouble if left unchecked. And now, had he checked them sufficiently? Had he taken the appropriate action? Time would tell, but from the bile threatening to rise in his throat, and the hostility evident in Blondin's manner, he wasn't at all sure.

Along with his quite sincere belief that no wrong had been committed, he had not wanted to charge Folsum, and be forced to admit, even to himself, his own culpability. Had what occurred between him and Leona Jackson been any different than what might have taken place between the young seaman and Blondin's daughter? Were his past activities that much more criminal because she was another man's wife? Was he now truly regretting that relationship?

Or was he simply upset because one of his crew had very nearly succeeded in dancing horizontally while he hadn't, and it would be endless months before his reunion with Evangeline?

Over two years had gone by since he had last seen her, held her in his arms, and kissed her. During the intervening months he had sailed thousands of miles, journeying not only to the opposite side of the known world, but across an immeasurable chasm to a new and entirely different world. The immense distances and the dragging eons of time could excuse most of his recent wanton behavior. Yet despite his lustful wandering, his overriding goal was to complete the voyage, and return to England and the waiting Evangeline.

He had not thought much about her since leaving Brunswick, New Guernsey. That was fortunate, because when he did, the ache in his heart became unbearable, and often he found himself doubting the relationship. But now, recent events caused him to focus on Evangeline, and the knowledge that it would be several months, perhaps years until he saw her again, dampened his spirit.

He felt like a man trapped underwater, lungs burning, aching to take that breath of life-giving air, but knowing that a breath now would surely end his life. He would not be in the clear, nourishing air until he was with her once more. And with the plans now being made, it would be even longer before they set out on their voyage home.

He could not let this loneliness consume him. Whether they remained on Stone Island or served to convey messages, diplomats, or delegates to and fro, work had to be done. Life went on, and as captain it was his duty to see that it did.

Pierce spent the better part of the morning with his logs and journals. He hated the subterfuge of keeping two sets, and in his mind it was a breach of regulations to do so. But Smythe had suggested it, and in a practical sense, Pierce agreed with the necessity. Smythe, Pierce, and the others concerned with the British Island Expedition Organization did not want undesirables to know the route to the island. Specifically it was the French in their own world, or the Gallicians or Tritonish in this world, for whom the routes between worlds should remain a highly guarded enigma. A wholesale excursion by one entity into the other world would truly upset the balances of power as they now existed.

Therefore he kept one set that was open to all. It did not hide the fact of having found the island or that it was in another world. It even gave the course they had sailed, in a somewhat general manner. Unlike the second, more detailed secret set of logs and journals, it did not enumerate those precise points they had crossed in order to traverse the chasm between worlds. That information was only for those, both in the government and the Organization, who really needed to know. And once Smythe completed his calculations for the return voyage and verified them, those coordinates would also be Pierce's right to know as well.

Eight bells sounded, marking the end of the forenoon watch. The hands were piped to their dinner. Pierce thought to go forward, grab a plateful from the coppers, return aft, and eat in brooding isolation. But Smythe had extended an "if you can come" invitation for dinner, not only for this day, but for any day the schooner was in port. While Pierce was usually quite happy with shipboard fare, even that served forward, it occurred to him that he really hungered for a home-cooked, a shore-cooked meal. He put on his uniform coat, grabbed his hat, and went on deck.

"Mr. Andrews, I shall be at the Colonial Building for the afternoon. Should you see Mr. Cook and Mr. Neilson, tell them that I would see them, six bells in the morning watch."

"Aye sir. Mr. Cook and Mr. Neilson, six bells in the morning watch."

Ashore, Pierce strode purposely to the Colonial Building. He walked directly in, the forward street-side portions of the edifice being public or colony property. Familiar with the building's layout after two previous visits, he paused and knocked at the door leading to the after portions of the building.

Mrs. Packingham answered after a minute or two. "Why Captain Pierce! Harold...I mean Mr. Smythe indicated you might dine with us. Please come in, won't you?"

"I shall, indeed. And indeed yes, it is my fondest desire to share dinner with you--allowing, of course, that you will have me."

"Perish any thought that we would reject your company. Today I believe you are all the company we shall have. Now, come this way, sir."

Smythe was already seated when Pierce entered. Opposed to where they had dined the previous day, this small room was an extension of the kitchen, and the smaller table took up a large portion of it.

"Ah, Edward, I thought you would come. As good as Eubanks' culinary skill is, I knew you could not resist the change."

"I did debate momentarily."

"But you are here. So take off your coat, sit, eat, and relax."

"Aye," said Pierce as he sat down.

The meal was in large part remainders of the previous day's dinner. *Delicious*, thought Pierce. Some foods became better each time they were reheated. It had been delicious yesterday, and today, warmed again, it was heavenly. Such flavor! Such aroma! Such texture! Rather than a wine, or beer, or even rum to wash it down, Pierce drank two large glasses of fresh milk.

When dessert, a freshly baked apple pie, was nearly finished, Smythe asked, "And did you meet with our Mr. Blondin this morning?"

"I did, and I cannot say that I'm happy with the outcome, sir."

"You do seem hipped."

"I made the choice not to bring charges against Folsum, nor to punish him for any transgression. Yet I fear Blondin is not satisfied with the overall justice of it. Tempers flared a little. My temper, to be most forthcoming."

"I see," responded Smythe in a noncommittal tone. "Truly nothing occurred for which you could punish the man. But we must watch the aggrieved father, lest he take things a step too far."

"But that aside, I have made my decision, sir, that we will attempt use of the dry dock."

"Excellent!"

"Tomorrow morning, the carpenter and sail maker will accompany me to the site. We'll make a more in-depth survey, and determine if we can indeed use it."

"I would think, Edward, that with your crew, even on shore hours, and with many of those on the island, that it should be operational within the month."

"Do we to have her in dry dock for December, she would be ready to sail shortly after the beginning of the year. And since we are now committed to being here for at least that time, it is a means to keep the hands occupied."

"I know you hate to see them idle."

"Aye! But truthfully sir, were it not that we've already agreed, I would provision and sail within the week. Damn the schooner's condition! Damn protocol, diplomacy, and damn official Land of Stone Island official damn service! I'd sail on the next tide!"

"Ah, the impatience of the young. Evangeline?"

"Why indeed, sir, yes! But has she… I mean, sir, do you know of…."

"No, not in so many words, did she tell me. But I could see the way she looked at you, and indeed the way you looked at her. As her father, I too found it hard to leave her behind."

"Until today, sir, I have usually been successful at keeping thoughts of her in the background. But certain events of late have caused them to surface."

"Would you sail sooner if you could, Edward?" asked Mrs. Packingham, rejoining them.

Pierce was surprised at her instant familiarity, but he warmed quickly to it. "I think not, Vera," he replied in kind. "I have promised to carry word and a delegate, should that be required. And I do worry about the condition of the schooner. I'll bide my time and see that all obligations are met."

"We must remember your encounter with the Gallician frigates," said Smythe. "Their actions and motives may account for more than we know."

"True."

The next day Pierce, the carpenter, the sail maker, and the master revisited the ancient dry dock. They made a more in-depth survey of the site, and determined they could indeed make it operational. Once that had been positively decided, Pierce announced that work would begin in earnest the next Wednesday.

For the remainder of the week, and through the weekend, he kept the schooner on minimum schedule, detailing enough men aboard every day that the vessel was secure and the required work was done. Otherwise the hands were given their full share of liberty. On Sunday, they held a memorial service for the seven killed in battle with HRMS *Hawke*. Pierce was grateful that the clergyman, a Vespican Reformed Episcopalian, led prayers for the dead and injured aboard that vessel as well.

As Pierce listened to pleas for the repose of the souls of the departed, he was amazed at the similarity of services in this and his own world. True, he noted, there were many differences between the two worlds, but many things were the same. Matters of faith seemed to very closely parallel one another; the biggest difference was one of name. From what he noticed at this particular service, and from what he had seen in Brunswick, this world had the three major monotheistic faiths of his home world. Further, days of the week, names of the months, and enumeration of the years matched perfectly. These similarities made passage between the two worlds much easier.

Monday was Guy Fawkes Day, and the entire community celebrated noisily. The Vespicans now residing on Stone Island, while not sure of the reason, celebrated as well. A few with more recent ties to Kentland concluded that the festivities paralleled their own Sam Whyte Eve.

Pierce retired early Tuesday night. He wanted a full night's rest before they began the chore of fully restoring the dock. As he drifted off to sleep, he wished the majority of the hands would think to do the same. But he knew that the only ones well-rested would be those whose duties kept them aboard. The majority would be at their rum and ale, and in the arms of any willing female. Most, if not all, would be back before six bells in the morning watch. Of those who might miss muster, he would take their names, and unless they were repeat transgressors, having their names would be enough. For those guilty of the same offense once again, something more would be called for, and as he lost contact with wakefulness, he could not imagine what.

In the morning, when all hands had mustered by division, when the division officers had reported to Lieutenant Hotchkiss, and that individual had reported to Pierce, only one man amongst the entire crew was absent. Questioning his messmates and division companions could not produce any idea of Folsum's whereabouts.

Pierce feared Blondin had become so enraged by the young seamen's relationship with his daughter, that he had harmed Folsum. And had Folsum disobeyed orders and attempted to spend time with Abigail Blondin? Had he been so overcome by desire for the young lass as to willfully disregard his captain's direct order? That possibility irritated Pierce, as he had carefully explained to the lad that it was for his own protection, and not any condemnation of the relationship. Pierce had even explained the order to the girl, having stopped by the makeshift tavern where she worked.

As he silently debated these things, he had other tasks ahead of him. He could not disrupt the well-laid plans for the entire ship because of one unaccounted-for crewman. Nor could he forget the man's absence. Despite his suspicion that Folsum had left in defiance of orders, Pierce was concerned for his well-being. Mentally scanning the lists of the day's assigned duties, he decided to designate a few from each group to form a search party. Whether Folsum needed to be rescued or arrested was not known at the present time.

"Mr. Hotchkiss!"

"Sir!"

"Four trustworthy hands from those going to the dock, if you please. We'll start a search for our young man."

"Aye aye, sir."

"And Mr. O'Brien, three hands of those remaining aboard!"

"Aye, sir."

"Mr. Andrews, take charge of the search!"

"Shall we consider him as 'run' or not, sir?"

"Not until he gives reason for you to believe so."

"Mr. O'Brien," said Pierce. "You will see to the work at the dry dock. You know what needs to be done, and with the present circumstances, it is best I remain."

"Aye, sir. Of course, sir."

The seven detailed to search for their shipmate formed up, and at a word from Andrews went ashore. As they did, a young woman, running wildly, nearly in tears, and gasping desperately for breath, approached the quay. "He shot him! He shot him!" she gasped, as she reached Midshipman Andrews and the search party.

"Who shot him? Who shot who?" asked Andrews as he offered her support.

She sank to the stones paving the quay. "Pa shot him! Pa shot him!"

"Shot who?"

"Why, Tim, of course!" she said with indignation.

Upon witnessing the girl's arrival, Pierce hurried down the brow and quickly arrived. "Miss Blondin, I must ask if our shipmate is fortunate enough to be alive."

"Oh, he was. Now, I don't know! So much blood! And he's fainted!" She looked faint as well, even as she sobbed vigorously.

"Can you show us, miss? Quickly, before your father completes the deed?"

"I can! But don't worry about Pa."

"Why?"

"I shot him!"

"Is he...?"

"Dead?" She wailed louder. "No, he's not dead! But he can't be trying to kill Tim no more! And he's not keeping me under his thumb no more neither!"

"Deck there! Doctor Matheson!"

"Doctor's gone below, sir!" responded Hotchkiss.

"Well then, send for him! Have him bring his medical bag!"

"Aye aye, sir!"

The doctor arrived within a few minutes, although to Pierce it seemed a much longer time. "Surely, Doctor, in your service, you have learned the need for preparedness and promptness."

"Indeed sir, I have. I foresaw no need for my immediate services...."

"But you are with us now. Come along, as we do have need for your skills. Miss Blondin, will you lead!"

She led the party south along the shore and then turned inland. As the trek grew longer, Pierce worried more about the condition they would find young Folsum in. She led them around a wooded hillock, up a narrow overgrown draw to a small clearing. A small cabin stood there, half of logs and half of stone, remnants of an Ancient Ones' structure.

"My home, Captain," she said, neither boasting nor ashamed. Her tone was one merely of fact. "Pa's over there, near the door! Tim's just inside the shed."

"Doctor!" commanded Pierce.

He was relieved to find that neither individual was in immediate danger of dying. Still, the injuries were quite severe, and Dr. Matheson insisted that both would require some time to recover. "Perhaps," he suggested, "we might transfer them to the Colony Building?"

"A most distressing turn of events, Edward," said Smythe that evening. He sipped slowly at his glass of port. It was from the last bottle of all they had brought from England. "Disposition of this will be a most delicate undertaking."

"Indeed?"

"This colony, this island, this minute outcrop of civilization is based on freedom and individual rights. Yet crimes of a most serious nature have been committed. Even here, we cannot allow such actions to go unpunished. Do we not take action, immediately and decisively, I'm afraid we will stray into chaos."

"And yet the very parties we would charge are also the victims. Should Folsum recover, and Dr. Matheson assures me he shall, I must deal with his violation of my explicit orders."

"Would we bring charges against Blondin? Indeed for an attempt at murder?" asked Smythe. "And the girl? Surely she is guilty to some degree."

"Aye, so it would seem. Perhaps not murder, but assault? We do know he shot Folsum, but not that he truly intended his death. Her action was one of defense, and yet inexcusable in its own right."

"Do we make arrests? Do we detain them? Miss Blondin?"

Pierce sipped as he thought. "Due to the severity of his injuries, I'm confident that Blondin will not flee. He is here, invalided and quite closely watched. She is caring for the two of them, and I believe she has no intention of flight. Indeed she may not realize that she also faces consequences."

"You did not mention it to her?"

"I thought it best not to. I do not want to intrude into colony affairs and usurp your authority, sir."

"Most considerate, I say. Perhaps we have been remiss to not consider such situations. I see now that development of a legal system and a means of enforcement are paramount."

"Quite so, sir. I can handle transgressions committed by the crew. When he is sufficiently recovered, I will deal with Folsum. Of Blondin and his daughter, I will allow that you and the colony are best suited to determine their punishment."

"But before we should decide upon suitable punishment, sir, we must ascertain their guilt. While we understand that they have committed these acts of violence, to summarily condemn them strains the very concept of the colony and the true meaning of justice. We shall need to try them, and allow them every chance to assert their individual or collective innocence."

"Would you suggest I try Folsum as well?"

"No. As a member of your crew, he comes under the rules and regulations of the Royal Navy. You surely have the right to maintain discipline and order what punishment you think appropriate."

"Aye. But what of the others on the island? Do we wait until the two are recovered and procedures begin, it may appear that there is no law in effect here."

"I agree, Edward. Tomorrow I shall let it be known that the two are under guard and face justice upon recovery of the injured. I'm sure that when explained appropriately, Miss Blondin will see our position and offer no opposition."

"Let us hope so."

"We must be most careful in this matter. We do not want to create an aura of false justice, such as caused so many to journey here."

"Aye!"

The two were silent for some time. Mrs. Packingham entered. "Coffee, gentlemen?" she asked. "Might I join you?"

"Of course, my dear," replied Smythe, a slight smile upon his face.

"I would welcome a cup, ma'am," said Pierce.

Anticipating their acceptance of both her presence and the coffee, she had brought with her the pot and three cups. She placed it on the side board and poured for each of them. Then she sat.

"May I ask, Edward, how things go at the dry dock?"

"We made progress, to be sure. But it has been only one day. Do they all have other activities, as this one did, it may be a long and tiring process to make it operational."

"Surely, the days ahead will go smoother."

"I pray you are right."

## Chapter Ten

# Overhaul

Despite Pierce's gloom that evening, the victims of the incident healed rapidly. Two weeks later, he declared the twenty-first as make and mend, a general day off for all hands. That evening he hosted the schooner's officers for a light supper.

When the meal was over, toasts drunk, and coffee served, Pierce said, "Gentlemen, remarkable progress is being made in clearing out the dock. It will soon be operational. While we are no longer forced to careen, placing the schooner in dry dock will be a tremendous undertaking. Fortunately, we can rely upon the island residents to complete the dock while we prepare the vessel to utilize it.

"We must send down all upper masts, yards, and spars. In general, we must lighten ship. To best accomplish this, the entire crew will move ashore. Mr. Smythe has asked Mr. Gibbons to arrange for berthing ashore, and that gentleman will be aboard later this evening with details."

"The entire crew ashore, sir?" said Morgan, his wooden leg sticking out awkwardly. "Surely that will be a source of trouble."

"No doubt, were we in England, and with another crew. Yet it is a unique situation. Rarely if ever, does a captain have a crew journey to the ship every day."

"Folsum?" asked Hotchkiss. "He's recovered nicely and won't long remain at the Colony Building. Billeting the hands ashore will pose difficulties with any restrictions you may impose upon him."

"Not that being aboard was enough for him to follow the order. It may have been followed closer, had others not looked away." Pierce glanced with fleeting disapproval around the cabin. "I do not want to think that ship's officers may have been remiss in their duties.

"As to the hands living ashore, and any in a restricted status, I do not see it as a problem, provided that all with the duty perform it to the letter. We will discuss any particular arrangements for those situations when it is time."

"Aye, sir," answered Hotchkiss. The others relaxed slightly, relieved that Pierce chose not to pursue any apparent lapses in duty amongst those present.

"Now, Mr. Morgan, if you would pass the decanter, I see several with empty glasses."

"Certainly, sir."

"Beginning tomorrow, the majority of hands will be working aboard or in the vicinity of *Island Expedition*. Only those with special skills needed at the dock will continue there. It is, as I said, to the point that the colonists can finish it.

"Gentlemen, when we commence, Mr. Andrews, Mr. O'Brien, and Mr. Cartney will send down spars, yards, and upper masts. Place them ashore on the quay."

"Aye aye, sir," they replied.

"Mr. Gray, you will have all stores removed, inventoried, and placed ashore. Inspect for spoilage, and discard any that are not at their absolute best."

"Aye, sir. Should I retain as much as possible against our return home?"

"The island now produces sufficient that we can replace any that are condemned. The Vespicans are also providing supplies, and we most certainly can avail ourselves of those."

"Aye, sir. Thank you, sir."

"Mr. Cook, you shall roust out the schooner's building plan that Sir Ronald provided. You and your mates will cut timber and construct cribs to support the vessel when the dock is pumped dry."

"Aye aye, sir."

"Mr. Hotchkiss, when Mr. Gibbons arrives with berthing

arrangements, see that billets are assigned appropriately. At the start of the first dog watch, all hands are to be dismissed for the move ashore."

"Aye aye, sir."

"Mr. Morgan and Mr. Harris will see the guns ashore. When it is convenient to do so, we will also unload powder and shot."

Following further work assignments, Pierce finally said, "And now gentlemen, other than those with the duty, we should turn in. We've had a day's rest, but tomorrow promises to be one of great endeavor. We have a great deal to do, but by God we won't spend the rest of the year doing it!"

The next day, with work underway, Pierce sat at his writing table and updated his journal and added to the continuing letter to Evangeline. It had been so long since he had seen her. Since those treasured moments had occurred so long ago, did he remember them, or did he conjure images and sensations to keep the memories alive?

He sipped at his ever-present coffee, put his pen down, and closed his correspondence. Then he packed his writing materials and other miscellaneous possessions so they could be taken to his temporary lodgings. He locked the small chest and dropped the key in his pocket. As he left the cabin, voices filtered through the open skylight.

"Damn, Joe, ye'd think we was careening the barky now! Never seen so much bilge! This ashore! That ashore! Strike that below! Off load this! Off load that! Off load yerselfs as yer at it!"

"Aye! Might as well careen her. And not to take all damn year! We'll be two, just gettin' the shit outta her."

"Knock it off, ya louts! D'ya need the captain t' hear ya?" Campbell's voice flooded below. "On the quarterdeck at that! Now put your backs into it! Heave!"

Pierce considered yelling through the skylight. It would give the grumbling seamen a start to know he had heard them. Further, it might add to the mystique of a captain being aware of everything happening aboard his ship. But he recognized their tone and knew it was typical seamen's grousing. While they crudely and at times profanely complained, they also were quite willingly going about their work. Despite their apparent dislike of the move ashore, he knew that they saw it as a change, and a chance at adventure. There was nothing dangerous in their tone. Still he was thankful that Campbell, the duty bo'sun's mate, had happened by and put an end to it.

By the end of November, preparations for putting *Island Expedition* in dry dock were nearly complete. Alone along the quay, the schooner rode high out of the water, her equipage piled nearby and covered with tarpaulins. With her crew living ashore, her holds and decks emptied, her guns removed, and only the huge lower masts remaining, she looked abandoned. The starkness of her apparent desertion was made more noticeable in that she no longer shared dock space with *Evening Star*. Randolph Cooper had sailed for mainland Vespica a week ago.

Pierce was pleased with progress to this point. Yet as he stood idly on the quay, looking at his denuded command, he fervently wished for the procedures to be behind them. He felt helpless, being in command of a vessel that could not sail. And he did so want this particular vessel to sail. Not only was it his home and his transportation, it was his link, his return to England. Until *Island Expedition* was afloat and fully outfitted for sea, Pierce could not come close to being content.

Tim Folsum had recovered enough that Dr. Matheson had discharged him from the makeshift hospital in the Colony Building. Folsum's disobedience of direct orders was not in question, but determining a suitable, just, and yet humane punishment troubled Pierce. The most obvious answer would be to seize the man to the gratings and have him flogged. Pierce had always had an aversion to that brutal punishment, and after witnessing it used to an excess in HRMS *Furious*, he had silently vowed never to prescribe it.

He understood that a just and appropriate punishment accomplished several things. It made the defaulter aware of and hopefully sorry for his transgressions. Additionally, a correctly applied sentence served to warn others. Judicious use of suitable punishment maintained good order and discipline. Nor was Folsum his only disciplinary concern. In the weeks since their return to the island, several other crewmen had managed to find themselves on the defaulters list.

After several minutes of contemplation, Pierce made up his mind. He turned from the quay and headed towards the Colony Building. He, Hotchkiss, O'Brien, and the senior midshipmen and master's mates now lodged there while the schooner was under repair. Upon arrival, Pierce found those individuals seated comfortably and in conversation with Smythe and Mrs. Packingham.

"A glass with us, sir?" asked Dial. The invitation was echoed by them all.

"Why, thank you, gentlemen. Mrs. Packingham." Pierce accepted the offered glass.

Talk was of a general nature and progressed easily, as it was amongst friends of long acquaintance. Pierce joined in from time to time, but focused on enjoying his glass of claret. When the time seemed appropriate, he said to Hotchkiss in a low voice, "Defaulters at morning muster."

"Aye." Hotchkiss nodded slightly.

When the schooner's crew mustered the next morning, all were present or accounted-for. That was a relief, because Pierce would not have to add to the list of those to be dealt with.

"Defaulters aft!" bellowed Hotchkiss after a significant look from Pierce. While they now mustered ashore, the crew was alongside the schooner, abreast their normal onboard muster locations. A few hands fidgeted slightly, and then hesitantly stepped from amongst their fellows. Self-consciously they made their way along the quay and stood where Cartney the bo'sun indicated. Folsum nervously made his way aft and stood toeing the line along with the others.

Pierce removed a list from his pocket, looked at it, and then looked at the assembled miscreants. He mentally matched the listed offenses against the faces before him. "We are a small crew," he said, loudly enough that the entire company could hear. "I'll not announce the specific charges against each of you. Your shipmates know them as well as you. Do any of you wish to speak on your own behalf?"

A few glanced about, moved nervously while still in their assigned spots, and a couple coughed apprehensively. But no one spoke.

"Do any officers wish to speak on behalf of their men?"

"I believe, sir, that all considerations have been covered prior to this, sir," remarked Hotchkiss.

"You are correct, Mr. Hotchkiss. I will tell you that your division officers had the most complimentary things to say about you, and begged me to consider the circumstances in determining punishment." A few surreptitious grins momentarily crossed the faces of the accused. Folsum's face remained blank.

"Will any shipmate speak on behalf of these men?" asked Pierce.

No one volunteered to speak, but there was an air of appreciation because Pierce had asked for input from the crew.

"For those with long experience at sea," he said, "you know the common answer would be to rig gratings and order two or three dozen, depending upon the offense committed and the individual having committed it. But the cat has not been out of the bag since we commissioned in Portsmouth. I will not let it out now. Do not think me soft, lads, but I have witnessed flogging to where I wish never to see it again.

"Yet, a few individuals have committed offenses, and for those actions, they must be punished. Therefore, we shall have a new division on board. Defaulters will man that division, and will perform those duties specified by myself or Mr. Hotchkiss. A division officer will be assigned. The senior amongst you will be leading petty officer, and you will berth together in a specified location. You will be considered as a part of the on-deck watch daily, excepting Sundays. All will be in the defaulters' division for a minimum of thirty days. Is that understood?"

"Aye aye, sir," they replied.

"Good!" said Pierce. "Mr. Hotchkiss, you may dismiss the hands and send them about the day's work. The new division will stand by while we arrange for berthing and a division officer."

"Aye aye, sir."

"Mr. Dial, once hands are dismissed, I would see you privately."

"Aye aye, sir."

A week later they towed *Island Expedition* away from the quay, and north a mile and a half to the dry dock. While the majority of the crew had been lightening ship, Mr. Cook and his mates had constructed timber cribs and had placed them in exact spots in the dock. The gates had been opened and a smooth unbroken stretch of water led into the dock.

They towed the schooner into the dock, cast off the boats, and made the vessel fast to bollards along the dock's edge. Hands manned the capstan and positioned *Island Expedition* exactly over the emplaced timbers. When the master, the carpenter, and the first lieutenant determined that the schooner was in the correct location, they reported the fact to Pierce. He sighted various marks painted on the edges of the dock and indicated on the hull. He agreed that the vessel was positioned correctly and nodded his concurrence to Lieutenant Hotchkiss. "Close the gates!" he ordered.

When the gates were nearly closed, the first lieutenant turned to a young boy standing by, waiting for the moment. "Now lad, would you run to the dam and desire them to release the flow!"

"Aye aye, sir!" The boy was off at a run, scampering across the stone surfaces of the dock edge and then across the rise to the dam. Jack Haight returned moments later, breathing heavily from his exertions.

"Water's flowing, sir!" he panted. "Should be turning them wheels anytime now, sir."

"Thank you, Haight. Your effort is appreciated."

"Thankee, sir!"

As they watched, water trickled and then roared through the stone channels cut and shaped so many years ago. The fast-moving streams struck the buckets constructed on the circumference of several large wheels, and soon they began to rotate. As they did, shafts and gears attached to them turned as well. The result of all this movement was that several long enclosed auger-like devices, which extended into the water supporting the schooner, began to rotate. Ideally these water-powered Archimedes screws would serve to remove the water from the enclosed dock and eventually leave *Island Expedition* sitting high and dry on the timber supports.

But there was no discharge of water from the top of the pumps, no flow of water through the discharge channels that led to the bay. There was, however, a certain turbulence around each of the tube-like pumps, and occasionally a burst of bubbles at the surface.

"Damn my eyes!" said Pierce. "Do not the laws of nature follow in this world?" He was tired, exasperated. It had been the idea of water-powered pumping to empty the basin that had convinced him to use the dock rather than careening the schooner. Now it seemed they would have to resort to that more primitive and strenuous method of accessing the lower portions of the hull. It was that, or rig their own pumps and laboriously empty the dock.

Pierce toyed with the idea of ordering pumps rigged and detailing hands to the back-breaking task of pumping the water out of the dock. But it had been a long busy day, and he knew the men were more exhausted than he was. Whatever they might accomplish in the remaining daylight would not be much. Instead, he turned to Hotchkiss. "Let the men stand down, Isaac. We'll begin anew, along with the new day. Perhaps those screws will take a prime overnight, or rested, the hands will better evacuate the basin."

"Aye. Perhaps." Hotchkiss nodded.

"Mr. Dial!" Pierce shouted.

"Aye, sir?"

"Your defaulters' division will remain on watch. Supper will be brought up, along with hammocks. Two men on watch at all times, and mind you, does the water start, you will need to pay out mooring lines." Thoroughly disgusted with the final turn of events, Pierce harbored little hope that conditions would reverse, although he mentioned the possibility to Dial, primarily to provide him with additional responsibilities.

"Aye aye, sir!"

It was a long walk back to the Colony Building and his temporary quarters. Pierce was tired and knew he should go straight to bed. But he was hungry as well, and Mrs. Packingham had prepared a very delicious, warm, and filling venison stew. After eating, he sat with a glass of wine and conversed briefly with Smythe. He needed those few moments to relax and ease the anxiety he felt. If he did not ease the tension, he would not sleep, tired though he was.

"Perhaps," he said with a weary sigh, "I should have careened."

"But the dock may yet be made operational. To think that it would operate perfectly to begin with is asking a bit much, is it not?"

"Perhaps." Pierce sipped at his glass.

"And without the attempt, we would never know of the problem. With a little time and diligence, it may yet work."

"I pray that is so. With all the labor expended to this point, I have no urge to pump the dock dry manually, or to revert to careening."

"But must you access the lower hull, Edward?"

"I would know the true condition the schooner for the return voyage."

"Aye."

Smythe was silent for a moment or two, and Pierce maintained the quiet. Then Smythe spoke again. "It would have been easier to have simply flogged the defaulters and be done with it."

"You do know my views on that."

"Indeed. That you come up with the defaulters' division speaks well of your ability to find alternatives. Is it proving satisfactory?"

"For all involved. We have a group that can be assigned the most mundane and distasteful tasks. And yet they perform their duties with a will and a cheerful good nature, knowing, of course, that someone would need to perform them."

"Discipline, justice, and punishment seem so simple for those in military or naval service," said Smythe. "You need not worry about the complexities faced in the public arena. As captain, you rightly act as accuser, judge, and jury, determine guilt, and impose sentence. Even as de facto head of the colony, I cannot take on those roles, lest I be seen as a tyrant. I must be aware of the public sentiment and exhibit a sense of fairness to a much greater degree."

"I'm sure that it is a difficult task, sir. But it is not always easy in the service. I trust you are speaking of the Blondins' situation?"

"I am."

"Might I suggest you bring it up with the council?"

"I have, and therein is the problem. We are at an impasse as to how to proceed...if, indeed we proceed at all."

"Might you consider some arrangement? Admitted guilt to a lesser charge? Agreed fair and just punishment? It might allow justice to be done without the necessity of trial."

"It could work that way. Neither has denied their actions. Perhaps I have been over-zealous with the idea of perfect justice. I'll see what transpires when the council meets next. Now, I must have some sleep. And I believe you need the same."

Pierce slept soundly that night, but he awoke, still tired and a little sore. A quick wash and two cups of hot strong coffee partially revived him. He wearily set out to the dry dock. As the facility came into view, *Island Expedition* seemed to be lower and less exposed than it had been the evening before. The tides? No, the basin was enclosed, and the water contained would not be affected by the sun and moon.

As he approached, he saw that the waterwheels were still turning, driving the pumps submerged in the water. But now, a steady stream of water burbled out of the top of each, spilled into its particular discharge channel, and flowed away. Could it be the pumps were finally working as planned?

Dial came up to him, grimy and exhausted. "We did it, sir! We did it!" he said with weary enthusiasm.

"I see, Mr. Dial. But may I ask, how?"

"There is a story to that, sir."

"I would hear it, if you so please."

"Aye, sir. You know, some of these lads are right sharp with these sorts of things. And to see to it they had more to do while awake and on watch, I challenged them to find and fix the problem.

"Not long after eight bells in the evening watch, Folsum comes by and says to me, 'Maybe they ain't pumpin' water out, 'cause maybe they're pumpin' air in.' I'm wondering if he's gotten into the spirits, sir, and so I ask him what he means. He says, 'Today, when the barky was set on her mark, young Jack says to me, "She'll never pump out. Screws ain't turnin' the right way." And I've been watchin' them, sir, and young Jack is right.' Maybe they are, too, so I had him find a way to reverse the turning so we could check."

"Evidently he found a way!"

"Oh, indeed, yes! Just repositioned one cogwheel in relation to another. Made the pump spin t'other way, and right away, she started pulling up the water. So we switched the rest, and just got done, afore you come up, sir."

"A most excellent night's work, Mr. Dial! You and your division are to be commended!"

"Thank you, sir."

"There is a chance, lad, that some of this division will see their assigned days reduced." Dial beamed. Pierce noticed and continued. "Unfortunately, as long as any are assigned, an officer will be required. As officers, our duties and responsibilities are greater, and thus so should our penance be, should we fail in those duties. But satisfactory performance while under discipline has a way of erasing past errors."

"Then I am to remain, as their division officer, sir?" asked Dial. "And if more defaulters are assigned?"

"If none are assigned, prior to these finishing their times, you shall be relieved. And does the division need to be reformed, perhaps another will become division officer. Your performance, now and in the future, will surely count for or against you in such matters."

"Aye, sir. And now, do you excuse me, but I must see that mooring lines are extended."

"As you will, Mr. Dial. Pass along my gratitude to all in your division."

It took the system two full days to empty the dock to the point that they could access the schooner's bottom and stay relatively dry. Pierce, Hotchkiss, O'Brien, and Cook spent three days in the dock and went over every square inch of the lower hull. They found the underwater portions of *Island Expedition* to be in very good condition for having sailed halfway around the world. Even though afloat only a couple of years, a considerable amount of marine growth adhered to the hull, in spite of the copper covering her bottom. Some sheets were battered and worn, and needed replacing. There were also three shot holes from *Hawke* that could now be fully repaired.

Pierce crawled in the mud lining the lower portions of the dock for a look at the underside of the keel. It was slimy with marine growth, which he wiped away with old burlap sacking. For most of its length, the vessel's spine and the copper sheets covering it were undisturbed, in perfect condition other than the result of months underwater. But aft of amidships, slightly nearer the stern, something caught his eye.

A nail, meant to hold the copper in place, had pulled loose and protruded perhaps a quarter inch. It could easily be hammered back to being flush. But wrapped about it were fibers, the remnants of spun yarn. Pierce carefully removed them.

Slightly farther along towards the stern, another nail was loose, and close by, a hole in the copper where another fastener had come completely out. But this nail hole did not fit the pattern and sequence that ran for the massive timber's entire length. Puzzled, he continued his inspection. Several more random nail holes became evident, some with larger-sized nails still in them, and additional strands of yarn twisted about. Other original nails were loose, and again had fibers twisted or tied about them.

He reached the sternpost, sighed with disgust, and got to his feet. Wet and muddy, he climbed out of the dock. "Mr. Hotchkiss!" he shouted upon spying the first lieutenant. "A word with you, sir!"

"Aye, sir!" answered Hotchkiss, himself equally filthy from having inspected other portions of the lower hull. "What a sight we present, Edward!" he laughed. "Not at all the way the King's officers are represented to the mob, eh?"

"I suppose not, Mr. Hotchkiss!" Pierce maintained quarterdeck formality, angered by what he had just seen. "At your earliest opportunity, do look as I have, at the very underside of the keel, amidships and aft. Then we both might know why this vessel did not so easily show her heels to those fucking frigates!"

"Aye aye, sir," replied Hotchkiss. "From the portions of fiber you hold, I surmise we had been stealthily fitted with a sea anchor." Perceiving his friend and captain's extreme ire, he did not wait for additional remarks, but immediately descended to look at the designated areas.

*Chapter Eleven*

# A Holiday Interlude

With the state of *Island Expedition's* underwater hull now determined, efforts to correct, upgrade, and repair began in earnest. Pierce kept the hands hard at it and drove them relentlessly to return the vessel to a condition better than when she had been launched. He was at the dry dock every day, often the first to arrive, and usually the last to leave. He crawled about the schooner, examining every part of her, calling for this to be corrected and for that to be corrected again. Exhausted at the end of these long days, he returned to his quarters in the Colony Building, ate a cold supper, and went straight away to bed. His association with Hotchkiss and members of the crew was short and businesslike. He spoke briefly and with careful attention to civility when forced to be in the company of Harold Smythe or others of the colony.

As tired as he appeared to be, and as tired as he actually was, there were many nights when sleep did not come until long after he had crawled into his cot. On those evenings, he lay awake, his mind strangely detached from the reality of his current driven temper. Out of the recesses of a long-forgotten conscience came questions as to why he was in such a state. From other long-buried regions came answers. And yet, when he did fall asleep and later awaken, groggy, tired as ever, the questions, if remembered, did not match the answers he thought he had found.

Ill-tempered due to a lack of sleep, amongst other things, Pierce gulped his coffee, ate his eggs and toast, and set off once more for the dry-docked *Island Expedition*. He wondered, as did everyone around him, what caused him to be in such a condition. Was it the delay in sailing as requested by Smythe and others in the colony? Add that to the year or more he had spent detained in Brunswick, and it marked a considerable period of his life, as he impatiently waited for the voyage to resume. Did the ongoing intrigue and the continuing efforts to circumvent Vespican neutrality he had seen there provide the means of his unrest? Or had the discovery that his vessel and in connection, himself, had been violated by unknown agents while restricted from leaving the Vespican mainland feed his continuing and silent rage? So much was happening in this world that he did not understand. In his confusion, perhaps he simply wanted to be away from it all.

Certainly, finding that someone had secretly attached devices to cut the schooner's speed upset him greatly. Looking back on that revelation, he recognized it as a significant contribution to his current angry state. He had, after all, used words in reaction to its discovery that he normally did not use. Was that situation so much worse, or was it merely the one that pushed him into his present mood?

On Saturday the 22nd of December, Pierce considered not allowing the hands the usual Sunday routine. Instead, he might push them through that day as well, and get a little more work done on the schooner. Doing so would not be welcome amongst the crew, and he normally prided himself on being cognizant of the men's needs. Even so, the question remained on his mind for a good part of the morning. Restlessly he checked his watch, nearly six bells in the forenoon watch. A bit more than an hour remained until noon and dinner for all hands. He would arrive at a final choice by then.

Some minutes before the eleven o'clock bells sounded, a young crewman arrived, breathing hard, having run from the quay and the makeshift signal tower there. "Mr. Spencer's compliments, sir!" he said, struggling to catch his breath.

"Yes! Yes! What is it?" Pierce was impatient.

"I'm to say, sir, that a ship has been sighted, entering the bay. The lookout on the hill just signaled, sir."

"Can you tell me more?"

Somewhat recovered from his run, but nervous at being face to face with his lately cantankerous captain, the lad thought desperately for a long minute. Pierce forced himself to be patient. Finally the crewman recovered his wits enough to say, "The ship flies the White Star. Doctor 'R' is aboard."

Dr. Robertson! God, thought Pierce, it would be good to see that man of medicinal miracles and diplomatic success again. "Thank you, lad," he said. "You may tell Mr. Spencer I have the message. Have a drink at the scuttlebutt first. As it is fast becoming very warm, you need not bother running on your return."

"Aye, sir! Thank you, sir!"

Six bells sounded and Pierce went in search of Lieutenant Hotchkiss. He found him deep in the bowels of the schooner. Hotchkiss was soaked through with sweat, having been in the airless hot interior for hours, supervising the installation of added bracing and stiffeners. There for only a matter of minutes, Pierce felt his clothes rapidly growing damp as well.

"Mr. Hotchkiss!"

"Aye, sir?" he replied warily, accustomed by now to the cross-grained temper exhibited of late by his friend and captain.

"Following the afternoon watch, Mr. Hotchkiss, all hands to be in a liberty status, other than those of the defaulters' division!"

"Aye aye, sir!"

"Rope yarn or make and mend tomorrow, as well, I think."

"Aye, sir. All hands again come Monday, sir?"

"No, I think not, Mr. Hotchkiss. We will go with watch on deck only, through Wednesday, Tuesday being Christmas. Perhaps some will desire to celebrate."

"Aye, sir."

"I believe, Isaac, that Mrs. Packingham and other ladies of the colony have a feast in the works. With nothing but coffee, eggs, toast, and cold suppers, I look forward to it."

"As do I," replied Isaac Hotchkiss, who wondered at this sudden change in Pierce's temper.

"And lest I forget, we have just received word of a ship arriving, bearing the estimable Dr. Robertson!"

"That answers that."

"Your pardon, Isaac?" questioned Pierce. "No, I grasp your meaning. Perhaps the good Doctor's pending arrival is already working a cure for my dark state."

"Aye."

This was the third Christmas celebrated during *Island Expedition's* voyage, and the second since their arrival on the island. For Pierce, it was his first here, having spent the previous year's feast amiably detained in Brunswick, New Guernsey. While he understood perfectly well the effects of being in the Southern Hemisphere, it felt strange to mark the occasion of the Lord's birth on a warm and sunny summer's day. He held long-cherished childhood memories of dampness and cold, perhaps even the fall of snow, and the warmth of family, a roaring fire, and a sumptuous meal inside.

That Tuesday was given over entirely to the festivities of the season. Religious celebrations occupied much of the morning, conducted by the same Vespican Reformed Episcopalian who had led the memorial services for those lost against *Hawke*. Pierce attended, not so much out of any spiritual obligation, but out of a sensed social requirement. Yet it was good to once again hear the familiar story of travelers, a lack of lodging, and the birth in the stable. How remarkable, he thought, that even here the story was so remarkably the same. He noted that a few names (primarily of locations) differed, but in all, it was the same story he had heard every year of his early life.

In the afternoon, nearly all of the island's residents gathered in a large meadow located south of the partially restored village. It was relatively flat and the grass had been cropped close by the sheep that had recently grazed upon it. A game of "keggers" was organized, reminding Pierce somewhat of rounders, that working-class version of cricket. Keggers was the Vespican version of whatever similar contest was played in Kentland. He was not unfamiliar with the game, having witnessed a few matches while in Brunswick.

Play involved a tightly wound, leather-covered ball, roughly the size of a four-pound shot. Remembering the few times he had tried to catch one, Pierce thought that it was almost as hard as the comparable cannonball. Play also involved clubs, used to strike the ball and put it into motion, and players running to specified locations. The most common means of designating those points was to use empty kegs, hence the name. Rather than the four points or bases of rounders, this game used five, arranged in pentagonal form.

Participation in the game was fluid and constantly changing. It had started out as British versus Vespican, but as it progressed through the prerequisite eleven settings, that exact method of defining the teams faded away. Nor did the players strenuously confine themselves to the traditional thirteen to a side, and in the back of the sixth setting, no fewer than twenty-one defenders intimidated those presuming to strike. Had those twenty-one not obtained the needed five kills, every one of the twenty-two on the other side would have taken his turn as striker. But once many players had a chance at striker, their interest waned, and they went in search of something to eat or drink. Others, eager to join in the play, took their places.

Pierce watched the front of the seventh setting with some interest. Several crewmen from *Island Expedition*, hands who had experienced the game in New Guernsey, now played on both sides. He noted that most of the British seamen acquitted themselves very well, in spite of their relative unfamiliarity with the sport.

As the eighth setting was about to get underway, a hand bell rang. That being the signal for the Christmas feast proper, players rapidly abandoned the game and the field. Still, there were those few nearing their turn as striker who pleaded in vain to let the game continue a while longer.

While this game of keggers had continued throughout the afternoon, Mrs. Packingham and the other ladies of the colony had labored in a makeshift outdoor kitchen to prepare a feast for all. Now the rough tables that sat beneath the trees at the southern end of the meadow groaned with the weight of the meal. Even before the bell stopped ringing, people lined up, jostled for position, and scrambled to obtain dishes and utensils. There were so many people eager to eat in the rustic and rural setting that it would have been impossible to establish any priority based on rank. It also would have proven impossible to have detailed anyone to serve anyone else. A queue of sorts was established and folks moved passed the tables, serving themselves from the heaping bowls, platters, and trays.

Although a naval officer and one trained in a more genteel method of dining, Pierce did not object. Over the years he had come to rather enjoy these occasions, where the emphasis was on eating and not the protocol surrounding it. He obtained a plate and flatware, falling in behind two laughing crewmen. They saw him and became somewhat more somber. "Why now, Captain! You should be first, sir!"

"Aye, sir! Take our place, sir! Not right that we eat first, sir."

"That's quite all right, Jones. Williams. Aboard, aren't hands piped to dinner prior to the officers?" asked Pierce. "There is plenty for all, and time for all. I will maintain my present position in the line."

"Aye, sir!"

"Thank you, sir!"

The two resumed their conversation and Pierce was alone with his thoughts. He noticed, however, that his presence restrained their spontaneous gaiety. It was a shame that he could not step completely away from being the captain at these times. Even had he chosen not to be in uniform, his status could not be easily ignored by those under his command.

At last he reached the tables groaning with food, and piled his plate high. He moved out of the way and stood momentarily, looking for a place to sit. Then he saw Smythe and Dr. Robertson waving to him. "Join us, won't you, Edward?" said Smythe.

"Why thank you, I will." Pierce sat down at the rough-hewn table. Soon, others joined them, and with the table filled to capacity, he found that he could concentrate on the meal and not be required to exchange pleasantries with newly arriving diners.

"Gentlemen," said Pierce as the meal neared an end. "I shall refloat the schooner immediately after the first of the year. Is there any reason that it cannot be so?"

"Not to my knowledge," affirmed Hotchkiss, one of the last to arrive at the table. He took another bite of ham. "From the point of overhaul and repair, there is no reason that it could not happen tomorrow, sir."

"But surely, Isaac, Edward will allow the crew a bit of holiday through the next week!" protested Smythe. "Are a few more days of that much importance?"

"Perhaps not," replied Pierce. "I do have reasons to be afloat and on the return voyage as soon as possible. Yet, I know you have need of our future service."

"In truth, sir, we do. And it is fortunate that you and your crew have the opportunity to celebrate the holidays ashore rather than afloat."

"A fortunate occurrence indeed, sir. But I must remind you, a King's ship does not sail according to the celebratory whims of her crew and the calendar's significant days." Pierce was silent for a minute as he took another bite from his plate and a swallow from his glass. "But I am glad to celebrate these joyous times ashore. Despite Mr. Hotchkiss's apparent zeal on my behalf, I do intend that the hands enjoy as much holiday as they can. We won't refloat *Island Expedition* until after the New Year."

"Perhaps then sir," mentioned Gray the purser, "we could turn the on-deck watch to scouring and filling water casks?"

"Aye, we can maintain a minimum of tasks, even while in holiday routine," emphasized Hotchkiss.

"Might I suggest, Captain, that should you choose to act upon Mr. Gray's thought, that you allow me to assist. I am aware of some procedures and herbal applications that will aid to keep water fresher on your upcoming voyage."

"Your attention in that matter would be most welcome, Doctor. Maintaining fresh water is a continuing battle to all sailing the seas."

"Indeed, sir," commented Morgan. Then the table was quiet as everyone's attention turned to the meal before them.

"I believe your presence during the holidays truly benefits those we have brought here. A last tie with England, I would think," said Gibbons.

"How so, sir?" asked Pierce.

"Simply put, it is fitting that all who left England together are united for these holidays. Whether transported or providing transport, we have shared a voyage and over two years together. That you have remained proves a unity amongst us. Had you departed immediately, it might have been seen that the colonists are of lesser worth."

"I never thought of it that way," said Morgan. "But you do know that I would gladly stay."

"If I have failed to mention it, Tom, Cecilia sends her affections," said the doctor.

"He would stay for the same reasons many of us are so anxious to return home," Pierce said, allowing an image of Evangeline to form in his mind. "I do see the point of our delay. Yet once we have done our duty to the Joint Council and the Unity Congress, gentlemen, *Island Expedition* will be England-bound."

That evening Pierce sat with Dr. Robertson in the quiet of the Colony Building parlor. Each had a glass of wine. The half-empty decanter rested on a nearby table. Pierce rather absently thumbed through a volume of Kentish poetry, and the doctor made entries in his journal. With a final scratching of his pen, he closed the book and glanced at his companion. "I do not wish to disturb your perusal of verses, Captain, but if you are not deeply engrossed, perhaps a little conversation, sir."

"I find the work interesting, but perhaps I am too full, as I cannot fully concentrate. Conversation would better suit, I believe." Pierce shut the pages and laid the book on the table.

"I didn't think to discuss it earlier, but word has reached the mainland concerning the Gallician aggression you experienced."

"Cooper did promise to look into it."

"Indeed he has," said Dr. Robertson. I chanced to meet with him upon his arrival in Bostwick."

"I trust you found him well?"

"Quite so, I believe. He told me of the pursuits, such as you had related the details to him. We discussed it with members of the Unity Congress and the Joint Council still in the Bostwick area. I first thought the news should be kept from the general public. Nevertheless, word soon spread, and a general cry of condemnation went up. There is a very strong anti-Gallician sentiment right now, even to the point that some are calling for war."

"War? That would be quite foolhardy in my humble estimation. The Lands have no real capability for waging one, that I can see."

"There is no real chance of it. It's the man in the street sort of thing. The populace did take notice of your successful evasion, and I must say that again you are somewhat of a hero in Vespica."

"Again?" Pierce frowned and cocked his head in puzzlement.

"Surely you have not forgotten the acclaim over your taking of HRMS *Hawke*, and the subsequent triumph of your release from

Tritonish custody. You and your crew were counted as heroes, not only in Brunswick, but throughout all the lands of Vespica."

"I imagine it was noted by a few, to say the least."

"And now that you successfully out-sailed the two fastest frigates in the Gallician fleet, your status is elevated once more."

"Weather did play a part, sir."

"Of course."

"But had we not been subject to methods meant to reduce our speed, our escape would have been even handier!" The anger that Pierce had kept buried since the doctor's arrival seethed near the surface.

"I don't follow, sir?"

"The benefits of a dry dock and the ability to inspect underwater portions of the hull cannot be discounted. Our hull was purposely and artificially fouled. Indeed, not so much that we would directly notice, but enough that they had a better chance to overtake us. We found many of the nails for the copper pried loose, and rope yarn and oakum twisted about them. Perhaps some small devices, sea anchors if you will, were also attached."

"That does account for it, Captain."

"For what?"

"That, according to Mr. Smythe, you had been in a most antagonistic mood until recently. And dare I say, discussion of this matter seems cause for its reappearance."

Mentally, Pierce bit his tongue and held back his most immediate response. He took a deep breath and a long sip from his glass. "Yes, I suppose I was. It was upon learning of your arrival, good sir, that my general good nature was restored."

"You're too kind, sir!"

"Still, it seems that every time you appear on the horizon, skies clear and seas calm. Now I only need know of your eminent arrival and...."

"You credit me with too much, sir."

Pierce was silent for several moments. He sipped once again at his wine. When at last he spoke, he said, "It is true that I allow your presence more influence on my state than I should. Still, I do wonder as to their motives."

"As do members of the Unity Congress and Joint Council, Captain. Surely such actions could not have been planned and executed in the few days following your release and sailing. It appears the Gallicians planned this action for some time prior to your release."

"Then they must have known of it, even before it occurred," surmised Pierce. "But how did they know, when apparently Lord Sutherland didn't? If I am not far off in my estimation, Lord Lancaster was not privy until right before our meeting."

"My immediate answer would be espionage. It takes no stretch to see that these two warring powers, Grand Triton and Gallicia, seek to gain every advantage over each other. I would not be surprised that each has agents involved in the highest levels of the other's decision-making process. Perhaps there are individuals within the highest Tritonish offices that secretly serve the other side. A decision is made, supposedly in great secrecy, and yet within a matter of days, knowledge of it is in the hands of Nicholas B. himself."

"I can certainly see that, Doctor. Still, I do not understand the Gallician reaction, regardless of having prior information or not. Were they hoping we would grant them access the island, they would have acted in a friendlier manner."

"Oh, one would think so, but what information did they receive? As we are not privy to the decisions of the Tritonish Government, was their decision to free *Island Expedition* as straightforward as it seems?"

"Explain!"

"Simply put, Edward, did Grand Triton really give up hope of being invited to utilize the island? You did tell me of Lancaster's discomfort and irritation with Chesterfield's comments."

"Yes."

"Were they really ready to let a prize such as Stone Island slip so easily through their fingers? I daresay they were not. I imagine that your freedom was a calculated act of kindness, which they hoped would be repaid by an invitation to visit and utilize the island."

"Perhaps the Joint Council's demand that they free us as Vespican citizens had no real effect. It merely furnished His Regal Majesty's Government an excuse to release us, with no one questioning their motives."

"You are possibly right, Edward."

"Yet I do not understand the Gallician reaction."

"Nor do I. It may depend upon what intelligence actually reached them. While we assume they have agents well-positioned within the Tritonish Government, it is likely that that nation also has persons equally well-situated. They may have embellished or changed the true nature of the information that eventually reached Gallicia's leaders."

"Tit for tat, eh?"

"Indeed! We will never know what the Gallicians understood about your release. They may have thought an understanding had been reached between Vespica, the Unified Kingdom, and your people."

"That we had invited the Tritonish to occupy the island?" Pierce reached for the decanter. "Another glass, Doctor?"

"One more, yes. But I believe that will suffice for today." He took a small drink of the freshly poured wine. "And yes, quite possibly they did believe Grand Triton had received your invitation."

"It would seem, sir, we are being played against both sides. I refer both to Vespica and those of us now on the island. I couldn't help but see signs of it in Brunswick, although I thought we British would somehow be left out of it."

"Then the Joint Council did a disservice in declaring you Vespican citizens. That ended your detachment, I believe."

"Quite possibly. Whether Smythe desires it or not, it would seem that our fate and fortune are now directly linked with the Independent Lands."

"It appears so. Smythe has mentioned that you will vote early in the year regarding annexation. Practically speaking, it would be foolish not to accept it," said the doctor. "The Independent Lands may be weak and unorganized when compared to other nations, but they are so much more than this one colony would be, should it stand alone."

"I agree, sir. Perhaps a small group such as we are would survive alone, provided we were not settled on such desirable soil."

Dr. Robinson swallowed the last of his wine. "I am at the point, Captain, where I prescribe a good night's sleep for both of us. I hope and pray that the people of Stone Island choose annexation. I believe it will be in their best interests, and that it would bode well for Vespica. I believe annexation is one of the steps my father has foreseen."

"Quite possibly. For more personal and perhaps selfish reasons, I pray the vote is taken soon. With the schooner afloat once again, and the results delivered to Bostwick, I can, at long last, be on my way home."

*Chapter Twelve*
# At Sea Again

With the holidays behind them and the infant days of 1805 marching smartly across the calendar's pages, Pierce once again set the crew to work. The vessel was refloated during the second week of January. The next few days were spent putting aboard all that had been removed. Many casks of salt beef, salt pork, and other victuals, which had been discarded as old or spoiled, were replaced with new. Stores came either from the growing bounty of Stone Island, or were brought from Vespica by *Evening Star* and other vessels.

Under Dr. Robertson's supervision, the water casks were boiled and rinsed with an herbal solution based on his Kalish medicinal knowledge. Its sundry ingredients would delay the onset of spoilage and allow the water to remain fresh for longer periods of time. Some of the crew thought it a waste of time, but Pierce remembered the doctor's successful use of native medicine in treating Morgan's leg and insisted that it be done.

By the afternoon of Saturday the 19th, *Island Expedition* was again tied up at the quay. The crew had restored their berthing accommodations, and earlier that day moved back aboard. Pierce and the officers had returned and resumed living in their respective cabins. He was greatly pleased with the progress of the overhaul process. While he had demanded a full day's work from everyone, as well as himself, he had not pushed as before Dr. Robertson's arrival. All hands had been allowed ample time off. Tomorrow would be one last instance of holiday routine for the crew. Then they would go to sea and work to regain the skill and precision that had been lost during the months in port.

Even though the crew now berthed aboard the schooner, they were not as self-sufficient as when at sea. Meals were not prepared aboard, and Pierce and several of the officers still dined at the Colony Building. As eight bells struck, ending the afternoon watch, Pierce grabbed his hat, shut the door to his cabin, and hurried ashore. He had been active enough throughout the day that his appetite was sharp, whetted by the thought of another of Mrs. Packingham's delicious suppers. He looked forward to the well-laid table, convivial conversation, and the usual informality of a meal presided over by Harold Smythe.

That late afternoon found many of *Island Expedition's* officers apparently desiring the same thing. When Pierce arrived at the Colony Building, he heard sounds of conversation, bursts of laughter, and occasional but ineffective calls for quiet and restraint. It was a happy and even boisterous group that he joined. Other than those on watch, all of the schooner's officers were there. Also seeking the pleasure of the meal and enjoyment of such a good natured company were several of the community's leaders, and other guests of some importance.

"Why, Edward," said Smythe near the end of the meal. "You do appear to be in a most amiable state today! Wouldn't you all agree?"

"Are not we all?" asked Hotchkiss.

"I would certainly say it was so," ventured Pierce. "If my personal affectations are indeed so noticeable, it must be that we are once again afloat and ready for sea. It is most trying as a sea officer to have one's vessel high and dry, one's crew berthed ashore, and only solid earth under one's feet."

"Most folks would welcome that, sir."

"Indeed, my dear Mr. Mally," said O'Brien between bites. "But to those of the sea, being at sea is the only natural condition, and the one condition we aspire to."

"Well said, sir!" Pierce raised his glass. "A toast if you will, to the refloating of His Majesty's Schooner *Island Expedition*! And may it please you to know that with the tide Monday morning, we intend to stand out to sea for a few days. It is quite time we ensure the hands have not forgotten their skills. As well, we need to observe the effects of our recent repair efforts in a dynamic and real environment."

"How long do you plan to remain, sir?" asked Gibbons.

"I would say no more than a week, two at the most. I know you will be voting tomorrow to accept or refuse annexation. Soon then we will be needed to fulfill our duty and carry those results to Vespica. Following that task, I believe we shall depart for England."

Following that remark, the schooner's officers simultaneously raised their glasses in salute. "To England!" they said, to the clinking of a heartfelt spontaneous toast. "To home!"

"Home!" echoed Morgan. "Surely England is home. But can one feel the magic of that word with respect to another place?"

"Perhaps one can," responded Pierce. He imagined the struggles that surely must be raging in Tom Morgan's heart. While he certainly desired to return to the land, indeed the world of his birth, Morgan had reasons and attachments far beyond those of the others for remaining here.

Pierce, with his overriding desire to see Evangeline, and his almost fanatical drive to be on the return voyage, could detect a slight desire within himself to stay. As he thought of it, he momentarily felt a strange fear of returning. It was not the actual return, but the imagined reaction he would face when he told of the entirely different world in which they had found themselves. Would he be able to withstand the ridicule and disbelief that would surely come his way?

Imagining the negative reaction, Pierce wondered why those here so readily accepted the possibility. While many of them--Horatio Newbury came to mind--voiced disbelief and uncertainty, the idea of different existences was not summarily scoffed at. Here, amongst those of both worlds, the possibility that it could be, was quite readily accepted.

"You have made arrangements for your crew to vote, have you

not, Edward?" asked Smythe. The question brought Pierce out of his contemplation.

"But surely they are not eligible, sir. Nor would I think any in His Majesty's Service, even those at this table, would be allowed the privilege."

"Nonsense, sir! Vespican citizenship was granted us all. Specifically it was granted to you, to obtain your release. If any amongst us should have a say in deciding our future, it is you and your crew. You are as much a part of this colony, this potential eleventh Land, as are the rest of us."

"True enough, Captain. Do you forget the advice I offered in Brunswick?"

"That was, Doctor?"

"To regard yourself as a Vespican while here, and an Englishman while there."

"Oh, I do remember, sir. However, I have always applied it internally, allowing it to guide me past any divided loyalties."

"But don't you see, sir," offered Hadley, glad to be at supper here and not aboard, where tradition demanded he not speak unless addressed by the captain. "If we are Vespican while here, it is our privilege, even our duty, to help decide the colony's destiny."

"True enough, I would think, sir," added Hotchkiss. "Perchance we are duty-bound in helping determine the path of all the Independent Lands?"

"Aye, I will yield the point, gentlemen. I will charge the lot of you, that with the morning's muster; you ensure all hands know of their voting privileges. If they are not familiar with the situation, be so kind as to explain it. I caution you, however, regardless of your views on the question, do not influence the way in which the hands might vote."

"Aye, sir!"

"I am glad, sir, to have you in agreement regarding this matter," said Smythe.

"It is a relief, sir, that we are permitted our say. Yet, I would have understood had we been excluded from the poll." Pierce took a bite of cherry pie and washed it down with a swallow of coffee.

"I pray you will be careful when at sea, Captain," said Talbot. "You must keep watch for any Gallician frigates."

"Quite so," agreed Dr. Robertson. "A successful evasion may not have ended the matter. As much as I hope the previous aggression was a matter of diplomatic disgruntlement, I cannot but wonder if there is more to it. I agree wholeheartedly, Edward, that you should be most wary of any sail sighted!"

"Well-found advice, I would say," echoed Mally. "Never have trusted the Gallicians."

Sunday, *Island Expedition* was nearly devoid of personnel. Pierce had declared the day holiday routine, and had even disestablished the defaulters' division. Only those few who had volunteered, or those who had committed some minor trespass remained on board. Of the majority who were not so restrained, or who did not simply wish to remain on board, one final adventure of shore leave was in full progress.

But regardless of their individual pursuits ashore, nearly all of the schooner's liberty party made their way to the Colony Building. There each stated his name, had it checked off a list, and was given a single Kentish penny. "Now, sir," said Gibbons to each. "Drop the coin in the white bucket should you favor annexation by the Independent Lands of Vespica, or in the black one if you oppose to it." With those simple directions, each man of the crew voted, many for the first time in their lives. And as they arrived in twos and threes and cast their ballots, others of the community arrived and voted as well. To be asked to simply place a token, the Kentish coin in one container or the other, simplified matters and compensated for the fact that many could not read or write. To accommodate those who were literate, the two pails were labeled "yes" and "no."

Pierce voted as well, quite early in the day, and spent the remainder of that Sunday taking his leisure. He tried his hand at painting, a hobby he had taken up in Brunswick. He wasn't impressed with the results. What he produced, and what looked back at him from the canvas, was not what he had imagined when he first set up his easel and laid out his paints, brushes, and palette knives. Still the effort was not completely wasted. Upon repacking his small painting kit, Pierce felt calm and relaxed, more so than he had felt in weeks.

He dined early in the afternoon with the doctor, Smythe, and Mrs. Packingham. It was a quiet meal, and one in which nothing of import was discussed. As they had gathered for the meal, they determined that they would not talk of serious matters, and for once they met their goal. As a result, conversation was light and about mundane everyday things, although Pierce felt a bit constrained in his efforts to keep it that way. By agreement throughout the colony, the balloting was not discussed, nor would the results be tabulated until noon of the following day.

By the time the decision regarding annexation would be determined, Pierce intended that *Island Expedition* be well on her way to sea. It would be better to sail with the results still unknown, concentrate on regaining their skills and not be forced to contend with joy or despair at the outcome. Knowledge of the verdict could wait until the schooner returned in a fortnight.

On the last day of January, *Island Expedition* sliced through the sea some two hundred miles northwest of Stone Island. Pierce had pushed the schooner, the crew, and himself very hard for the previous nine days. They had drilled, practiced, and repeated every maneuver and scenario he could devise, and they had done it in such heavy weather that only a scrap of canvas could be spread to the howling winds. Conversely, when the seas hadn't been battering the vessel about, or the very air attempting to rip it apart, the wind had died to nothing

and the blue sky had become home to a relentlessly hot and murderous sun. Two hands had fallen from aloft, one dead on impact and the
other below in sickbay, his pain eased by massive doses of laudanum
doled out by Dr. Matheson. In spite of orders to cover themselves
against the sun, five others had been horribly burned, and they too
spent their time below in agony.

Today the weather finally reached a comfortable compromise.
There was wind, but only enough that they enjoyed a breeze and
moved easily through the lightly tossed seas. A few high clouds dotted
the sky. The sun was warm and pleasant, and having determined that
most of their seafaring skills had been reclaimed, Pierce had declared
the day as make and mend. Heading southeast in the general direction
of the island, they did not drill or practice.

The afternoon was warm enough that Pierce was on deck in his
shirtsleeves, his uniform coat and waistcoat having been discarded and
left below. Hotchkiss and the others on deck and on duty were all
similarly attired, the prevailing thought being one of comfort rather
than appearance. It would have been a very fine day, except Pierce
mourned the loss of Stevenson, Able Seaman, who had slipped from
the main topsail yard four days ago. His fall had ended with a bone-
cracking bounce off a starboard twelve-pounder. Hooper had fallen a
day later, but his plunge had been modified by the lower shrouds so
that now he lay mending three broken bones and a cracked skull. The
fractured limbs and ribs had posed no problem for Matheson, but the
skull worried him. As it worried the surgeon, it worried Pierce.

He was aft at the taffrail, staring at the slight wake of the vessel's
passage, deeply alone with his thoughts, second-guessing his choice to
be at sea during this time. Had he waited another week, perhaps the
weather would have proven more amiable to sailing. Had he waited,
perhaps there would not be one less member in the crew and several
suffering in sickbay. Even as he wondered whether a few days' wait
would have been prudent, it occurred to him that if his plans had been

altered, perhaps the weather patterns might have shifted as well. He could have waited a week, two weeks before sailing, and yet gone to sea amid the storms and squalls they had encountered.

Despite the tragedy of loss and injury, Pierce was well satisfied with the performance of *Island Expedition* and her crew. Perhaps the heavy adverse weather had helped them recover, refine, and re-hone their maritime skills. The vessel itself, fresh out of dry dock and having undergone intensive repairs and upgrades, answered nicely and responded most favorably to the harsh conditions it had so recently encountered. Truly, she and all who sailed in her deserved a day of rest, and with the day's calm and pleasant weather, Pierce was more than willing to oblige that need.

He turned from the rail and looked forward. As he was deciding whether or not to order a reef out of the foresail, the lookout, high in the foretopgallant crosstrees, hailed. "Deck there! Sail to starboard!"

"Shall we investigate, sir?" asked Hotchkiss, who had also been on deck, but who had allowed Pierce his privacy over the past hour and a half. "Or do we stand clear?"

"It would make sense, Isaac, to at least determine identity. I'm sure we would out-sail anything afloat, should she prove hostile."

"Quite so, I agree. We cannot let memory of those Gallician frigates cause us to shy away from every sail sighted."

"True enough, my friend."

Morgan, currently officer of the watch, bellowed aloft. "Is that all, Jacobs? Is she off the bow, off the beam? What course?"

"Near the opposite course! On the port tack! A point, no, two points abaft the starboard beam?"

"Aye aye," acknowledged Morgan, who started to pass the information on to Pierce. But Pierce caught his eye, nodded, and Morgan said no more. Instead he noted the particulars of the sighting in the rough deck log.

Jacobs called down again. "She's wearing ship!" The vessel had sighted them. To make a course change at this exact time could only be mean she had sighted the schooner. It was too much a coincidence that the stranger should alter course at this exact moment.

"Do I call the watch below?" asked Hotchkiss.

"I think not. Most are already on deck as it is. Should we need them, they will be available." Pierce moved forward, closer to the wheel and the grouped quarterdeck watch.

"Mr. Hadley, if you would, aloft with a glass."

"Aye aye, sir." Hadley's voice was changing and one "aye" squeaked in a boyish soprano, and the other grated in a manlier bass. He reddened slightly, fetched a glass from the case, and started up the main shrouds. Young, strong, and agile after having made the ascent hundreds of times, he climbed without stopping, going with his back down to the water as he traversed the futtock shrouds and moved into the topmast shrouds. He continued on and moved up the topgallant shrouds until he was at the mail topgallant crosstrees. There, the lookout moved out onto the yard and allowed Hadley a position against the doubled topgallant and royal masts.

Pierce gave him a minute or two to get situated and to find the strange sail in his glass. When he figured the midshipman had accommodated his view to the roll and pitch of the schooner and could keep the far vessel in sight, he hailed. "Well, what can you tell me, Mr. Hadley?"

"A ship, sir!" came the lad's reply. "Settled on a port reach!"

"Can you identify?"

"No colors visible! Looks familiar, sir."

"Very well. We will know shortly." The schooner and the ship were now on converging courses, and every moment brought them closer together. As each minute passed, each would be able to make out more and more detail about the other.

"A ship-sloop, sir!" hollered Hadley. "Tritonish white ensign!

"Slightly less threatening than the Gallician tri-color, I would think," said Hotchkiss quietly.

"One would hope," stated Pierce. "Mr. Morgan, see that our colors are hoisted!"

"Aye aye, sir! British or Vespican, sir?"

"As we are still in this world, I would say we hoist Vespican colors, unless you do not agree, Tom?"

"Oh, I positively agree, sir," he said, and turned to see the task carried out.

The sail was now visible from deck and Pierce stared at it. It had a most familiar look.

"My God! 'Tis the *Hawke*, sir!" shouted Hadley enthusiastically. "'Tis the *Hawke!*"

Hotchkiss grinned at hearing that, and even as he did, a good-natured murmur went up aboard the schooner.

"Silence there!" the first lieutenant roared. Then quietly to his friend and captain he said, "If it is *Hawke*, it's even less of a threat, if indeed a danger at all."

"One would think so, Isaac, but we do not know the latest from Kentland and what orders our friend Newbury now sails under. We shall observe caution for the present time."

"Aye."

After some time had passed and as *Hawke* became hull up from deck, Hadley reported signal flags breaking out in her rigging.

Spencer was able to make out the signal from deck, and after briefly consulting the Tritonish signal book, turned to Pierce and said. "As best I can make it, sir, she says, 'I E,' I think that's *Island Expedition*, 'shall we heave to? Will you visit, or shall I?' Most polite, should you ask me, sir."

"Indeed, Mr. Spencer. You may reply that I will visit. And take the time to spell out and send 'hello.'"

"Aye aye, sir."

Three-quarters of an hour later, Pierce, Hotchkiss and Morgan sat in *Hawke's* small but elegantly furnished stern cabin. Newbury apparently had richer tastes than Pierce, or at least he had the means to fulfill them, and had equipped his personal quarters in a more lavish fashion than Pierce would have.

As relieved as he had been to find that the strange sail was *Hawke*, and as friendly as Newbury's invitation had been, Pierce felt somewhat uncomfortable as he sipped at a glass of wine. The visit and the association with a one-time foe and now amiable acquaintance did not bother him. But on this particularly warm day, the visit had forced him to dress completely and don his uniform coat. If he was uncomfortable in the heat, his companions from the schooner, and his hosts aboard the sloop-of-war, suffered from it as well. Should he have invited the Tritonish captain aboard *Island Expedition* and passed the word that shirt sleeves would be permissible? However, with wind sails rigged and stern windows open, a bit of breeze drifted through the cabin, and as he sat quietly, Pierce grew more comfortable.

The visit was at that awkward time, late enough that dinner had already passed on both vessels, and yet too soon for any sort of supper. Yet as a generous and kind host, Newbury had caused a tray, laden with comfits, maids of honor, and ratafia biscuits to be set on the table. Pierce nibbled slowly, eating enough to please his host, and hopefully little enough that the food would not add to his discomfort.

As he poured Morgan another glass of the most excellent wine, and then one for himself, Newbury said, "It is a surprise to find you in these waters, sir. I thought you well on the way to your world and England."

"The truth, sir, I would have hoped to be well on our way at this time. Certain things require us to remain. I do hope in a scant number of weeks to undertake that voyage."

"It is always wise to ensure one's vessel is in excellent condition before such a journey. Amazing that you found a usable dry dock on the island. No doubt it would have served us well, had you made the proper invitations. But I rejoice sir, that it is not available to the Toads."

"With what we experienced upon leaving Brunswick," interjected Hotchkiss, "our distrust of them grows daily."

"And to the point, sir," continued Pierce, "that when I discovered the attempt to foul our hull and diminish our speed, I used language that I usually do not."

"The revolutionary bastards have that effect, sir," said Jarvis, *Hawke's* first lieutenant. "Of course, should they be confronted with it, they will deny it."

"I'm sure."

"Beyond the chance for repairs and upkeep, there is the matter of Vespican annexation of Stone Island," Pierce said. "We have been asked to remain until such time that the islanders have decided for or against, so that we may carry word to the Vespican capital."

"As I understand your great desire to return home, sir, I truly hope they decide soon and that you may quickly be on your way."

"As it was, a vote was taken the day before we sailed. We do not know the outcome, but when we return, it shall be revealed, and then hopefully the requirement for us to remain will soon pass and we will be homeward-bound."

"And while you remain in these waters, Captain Pierce, I would advise you take all precautions. It is possible the Gallicians will again attempt a capture or sinking. Unfortunately, the Flying Squadron is no more. The various ships and vessels that constituted it have been ordered home. The main Gallician fleet broke through our blockade some months ago. Lord Kershner is in pursuit, but as to his success, we have no idea. News travels so slowly in these matters." Newbury swallowed the remnants of his glass and reached for a kickshaw from the tray.

"A dark day and a true threat to Kentland, I imagine," said Pierce.

"Indeed, a most apprehensive time, sir. And I must caution you with regards to another possible threat, one more directly aimed at you."

"If you would be so good as to tell me, sir?"

"When you previously met with the captains of the Flying Squadron, you may have ascertained that if we were a family, Jackson would be considered the black sheep. He has sorely tried the commodore's patience, both with his heavy-handed discipline and his rather broad interpretation of orders. Even as we have been ordered home, he has pressed for and has received permission to remain in Vespican waters a few more weeks. He says that a lone frigate may accomplish what an entire squadron could not, and that he might deliver a mighty blow that would send the Toads scampering back to Gallicia.

"Yet rumors abound in the squadron that he pursues a personal vendetta. He has a certain reputation for jealousy, and many believe his real purpose is to hunt down his wife's latest lover."

"I have heard that about him, and I have witnessed the true measure of his excessively harsh discipline. You do remember, sir that I voyaged to Brunswick in *Furious*."

"An experience I would not wish upon any officer of His Regal Majesty's service, let alone a prisoner suspected of piracy and rebellion. Sir James has confided that he regrets his choice to send you in *Furious*, and begs forgiveness for doing so. But, it was a matter of expediency, and Jackson was due next for resupply."

"I hold nothing against Commodore Hargrove in that matter, sir. I'm sure it was decided quite directly and did not involve Jackson's devilish devotion to brutal and excessive punishment."

"He will be happy to hear that, sir." Newbury reached for and ate one of two maids of honor remaining. "A strange facet of the rumors about Jackson, sir, is that he suspects you of being the one he seeks."

"Indeed," said Pierce nonchalantly. Even though he had lately managed to cool off and be somewhat comfortable in full uniform, he felt himself growing warm. A trickle of sweat ran down his back. "The man has some strange ideas."

He would have left at that moment, gone back aboard *Island*

*Expedition*, and crowded on sail until Stone Island was once again in sight. But he did not want to provide Newbury with any sign that he might actually be the party Jackson searched for. It would lower him in Newbury's esteem, should that individual realize he had been the latest to cuckold Jackson.

Therefore Pierce and the others remained on board the ship-sloop for another hour. He fervently hoped the delay would help dismiss any thoughts of his guilt that Newbury might entertain. Yet, as their visit stretched onward, he found himself growing warmer by the minute. Evidently his discomfort was noticeable, because at one point Newbury interrupted a genial discourse on Gallician warship design to remark, "Are you quite all right, Captain Pierce? You look somewhat heated, sir."

"No, I'm quite well, sir. It is warm, and perhaps a glass too many." Pierce lied, even though he had drunk a little more wine than he should have. Against his better judgment he had eaten more than enough from the tray, and had sampled a particularly potent but delicious brandy.

He was ultimately relieved when a Tritonish midshipman knocked at the door and told Newbury the wind was veering and getting up. That gave Pierce and his party an excuse to return to the schooner.

## Chapter Thirteen
# The Diplomatic Voyage

Pierce fidgeted, looking at his watch, anxious for the last members of the official delegation to be aboard. They milled about on the quay, halting the loading of their dunnage as time and time again, it seemed, a needed item was discovered to be in a chest destined for the very depths of the hold. At the same time, as members of the group tried to make their way on board, they were waylaid by residents, or those being left behind with some sort of authority. In the not-so-distant future, a future measured now in portions of an hour, they would lose the tide, and sailing would have to wait.

Why had he agreed to convey the results of the vote and the island's representative to the Vespican capital? Why could he not have insisted that *Island Expedition* sail for England as soon as repairs had been completed? That had been his original plan, but at the insistence of Smythe and others, he had been convinced to remain and make this additional trip to the Vespican mainland. Quite possibly he could have refused the request, even though his orders placed him in service to the British Island Expedition Organization and those in charge on Stone Island. As the delays mounted, and as each small sign of progress conversely brought forth additional detours, he sincerely wished he had followed his initial desires.

Now he would have to make the voyage to Bostwick and wait while the delegates from the newest Independent Land of Vespica proceeded through the ceremonies of diplomacy and annexation. Then there would be a return voyage to Stone Island, against the prevailing westerly winds. More time would be lost before they were ready to sail on their homeward journey.

Exasperated by the endless delays and tired of watching the circus being staged on the quay, Pierce all but gave up hope of sailing on the current tide. He forced himself to stand immobile along the starboard rail and gaze idly across the bay. When his patience could wait no longer, and he was about to check his watch once more, Hotchkiss approached him.

"Sir!" the first lieutenant said quietly. And when Pierce did not respond, he said again, "Sir!"

"Yes, Mr. Hotchkiss?"

"I am happy to report that everyone and everything are aboard. With your permission, we may get underway."

"The tide?" Pierce asked, even as he looked at his watch to check for himself.

"Still time, sir."

"Well then, let us be at it. Allow Mr. Townsend the honor of taking us out. Quite naturally, we shall have Mr. O'Brien as well as ourselves nearby to see that all goes well."

"Aye, sir!" Hotchkiss tipped his hat in salute and turned to the master. "Mr. O'Brien, we shall proceed to sea. Mr. Townsend is to have the conn."

"Aye aye, sir."

"Mr. Townsend!" shouted Hotchkiss, for the midshipman was forward, dealing with a last-minute problem. "Leave that until later! You are to take us out!"

"Aye aye, sir!" Townsend hurried aft, shouting as he came. "Cast loose fore and aft! In the boats, take up the slack! Put your backs into it now! Pull!"

Because the wind effectively pinned the schooner against the pier, the boats would pull her far enough away to allow a minimum of sea room and permit them to sail on a starboard reach or tack, roughly parallel with the shore.

"All free forward! All free aft!"

"Shove off, lads!" roared Townsend, directing his voice to those hands standing by with spare oars and sweeps. Their push against the quay would help give the schooner an initial impetus to move away from the dock. That first push would also impart some momentum and make the work of those in the boats just a little easier.

"Damn it, sir! The brow!" shouted Davis, the bo'sun's mate. In trying to make the tide, the boarding plank had not been detached and set ashore. Now, as the slightest movement came upon the vessel, that walkway betwixt ship and shore twisted in the entry port and dragged across the quay's stone pavement. The lines that secured it to the rail grew taut.

Pierce had been watching the procedures with a certain detachment, confident in young Mr. Townsend's abilities, and in the knowledge that several senior and experienced individuals were there and ready to assist if he should face any difficulty. But with Davis's shout and his own notice of the problem, Pierce became more attentive. Still, he did not take charge, and for the moment he sincerely hoped that no one else did either. He wanted to see how Townsend would deal with it.

"Avast there! Avast all hands!" shouted Townsend. Even though the efforts to push and pull *Island Expedition* away from the pier ceased, enough effort had been instilled in her that she kept moving. She crept away from the solidarity of land and because of the initial pull of the boats, now made slight but noticeable progress sternways. The shipboard end of the brow had been secured to the rail, lashed into place with several turns of stout line. The shore end had been free to roll on small trucks, in and out, as the schooner's draft and the tide changed. Those minute wheels caught in grooves worn by similar devices used by the former inhabitants. As the vessel slowly moved along the quay, the plank twisted in position. The schooner's momentum could not be halted before the twisting action would wrench the brow hard enough to damage the rail or finally deposit the structure in the water.

"Mr. Cartney!" roared the embattled midshipman. "Cut the lines!

Cut the lines!" Those were now so tight that no man could force enough slack to untie them.

The bo'sun and his mates, Campbell and Davis, grabbed boarding axes and chopped away at the lines. With each blow, fibers parted and wood chips flew in the air as the sharpened blades found wood along with rope. Mr. Cook, the carpenter, looked on in disgust. He would have to repair the gouges in the ship's structure.

Cartney gave a final massive blow. The last remnants of line, good manila line, parted with a snap, and the end of the brow slid freely from the entry port. Unsupported, the free end fell. It had been pulled too far out, and teetered momentarily before plunging towards the water. The trucks caught on the quay edge, and it hung precariously over the water.

Talbot yelled from the pier, "Go on with you now! We'll take care of it!"

"Aye sir! Thank you, sir!" said Townsend with noticeable relief. However, his duties were not finished. "Another shove aft! In the boats, put your backs into it!" Then to the helmsman he said, "Port your helm!" That would swing the stern farther away from the shore.

As the aft-moving *Island Expedition* reached forty-five degrees to the pier, the midshipman directed the helmsman to halt the shallow turn. Then he ordered the boats to pull towards the quay and had the helm put hard over, bringing the stern back towards the quay and the bows into the wind. "Mainsail and jib!" he ordered. "Starboard tack! Get those boats aboard!"

When they were well out into the bay, Townsend wore ship and settled on a port tack, heading north northwest and out of the bay. There was some time before any further maneuvering was required, and he slumped visibly with relief.

Pierce moved forward and sidled up next to the midshipman. "A little excitement, eh, Mr. Townsend?"

"Oh no, sir! I'm sorry, sir!"

"No real harm done--and you have learned something, I believe. If the lesson is remembered, perhaps a few nicks and scrapes in the paint are worth it. Mr. Cook, I'm sure, will not agree and be vexed that he can't equate it to copulation."

Townsend grinned, relieved, and put at ease by his captain's reference to the carpenter's habit of relating nearly everything to coitus.

"Someday, William, I'll tell you about Saumarez's barge in *Orion*. Do remember you cannot overlook details, nor do you focus on them and lose sight of the entire situation."

"Aye aye, sir!"

Pierce moved away to let Townsend have some room as he continued to guide them out to sea. Cook made his way to look at the damage. "Damn!" he muttered, half to himself. "Which they're always a-hurrying! Can't wait for the thighs to part, what they're tryin' to board and spillin' the spirits afore the keg is stowed!" He looked over the mangled wood, eyed the scratched and gouged paint, squinting against the sun, and went below.

Despite Pierce's prediction, Cook had managed to relate the damage and the incident to sex. He usually berated the carpenter about his sexual connotations, but today he did not. He thought to do so, but decided against it when he noticed that his overall mood had changed. The anger, frustration, and impatience he had felt earlier were gone. He was calm enough not to react to the carpenter's licentious comments. A brief smile crossed his face as he thought of the schooner leaving the quay with the brow firmly attached.

The incident was of course a black mark against Townsend. Still, he had reacted quite properly once the error had been pointed out to him. He had taken the only reasonable course of action and freed the schooner of the unwanted attachment with a minimum of damage and fuss. He was, as Pierce already knew, a quick thinker, and from experience he knew that that trait could ease many uncomfortable situations.

When they cleared the last point of land, a small island off the starboard quarter, Pierce relieved Townsend and re-established the regularly scheduled watch. He ordered a course change to northwest by north. He left word to alter it to due north when the second dog watch ended and went below. By the end of the evening watch, they would be clear of Stone Island's northernmost points and could bend their track further to the east.

It was a quite crowded table at supper that evening. Smythe was aboard, on his way to pay an official and diplomatic call upon the Independent Lands government. In effect, his was a "state visit," as he was in all practical sense the governor of Stone Island. Gibbons was along as well, for he had been nominated and confirmed as the island's representative to the Joint Council. Dr. Robertson had elected to return to the mainland aboard *Island Expedition*, rather than waiting for the merchantman that had brought him. The doctor had also agreed to temporarily represent them in the Unity Congress.

Mrs. Packingham had come along as well, invited by Smythe as his personal associate, and no doubt as someone with whom he would be comfortable in any foreseeable social setting.

These additional personages not only crowded the great cabin on the occasion of meals, but they forced a massive shift in berthing arrangements. As a person of great importance, Smythe resumed his occupation of the aftermost starboard cabin, the one that he had lived in during the voyage from England some two years earlier. Hotchkiss had appropriated it for use in the meantime, and would have moved back to his original accommodations. However, to avoid any appearance of impropriety, Mrs. Packingham now occupied Pierce's sleeping quarters. Pierce would have shared with Hotchkiss, but that cabin was used by Gibbons, and the master's berth was lent to the doctor. As it was, Pierce and Hotchkiss found themselves in Morgan's space. So it went through the wardroom and gunroom establishment, until every officer, warrant officer, or midshipman found himself moved or doubled up.

The cabin was crowded, yet cheerful and animated as they dined that early February Thursday evening. Despite the lingering heat of the day, the breeze through the open stern lights cooled them. The meal itself had been prepared ashore by Mrs. Packingham's acquaintances. For convenience and to combat the heat, they ate it cold. There were ample amounts of chicken, roast beef, a vegetable relish, fresh soft bread, and a pie to top it off.

The islanders, in sending off their first official delegation, had also produced a meal for the hands, and as Pierce and his guests sat and ate in the stern cabin, the hands enjoyed the same meal forward. However, the hands were more limited in their choice of drink. They could have water, which at this point--and after Dr. Robertson's treatment of the casks--wasn't bad, or they could have a weak beer, so diluted that one would burst his bladder before getting drunk. Pierce thought to allow an additional spirit ration, the traditional rum and water grog in accompaniment of the meal, but decided against it. After the recent short time at sea, they had spent nearly another week ashore, and he doubted that any of the hands had not had a share of intoxicating beverages.

Aft, the strictures on drink weren't so tight, and as they ate, several bottles of wine were available. Most were of that world, although Pierce did have a few bottles remaining of what he had brought from England. Trying to be a good host, he gently insisted that those vintages should be allowed first to those who were not from his world.

"My my!" said Mrs. Packingham as she delicately finished her glass of Marsala. "This is most delicious. I'm sorry to not have words to adequately describe it. I do fear I like it well enough to overindulge."

"We would not think less of you," said Smythe. "Would we, gentlemen?"

"Indeed not, ma'am!" Townsend replied, and the several of them nodded in agreement.

"You do appear a bit flushed, Mrs. P. Perhaps you have had your measure. As it is, the warmth of the day can only add to the effects."

"I'm certain you are right, Doctor. Maybe coffee will answer for me."

"As it would for all of us, my dear."

"Perhaps a turn on deck," suggested Pierce. "It is certainly cooler than the cabin and less crowded as well."

As they were leaving, which due to the tightly packed seating arrangement they had arrived at to allow them all at the table, was a highly choreographed exercise of its own, Dr. Matheson spoke. "Perhaps our medical guest would join me in sick bay. I would value his further opinion regarding Hooper."

"I would be intrigued, sir. I am grateful you hold no animosity for my succeeding with Mr. Morgan when you did not. I am touched that you would consult me in your present case. But unless we are urgently needed below, let us gain a little of the cooler air first. I too may have reached my mark with the captain's excellent wines."

On deck it was indeed cooler. There, shipboard tradition prevailed and the more junior individuals moved to the lee, leaving the windward portion of the deck to Pierce and members of the official party.

"I feel much better, Captain," said Mrs. Packingham. "The air does work wonders."

"Ah, here is our coffee, now. Thank you, Franklin." The cook's mate set the tray with its steaming pot and array of cups on the pin rail, where with two belaying pins removed, it fit quite perfectly. "May I pour you a cup?"

"Certainly. Please do."

"My pleasure." Pierce poured carefully, instinctively balancing himself, the pot, and the cup as he did so. "Gentlemen," he said, slightly louder. "Coffee is at hand. Please do avail yourselves of it as you will.

"Mr. Dial," he continued, directing his communication now to the current officer of the watch. "I believe Franklin has brought sufficient that should you and quarterdeck watch-standers desire, you might share our bountiful brew."

"Aye, sir. Thank you, sir."

"There is plenty of the meal left as well for when you are done with the duty."

"Aye, sir."

As the sun sank into the sea, the air cooled, and the breeze freshened. Those members of the supper gathering milled amiably about the deck. The group was in fine spirits, as if it were a holiday or special occasion. Indeed, the whole of the ship's company were in high spirits. Forward, the hands with musical ambition, including a few with actual talent, struck up a tune. Several danced a hornpipe. As the stomp of their steps became more pronounced, others joined in, dancing, clapping, or beating time on various deck furnishings. Aft, Midshipman Townsend, who had been quite morose following the day's mangled departure, and who conversed with Master's Mate Spencer, absentmindedly tapped his foot to the beat.

"A most pleasant evening," said Hotchkiss, as he emptied his cup and placed it back on the tray. "We've not had many like this for a long while."

"I can speak only of my journey from Bostwick a year ago, sir," commented Mrs. Packingham. "But I did wonder if life aboard all ships was such as I experienced then?"

"I'm sure it's different aboard each vessel, ma'am. Indeed, it can vary from day to day on a single hull."

"A person's status aboard can also determine one's view of it," said Pierce.

"I'll agree to that," said Smythe. "As one who served before the mast years ago, and in a service not noted for humane treatment of foremast jacks, the difference is truly amazing."

"Yet the men seem happy?"

"They are. Edward is a good captain, and sees to their well-being. He depends upon them, just as they depend upon him. That is why he insisted that the provisions your friends provided be made available for all. And you will see that as stores are depleted, those of us living aft will eat the same as they do forward."

"And I doubt, ma'am," added Hotchkiss, "that we'll dine quite so lavishly, even with the morrow. I should not expect that we'll all gather for coffee and a stroll about the deck as we have tonight. Perhaps in a week, or upon nearing Bostwick."

"I had never thought that it would be so every night. Still, I believe this voyage will be much more pleasant than my last. And now if you will excuse me, I'll retire."

"Yes, ma'am," said Pierce. "But before you go below, might I ask...."

"Yes, Captain?" she answered.

"You see, ma'am, this is a man-of-war, or at least we tend to think of her as such. We try to drill on a regular basis to keep our skills sharp and our wits keen. I had thought to exercise the great guns tomorrow, but if you think it would disturb you, we will refrain."

"Oh, I think I would like to see that!"

"'Hear it!' you should say, ma'am," offered Hadley.

"Of course. And now I bid you all a good night. I think I shall sleep very well tonight, what with the gentle motion of the sea and a fine meal tucked away. Good night!"


The voyage to Bostwick went smoothly. The weather was fair and the wind favorable. As Hotchkiss had told Mrs. Packingham, meals were not quite the special occasions they had been that first evening at sea. Still, it was a pleasurable journey.

While Pierce enjoyed the journey and marveled at the lack of difficulties encountered, an ever-present foreboding prevented him from finding true pleasure in it. Daily, his first thought was, please God, they did not sight *Furious*. It was not only that Jackson was searching for him, but that to satiate his appetite for vengeance he might bring injury or death upon the others. Because of why Jackson sought him, he could not discuss it with those aboard the schooner. Hotchkiss, Dr.

Robertson, and Morgan would know what caused Jackson to seek him out. As shipmates, the two would not broach the subject or speak of it, even amongst themselves. As a friend, the doctor would not mention it either. Yet he didn't know who amongst the crew might have guessed at his nocturnal adventures in Vespica, nor to what extent such actions might be discussed.

His one wish was that Smythe would never know of his escapades with Leona Jackson. If Pierce's dreams were ever realized, Smythe would be his father-in-law. It would be an insult to their friendship, as well as to his relationship with Evangeline, should either discover the entire truth about his stay in Brunswick. For the time being, all that Pierce could do was to hope to avoid Jackson and *Furious*, and pray that someone did not inadvertently say something.

Despite Pierce's apprehension, that particular Tritonish frigate was not sighted. They did come up on several merchant vessels of varying nationalities, with which they exchanged pleasantries and general information and news. A Gallician corvette was also seen, but she behaved in a most civil manner and did not attempt any hostile act, unlike the two Gallician frigates some months previously.

Bostwick was somewhat farther south than Brunswick, but with new and updated charts, they reached their destination in timely fashion. Saturday the 16th of February saw them alongside the pier in Bostwick harbor, having exchanged salutes with the militia artillery batteries at the entrance. Even with their unannounced and unplanned arrival, the town's citizenry turned out in great numbers, and a vast and boisterous crowd of well-wishers welcomed them. News of *Island Expedition's* triumph, and indeed the Independent Lands' triumph over Tritonish dominance, had long ago reached the populace, and the schooner and her people were greeted as and treated as heroes in every sense of the word.

The official Stone Island delegation was hustled ashore and

provided with accommodations at the best inn in town. Conveniently, it was directly across the square from the large hall where the Joint Council met, and a few buildings removed from the tavern that hosted the Unity Congress. Situated nearby were the Tritonish, Gallician, and Cordoban embassies.

Pierce would have been content to remain aboard for the duration of their stay, but members of the Joint Council, the Unity Congress, and the local inhabitants insisted that as he was a hero to them, he should be quartered ashore. As it eventually worked out, Pierce and the other officers were comfortably lodged in the same establishment as those of the primary party. Although he resisted at first, members of the New Sussex naval militia volunteered to look after the schooner, and all hands were provided berthing in a nearby inn.

Nothing of any importance happened the day after their arrival. It was Sunday, and was given over to a day of rest, both for Bostwick's inhabitants and their newly arrived guests. Pierce, Hotchkiss, and O'Brien were given a tour of the town by Captain Stanton of the naval militia. Despite their efforts to remain anonymous, their presence was soon discovered everywhere they went. Small crowds of excited well-wishers formed and grew larger as word of their presence spread.

Finally, Stanton led the three Englishmen down a dismal-looking alley and through the back door of a modest and common-appearing public house. It was quiet and cool inside, and the beer was refreshingly chilled. The few other patrons acknowledged and welcomed them warmly, but did not run into the streets to announce their presence. After a few minutes of conversation they returned to their own business and the drinks sitting upon their own tables. Checking his watch in elaborate fashion, Stanton asked if they might have developed an appetite during their tour and the constant avoidance of the crowds.

"I do feel a small pang, sir," answered the schooner's master.

"In that case, then, I shall see what they might have available. It is quite common victuals here, more akin to what you would find forward, rather than in the wardroom or captain's cabin. But it is prepared very well, and invariably they have a most excellent boiled baby."

"We have been lacking in our puddings of late, Edward," said Hotchkiss.

"Quite true, Isaac. And you will find, Captain Stanton that our appetites and preferences are quite pleasantly served by those dishes of the lower deck."

"I did despair to bring you here, as it caters to a more common crowd. Yet it is quiet, and we will have a meal in peace."

"A most excellent plan, sir," said Hotchkiss.

With that, their host caught the eye of a house boy and inquired as to the day's dinner offerings. Told that a large kettle of venison stew meant to be served over rice had just been pronounced ready, they agreed that it would answer very well, and Stanton sent the lad to fetch each of them a generous portion.

It was a satisfying and delicious meal. Pierce realized much too late that he had eaten more than enough. He was full to bursting, and the effort of digestion had him warm and sweating. Perhaps if he had not eaten that second helping of pudding? But it was a very fine boiled baby, of a quality that he had not been allowed of late, and an emerging gluttony had made itself known.

As they eased away from their plates and traded coffee mugs for beer steins, Stanton renewed the conversation. "You have set all of Vespica abuzz. To solidly whip one of the Kentish Navy's finest is enough in itself, but then to offer and render aid to a defeated foe, even to the point of your capture--no finer action could have been taken, sir!"

"The combat success, I fear, is a result of the continual warfare experienced by my country, and thus myself over the past several years. I have always believed the humanitarian aspect in conducting war is necessary to prevent falling in to total barbarism," responded Pierce.

"But should one not observe such niceties only to a certain point?"

"True enough, sir. Your point is willingly conceded."

"The big stir in these parts isn't so much your defeat of *Hawke*, but that you caused the Joint Council to act together. While the common man cheers your success in battle and the victory of your freedom, more knowledgeable persons celebrate because of the obstacles overcome."

"Once again I must say that we are very grateful of the outcome," said Hotchkiss.

"Indeed we are," said O'Brien as well.

"Happy as I am that we are free of Tritonish rule, they do have something I envy. And I believe from what I've heard of this Great Britain, you have it as well."

"Sir?"

"A truly disciplined naval force, one that will follow orders and not question whence the orders came."

"It would be a poor showing if a fleet did not perform as ordered or expected."

"Aye. And that is the trouble we have in Vespica. Each Land has its particular naval militia, and some are quite well equipped and provided for. Yet, like the Joint Council, trying to get the various naval militias to act in concert can be a fool's errand."

"Indeed?"

"Since winning our independence, a group of pirate states along the Darnahsian coast, north of Baltica, have preyed upon Vespican merchantmen. They seize ships and cargos, and enslave the crews. While many say it has a religious basis, most believe any worship involved relates mostly to gold. They demand outrageous ransoms for the release of captives, and yet with impunity, take more and more. Five years ago, the majority of the lands tired of paying the bribes, and decided that a show of force might cause them to cease attacks on our ships.

"I believe the Americans have recently done much the same, sir," remarked O'Brien to Pierce.

"The Barbary Coast of North Africa, I believe," added Hotchkiss.

"Then you are somewhat familiar with the overall situation?"

"Indeed, sir," answered Pierce.

"I do not know of these Americans, nor how well met with success they were. But I am ashamed to say that our effort was largely a failure. Oh, we had the ships, gentlemen, a great fleet as it were, primarily frigates, sloops, and brigs-of-war, nothing as large and powerful as to go against up the Tritons or the Gallicians, but a force that should have overwhelmed those conniving Darnahsians.

"But we were seven separate squadrons, and no one individual flew a flag that the rest would answer to. There were several incidents of near combat between vessels from the various Lands, and the few attempts to actually go after the pirates generally ended in dismal failure."

"Too many admirals and not enough captains, it would seem, sir. My sympathies!"

"Oh, we have no admirals, sir, not in any of the various naval militias. But your point is taken. It is for that very reason that I fervently support the efforts of the Unity Congress. If we can cease quarrelling amongst ourselves in matters of government, perhaps we can reach the point that we no longer quarrel when at sea as a unified force."

"Do you foresee any new attempts to subdue the pirates?"

"Sadly, no. While the Joint Council may have acted in concert regarding your situation, it appears that it is still just as divided as ever in other matters."

"A true shame, sir. A true shame," lamented O'Brien, expressing the Englishmen's combined regret.

"Quite honestly, sir, I am surprised that you should tell us of these matters."

"Shall we say, gentlemen, that I would prefer you know just what you are getting into. It may seem like Stone Island's answer to everything, joining as the eleventh Independent Land of Vespica. Do remember that the key word in all this is *independent*."

"I have long conjectured that that is a part of the problem, sir," said Pierce. "I do feel for Mr. Gibbons. His stint as our representative may prove to be more than he planned for."

"But I primarily tell you, captain to captain, not to expect any real cooperation amongst the various naval militias, should you ever be involved in any similar operation. Oh, I know you plan to return to that England of yours. But as the only insular Land; I see that some sort of fighting fleet will eventually be established. You must pass along to whomever should lead it, the impracticality of cooperation with other naval militias."

"We did jest some time ago, that *Island Expedition* constitutes the Stone Island Navy, but what will be done upon our departure, I cannot say. Still I would hope that should the situation arise, that you and I, and any forces we should command, might cooperate to the fullest."

"I would welcome such an opportunity. And now, perhaps it is time that you returned to your quarters. I would advise a light breakfast on the morrow. The activities at both the Joint Council and in the Unity Congress will be somewhat long and, quite possibly, boring. At this time of the year, the meeting chambers can grow quite warm. It would not do to fall asleep."

"Indeed not, sir," agreed Hotchkiss.

As if by some unseen agreement, the four stood and made their way outside. In the early evening, the sun had sunk low enough that the narrower streets were in shadow. But the air itself was hot, and as they strolled the few blocks to the inn, Pierce felt as if he were in an oven. Stanton sniffed at the air. "You are likely to encounter fog during a return to Stone Island. If you do not have the latest local charts, I will provide!"

"I would have said squalls and thunderstorms, sir, with the way the air feels. But you know the local weather better than I do.

Perhaps you would be so good as to review our charts to see if they are adequate."

"Most assuredly, Captain. Now, here is your inn. I will go aboard and see that your vessel is safe and secure for the night. I bid you a good night, gentlemen."

Chapter Fourteen

# Out of the Fog

Pierce did not sleep well that night. The unfamiliar room was too warm, and even with the window opened wide, very little breeze came through to cool him. He still wasn't comfortable with the insistence that he and all the crew berth ashore and not aboard *Island Expedition*. It didn't feel right, and continued reflection upon Stanton's revelations about the Vespican naval militias contributed to his insomnia.

When he finally slept, the sun was already creeping into the morning sky, burning its way through the lingering mist that had settled during the night. Finding slumber just before the day began meant that he did not readily respond when Hotchkiss rapped at his door a short time later. In fact the lieutenant knocked twice, and receiving no response, entered the room and gently shook him by the shoulder.

With a groan, Pierce rolled over and opened his eyes. The morning had progressed far enough that the light was quite bright, and he immediately closed his eyes against it. He blinked several times and yawned. Besides the painful brightness, he felt that deep-seated scratchiness so familiar to those with too little rest. His eyelids were heavy and uncomfortably sticky.

"Good morning, Edward," said his friend. "I hope you slept well."

Grumpily, trying to focus, Pierce moaned unintelligently. He thought he had said "Good morning as well. Truth! I slept not a farthing's worth." But even as he uttered the words, he knew the words were not understood by his friend.

"Coffee? I've brought you a cup. Hot and fresh, as you like it."

Pierce yawned again and took a deep breath. The odor of the

coffee penetrated his senses and he awoke a bit more. He swung his feet to the floor and sat up, slumping upon himself as the urge to sleep returned. "Thank you!" This time it was clear enough that Hotchkiss could understand. He placed the cup in Pierce's hands, and yet retained a touch upon it in case his friend did not yet have the wherewithal to control it.

Groggily confused, Pierce wondered why he was so tired, and why he seemed to struggle so to become fully awake. After all his years of naval service, he was quite accustomed to being awakened at all hours, sometimes having just fallen asleep. He had long ago learned to transition between the two states in rapid fashion. This morning, for some reason, he could not. In the early morning, the room was comfortably cool, and yet Pierce was damp with sweat, and while he felt warm, nearly hot, at the next moment he was cold.

He raised the coffee mug to his lips and sipped experimentally. It was exceedingly good coffee, nearly as good as he remembered at the Frosty Anchor in Brunswick. He gulped a bigger swallow, let it course down into his stomach, and slowly he felt life itself returning.

"I've taken the liberty, sir," said Hotchkiss, still assisting in holding the cup, "of requesting a tub and hot water for you. It will be here shortly. We have a most momentous day ahead, and I'm convinced you will want to be at your best."

"Aye. Thank you kindly, Isaac." Pierce sipped at the coffee again. As he did, certain particular sensations made themselves known and as quickly departed. "Have you arranged for yourself as well, friend?"

"Most assuredly. And I've sent Mr. O'Brien to muster the hands and see that none have become lost."

"Thank you. I seem not to have my wits about me this morning." Once more he drank from the cup, nearly finishing it. "I could use another, Isaac, and perhaps then I will be fit to be about the day." The sensation experienced earlier returned, this time a bit stronger and of a more lasting duration.

"Should you wait momentarily, I'll see another is sent along." Hotchkiss took the cup and sat it on the table next to the bed. He got up and headed towards the door.

Pierce noticed the particular feeling return, stronger than before. Now he recognized its urgency. "I believe I must be up and about, Isaac, even before I have that second cup." He got to his feet and headed to the door as well.

"Of course, my friend. But first, do don trousers and shirt, lest there be any improprieties of dress."

As the need to leave rapidly became stronger, Pierce nodded his understanding, hurriedly struggled into the most basic of clothing, and left.

After a refreshing bath and a close and comfortable shave, Pierce felt much better. In fact, he had felt much more human on his return to the room. Because of the day's significant events, he dressed carefully and departed wearing his seldom used full dress uniform. Even at that fairly early hour, he felt a trickle of sweat run down his belly. Pierce sighed to himself, knowing that as the day wore on, the increasing heat would make the ceremonial regalia more and more uncomfortable.

He found Hotchkiss, O'Brien, and Smythe in the dining room, having coffee and a bit of late breakfast. They ate heartily, and the sight and aroma of familiar and delicious delicacies stirred Pierce's appetite into full appreciation. While he greatly desired to join in and greedily devour the bacon, eggs, kippers, toasted soft bread with marmalade, and oatmeal, recent memories encouraged him not to. He ate sparingly of toast, oatmeal, and coffee.

"You are not hungry, Edward?" asked Smythe, noticing the minute amount that Pierce ate.

"No, I suppose I am not. Captain Stanton did advise that a light breakfast might be the thing before the day's events."

"Perhaps," said O'Brien. "I do remember him saying so, but this is most delicious bacon, and I'll not let it go to waste."

"Nor I, the toast and marmalade," said Hotchkiss. "Is it possible, friend, that something consumed yesterday has had a telling effect upon you this morning? You did not seem at all well earlier."

"Quite possibly, Isaac."

"And now?" queried Smythe.

"Better! Much better indeed!"

"It appears that we have nearly finished this excellent breakfast. I have a few things to collect, and then I shall be off to the meeting hall."

"Very good, sir," said Pierce as Smythe stood to leave. "We shall be along shortly."

A serving girl, the same one that had brought him three cups of coffee the day before, appeared and cleared away their empty and dirty utensils. Unconsciously, Pierce noticed her form and the cleavage revealed as she leaned and reached across to pick up a plate on the near side of the table. She caught the direction of his glance, smiled, and bustled the dishes off to be washed.

He let his mind wander amid thoughts of pleasure for a brief minute, and then dismissed them and brought his attention back to the table. He finished the coffee in his cup. "I would hear the status of schooner and crew, should any of you know it?" It irritated him to have to ask, for as captain it was his duty always to know these things.

"I was aboard earlier," said Hotchkiss. "The New Sussex naval militia has maintained a close and watchful eye over our vessel. All appears to be in order, sir."

"Hands are all accounted for. Most are reasonably sober. Two involved in fights. I have their names here, sir." O'Brien handed Pierce a scrap of paper. "Currently they are at make and mend and readying their best shore-going rig for later."

"Do they know when and where, Mr. O'Brien?"

"Aye, sir, they do. The meeting hall at seven bells in the forenoon watch, sir."

"Very well. If we have any last-minute details to be concerned with--now, gentlemen, would be the time."

At a little before eleven-thirty that Monday morning, a crowd began to gather in the square before the town's meeting hall. Not only was a considerable percentage of the Bostwick populace there, but the entire crew, to a man, of HMS, or as it was now known, OGS *Island Expedition* mustered and hung about in some semblance of order. The doors were opened and the crowd of spectators flowed into the building until seats allotted for viewing the day's events were full. Still more entered, and it was only when the queues into the building stopped moving that a lack of room was announced.

Now all that remained within the square were those participating, or those whose office determined that they should arrive with ceremony. As noon approached, the remaining dignitaries arrived and soon were clustered somewhat haphazardly amongst their own. Pierce, the officers, and men from the schooner gathered to one side of the square, and directly opposite of them, the entire Joint Council formed a tight mass of humanity. Nearby were delegations from the various embassies, as well as from the unofficial but highly respected Unity Congress.

As he looked about the reduced but now-distinguished crowd, Pierce saw several familiar faces. He nodded respectfully in the direction of Lord Lancaster, but the Tritonish Ambassador either did not see the gesture or chose to ignore it. On the other hand, Sir Vaughn Chesterfield promptly and quite cheerfully returned Pierce's acknowledgment.

The bells high in the tower atop the meeting hall pealed out the noon hour and created such a din that any conversation was momentarily impossible. When silence returned, the center doors leading to the hall opened and a solitary figure appeared.

"The sergeant-at-arms, sir," said Hotchkiss. "He'll call us to enter in turn."

"Of course," replied Pierce. He had assumed that that was the case, but he was grateful for his first lieutenant's explanation. The council staff had briefed them on the proceedings earlier that morning, but Pierce had been involved in other matters of a more pressing and personal nature. Now he followed the lead of the others, and hoped they led well.

Sweat trickled from underneath his cocked hat, and he moved into the shade of a large cedar, one of a very few that had been left standing in the square.

"Joint Council Delegates Jonathan Fox and William Jefferson, of the Independent Land of North Charlenia!" the sergeant-at-arms called out, and the two named individuals stepped forward and disappeared into the building. As they passed close by those from Stone Island, they nodded in polite and even friendly recognition.

"Friends?" asked Smythe.

"Indeed, sir," replied Hotchkiss. "They were of the delegation that delivered the good news of our release this last October."

"Joint Council Delegate Gerald Lee, of the Independent Land of New Somerset!" The voice at the doorway sounded soon after the first two had disappeared inside. That individual, also a member of the small delegation to Brunswick the past spring, nodded his greetings as well as he passed and entered inside.

"I'm afraid this could take a while," said Pierce as another trickle of perspiration made itself known under his clothing.

"Aye," responded Hotchkiss.

So it went, delegates of each of the ten Lands being called to enter the meeting hall. A few of the Lands had but a single delegate, many had two or three, and one or two Lands had four or even five delegates. "At least they are not calling them individually, sir," observed Andrews. "They do group the multiples together."

"Thank God for that!"

With the Joint Council delegates in the building, the chairman, James Warren, and the secretary, Elias Johnson, were ushered in next. Warren was a part of the delegation from New Sussex, and Johnson hailed from Geoffreyland. There was a short pause and Hotchkiss explained to Pierce, "They are being called to order and into session for the day. When that is done, entry of guests will proceed."

After a quick turn and look back into the doorway, the sergeant-at-arms continued. Perhaps in an effort to speed the process and get the remaining personages out of the sun, or because the Unity Congress was a non-sanctioned body, the only person named was the president, Joseph Braxton. They entered as a group, Dr. Robertson among them, his darker Original Peoples' features contrasting with the remainder. The other guests, delegations from the various embassies, trade missions, and consulates were asked to enter as well.

The doorman, for such he really was, announced: "Petty officers, seamen, landsmen, and boys of His Britannic Majesty's Schooner, Stone Island's Good Ship *Island Expedition!*" Pierce was pleased and just a little astonished to see the hands march in smartly, two by two.

"Officers, warrant officers, and midshipmen of His Majesty's Schooner, Stone Island's Good Ship *Island Expedition!*" They disappeared through the doorway and Pierce was left, along with Smythe and Gibbons in the square.

He was called next, by name, rank, and position. He strode up the five steps and through the door. It was a relief to be out of the sun, and inside it felt slightly cooler. There was a minute breeze as well, and he looked up to see fans moving back and forth in the highest points of the ceiling. They were linked by rods and apparently set in motion by servants hidden somewhere on an upper floor.

Another individual announced him again. "Master and Commander Edward Pierce, Captain of His Britannic Majesty's Schooner and Stone Island's Good Ship *Island Expedition!*" Amid polite but enthusiastic applause, he was directed to his seat. It was quite near the front and placed him at the lead of his officers and crew. He removed his hat.

Gibbons was called next, followed by Smythe. Pierce was surprised that they were not identified as Stone Island's Joint Council Delegate or Governor. That they weren't was explained when Warren gaveled for silence and said, "Before us, gentlemen, stand official representatives of Stone Island. Have you accepted the offer of annexation, and do you now ask to become the eleventh Independent Land of Vespica?"

"By the wishes of those now residing on Stone Island, sir, that is indeed our goal," said Smythe with simplicity, dignity, and candor.

"Very well! Does the Joint Council favor such annexation? If so, signify and say 'Aye!'"

The Joint Council erupted in a roar of approving "ayes," aided by others in the chamber.

"If any are opposed, indicate by saying 'Nay!'"

After a moment of relative silence, Warren continued. "I believe the Council has agreed. Stone Island, the Independent Land of Stone Island, is now the newest and the eleventh Independent Land of Vespica!" Cheers, calls, applause, and desktop-drumming sounded as the words were spoken.

When silence returned, the Joint Council Chairman said, "Do you have one designated to sit on the Joint Council and represent your Land amongst the others?"

"Mr. Chairman! I am Jonas Gibbons, and I have been asked to represent Stone Island at this Joint Council."

"Excellent! Excellent! Ladies and gentlemen, I give you Jonas Gibbons, the Joint Council Delegate from Stone Island." And as the applause died away, Warren said quietly, "You may take your seat, Mr. Delegate.

"And might there be amongst you one representing the executive office, or indeed one holding the executive office of Stone Island?"

"Mr. Chairman! Harold Smythe, Governor of the Independent Land of Stone Island, at your service, sir!"

"Welcome! We are honored by your presence. Please be seated!"

So far, thought Pierce, things were moving along nicely. Looking at his watch, he saw that the activities had not taken long. Sitting motionless out of the sun, and with the slight breeze provided by the overhead fans, he was, for the moment, quite comfortable. He silently knocked wood for luck, hoping that the proceedings would progress rapidly and be over soon.

Luck was not with Pierce or any of the Stone Island contingent that day. While the official program, the acceptance of annexation, and the admission of Stone Island were carried out in the briefest of times, the unofficial part dragged on. Warren spoke, welcoming the newest of the loose confederation of Vespican Lands. He even mentioned that the plight of seamen from that new Land had caused the Joint Council to uncharacteristically act in unity.

Smythe was called upon to address the assembled masses. His speech was short, even though he mentioned his childhood, the old legends, searching for a route to the island, the desire to found a "freedom colony," and his initial resistance to having even the most basic contact with other lands. As Smythe spoke quite freely about the passage between two worlds, Pierce wondered how many understood the reality of travel between them. How many of them grasped the possibility of other worlds? Or did most of those present scoff at their tale of being from another world, believing the British to be from an unknown place in this world?

By now, the boredom of the afternoon began to tell on Pierce. He sat immobile and unthinking, nearly in a trance, his mind far from the activities around him. He did not hear his name called, and Hotchkiss had to nudge him awake. But he had known that he would be expected to say a few words, and during the voyage, he had formulated and practiced a little speech. As he drew a couple of deep breaths to hasten complete wakefulness, Pierce was glad for the idle time spent watching the schooner's wake, and the chance to plan his remarks.

"My friends," he began. "I can think of no better address to honor and signify what you truly are. Over the past months you demonstrated that the plight of strangers can overcome petty differences and lead to better days for all concerned. On behalf of the officers and men of His Majesty's Schooner *Island Expedition*, I extend our sincerest thanks for the efforts put forth on our behalf. We are strengthened by your concern and believe that the success achieved has added to the prestige and power of these august bodies.

"Whether you believe we are from a different world does not matter. It is enough that we are here, and that with your aid we are again free men. We are most grateful for the citizenship extended to us, and we accept it proudly yet humbly. I fully intend to meet all that is expected of me as a Vespican citizen when I am in this world. When I return to my world and my England, I shall again be a subject of the British Crown. My duty and allegiance shall lie there.

"I have had the chance to be associated with many of the fine gentlemen in this room, and I have come to understand that in aid and compassion there is unity. In unity, my friends, there is strength. I charge you all to remember that.

"Soon we will return to Stone Island and prepare to voyage back to the world we left behind. It is our home, and we long for it. Yet we have found a home amongst you. I cannot say with certainty whether I or any of us will return. That we can return home is due to all of you, and for that we will be eternally thankful. Thank you!"

There was a smattering of applause as Pierce returned to his seat. Soon, the individual hand claps joined and became a dull roar that reverberated around the chamber. Somewhere behind him he heard, "three cheers for the captain!" The "huzzahs" and "hurrahs" rang out, and Pierce's first instinct was to sit as inconspicuously as possible and let the din die down. Yet that would not suffice, so he stood and bowed.

Others, members of the Joint Council, those of the Unity Congress, and the more casual spectators arose. They clapped furiously, rapped repeatedly on the desks and tables, or stomped enthusiastically on the floor. Amid the resounding racket that ensued, shouts cried out in salute to Pierce, the crew, and the schooner herself. When the noise subsided a bit, Pierce raised his arms to further quiet the crowd. "In turn, will you not cheer yourselves? Three cheers for the Joint Council! Three cheers for the Unity Congress! And three cheers for the Independent Lands of Vespica!" The cheers rang out once more.

Pierce was in a daze for the first half of the week. One dinner followed another as members of the Vespican government vied with each other to produce the greatest feast. Others with certain power or influence also scheduled various events, and for a while it seemed that the round of celebrations would never cease.

Friday afternoon found the schooner underway and out of sight of land. It had stormed furiously two days before, cooling the air and bringing relief and refreshment to the succeeding days. The added humidity and cooler temperatures also brought fog, just as Stanton had predicted some days earlier.

The wind was light as *Island Expedition* crept slowly through the patchy fog and intermittent areas of rain. It wasn't raining hard, and what did fall was more of a mist or a gentle drizzle. Yet the fog, low clouds, and easy rainfall conspired to noticeably lessen the visibility. For that reason, Pierce had minimum sail set, enough that they might make slow progress away from the Vespican mainland. He had the latest in charts, generously provided by Captain Stanton, and he understood that in these specific waters, no unseen dangers lay in wait for them. Still, as they were near the mouth of a busy harbor, there was the possibility of other ships. Lookouts aloft had been doubled since sailing, and many others stood their duty along the rails. In the gloom of the dreary afternoon, top lights and stern lights glowed brightly, and hopefully would announce their presence to any other vessel afloat. The ship's bell was also struck vigorously at one-minute intervals to identify their location to anyone else afloat in those same waters.

The seas were calm in the gentle wind, and the schooner rode easily over them. The wake showed only the slightest disturbance, and there was a gentle murmur of water passing easily along the hull. Pierce stood on the windward side of the quarterdeck, clad in his oldest and most dilapidated undress uniform. He was cold and wet but not seriously so, and despite his apparent discomfort, took real pleasure in the cool dampness. He had quite some time ago quit wondering if he should have worn a tarpaulin and his sou'wester during this time on deck. Even with the fog and mist, the weather was mild, and to have donned extra clothing would have made him too warm.

Forward at the belfry, Jack Haight watched the second hand of Pierce's watch creep towards the twelve. When it arrived, the boy dutifully rang the bell twice in rapid succession. Pierce and all on deck listened intensely for any reply that would mean the presence of a nearby ship. For a moment he thought he heard the swish of water along another ship's hull. Perhaps he had yawned and caused the sound of his own vessel's passage to change.

A moment later, Jones, who watched and listened along the starboard bow, quietly hailed the quarterdeck. "Ship to starboard, sir! Off the bow!"

Pierce moved forward. "Did you see it?"

"No sir. Heard it, I think!" Jones cocked his head and put his hand behind his ear. "Again, sir!" After a moment or two he continued. "Sounds like trucks, sir. Guns being run out?"

Pierce stared into the gloom. Faintly he heard the squeal, rumble, and thump of heavy guns being thrust against unseen bulwarks. "Jones! Find Mr. Hotchkiss and bid him join me."

"Aye, sir," the seaman responded, and slipped quietly away. As Pierce waited and listened, he too thought he could hear the sounds of a ship being made ready for battle. The schooner's bell rang again, startling Pierce. Should he cease sounding their position? Or would the stoppage alert the other vessel to their awareness of her? He said nothing to Haight, and let the regular ringing of the bell continue.

Hotchkiss arrived quickly, and upon listening for a short while, said, "It does sound like it to me, sir. I believe she is drawing nearer. Shall we alter course?"

"Perhaps we will let her fall off a bit. Douse the lights as well. Perhaps they see us and we don't see them."

"Aye!"

"And quietly rouse the watch below. Let us man for battle as quietly as we can. Hopefully we can load without telling the world we are doing it."

"Do you remember sir, that following our display for Mrs. Packingham, we did not fire the final broadsides? Indeed, we have been loaded this whole time."

"Aye, so we have. Do see that Mrs. Packingham and Mr. Smythe are safely below."

"Aye aye, sir!"

Pierce stepped across the deck and spoke quietly to young Jack Haight. "Now lad, we are going to fall off to port a bit. When you strike the bell, strike it slightly harder. At the next instance, strike harder yet."

"Aye aye, sir! Strike harder each time."

"The game is not to let any ship that might be out there know of our course change by the sound of our bell."

Haight concentrated on the watch, nodded, and struck the bell. Being so close, the tone echoed painfully in Pierce's ears.

The motion of the deck underfoot changed ever so slightly. The heel to port increased just enough that he noticed it. "Now, louder next time, Haight."

"Aye, sir!"

Those hands who had been below in the comparative comfort of the 'tween decks came topside now, quietly, and in ones and twos. Quietly and casually, gun ports were opened, guns cast loose and made ready. There was no time, and indeed no way to stealthily clear the deck for battle. About all that could be done was to prepare the already loaded guns and stand by.

Haight rang the bell once more, quite loudly this time. Dr. Matheson appeared on deck. "What is up, gentlemen?" he asked of those gathered on the quarterdeck. "The bell has wakened Hooper, who should not be awakened as per the good Dr. Robertson's directives." Before anyone could answer, the bell was struck again, and again with all the strength that Haight could muster. The surgeon cringed, and shot an annoyed look at the lad manning the belfry.

"I am sorry that it inconveniences Hooper, Doctor. But are you not aware of our situation? Have you not been told of the potentially hostile vessel off our lee?"

"I have not been so informed, Mr. O'Brien. I have been occupied tending to Hooper."

"The bell's increasing volume is to prevent yon vessel from knowing we are altering course away from her, Doctor. We are quietly manning guns in the event of a nasty occurrence. If such comes to pass, the loudness of the bell will be the least of your or Hooper's concerns."

"Mr. Hotchkiss is right," said Pierce. "I would suggest you return to him and as you can, prepare sick bay, should it be required."

"Aye, sir!"

"But do tell, before you go, how is Hooper?"

"Better! Much better! Trepanning was the key, sir. Dr. Robertson was correct in his assessment, and he is very skilled at the procedure. He has a chance now. Had we left him on the island, I'm sure he'd be gone by now."

"I quite agree, sir. Now to your station, if you please."

The bell rang out again. Matheson flinched at the sound, made his acknowledgment, and headed below.

Pierce originally thought to leave the badly injured man behind on the island during this diplomatic voyage to Bostwick. But it had been pointed out that both Dr. Matheson, the ship's surgeon, and Dr. Robertson would be aboard for the trip. That would have left Hooper, who suffered from several broken bones and a fractured skull, without benefit of any kind of trained medical attention. It was decided, therefore, to bring the seriously hurt seaman along so that both doctors could see to his care. While they had been in Bostwick, Hooper had been moved ashore, and in the afternoon following the special session of the Joint Council, Dr. Robertson had operated. He had carefully removed a small circle of the man's skull, easing the pressure caused by the depressed bone against the brain. With luck, and barring the ever-present chance of infection, it was thought that he would eventually recover.

The next sounding of the bell brought Pierce back from his momentary reflections. Once again he thought he heard the sound of water flowing along a ship's side. As he looked in the direction from which the sound seemed to come, the rain ceased and the fog eased. A murky, cloudy silhouette, unmistakably that of a vessel, loomed surprisingly near the schooner.

At the same time, several hands saw it as well, and nearly in unison shouted, "Ship to starboard!"

"My God!" shouted Hotchkiss. "It's *Furious*! She's on a collision course!"

The large Tritonish frigate was indeed on a course angled towards the schooner. Under fighting sail, her ports open and guns run out, she edged ever closer. In their current position, the schooner was relatively safe. Only the forwardmost portside guns of the frigate, those positioned in the curve of her bows, pointed directly at them. The rest of her broadside pointed aft. But with a slight nudge of her helm, she could be brought parallel with *Island Expedition* and unleash a devastating storm of shot.

Pierce fought down a sudden urge to visit the head. Nausea swept over him, and he was wet, not only from the weather, but from a nervous sweat. The vessels were close enough now that Pierce could readily distinguish Jackson on the higher windward side of the quarterdeck. He saw *Furious'* captain open his mouth to shout an order. He watched as the two helmsmen spun the wheel to starboard. She was turning and bringing her full broadside to bear.

Chapter Fifteen

# Witness to Mutiny

"**B**ack the topsails! Helm aweather!" shouted Pierce. "Turn into her!" He prayed the sudden move would diminish their time under the frigate's guns. Backing topsails would allow the larger vessel to forge ahead, and the turn into her would further alter their relative positions and lessen the chances of receiving a full broadside. With judicious and quick handling, the schooner could continue her turn, fall off on a port tack, and momentarily have the frigate's port quarter under her guns.

Yet Pierce would not fire unless fired upon. As much as he disliked Jackson, he would not fire on a ship that was not a declared enemy. Would *Furious'* captain show the same restraint? He tended to think the man would not, and that if any guns could be brought to bear on the schooner, a hail of deadly shot would sweep the deck. After all, the Kentish man-of-war had run out her guns when they could only hear each other in the fog. As visibility had increased she had edged purposely and ominously closer.

Jackson was sharp. No sooner had the schooner begun to slow and turn, when the frigate ceased her turn to starboard and came about to port. "Damn!" he said. *Furious'* countermove placed the British vessel in the line of fire again. With a sinking feeling in the pit of his stomach, Pierce watched Lowell Jackson wave his sword and issue the commands that would unleash death and devastation upon his schooner.

The two vessels were close enough that he could hear Jackson shout, "As your guns bear! Fire!" Pierce braced himself for the onslaught that would follow.

Still, he had the handling of his own ship to be concerned with.

Turning into the wind and backing topsails had brought the schooner near dead in the water. She did not have the impetus to continue the turn and fall off on the other tack. If he did not act decisively and quickly, they would be caught in stays and truly at the mercy of the larger ship. "Starboard your helm! Brace topsails around!" Hopefully the *Island Expedition* still had enough way on her that she could reverse the direction of her turn and with the wind once again aft of the large square sails, resume something akin to her previous course. It might place them under the frigate's guns for a slightly longer period of time, but now Pierce wanted steerageway and speed. Then, depending upon Jackson's next move, he could attempt a proper tack.

The schooner answered her helm's new position and sluggishly turned back to port. Wind filled the topsails, caught behind the jib, and exerted a push on the double-reefed mainsail. It had been some moments since he had seen and heard Jackson give the order to fire.

As he watched, Jackson shouted again and brandished his sword at his first lieutenant. Clearly his words reached the schooner's deck. "Fire I say! Fire! Damn you!" Jackson jumped about in a rage, and Pierce watched his face growing redder. "Damn you to hell, Rollins! I'll have the lot of you in irons! You'll hang, damn your eyes! All of you filthy bastards will hang! Now fire, and sink that damn schooner!"

Pierce looked on in amazement. Distraught and enraged, the frigate captain cavorted angrily about the deck. Three Tritonish marines, bayonets fixed, surrounded him, but kept a respectful distance from his flailing sword. Rollins, the ship's first lieutenant stood resolute, repeating the words, "Do not fire! On your life, men, do not fire!"

"I'll see every man-jack of you hanged, or flogged around the fleet!" Jackson shouted hysterically. "Sink that fucking schooner, now! Kill that bastard Pierce! Make me a fucking cuckold, will he!"

Rollins shook his head, almost in sympathy for his captain. Then he nodded briskly. The marines stepped nearer Jackson. He raised his sword threateningly, but the center of the three thrust his musket forward and with a twist caught Jackson's blade and sent it flying. Rollins joined the marines, and soon they had Jackson bound and defenseless, still standing on what had been his quarterdeck.

"Fire a gun to leeward, Mr. Nelson! And haul down the colors!" Pierce heard the frigate's lieutenant say. "Secure the guns and stand down!"

"Secure our guns as well, Mr. Hotchkiss!" said Pierce.

Soon thereafter, the frigate fired a single gun, but a shouted conversation convinced the Tritonish they need not lower their colors. Now the two vessels hove to, less than a hundred yards separating them. Pierce awaited the approach of the frigate's cutter. Having stern and quarter davits, it had been much easier for the larger vessel to put a boat into the water. When the boat came alongside, he would embark and return to *Furious* for in-depth discussion of the recent incident.

The immediate danger past, Smythe was on deck, having gratefully escaped the stifling confines of the hold. "A near thing, I would say, sir," he said to Pierce. "I was not aware of hostilities between the Independent Lands and Grand Triton."

"There are none, to my knowledge," said Pierce. "This is a misguided and unauthorized attempt on the part of a particular individual. It had nothing at all to do with his nation's interest, but was based solely upon personal motives."

"I see, but I do not understand. I am surprised that we find a Tritonish warship in these waters. Lancaster led me to believe the Flying Squadron and other Kentish ships had been recalled. Something about a major Gallician fleet being at sea."

"I was told the same last month upon meeting with *Hawke*. However, Newbury informed me that Jackson had obtained permission to remain for a few more weeks."

"For what purpose?"

"Ideally, it was to scour these waters one last time, searching for any Gallician vessels. Practically, I believe it was for strictly personal reasons."

"As he attacked and nearly fired upon us, could we somehow be the object of his quest?"

"While he surely has no fondness for us as a whole, I confess that perhaps I am the target of his obsession."

"A result of your passage aboard *Furious* these many months ago?" Smythe was quiet for a moment. "Or did other events occur during your time in Brunswick?"

Pierce knew what events had occurred, and that lately Jackson had come to suspect him. Still, they were episodes of which he was not particularly proud, and ones that he would prefer not to admit to Harold Smythe. Besides regarding the man as his employer, current mentor, and leader, Pierce thought of him as his potential father-in-law. He did not want his beloved Evangeline's father to know or even suspect his involvement with Leona Jackson, nor to know that Jackson suspected him of that very thing. But Jackson, in a vengeful thirst, ready to sink *Island Expedition* and kill many others in the process, left him little choice.

As the moments since Smythe's question stretched into eternity, Pierce wondered if he might truthfully answer and yet not really admit to his transgressions. "Lowell Jackson has gotten it into his mind, sir, that I bedded his wife in Brunswick."

"I see, Edward. And did.... No! I will not ask. You would answer truthfully, and if true, despite any reassurances, you would feel diminished. Should it not be true, and should you respond thusly, or should it be true, and you uncharacteristically reply falsely, there would always be doubt."

"Then if you do not ask, sir, I will not answer."

*Furious'* cutter came alongside and hooked on. Her first lieutenant, Rollins, came aboard, followed by Nelson, her third, and Barry her fourth. There was no ceremonial piping or presenting of arms to welcome the visitors. Under the circumstances it would have been unwarranted, and from the expressions worn by the three, would have been quite uncalled-for.

"Might I welcome you aboard *Island Expedition*, gentlemen?" offered Pierce. "So good of you to come for me."

"It is good to see you again, Commander, alive and unharmed," responded Rollins. "Had things not occurred as they did, perhaps I would not be allowed to so remark."

"Indeed, sir."

"You may have my sword, sir, should you wish it."

"Surely I do not need another, sir. Do not consider that there is any sort of surrender or capitulation involved in today's occurrences."

"Very generous of you, Commander Pierce. Truthfully, sir, I am quite at a loss regarding this incident and the resulting aftermath. As we discussed earlier, perhaps you would accompany us aboard *Furious* for further talks. Please bring any of your officers you might prefer to have along. Should you wish it, Mr. Barry will remain aboard to guarantee your safety."

"His presence will not be required, Mr. Rollins. I do not consider you to be enemies. I will ask that Mr. Hotchkiss, my first lieutenant, and Mr. Smythe, Governor of Stone Island accompany us."

"Excellent, sir!" The Tritonish lieutenant bowed in reply and then said, "Mr. Hotchkiss, it is good to see you again as well. Mr. Smythe, I am pleased to meet you. Now, should you step into the cutter, we will be off. More room aboard *Furious*, you know. We may want testimony from some of the hands as well."

On the deck of the Kentish frigate, things were as Pierce expected them to be: shipshape, squared away, clean, and polished to high perfection. Yet there was an air of decay about the frigate because of the relentless way Jackson had driven the crew in the year and a half since Pierce was last aboard.

Rollins showed them below and into the great cabin. Seated about the table were the majority of the frigate's warrant officers, two master's mates, and the senior midshipman. They rose when those from *Island Expedition* and their own lieutenants entered. "Commander Pierce, Mr. Hotchkiss, I believe you know everyone? Governor Smythe, may I present Mr. Belknap, sailing master; Dr. Lycoming; Forbes, second lieutenant; Manley, our gunner; King and Sullivan, master's mates; and Roberson, midshipman?"

"I am pleased to meet all of you, gentlemen," said Smythe.

"Commander Pierce and I are relieved to see all of you in excellent health," said Hotchkiss.

"Aye," said Pierce. "I'm glad to once again make your acquaintances." As he spoke he noticed the gathered officers of *Furious* appeared nervous and afraid. While they did their best to welcome Pierce and his party, other concerns weighed heavily upon them.

"Commander, some wine? Or would you prefer coffee?" asked Rollins. "I remember your taste for the brew."

"Coffee, if you please, sir," said Pierce. He glanced at his companions, seeking their agreement. They nodded. "A cup or two would serve admirably."

"Grayson there! Light along the coffee pot and the cups! Lively now!" Rollins spoke to the steward.

When the coffee arrived, and a cup was poured for each that wanted one, *Furious'* first lieutenant continued. "This has been a strange day indeed. In our actions we prevented what surely would have been a tragedy. Yet in those actions we may well have damned ourselves and the remainder of this ship's company. Quite frankly, gentlemen, I am frightened for our future. It is because of my personal regard for Commander Pierce that I have asked him to join us as we attempt to plot our course ahead.

"Like as not, we have mutinied. We have defied orders of our captain, one placed in command of this vessel and whose sacred authority

derives from the crown itself. In doing so, we prevent the probable destruction of a smaller and less capable vessel, one that is not an enemy
of His Regal Majesty or of his kingdom. It certainly was criminal for
our captain to press home an attack on this vessel, especially as it was
apparently motivated by personal matters. Yet, we have mutinied, and
I fear the consequences. We must deal with it promptly."

"I understand your concern, gentlemen," said Pierce. "While I am
not familiar with the regulations of your service, I know that such action in His Britannic Majesty's Service would be viewed with disfavor.
Perpetrators would be dealt with swiftly."

Hotchkiss nodded in agreement.

"We acted in the best interests of the service," said Nelson, sitting
pale and trembling at the far end of the table. "That should override
any consideration of guilt on our part."

"It would be so, if we are judged by an impartial jury. But are we
tried, it will be before a court of Regal Navy captains. We will be
considered guilty, even as it begins," expounded Forbes. "The reasons
for our actions, the actions of our captain will not matter. What will
matter is the action we took. It is not fair, Mr. Nelson, but centuries of
naval tradition insist that it be so."

"Aye," agreed Pierce. "It would be the same in the Royal Navy as
well. The burden of proof would be upon you." He took a deep drink
of coffee. "Still, I know of officers who rid themselves of a captain they
deemed unfit for command. A couple of them survived the experience
with no apparent harm to their careers or reputation."

Hotchkiss looked questioningly at his friend. Smythe chimed in.
"What would you be talking about, Captain?"

"*Atlas*, sir. Captain Palmer. It wasn't in the *Gazette*. The real details
of the story were not printed or told. But you remember that my
brothers served aboard, and from them I learned what was kept from
the public. I've never spoken of it, so I might protect any involved and
the official good name of the late Captain Palmer."

"But what did happen, Commander Pierce?" asked Roberson. "If I may be so bold as to ask, sir."

"I have wondered as well," stated Hotchkiss.

"The situation in HMS *Atlas* was similar to that aboard *Furious*. Palmer favored certain individuals and thought others conspired against him. Eventually the captain was severely injured, the circumstances of the accident never having been satisfactorily explained. The captain was ruled by the surgeon as unfit for command, and the first lieutenant took over.

"Later, French prisoners attempted to seize the ship, and Palmer was killed in the resulting fight. Officially he was allowed to have died a hero, killed defending his ship. With an exception or two, the surviving officers' actions were lauded. Any improprieties were erased as to not disgrace the service."

"Rowley?" asked Hotchkiss.

"Aye."

"But could we apply it here? Surely you do not suggest we kill him in cold blood, sir!"

"No, Mr. Barry, I do not. But may I inquire as to his current disposition?"

"He's in sickbay, sir, sedated. He slipped and fell on a ladder. Cracked his head on the step and has a nasty knot. I gave him a double dose of laudanum, primarily to keep him quiet. He's under guard, not that he'll escape, but for his own safety. Certain crewmen might do him harm," explained Dr. Lycoming.

Pierce nodded in agreement. "His mood, sir?"

"Before the dose, he was angry and confused. But the blow seems to have obliterated his recent memory. He thinks he dreamed that we tried to sink you."

"And perhaps, sir," said Manley, "had you not enjoyed the pleasures of his wife's bed, all this would not have occurred." *Furious'* gunner glared at Pierce, and a low angry buzz filled the cabin.

"You do not know that such events occurred!" shouted Hotchkiss. "Jackson's suspicions are based on rumor and supposition. Regardless, his actions were purely for personal reasons, and ought not to have involved his ship, officers, or crew!"

"From what I've heard of his disciplinary measures, your actions may have occurred eventually?" asked Smythe. "If he should sentence one too many to an uncalled-for flogging, what might be your reaction? If he ordered other unlawful or unethical actions, how might you respond?"

"Well spoken, Governor," agreed Barry. "Regardless of the root cause, we well might have eventually taken similar action."

"And been in the same dammed predicament," mourned Forbes.

As *Furious'* officers argued, blaming their captain and at times, each other for their current predicament, Pierce and the other Englishmen sat silently. Pierce was soon in deep thought. For the moment, Justinian's officers and crew were safe. Jackson's fall and the subsequent blow caused him not to remember their rebellion and failure to follow orders. To him, the attempt to sink and destroy the schooner, and Pierce along with it, had been a dream. That the action, so near reality, had been thwarted by his own men did not register with him.

Pierce was not a medical man, and yet he knew that a permanent loss of memory could not be guaranteed. Jackson's recall of the mutiny might never occur, and yet, even as they sat debating amongst themselves, he might be recollecting the morning's damning events. An idea flashed in his mind. Foolhardy! Rash! Uncalled-for! Yet it might offer a final solution to the frigate's crew. And if it worked, it might also rid Pierce of Jackson's haunting thirst for vengeance. As he thought more of it, he felt those old and familiar symptoms of fear creeping into his gut. When the need to visit the head passed, and when the nausea and weakness subsided, he sat with a firm resolve, knowing what he must do.

*Furious'* officers continued to explore one dead-ended idea after another. Pierce remained quiet. He felt strangely detached from the reality of the hot and humid cabin, more like he was someplace far away, observing the discussion through a spyglass. He heard the sometimes heated words, but they did not sink in.

During a momentary pause in the flow of verbiage, Midshipman Roberson glanced his way. "Captain Pierce, sir! You've been quiet these last several minutes. Might we know what preys upon your mind?"

He did not answer immediately, as he was trying to formulate the most appropriate response. However, Pierce did tilt his head toward the young gentleman to acknowledge the remark and question. What he had in mind was the obvious solution, even if its execution placed him at a rather great degree of risk.

"Friends," he said with a soft familiarity. "I can settle this. I can solve the dilemma, such that you needn't worry about restoration of his memory and charges of mutiny being leveled against you. It would also remove his charges against me."

Some of the Tritonish looked puzzled. A couple of them wore looks of understanding, similar to Pierce's British companions.

"What have you in mind, Commander?" asked Dr. Lycoming.

"His memory of this morning's events is gone, I believe. How much of the morning, would you say, Doctor?"

"He does not remember our refusal to fire upon you. Nor does he remember his raging profanity upon the quarterdeck and his subsequent seizure by the marines. He does remember attempting to close an unknown vessel in the fog."

"Was he aware of whom we were?"

"Not until you broke out of the fog," replied Rollins. "He suspected a Toad corvette. There are rumors of one plying these waters. But being you, it played into his craving for vengeance."

"That bodes well, gentlemen. It may make things a little easier. But first, before I reveal what I plan, please send someone on deck, that there are no ears at the skylight or cabin door. The fewer who know, the fewer chances that any inquiry will find the truth."

"I'll go, if I may," said Barry. "A bit of air would serve me well, sir."

"Aye, go," said Rollins. "I am almost afraid to ask what you are considering, Commander."

"As I am dearly afraid to reveal or carry it out, sir. But for your sakes, and mine, I believe it the only chance we have."

"Do carry on, sir."

Pierce swallowed hard. "You are safe, as long as his memory does not return. Does it manifest, you are doomed. But until memory returns, we can provide him with details of events more favorable to our situation."

"What are you saying, Edward?" asked Smythe.

"He has a bump on his head. He has the pain and presumably the headache. There is a period he does not remember. Let us fill it in for him."

"Aye, go on, sir," nodded Forbes.

"Simply put, gentlemen," said Pierce. "When our two vessels became visible, he hailed and demanded that I come aboard. To prevent a threatened broadside from destroying my schooner, I complied. Jackson escorted me below, and in the privacy of his day cabin, made certain accusations and issued a challenge. I accepted that challenge, and as we left the cabin and proceeded on deck, he slipped. The upper decks were quite wet from the rain and fog, as you are well aware."

"Quite so!" said Nelson. "I nearly copped it myself."

Hotchkiss looked up from his coffee. "He challenged you?"

"Yes, and I accepted."

"Surely you don't mean to go through with it! He never really issued a demand for satisfaction. You never offered any agreement that he would have the chance!"

"I'll not have the captain of Stone Island's only vessel killed in an unnecessary duel, sir!" said Smythe.

"Aside from out and out murder, sir, I see no way out of the present predicament. Should he remember, this frigate's crew will be hanged or flogged around the fleet. As long as he's alive, two hundred and fifty odd souls are in jeopardy. While he lives and suspects something between Mrs. Jackson and myself, all in *Island Expedition* are in danger."

"The captain has fought his share of duels, sir," mentioned Rollins, "and has had a great run of success. May I inquire as to your experience?"

"None of a formal nature, as I honestly deplore the practice. But I have often been in battle, and in countless individual struggles, I have survived."

"But such a risk, sir!"

"Yet the risk is equally his. And think, gentlemen! Should I succeed, there would be no need to falsify the logs regarding his death. 'Captain dead of wounds inflicted in an affair of honor' would indeed be the truth."

Lieutenant Rollins, now effectively in command of HRMS *Furious*, sat quietly, deep in thought. When he did speak, it was to say, "Gentlemen, I am touched by Commander Pierce's offer. But we must be in complete agreement before we accept or reject it." Heads nodded and an undertone of compliance filled the room. "Might I ask that our guests retire to the quarterdeck for a few minutes? I would prefer we discuss this privately."

"Assuredly, sir," answered Smythe. "We need to discuss it as well."

On deck, Pierce led them to the forward part of the quarterdeck. He did not want to be directly above the cabin and inadvertently overhear the discussion below. A glance to leeward revealed *Island Expedition* resting upon the gray waters. The rain had stopped and the fog was breaking up. He saw small patches of blue sky that became larger as the minutes passed.

A movement aboard the schooner caught his attention. O'Brien stood with one arm held aloft, moving his hand in slow circles. It was an inquiry concerning the status of Pierce and the other Englishmen aboard the frigate. In reply, Pierce raised his right arm and repeated the gesture, indicating that all was well.

"Edward! Are you mad?" demanded Hotchkiss in a low but determined voice. "I know it is your strongest desire to complete this voyage and return to England. There is enough risk in that, and now you wish to increase it by fighting a duel?"

"Mind what he is saying, Edward!" advised Smythe. "I had always thought you beyond such affairs of so-called honor. Are you so hipped because of his accusations as to risk your life?"

"Truthfully, sir, I could care less about his charges, and normally I would not give a farthing for the plight of mutineers. Should this matter concern anyone but Lowell Jackson, I would suggest they turn themselves over and face the consequences. As a naval officer, I hold mutiny in great distaste.

"Isaac, surely you understand that what I propose is not for myself, nor is it for the officers of this vessel. It is for the hands, those men beaten and flogged half to death on a daily basis. It is for Whitcomb and the others who have died as a result of one man's overenthusiastic application of the lash, that I suggest it.

"My friends, I pray you will support me in this endeavor. When we return below, we must do so with your full support for my offer. I beg each of you that I will have it."

"I had not thought of Whitcomb, sir," said Hotchkiss. "But for the sake of his soul, I will stand behind your decision."

"As will I," said Smythe.

Chapter Sixteen
# An Unexpected Intervention

A rather desultory conversation continued as the three Englishmen stood on *Furious'* quarterdeck. They had agreed to Pierce's decision about Jackson and the mutiny on the Kentish frigate. In light of that, no one had much to say, and for the most part, each of them kept his own counsel as they awaited recall to the great cabin.

Once again Pierce signaled the master of *Island Expedition*, who waited and watched aboard the schooner to assure the safety of his captain, first lieutenant, and governor. Having once again indicated that everything was all right, Pierce noticed O'Brien visibly relax and expel a large breath in relief. Moments after that visual communication, Midshipman Roberson appeared on deck.

"Captain Pierce," he said politely, "if you would care to return, sir."

"Ah, yes, I take it you have reached a decision?"

"Indeed, sir, we have."

The frigate's officers stood as Pierce and the others entered. "Let us be seated, gentlemen," said Rollins. "We shan't waste time, as I'm sure these gentlemen wish to return to their vessel immediately. But before we announce our decision, I would ask once again if we all agree?"

"Aye! We agreed, and we continue to agree!" answered the others.

"I wanted you to know that our choice is unanimous, sir."

"I would hope it would be so, regardless of the final choice."

"Commander Pierce, in light of recent events aboard His Regal Majesty's Frigate *Furious*, we believe your offer provides the best solution to the problems currently besetting this vessel. We do offer our sincerest thank you, and pray for your success."

"I am relieved to find us all in agreement on this matter," said Pierce. "It is a task that I approach with great apprehension and misgiving, even though I believe it the only way. I am strengthened by your total support, as well as by the support of my own people. Now, may I ask, when and where shall this take place?"

"There is a stretch of Vespican coastline, two days' sail from here. It has a small beach with hard-packed sand that should serve our purposes. I will provide the coordinates, or you may simply follow in our wake," stated Belknap.

"The position will serve, sir. Yet we will follow your lead."

"Very good, sir. Now I would imagine you to be most anxious to return aboard *Island Expedition?*"

"Quite so," answered Pierce. "But may I suggest to Dr. Lycoming that he prescribe and administer to Jackson just enough of what he might have in his pharmacy that the man is never completely lucid. If it can be done by telling him it is to treat the blow to his head and restore his memory, it may aid in planting a revised version of that memory."

"Certainly that is something to consider," said the doctor.

"When he is awake, and you are supplying him the details of that lost time, you might also suggest that he relieved himself of command until after the affair is settled." Pierce moved towards the cabin door. "Lieutenant Rollins, if I might speak to you privately for a moment?"

"Of course, sir. Mr. Roberson, if you will see the cutter manned!"

"Aye aye, sir."

Pierce and Rollins remained behind as the others departed and went on deck. "And now, sir, what is it you wish to discuss?" Rollins asked.

"It is not so much a matter of discussion, sir," said Pierce, "but a means of ensuring final success."

"Indeed, how?"

"It may be advantageous to have someone standing by, perhaps hidden from view, and armed; someone who is completely trustworthy and also an excellent shot. While I certainly intend to survive this event, whether I do is not important. But it is imperative that Lowell Jackson does not."

"I understand, sir."

As Pierce and *Furious'* first lieutenant stepped out of the cabin, Roberson reported the cutter standing by. "We will endeavor to remain in sight. Do signal if things go awry. Mr. Roberson, I hope that as you progress towards your commission, you learn that an officer must be aware of the limits of his men. Go beyond very often, and it will result as it did in this ship. That is true, both of the hands and any officers who may be junior to you," Pierce remarked prior to climbing down into the boat.

"Aye, sir." The midshipman nodded in agreement and thanks.

"Most excellent advice, Captain," added Rollins. He reached for Pierce's hand, shook it, and added, "Thank you, sir."

As the cutter made its way across the water, returning the three to *Island Expedition*, Pierce leaned in towards the other two. "Not a word to the others of what is planned. I'll not have half the crew attempting to talk me out of it!"

"Aye, sir," said Hotchkiss quietly. Smythe said nothing, but nodded silently.

Once aboard the schooner, Pierce told Dial, officer of the watch, to follow the frigate and match her speed and course. After instructing the master's mate to pass that along to his relief, he went below and secluded himself in his sleeping cabin.

There he added to his personal journal and brought his continuing letter to Evangeline up to date. While he had previously mentioned meeting Mrs. Jackson, he had not delved into the real nature of that relationship. Now he omitted Jackson's suspicion of him and their pending duel. He did write a second, shorter letter in which he mentioned the combat, saying that if she were reading it, he had lost.

Eight bells sounded, marking the end of the afternoon watch. Hands were piped to supper, and dimly Pierce heard the sounds of the meal being set out in the cabin. He had not eaten all day, and yet he had no appetite. He remained in the small room, aware of those in the cabin as they enjoyed the repast and each other's company. He brooded, silently and alone, wondering if he had made the wisest decision, the best choice after all.

When the noise of the supper faded, indicating that it was nearly at an end, he cautiously opened the door and looked out. He saw Hotchkiss sitting and looking rather preoccupied. A glass of brandy sat untouched by his hand. "Isaac, my friend," he whispered. "Be so kind as to send for a cup of coffee. Then heed what I say."

"Aye aye, sir." When the coffee arrived, Hotchkiss sent Franklin on his way and brought the steaming cup to Pierce. "You are troubled, my friend."

"Would you expect anything else?"

"Not in the least."

"I am afraid, Isaac, that I shall be unfit company for the next day or so. Do extend my apologies to the others. Explain it as…as…."

"I will find something, Edward."

"I'm sure you will, friend. But now, do listen closely. Because of what I intend, I am not fit to command this vessel. I give that responsibility to you. I pray the endeavor will be successful, and when it is over, I will reassume my duties."

Hotchkiss nodded, not so much in agreement as in understanding.

Pierce continued. "Should the future not go as we plan, there are letters in my desk that I would ask that you see delivered."

"Aye."

"One will be for you, detailing the location of documents with complete details about the nature of this voyage. Guard them well my friend, and above all, bring this schooner safely back to England."

"Aye aye, my friend." Hotchkiss reached, shook Pierce's hand, and briefly clasped him about the shoulders. "I'll leave you now," he said as he quickly turned away.

"Yes. But while I'm thinking of it, do see the guns are drawn. Those charges have been in place much too long."

"Aye aye, sir."

Pierce had other correspondence to finalize. He had written his last word to Evangeline, but still he needed a final message to his parents and brothers. He wondered, for a moment, if they were still at home. Or had the war resumed in his world as it had in this one, and had John and Robert returned to the service? There was so much that he wanted to write, and having temporarily relieved himself of command responsibilities, time in which to do it. But thoughts flooded his mind faster than he could set them down on paper, and he sat there into the late hours of the night and did not put a single word on the page.

He awoke at the muffled sound of eight bells. Midnight and the end of the evening watch. He heard the soft calls as the new watch was established. Noting that he had been sleeping, he glanced out the window. The fog had returned. He thought to return to the task of writing those final letters, but weariness won the day and he decided to sleep. As he shrugged out of his shirt and trousers, he was grateful for Gibbon's and Dr. Robertson's departure in Bostwick. There had been another reshuffling of accommodations, and now he found himself back in his own cabin. He had graciously lent it to Mrs. Packingham for the voyage to the Vespican mainland, but now she had in return insisted that he resume occupancy, and had established herself in what was normally Hotchkiss's space. Under the present circumstances it was best that he berth alone. He did not want the presence of anyone, even his longtime friend, intruding into his solitude.

Pierce lay back on his cot, suddenly wide awake, and wondered if he had made the wrong choice in deciding to sleep. But even as he debated the issue, his eyes grew heavy and finally closed.

He awoke to find the cabin dark, the lone candle having long since burned itself out. As he tried to comprehend what had awakened him, a dull flash momentarily illuminated the space. Lightning? No, it wasn't bright enough. Then he heard the far away rumble. Thunder? No, if the flash had not been lightning, then the sound was not its resulting report. Gunfire! Pierce sat up, wide awake, as the realization of what he had heard and saw became clear in his mind. More flashes lit the cabin and within minutes the reverberations of a not-too-distant broadside rang in his ears.

Pierce got up and struggled into his trousers. The early morning was warm and he didn't need his uniform coat. As hurried as he was, he didn't make it out the door before there was a hurried knock upon it. "Yes?" he said, still a little groggy.

"Mr. Hotchkiss' compliments, sir," said Steadman. "*Furious* appears to be engaged with an unknown vessel, sir."

"Very well, Mr. Steadman. I shall be but a moment."

On deck he nodded in Hotchkiss' direction, and that individual pointed forward. Some distance forward of the schooner, Pierce could make out the dim shape of the Tritonish frigate. The fog was thinner and she was easy to see. Yet there was something disconcerting about the image, if there was something more. Flashes of gunfire came again, and now Pierce saw the second ship. It was beyond *Furious*, and had just fired a full broadside into the Kentish vessel.

"Gallician, I believe," said Hotchkiss. "I got a glimpse of her ensign as the last shots were fired. It came out of the fog at her, just as *Furious* did to us."

"With the day's events, Isaac, could they have relaxed their caution?" As Pierce asked, the clouds and fog lit up from another broadside.

"I'm not certain, but they did respond in a timely manner. That's the second full broadside they've given in reply, against only three fired at them." The rumble of gunfire echoed across the water. The smell of gun smoke wafted over the schooner's deck.

The mist and fog illuminated again and for a brief instant Pierce saw the attacking Gallician ship. "Damn my eyes, Isaac! That's no corvette they've tangled with. From my brief look, I'd say a very large frigate, at least."

"Perchance they've met their match?"

"Perhaps."

"Do we stand by and watch? We are neutral, are we not?"

"Aye, but according to the last prick of the charts, we are in Vespican waters. We would be right to detain them both."

"Are you quite mad, Edward? Sail this schooner in amongst two battling frigates?"

"We would not take both on. I'm sure we could add to the force of one or the other. And should you beg to ask which, Isaac, you do not know me as you think you do. Call all hands, and beat to quarters!"

"Aye aye, sir!"

Hotchkiss passed the word to the bo'sun's mates, and soon their shrill pipes filled the night air. The marine drummer arrived on deck, wiping the sleep from his eyes, and half-dressed, began the rapid tattoo signifying action stations. Many of the below-deck watch had already been awakened by the distant cannonade, and all stations were manned quickly.

Smythe and Mrs. Packingham appeared on deck as well, looking quite bewildered, confused, and slightly annoyed. "My word, Edward!" said Smythe. "What is with the noise?"

"Nearly frightened me to death, I must say!" added the lady.

"My apologies, sir, ma'am, but we must aid *Furious*. She has come under attack by a Gallician frigate. I must ask you both to retire below. Sick bay may prove safe, and if you are of a mind to do so, Dr. Matheson might appreciate your assistance."

"Surely suicidal to take on a frigate, sir!" astounded Smythe.

"I don't plan to match her, sir. But can we prove a distraction, a thorn in her side, and then *Furious* might have the advantage. Now below with you both, while there's time!"

Hotchkiss approached. "Guns are manned, sir, and we are ready for action. We did not clear away on the lower deck, if that is all right with you."

"Yes, yes--quite all right. Now a touch more canvas; topgallants, I think, that we may close with them." Flashes of another broadside brightened the mist and clouds. The rumble of gunfire echoed over the deck.

Since their initial encounter, *Furious* and *Island Expedition* had been on a starboard reach, heading to the south and the uninhabited beach upon which Jackson and Pierce would settle their dispute. During the night, *Island Expedition* had purposely fallen some distance behind, to avoid a collision if the fog and mist became too thick. The Gallician frigate had come out of the fog from windward, and had fired its first devastating broadside into the Tritonish frigate from near point-blank range. They paralleled each other, mere yards apart, and made no effort to alter course or maneuver for an advantage. With more sail set now, the schooner forged ahead and rapidly closed with the frigates. "Ready the port battery!"

"Aye aye, sir!"

"Helm, steer as to pass between them!"

"Aye aye, sir!"

"Sure madness, Edward!" warned Hotchkiss.

"But a method to it, Isaac! When I give word, we must put into the wind, and as our guns bear, concentrate fire on the Toad's starboard quarter. Let us then fall off the wind and repeat with the starboard battery."

"Aye!" Hotchkiss nodded with understanding.

Fully awake and alert, his senses at their sharpest, Pierce watched the battling frigates grow larger. The damp night air whipped past, mingled with spray thrown up by *Island Expedition's* hurried dash through the sea. Despite the apprehension in his gut, Pierce felt alive.

"Mr. O'Brien! See that all hands are ready. We shall be making precise and rapid course changes momentarily!"

"Aye, sir."

The gunfire grew louder. It was more constant and incessant now as individual guns aboard the frigates fired faster than others. Pierce could smell the remnants of the noxious smoke as it wafted over the deck. They were close enough that he could make out details of both battling ships. The Gallician frigate was off the starboard bow, and her Tritonish opponent off the port. If the schooner continued on her present course and at her present rate, she would soon be between the two, and in a dangerous and devastating zone from which they would not emerge unscathed. Their arrival had not been noticed by either combatant.

He wanted to get as close as possible before turning and crossing the Gallician's stern. His primary concern at the present was not to get too close and entangle the flying jib boom in the Toad's mizzen rigging. Still, he wanted to be close enough that the risk of fouling would be real.

"Now! Mr. O'Brien! Lee helm! Man the braces!"

The wheel spun, and the schooner nosed into the wind. Pierce watched the bow swing towards and then past the Gallician's stern. Close-hauled, *Island Expedition* sped to windward off the frigate's starboard quarter.

"As your guns bear, Mr. Hotchkiss!"

"Aye aye, sir! Port battery! As your guns bear! Fire!"

In ones and twos, the port battery's guns banged, bucked, and recoiled. Smoke billowed across the deck. Close enough that the frigate presented an ideal target, and with gun captains trained in accurate fire, Pierce was sure that all of the double-shotted guns had found their mark. Splinters flew aboard the Gallician vessel. Several figures on the quarterdeck looked aft with surprise and animated anger.

"Weather helm! Braces! Starboard battery!" Pierce shouted. "Reload port battery!"

With her bows now pointed directly at *Furious*, *Island Expedition* angled across the Gallician's stern. Her starboard battery roared out and sent its destructive wave of shot straight into the frigate's stern and port quarter. Directly before the wind, the schooner crossed astern of the Tritonish frigate. Someone on board, Pierce could not tell who, waved as if to thank them.

"Starboard your helm, Mr. O'Brien. Continue around until we are again on the starboard tack. Then we'll do as before. Port battery, stand by!"

"Aye aye, sir!" Pierce would rather have turned the other way, but they were too close astern of the dueling frigates. By circling away from them, the schooner would have the advantage of sea room and wind direction. Rapidly *Island Expedition* swung north and beyond, now on a port tack, and now with her bows directly into the wind. She passed through the wind and fell off on a starboard tack again. Nearer and nearer she raced, and the Gallician grew ever larger.

But this time there would be no surprise broadside from a vessel the Gallicians were not aware of. They saw the schooner approaching and abruptly turned into the wind, hoping to get a shot at it from their unengaged starboard battery.

Pierce saw the beginning movements of the maneuver and shouted, "Lee helm! Port tack! Fire as you bear!"

*Island Expedition* swung into the wind again, and as she did so, her guns bore fleetingly upon the Gallician. They roared and sent a third broadside into the frigate's stern windows.

The Tritonish had noticed the course change by their opponent as well. They backed topsails, and for a brief moment had the Gallician's stern and port quarter under their guns. At last they were able to fire an unanswered broadside into the enemy frigate.

The Gallician frigate visibly shook and shuddered from the impact of the twin broadsides that thundered into her. Debris and splinters flew high into the air. Lines parted, blocks and smaller pieces of top hamper rained down. With a crack and ripping report heard above the constant din of gun fire, the frigate's main topmast twisted from the vertical. It fell across the waist, shattering the boats stowed on the cross beams. The excess portions of the mast trailed overboard on her port side, hampering the gun crews as they attempted to slew them aft at *Furious*.

*Island Expedition* continued her turn through the wind, and once again headed across the Gallician's stern. At Pierce's order she once again let fly with her double-shotted starboard battery.

"Put us before the wind, Mr. O'Brien!" bellowed Pierce. "Mr. Hotchkiss, a quick check of any damage or injury!"

"Aye aye, sir!" they both acknowledged. Pierce wanted a few moments to allow the guns to be properly served, and for the schooner to regain some momentum. In a few minutes he would reverse course and once again attempt to cross astern of the frigate to inflict two more double-shotted broadsides.

"The Kents are boarding!" said Townsend with misplaced enthusiasm, and a certain degree of action-induced bloodlust.

"Indeed they are, sir!" echoed Dial.

Pierce looked to see that *Furious* had braced around her backed topsails and had pivoted into the wind to come up on the Gallician's relatively unscathed starboard side. Each frigate managed to get off a full broadside as the distance between them narrowed. The gap lessened until they collided with a crash heard aboard the schooner. A mass of men, dark and indistinct, flowed over the lashed-together bulwarks and spilled onto the Gallician's deck. Small arms fire popped, men grunted and screamed. Yells of savage destruction and absolute terror filled the air. Swords, cutlasses, axes, and boarding pikes glistened and flashed in the pale suffused light. Below, on the blood-strewn, hellish gun decks, crews feverishly reloaded, only feet away from their foe doing the same. Firing as guns were loaded, a continuous din of reports and blasts filled the small space existing between the vessels. They were so close that flaming wads expelled from the guns set fire to the enemy's hull. Fearing fire more than the enemy shot, crewmen on each vessel flung buckets of water at the flames sprouting on the hull opposite them.

"Do we make another pass, sir?"

"One more, I would think, Mr. Hotchkiss. Stand by the port battery! Mr. O'Brien, port your helm, and bring us around onto a port tack! After we have fired, continue the starboard turn until we are on a starboard broad reach!"

"Aye aye, sir!"

Once again *Island Expedition* crossed astern of the Gallician frigate and poured her twelve-pounder broadside through the shattered stern. She completed her turn and came back again. This time the six twelve-pounder long guns and the two twelve-pounder carronades of her starboard battery blasted away. Splinters flew as the shot struck home.

"Again, sir?" asked Hotchkiss.

"I think not, sir," answered Pierce. "We do not want to hit any from *Furious* that might be aboard. Mr. O'Brien, heave to if you please! Mr. Morgan, do allow gun crews to stand down momentarily. I hope we have given them the edge they need."

"Aye," agreed Hotchkiss. "I for one am grateful to be here. Glorious, I'm sure, to be aboard with the enemy alongside. But the butcher's bill, sir? Surely it will be excessive aboard either, while we've got one broken leg and some powder burns."

"It is a captain's duty to inflict as much damage as possible on his opponent, while avoiding the same in return," said Pierce, summing up his basic philosophy of battle.

As the British watched warily, standing by to charge in and nip at the Gallician's heels again, the sounds of the cannonade slowed and died away. The din of hand-to-hand combat faded as well. Now there was only the occasional pop of a pistol, the solitary yell of pain, or the rare rasp of metal on metal. In a matter of minutes, all was quiet.

"They've surrendered, sir!" announced Haight, powder monkey at the starboard aft carronade.

"Indeed they have, lad!" said Pierce. He watched as the Gallician tri-color was hauled down. So like the French colors, he thought, the exception being that these were reversed in the order of colors from the hoist to the fly. But what colors flew above the *Island Expedition*? He had thought to ensure colors were hoisted as they had run down on the dueling frigates. A momentary detail had distracted him, and he had never given any orders to that effect. He looked aloft and saw both the Royal Navy's blue ensign and the alternate red, white, and blue stripes of the Independent Lands of Vespica standing out in the moderate breeze.

"I run up both, sir," said Spencer. "No time to ask, and I didn't want any accusations of piracy against us, sir."

"Thank you, Mr. Spencer. Your initiative is noted and appreciated. An oversight on my part, to be sure."

"My duty, sir!"

"Yes," said Pierce.

"*Furious* is hailing, sir!" announced Hadley, sweat-stained and powder-streaked.

With difficulty, Pierce heard the voice amplified by a speaking trumpet. "Can you come alongside? Can you assist?"

"Aye aye!" he replied, using a trumpet from the rack by the helm. "Stand by!" Then he turned to those nearby on the quarterdeck. "Make ready repair and aid parties! Mr. O'Brien, lay us along *Furious'* starboard side!"

It was a weary, bedraggled group that sat in *Furious'* great cabin. The sun had risen, and for once the day had dawned bright and clear. Looking through the stern windows, Pierce saw the Gallician frigate, *Seine,* as Tritonish and some of his own British sailors rigged jury masts. He took a drink of coffee from his cup and shuddered. He was tired, exhausted, and the coffee was old and bitter.

Rollins sat there as well, and sipped at a mug of chocolate. "We did not expect your assistance at all, Captain. I'm sure we would have prevailed."

"I believe so," responded Pierce. "But had you not, how would we have fared with the Toads victorious? I acted to ensure our own safety. You remember, sir, that upon leaving Brunswick, we were pursued with obvious hostile intent by two separate Gallician frigates."

"I am quite aware of that, sir. I do not protest your aid at all. Quite the opposite--I am most grateful for it. I believe you proved to be enough of a distraction that we more easily gained the upper hand. We've still a ghastly butcher's bill, which would have been much higher without your assistance."

"Still, any death or serious injury could be said to be excessive. Such carnage aboard the Gallician!"

"Aye. Her captain passes along his gratitude for the efforts your surgeon made in treating members of his crew. And I as well deeply appreciate the efforts your hands have made in restoring both vessels to somewhat seaworthy conditions."

"You are most welcome. And do pass along to *Seine's* captain that he is most welcome as well," said Pierce. "I am afraid, however, that this engagement complicates and possibly delays our original plans."

"I think not, Captain Pierce," said Dr. Lycoming from the far end of the table. He had been sitting slumped in his chair with his eyes shut, and Pierce had thought him fast asleep. "You have not heard?"

"Heard what, sir?"

"Why in the confusion of battle sir, Captain Jackson left sickbay, came to his cabin, and dressed. He went on deck, cursing and screaming, vilifying you, your schooner, your men, as well as the entire company of this frigate. He took a musket ball to the head and died almost instantly."

Pierce was silent for a long moment. "It seems, gentlemen, that our collective problem is solved. Perhaps contradicting my earlier statement, there is one death that may not be considered excessive."

"Perhaps," said Forbes, *Furious'* second lieutenant. "With judicious wording of the ship's log, we can eliminate the charge of mutiny that would otherwise hang over us. We can record the encounter with you as suggested, and mention his fall. That he came on deck from sickbay and died at the hands of the enemy can only show him to have died a hero."

"Quite so, Mr. Forbes," added Rollins. "Captain Pierce, would you have any other suggestions?"

"Yes, and a question, sir, which might dictate just what advice I pass along."

"Yes?"

"How long since *Furious'* hands have had a run ashore? How long since any of them have had a good day and night of liberty?"

"I don't recall, sir. The captain was very much against such things. He feared the crew would desert en masse."

"I'm sure his fears were well-founded. But if Tritonish seamen are like the British tars I've served with, they will put up with tremendous amounts of ill-use. Put forth the very minimum of trust, they will return it measure for measure.

"Should you have the chance, put in somewhere in Vespica. Allow all hands a good run ashore. Of those that may run, say 'good riddance.' Of those who return, you will have the nucleus of a loyal and well-trained crew. Let those hands that would prove undesirable winnow themselves from the ship's company before a new captain is assigned."

"Something to think about, sir," agreed Rollins.

"Aye," responded several of the others.

"And you, Captain Pierce? What are your plans, now?"

"As they always were, gentlemen; return to Stone Island, take on supplies, and sail for England."

*Chapter Seventeen*

# A Deeper Mystery

"Neither frigate is in condition to sail directly to Kentland," said Rollins. "With all the sick and hurt aboard, and providing a prize crew for *Seine*, I'm stretched beyond limits. Short-handed and with prisoners to guard, my only option is returning to Bostwick. Our embassy can handle the prisoners and perhaps act as prize agent."

"They might also provide additional crew for your return home," said Pierce.

"Aye, they might. But they will surely hold some inquiry into the captain's death. Would it ask too much that you accompany us and testify? Your presence might also ensure the Toads do not attempt to retake their ship."

"It is an honest request sir, and one I do understand, but I'm afraid I must refuse. I am considerably delayed in returning to England. It is my duty to return Governor Smythe to Stone Island, and as soon as possible depart on my homeward journey."

"I truly understand your desire to return home. We are much closer than you, and yet it has been two years since we were last in Kentland. I had thought to insist, to use force to see you accompany us into Bostwick. But I shall not detract from the noble act that you had proposed, or the gallant assistance rendered earlier this morning. I will ask that you write an account of recent events."

"I will, sir. Now, if you will permit me, I'll return aboard and begin."

"By all means," said Rollins. "Do not hurry yourself. There is still a great deal to be done before we can get underway."

"I shall leave Mr. Hotchkiss, along with the repair and assistance parties, aboard if they may be of further help."

"Excellent! Providing Mr. Hotchkiss does not object."

"I will gladly stay a while longer, sir."

"I'll return now and begin my work," said Pierce. "Hopefully two bells in the afternoon watch will have it complete. Naturally you should review it and ensure that it agrees with your understanding of those same events."

"Wise indeed, sir."

Back aboard the schooner, Smythe met Pierce with an anxious and questioning look. "A true battle, it seems, Edward. I can see from here that each took and delivered a fair share of destruction. I pray casualties were not too many."

"Enough, sir! Had we not intervened, there would have been even more."

"And soon we must add you or Jackson to that list?"

"Jackson was killed in the battle. It can be stated that he died, fighting his ship."

"A relief, I'm sure, Edward."

"Indeed! I did not look forward to what I had planned. Had this morning's events not occurred, it was the only option available."

"You are correct, of course."

"Yet," continued Pierce, "his death saddens me. Perhaps I have seen too much of it. Perhaps even such as Lowell Jackson deserve to live out a full life."

"I'm quite certain they do, Edward. Your lament at his passing is understandable."

"But do you excuse me; I have promised Rollins a written statement of the events since our vessels sighted each other."

"I see," said Smythe. "Perhaps I will toy with ideas for dealing with Blondin and daughter upon our return."

"That problem, sir, has not been on my mind for some time."

Pierce went forward and down the forward companion way. "Eubanks! Franklin!" he shouted as he neared the camboose. "How is the coffee?"

"Fresh made, sir. Would you like a cup?" answered Franklin.

"Indeed yes! And if it could be spared, a pot sent along to my cabin. I shall be busy for a while."

"Aye aye, sir."

For the rest of the morning, a morning already growing hot and sticky, Pierce sat in his cabin. He removed his uniform coat, neckerchief, and waistcoat because of the heat. He faced the paper on the writing table, drank cup after cup of fresh hot coffee, and began again and again to describe the past days' events. Finally he decided that he must write it from beginning to end before going back to make corrections. When that was done he could copy it fair, or call upon one of the young gentlemen possessing a fine round hand to do it for him.

Eight bells had struck, ending the forenoon watch, and hands had been piped to dinner when at last he finished. He had written it out smooth himself, and now there wasn't time to allow it to be copied any better than his own hand would allow. "Pass the word for Mr. Steadman, there!" he yelled. The call was repeated, and momentarily a knock came at the stern cabin door.

"Mr. Steadman, sir! You sent for me?"

"Yes, Mr. Steadman. Have you had your dinner yet?"

"Aye, sir."

"Then do a good turn and go aboard *Furious*. Take this and see it is delivered directly to Mr. Rollins."

"Aye aye, sir."

"And you may pass to Mr. Hotchkiss that if his repair parties are far enough along that *Furious* can spare them, he may return them and himself back aboard."

"Aye aye, sir. The letter directly to Mr. Rollins, and Mr. Hotchkiss and repair parties to return aboard."

"If *Furious* can spare them."

"If *Furious* can spare them. Aye aye, sir."

Steadman clattered noisily up the companionway. Normally Pierce would have issued a stern reminder about quiet, but he was far too tired to do so. He sat on the edge of his cot, yawned, and rolled over onto his side. He yawned again, closed his eyes, and in spite of the heat was soon fast asleep.

From habit, he awoke at each sounding of the bell, but each time he promptly fell back asleep. It wasn't until eight bells sounded, ending the afternoon watch, that his nap was disturbed. Immediately after the first dog watch had been set and hands piped to supper, Hotchkiss tapped lightly on his door.

"There is no need to arise, my friend," said Hotchkiss quietly. "I do want to tell you that the frigates are getting underway. Mr. Rollins sends his thanks for your statement. I merely need to know, do you desire we make sail as well, and what course we steer."

"Yes, set what sail you think prudent. Steer for Stone Island, the particular course as you think most appropriate."

"Aye aye, sir." Hotchkiss left and Pierce resumed his slumber.

Two days later, *Island Expedition* thundered along on a port tack. Weather was fair, the seas and wind moderate, and the blue sky unmarred by even a single cloud. With such comfortable weather, members of the wardroom and their guests enjoyed the air following their dinner. As was often his habit, Pierce remained apart from the gathering. He spent his leisure time at the taffrail, idly watching the schooner's wake. "Mind your helm, there!" he shouted as the vessel momentarily wandered off course.

"Aye aye, sir," the helmsman replied. Pierce resumed his quiet gaze and introspection.

"Do I disturb your thoughts, Captain?" asked Mrs. Packingham, joining him at the rail.

"Oh no, ma'am. There is often time enough at sea for one's thoughts. It has always helped me to watch astern."

"I see," she said.

"Perhaps as I watch the ship's wake, I consider recent events."

"Shouldn't one watch ahead, rather than seeing what has already been?"

"But we must understand the past so that we can plan for the future."

"True," she said. Then both were quiet for several minutes. At last she spoke again. "Harold has told me of your original intentions concerning *Furious* and Captain Jackson."

"I'm sure it is general knowledge by now. I truly wish it wasn't."

"I do understand, Edward. Be assured that very few know. He told me only because I strongly insisted. He has told no one else, nor has Isaac."

"That is a comfort, ma'am."

"Yet, you are troubled. Was there some truth to Jackson's charges?"

Pierce looked at her warily, but said nothing.

"Inappropriate to ask, I know," she continued. "Still one does wonder if what you had planned was for your sake or their sake."

He turned away from the taffrail to face her directly. "Vera, understand that any involvement with Mrs. Jackson had naught to do with it. My sole and overriding desire was that a ship's company, brutalized to the point of mutiny, should not suffer the consequences of that mutiny. Were it as he implied, I simply would have avoided him. Yet in his jealousy, he thought to destroy me, even at the expense of this vessel and all in her. You may add to it my wish to protect *Island Expedition* and those who sail in her."

"Would you have rather fought the duel?"

"I don't know. I don't really know." That was all that Pierce would say. He would not tell her of his immense relief upon learning of Jackson's death. Nor would he admit feeling deprived of the satisfaction of directly causing it. As he turned once more to watch the schooner's wake, he wondered if he also mourned for Jackson. If so, it was something he did not want to admit, even to himself.

The next week of the voyage back to Stone Island passed without notable incident. As one day followed another, Pierce's melancholy faded and he once again became a part of shipboard life and society. While his mood certainly changed, his memories of past and planned actions remained, seared into his consciousness. Perhaps, he thought, this was what it meant to gain in wisdom.

Weather had been remarkably fine since *Island Expedition* had parted ways with *Furious* and her prize. Mornings normally had a smattering of low clouds and fog that quickly burned away. The remaining daylight hours usually revealed blue skies and a few white and harmless clouds. The steady westerly wind was moderate, rarely stirring the seas to the point of spouting whitecaps. Under a large cloud of fore and aft sail, the schooner forged through the water on a port tack, certainly into the wind, but not close-hauled in the extreme.

No other ships or vessels had been sighted since the Tritonish frigate and her Gallician prize had sunk below the horizon eight days ago. As two bells into the afternoon watch sounded on Monday the 4th of March, it seemed to Pierce that this day might also pass without any sightings.

Yet as that very thought played in his mind, the lookout shouted from aloft, "Deck there! Sail off the starboard bow!"

"Course?" bellowed Pierce, today taking the duty as officer of the watch in person.

"Close-hauled, starboard tack, sir!"

"Do you make her?" Pierce asked, anxious as to the sighted vessel's identity.

"Too far, sir! Square-rigged!"

It was a description applicable to hundreds if not thousands of vessels, both in this world and the world Pierce knew as home. He was cautious, worried, because it seemed that nearly every unexpected sighting of strange sails resulted in danger or disturbing news. Yet he had a course plotted and a destination to reach. Only if the just-sighted unknown proved hostile would he alter course and seek to escape. Since finding the island nearly two years ago, *Island Expedition* had seen more than her share of combat. Pierce was not in the mood for any more.

"Watch her! Report any changes!" ordered Pierce.

"Aye aye, sir!"

"Company?" said Hotchkiss, just emerging on deck

"It would seem…" responded Pierce. "I've been grateful for the lack of it. Yet that a sail is sighted reassures me that we are not the only vessel upon these waters."

"True. Perhaps this will prove a more amiable meeting than most."

"We can hope, Isaac."

"Do we take precautions, sir? Beat to quarters? Call the watch below?" asked Hotchkiss.

"I don't see a need for it. Should she show hostile intent, we certainly would have time to prepare. It is my intention that we avoid conflict, should it be offered."

"Of course."

Twenty minutes later, the lookout hailed again. "She's backing topsails, sir!"

Pierce and Hotchkiss looked inquiringly at each other. Was there another vessel over the horizon? Did this action by the strange vessel indicate some unknown danger to the British schooner?

"Topsails aback, aye!" Hotchkiss acknowledged the lookout.

Before Pierce or Hotchkiss could speculate on the significance of this action, the man at the masthead hailed again. "She's braced around and back on course!"

"Very well! Maintain your watch!"

"I believe we can relax our guard, sir."

"How so, Isaac?"

"Surely you remember, both from conversation with Cooper and with others, that momentarily backing topsails conveys the message that a vessel has no aggressive intent."

"It would also indicate that she has seen us."

"Aye. And we must answer."

"You are right, of course. Now you may call the watch below. We shall come about, and once settled on the starboard tack, come about and resume our present course."

"Aye aye, sir!"

Each having established that the other harbored no hostile intent, the two vessels quickly closed the distance between them. By now the stranger's canvas was visible from deck. Still hull down, the nearing vessel looked familiar. Her rig was also recognizable to Hotchkiss, because he remarked: "I'd suggest she's *Evening Star*, sir."

"I'm thinking that as well, Isaac. Perhaps Captain Cooper will join us for supper."

"Perhaps," said Hotchkiss.

At that moment, the seaman at the mast head hailed: "Deck there! She's *Evening Star*, sir. And what she's signaling, sir!"

"Thank you Folsum!" said Pierce. He glanced at Hotchkiss, grinned, and nodded. Then he turned to Hadley, the midshipman of the watch. "Aloft with you, sir! Take a glass and the signal book. See what you make of her signals!"

"Aye aye, sir!"

That evening proved Pierce correct, in that Cooper did join them for a meal, wine, and conversation. The merchant captain had first suggested they gather aboard *Evening Star*, as there would be more room in her larger cabin. That idea was quickly shelved when Pierce mentioned Mrs. Packingham's presence aboard the schooner, and her hand in preparing the meal. Having often dined at the Colony Building, Randolph Cooper had quickly decided to play the guest, rather than the host.

The two vessels were hove to, only yards apart, and small boats plied the waters between them as crews visited the other. Having shared adjacent spots along the quay following *Island Expedition's* return to Stone Island, the people of each vessel had come to know, and had often befriended or aided those of the other. While the hands traded stories, tobacco, and secreted spirit rations, the officers did much the same. If the decorum and civility in the cabin were at a higher level, the spirit of relaxation and friendship was much the same. Laughter spilled forth from the schooner's stern windows, just as it did from her deck and the deck of the nearby merchant ship.

Pierce had initially been opposed to crews visiting ship to ship. As the evening wore on, he saw that the change in routine benefited the hands. Now that the supper had been consumed, and as a bottle of wine was passed around the table, he noted that having company aboard affected him as well. His lingering despondency over recent events abated further, and he told several of what he thought to be clever and amusing anecdotes. He chuckled heartily at those tales related by others, although Mrs. Packingham's presence prevented many from becoming too lewd, vulgar, or being told at all. Even when the conversation turned to more serious matters, Pierce's spirit maintained a rare light-hearted edge.

"I trust Dr. Robertson told you of public reaction to the Gallician pursuit you experienced?" asked Cooper.

"He did," replied Smythe.

"In return, we informed him of finding certain measures which had been taken to hinder our flight," Pierce observed.

"I'm not sure I understand."

"When this vessel was in dry dock," said Pierce, "we inspected the very bottom of the keel. We found evidence of small sea anchors or other drag-inducing items having been secured there. Intended, I believe, to slightly lower our speed, and as those particular frigates are reputedly the fastest in the Gallician fleet...."

"Which set the odds more to their advantage!" exclaimed Hotchkiss. "It is the 'why' of it that I still do not fathom."

"Nor I," said Smythe. "From what we understand, such action would have availed them nothing, even had they been successful."

"As the average man understands the superstitions, dear sir," said Cooper. "Since departing Stone Island, I have made several short voyages along the Vespican coast. On one I had a passenger, a somewhat clumsy scholar claiming knowledge in antiquities and ancient history. Professor Parks is unusual enough that he cannot be anything but as he said."

"I'm sure it made for interesting discussions at table," remarked Mrs. Packingham.

"Indeed, ma'am."

"But how does he relate to the Gallician actions, sir?" asked Andrews.

"On the second day of our trip--it was only a three-day voyage, you see--he asks if I've heard of the chase. I told him that in fact I had delivered the news to the Vespican mainland, having heard of it directly from Captain Pierce.

"Then he nods knowingly and says it may not have been the Gallicians after all. Of course I'm taken aback and ask him his meaning. I inform him you had seen both frigates in Brunswick and that they were surely Gallician. But he says that even if they were Gallician, their orders did not necessarily come from the Ministry of Marine."

"Nicholas B. himself? Directives from their embassy or consulate?" asked Smythe. "Were the frigates in special service to the highest levels of government?"

"That crossed my mind as well. He rejected the notion, although he did allow some highly placed persons to have had a hand in it."

"Beg pardon, sir, but this is becoming tremendously confusing!" Morgan looked exasperated.

"No doubt. Do understand that I was perplexed as well, and for that matter I still am. He did offer an explanation, couched in scholarly discourse and with such obscure references that it made little sense."

"Could you elaborate, Captain?" insisted Pierce. "We should all be as confused."

"Of course, sir. I realize that excepting the dear lady and me, the legends and superstitions concerning Stone Island are new to you."

"But it was Mr. Smythe's knowledge of them that allowed us to find it," objected Townsend.

"But those were legends of the island, centuries old, as told in your world, lad. True, they led you here, but I refer to more recent stories. Stories of what caused it to remain uninhabited after Baltican explorers first discovered it."

"I have surmised that much of it resulted from Original Peoples' actions, rather than any natural or supernatural cause," commented Smythe.

"I had the same impression," said Pierce, "even as we initially spoke with Shostolamie."

"Before we left Brunswick, I believe Captain Newbury suggested the same thing," added Hotchkiss. "He commented that Baltican powers are starting to see the constraints regarding the island as superstition. Events that occurred two hundred or three hundred years ago may no longer protect it."

"Many have realized that for years, Mr. Hotchkiss. But why has no Baltican power opted to occupy and utilize Stone Island? Are there other legends that are not general knowledge? Is there something else that curbs such ambition?"

"Magic? The supernatural? Heaven or hell, themselves?" asked O'Brien.

"I think not," considered Pierce. "Other than unusual phenomena experienced journeying to this world, nothing here appears to be un-natural or unexplainable."

"True! Quite true," allowed the master, who slowly nodded his head in agreement.

"I've heard the stories of failed settlements all my life. Upon my word, sir, I've not been told anything else." Mrs. Packingham fanned herself against the evening's heat.

Cooper continued. "As best I remember, that was Professor Parks' precise point. Are the stories and legends we are familiar with, all there is? What we know concerns the island since its discovery by Cordoban explorers, early in the sixteenth century. We know nothing of it before that time."

"Surely you could not be expected to know," observed Andrews as he helped himself to another glass of Marsala.

"Indeed," added Hotchkiss. "In like fashion, we know so little of the Americas prior to Columbus."

"Most understandable, in both cases, I would say," commented Smythe. The others nodded in agreement.

"Yet nothing has been clarified for us. How does this supposition relate to our being pursued across the sea by two Gallician frigates?" Pierce asked.

"Upon Cordoban discovery, Vespica was well-populated with those we call Original Peoples. Many in Central and North Vespica had highly developed and advanced civilizations. They were conquered and destroyed, of course. When Stone Island was discovered, it evidenced the same degree of advancement, even though it was much farther south than any comparable site on the Vespican mainland. Furthermore, it was devoid of people, apparently abandoned years or even centuries earlier."

"So far, Captain Cooper, you are not relating anything new. Everyone knows the island was deserted when de Vargas found it," complained Mrs. Packingham.

"But we must remember, ma'am, that these gentlemen do not know what we understand to be common knowledge."

"Yes, of course. Forgive me?"

"Certainly," said Cooper before continuing.

"General opinion, my friends, is that the more advanced Vespican civilizations originated on the island. For reasons unknown, those Original Peoples abandoned it and migrated to Vespica itself. Those whom Shostolamie and others call the Ancient Ones are conventionally thought of as the immediate ancestors of the Original Peoples."

"I assume that we are still in the realm of common knowledge?" asked Morgan.

"Yes," answered Mrs. Packingham.

"After the island was discovered, gold, silver, and many other riches were found. Several attempts to colonize and exploit its treasures were undertaken. It's believed that then the Original Peoples took many surreptitious and stealthy actions to cause the Balticans to abandon the island. Later stories and continuing interactions helped formulate the *rules* that dictate how we regard the island." Cooper drank the remaining wine in his glass, set it on the table, and pushed it away.

"In our short time here, we have arrived at much the same conclusion," said Smythe.

"I'm sure you have, Governor," said Cooper.

"I must ask, sir, just where is this leading?"

"I hope to get to the heart of Parks' argument shortly," apologized Cooper. "I want us all on the same course before the professor's reasoning leads us away from it."

"Understandable," said Pierce quietly.

"While nearly all believe the Ancient Ones to be the ancestors of the Original Peoples, Parks insists they existed much, much earlier in pre-history. He believes Original Peoples did occupy the island for a while, and that it is largely the ruins of their presence that we see today. Yet, he says, do you dig deeper; you will find traces of a much older civilization--one so ancient that it is not only the forerunners of the Original Peoples, but the progenitors of us all."

"If that is the case," said O'Brien, "I wonder, does Shostolamie understand just how ancient the Ancient Ones are?"

"He may not even consider them to be real. They may be more like gods to him," offered Smythe. "And I wonder as well if he has ever considered the true level of their advancement and knowledge."

"I am amazed, Harold," said Mrs. Packingham with surprise and spirit. "Until moments ago we saw the Ancient Ones only as the Original Peoples' ancestors. Now you assert some new knowledge of them and the state of their civilization!"

"I do not claim any great knowledge, my dear," said Smythe. "Yet, having found the dry dock, I have wondered if in our world, could the Mayans, the Incans, or the Aztecs have constructed such a monumental work? I would compare them with the more advanced Original Peoples, and doubt seriously they could have engineered it."

"When I told him of it, Parks thought it unlikely as well, Governor. While he believes they had the skills to build it, he doubts they ever needed it. 'More evidence,' he said, 'of the true Ancient Ones.'"

"I thought the inscriptions looked a bit odd, sir," added Townsend. "I mean those at the dry dock, opposed to what we've found elsewhere."

"Yes, there was a difference, but I paid it no mind, considering the nature of where the marks were found." Smythe thought for a moment. "I would like to be able to read them someday."

"I understand that many learned individuals have puzzled over various ancient writings for years." Cooper emptied his glass and set it on the table with a move of finality. "Professor Parks admits that they have concentrated more on that left by the Akhargians and other ancient civilizations in the Near West."

"If I may be so bold, sir, this is all quite interesting," said Morgan. "Yet it does not explain that the Gallicians were not responsible for their frigates giving us chase."

"You are so right, Mr. Morgan." Cooper's glass had been refilled, and he drank lightly from it. "It would take the rest of the night," he said, raising his glass in salute, "to follow in detail the course of the professor's reasoning. Simply put, he understands the Ancient Ones to have pre-dated other early civilizations. He says that obscure and little-remembered legends attribute them with great magic, perhaps knowledge and technologies beyond what we possess today. He thinks some believe that knowledge exists on Stone Island."

"And we dig ourselves even deeper into a world of superstition and magic," groused Andrews.

"But would you have considered the possibility of this world, Mr. Andrews, when we were blockading France in *Theadora*? Would Vespica, Grand Triton, or Gallicia have meant anything to you then?"

"Aye, I do see the point, sir. Still, I do not understand how all this relates to the chase."

"According to Professor Parks, it is quite simple," said Cooper. "He believes there are groups seeking that ancient knowledge, just as others work to keep it hidden."

"You suggest, sir, that one or more of these groups may be behind the Gallician pursuit?" questioned Hotchkiss.

"I don't suggest it, sir. Professor Parks suggests it, and truth be told, by the time he reached that point, we had drained more than a few bottles."

Smythe grinned somewhat sheepishly. "Perhaps the good captain has taken us all on a voyage outside of reality. Indeed, Captain, was there ever a Professor Parks aboard *Evening Star*?"

"Whether the professor exists or not, sir," said O'Brien, "It's a damned good tale, at that!"

"Hear! Hear!" said Pierce. "A toast to the professor! Does he not exist, than a toast to Captain Cooper for the most delightful invention of him!"

After the toast was drunk, and after the laughter died away, the merchant captain regained his composure. "My friends! I understand your amusement and lack of belief. Yet, Professor Parks is real as any of us. In fact, I have a letter for you, Governor, from him." Cooper reached into his pocket, withdrew the letter, and handed it to Smythe.

"As he traveled aboard *Evening Star*, he was en route to study ancient ruins recently found in Western Baltica. He expressed a great desire to one day go to Stone Island to study any remaining artifacts first hand. He is a rather quaint fellow who would not visit without first asking your blessings on his presence. Such, as I understand it, is the purpose of the letter."

"Do forgive us, Captain Cooper. I shall look forward to a visit from the learned gentleman," said Smythe. "In fact, sir, as you are accompanying us to Stone Island, I will draw up a letter for the professor, which you may deliver or send on to him."

"Excellent! I would be delighted to transport any correspondence for either of you," mentioned Cooper. He saw the expectant look on Morgan's face. "Indeed, I would delight in acting as courier for any and all of you."

## Chapter Eighteen

# Final Departure

Sunday, the 10th of March, found both vessels again moored along the ancient stone quay. Another Vespican merchant ship was there as well, having transported more settlers to the newest Independent Land. Of course, *Island Expedition* was returning to her current home port, bringing Stone Island's leaders from recent momentous events in Bostwick. *Evening Star* had sailed in consort with the schooner for the past week and bore a small but well-received cargo of woolen goods, cotton cloth, and leather for shoes and boots.

While Captain Cooper had visited aboard the schooner, and the respective crews had interacted upon the vessels' first meeting, Pierce was in enough of a hurry that subsequent social interactions had been few and far between. Most communication between them was by signal flags or speaking trumpets. Pierce's driving ambition had been to return as quickly as possible to Stone Island and when ready, depart for England.

That Sunday afternoon, his first thought was to begin preparing the schooner for the long voyage home. But he was a practical man and knew very little would be accomplished in what remained of the day. Since it was Sunday, a day of rest, Pierce granted liberty to all but the most essential hands. The largest part of the liberty party headed for the meadow south of the settlement. A challenge had been issued and accepted upon meeting with *Evening Star*, and that afternoon, the two crews were competing in a spirited game of keggers. For those remaining aboard, he declared rope yarn Sunday, granting them as much of a day off as could reasonably be had. Come Monday morning, these would be the ones without throbbing heads and churning guts.

Nonetheless, all hands would work more diligently following a day of relaxation.

As Harold Smythe, now officially Governor of Stone Island, prepared to go ashore, he turned to Pierce and said, "I'm not sure I understand all that Cooper has suggested about the island. Still, I go ashore with more reverence for the place we now call home."

"I sense it as well, sir," answered Pierce. "I would enjoy being here when Professor Parks visits. To hear his ideas and theories directly might prove most interesting."

"Quite so. You will see that my letter to him is sent aboard *Evening Star?*"

"Of course, sir. Tom also has four letters to Cecilia that I must pass to Cooper. He sails within the week, so anyone wishing to correspond with the mainland should avail himself of this opportunity."

"Word will get around, Edward, so you needn't worry. As you've noticed, we do have regular calls by various vessels these days. If a letter doesn't get aboard a particular ship, another will be along that can take it."

Pierce, Hotchkiss, Morgan, and Spencer dined at the Colony Building that evening. In spite of Smythe's protests and insistence that she rest from the journey, Mrs. Packingham took to her kitchen and prepared a simple but satisfying meal. Pierce was surprised that Cooper didn't join them, but he understood the merchant captain to be absent due to requirements aboard his vessel. However, they were joined by Mally and Talbot, who had been left in charge during Smythe's absence.

Quite naturally, their curiosity about the trip overshadowed questions about life on the island during the past weeks. It was well into the second glass of after-dinner wine before Smythe had a chance to query them.

"Thankfully, sir, we had no occurrences worth noting."

"A relief, I must say," sighed Smythe. "The Blondins?"

"The bloke has recovered from his injuries. Thought to set him at liberty, but wondered about his temper. Worried about the girl," said Mally.

"It occurred to us that he might do her harm, as she's the one that put the pistol ball into him."

"Some problems never go away, do they, sir?" mentioned Pierce.

"Unfortunately, no. But I did have time to reflect during our homeward voyage, and have a solution in mind."

"May I ask what?" asked Talbot.

"You may ask, sir," responded Smythe. "However I am not prepared to put forth the full details of my ideas. At the very least, we must try each of them. It must be a dignified occasion in which we establish justice and impose realistic but fair penalties upon any transgressors."

"If it is truly a fair trial, either or both could be found innocent," suggested Hotchkiss.

"That is always a possibility," said Smythe. "I would welcome such a verdict."

"Even if he did shoot my crewman?" said Pierce. "I think we all know he did just that!"

"And we all know she shot her father in retaliation. The fairness of our budding justice system is more important than retribution. We must firmly establish that all will be granted due process."

"You are correct, of course, sir," said Pierce. "I have been under naval discipline too long. It is certainly more direct and practical, but it does not always consider the rights of the accused."

"As we've discussed before, Edward," replied Smythe.

"May I ask, sir, what is an offense, and what is not?" asked Spencer from the far end of the table. "Certain things we all understand. Blondin shoots Folsum, and Miss Blondin shoots him? There's no question that chargeable offenses occurred. But what tells us what is or isn't a violation?"

"I'm not sure I understand, Mr. Spencer," remarked Talbot, reaching for a slice of cheese.

"I mean, sir, what's to stop a fellow from laying charges against someone for spite?"

"I still don't...."

"Perchance, what Mr. Spencer means," explained Morgan, "is that aboard ship we have the Articles of War and other King's Regulations that spell out what is acceptable or not. They also specify certain punishments for particular acts."

Talbot nodded with understanding, as did the others at the table.

"I believe what these young gentlemen imply, sir, is that this colony currently has no law beyond common sense. As the colony grows, common sense will surely fade in importance."

"Believe me, Mr. Hotchkiss," Smythe said, "I have realized that shortcoming for some time. We need a written code of law, not only for practical aspects, but because it is required of us as one of the Lands of Vespica. As I understand it to be in the United States, laws must be written. They must be *on the books*, so to speak. Tradition and unwritten precedence do not count. Am I correct, Captain?"

"No doubt you ask because of my interest in the American system. I believe what you say is true. I am less familiar with any such requirements in the Independent Lands."

"No one expects that you would be, Captain," added Mally.

"It is my intention, gentlemen, once the excitement of annexation and *Island Expedition's* departure die down, to begin work on a code of law for us all." Smythe continued. "Various members of the joint council were most generous in sharing with me copies of the charters and by-laws of their respective lands. Hopefully from those and my own knowledge of various legal systems, I will arrive at a system that is fair to all."

"Might I suggest, sir," said Pierce, "that you consider the Constitution of the United States as an example? I have always found it to be a very profound and yet practical document. As a loyal and true Englishman, I hate to say it, but the Jonathans may have surpassed us."

"I have had a copy for years, Edward. I would not consider such an undertaking without reference to it."

"But to return to the more immediate question, gentlemen," said Morgan. "May I ask when the Blondins shall answer for their offenses?"

"With what I have in mind, Mr. Morgan, perhaps it could be done tomorrow. That is, if your captain can spare himself and Folsum for the afternoon. I would need both as witnesses in the case."

"I will see to it that Folsum appears, sir," said Pierce. "And I will attend as well. Should you require any other officers or crewmen from *Island Expedition*; I can assure you of their presence."

"No, I think you and young Folsum will suffice. Do we need anyone else, it will not be difficult to fetch them."

"True, enough, sir."

Monday afternoon's trials, if indeed they could be called such, were proceedings carried out in a simple and yet dignified manner. Smythe, acting as judge, dressed in his finest. Pierce was in full dress, uncomfortable in the heat, and Folsum twitched nervously in his best shore-going rig. The Blondins, father and daughter, were scrubbed, combed, and in Jacob's case, freshly shaven, while attired in their Sunday best. As the small group assembled, Pierce noticed sly and apparently affectionate glances between Abigail and Tim Folsum. He also observed the girl's father looking at the two with obvious distaste.

The affair was conducted in one of the public rooms towards the front of the Colony Building. While they were in effect, public trials, Smythe had decided the night before that it would not be in the best interests of those concerned if the proceedings were public entertainment. Thus, only those directly involved with the operation of the eleventh Independent Land of Vespica were present. Smythe had kept his planned solution secret, and Pierce had no idea of what the colony's governor would do to see justice served.

When four bells sounded aboard the schooner, Smythe opened the proceedings by saying, "We shall begin!"

The room became silent and all eyes focused on Smythe. "Our duty today, good people, is to dispense justice--justice tempered with understanding and mercy. We are all aware that offenses occurred, and we are well aware of the causes. To begin, I shall ask each of those charged, how they plead.

"Jacob Blondin, you are charged with assault, in that you did purposely shoot one Timothy Folsum, able seaman in the schooner *Island Expedition*. Do you plead guilty or not guilty to these charges? Do you plead guilty; tell us why you undertook such action."

"Guilty, sir! He was getting too friendly with my child. It was to save her honor, sir." Blondin glared at Folsum.

"We note that you have pled guilty. But before any sentence is pronounced, I will ask the victim of your crime if he prefers that the charge against you remain in place.

"Able Seaman Timothy Folsum, do you wish to see charges remain and punishment meted out to Jacob Blondin?"

Folsum stood nervously, his hat in his hands. He looked quickly at Abigail. "No, the charges need not remain."

"Very well," said Smythe. "I shall consider your generosity.

"And Miss Blondin, you are aware that you face the same charge, in that you did purposely shoot and seriously wound your own father. Again I ask how you plead and for your reasons, should you plead guilty. Miss Blondin?"

"Aye, guilty, sir! It was only on account of him shooting Tim. Able Seaman Folsum, sir," she said in a quiet and yet defiant voice.

"Jacob Blondin, would you prefer that charges be maintained against her?"

"No, sir."

"This is as I have hoped, my friends," said Smythe. "From my time aboard *Island Expedition*, I know Able Seaman Timothy Folsum is a young man of honesty and integrity. Should you doubt that, I believe his captain will say much the same about him." Smythe looked questioningly at Pierce.

Pierce nodded in agreement, saying, "Aye, he is an excellent hand, sir, well-regarded and respected by officers and shipmates."

"It is generous of him to discard charges against Jacob Blondin. In like fashion, it is very noble of that individual to insist we do not charge Miss Blondin.

"Yet, of those crimes charged, the perpetrators have both admitted their guilt, and we are all aware that the offenses occurred. We cannot, for the sake of true justice, allow those offenses to go unpunished. At the same time, we must fully consider the circumstances and the persons involved. We will not order penalties in the spirit of revenge or retribution, but rather to guide wrong-doers and establish peace between our citizens."

"Ya mean I must let this young sailor-man be around and always at my daughter?" asked Blondin. He glared threateningly at Folsum.

"We sail in two weeks or less, Mr. Blondin," Pierce said.

"Until that time, sir, she is forbidden to see him," Smythe continued. "And you, Mr. Blondin, are directed to avoid him as well. To be restrained from others' presence for a short number of days is hardly a penalty to consider. Therefore, Mr. Blondin, you are directed to report tomorrow morning to Mr. Fitch and the land-clearing crew. One half of your pay will be forfeit to the Land over the next twelve months.

"Miss Blondin, in the morning you will return here to aide Mrs. Packingham in her duties as housekeeper. As with your father, you will forfeit one half of your pay for the next year. Does either of you wish to make a statement?"

"But may I see him for just a moment, sir?" questioned Abigail Blondin. "Just one moment before...."

"I'd as soon not, sir," declared Folsum, directing his words towards Pierce. "I'm leaving soon, and she just ain't worth getting shot!"

"Sensible lad at that," said Blondin quietly.

His daughter's distress peaked. Her expression lost all trace of hope and tenderness. She glared icily at the British seaman. "So be it, Timothy Folsum! You've missed your chance. May I go now?" she asked Smythe.

"A change of heart, Folsum?" asked Pierce as the seaman accompanied him back to the *Island Expedition*.

"More a practical matter, sir. What had we been allowed a final meeting, the blood would be running hot again. Maybe I wouldn't have let her stay away. Maybe she wouldn't have tried. Then it'd be the same trouble all over again, sir."

"Yes, quite sensible, lad. And with our impending departure...."

"Two to a hammock just ain't worth the trouble, sir."

Folsum was right, Pierce thought. While many men might relish the challenge of an overprotective father or an insanely jealous husband, were a few intimate moments really worth it? Was Folsum a stronger man and better able to resist temptation than he was? Pierce remembered that evening at the Mercers' and the overpowering seductiveness of Leona Jackson. He should have been stronger that night and stood by his initial decision to resist the pleasures she so boldly offered.

After all, rumors of their affair had reached her husband, and his jealousy had not only threatened Pierce's life, but the well-being of two ships' companies. In the end, it had cost Lowell Jackson, as despicable a person as he was in Pierce's estimation, his own life. Despite the fact that he and the girl's father had both been shot, Folsum had managed to disentangle himself from a potentially dangerous relationship.

Aboard the schooner, Pierce checked briefly with the officer of the watch and then went below to his cabin. Folsum, a member of the watch on deck, and ashore only by his captain's request, went forward to join his messmates. Pierce wondered briefly just what the young seaman would tell his friends about the day's proceedings. By the next day, he supposed, the tale would be that he had spurned her advances, and that the lass had clung to him bodily, even as he left the Colony Building. By the time they sailed, the story would have Folsum as a hero amongst his shipmates.

Now however, Pierce had something to do. He had thought of it often in the last days of the voyage back to Stone Island. Yet he had not been able to sufficiently organize his thoughts and emotions to be able to write the letter that he must write. The day's events, and the thoughts they had brought forth within him, emphasized that he must now take pen in hand and write a letter of condolence to Leona Jackson.

He had a difficult time writing that letter. While she often seemed to dismiss Captain Jackson as an annoyance in her life, Pierce did not know her true feelings for the man. Had she truly loved him? Did he have some emotional hold over her? Had there been a bond that even their lustful wanderings could not break? He did not want to trod unbidden into such territory. He also had to assess his own feelings. For him, their relationship had primarily been a matter of physical attraction and availability. At times he remembered her with affection, and at times near loathing, especially in light of the trouble their relationship had eventually caused.

He could not tell her that he had conspired to be the agent of her husband's death. Yet the letter had to be written, and written in such a way as to convey his truest sympathies for her loss, and not mention his intention of causing it, or his overall sense of relief at what had finally occurred.

Shortly after four bells sounded in the evening watch, Pierce finished the letter and signed his name at the bottom. He sanded it, folded it, and with a weary cramped hand addressed it. He laid it aside, ready to take aboard *Evening Star* the next day. Then he went forward for a somewhat fresh cup of coffee at the camboose.

As he returned to his cabin, Pierce knew that the night would be one of little sleep for him. The coffee he carried with him, and the three cups he had consumed while writing the letter, would not be the cause of his wakefulness. No, it would be that in writing his condolences and sending them on to Mrs. Jackson, he had started to think of Evangeline again. That was always a dangerous thing to do, as it caused interference with his required and desired rest. He sat for a while in the dim glow of a single candle, hoping his mind would relax and drift away from thoughts of her. If it did, and if he could keep it from returning to that subject, perhaps he could eventually fall asleep.

Every time he realized that he had quit thinking of her, and every time he felt ready to drift into slumber, doing so would bring Evangeline to the forefront of his memory, and once again he would be wide awake. Perhaps it wasn't such a bad idea to think of her at times. After all, in a week's time he would be departing Stone Island, en route to his world and her. With this thought, and the realization that sleep would elude him that night, Pierce slipped on his shoes, pinched out the candle, and went on deck.

If it had been entirely up to him, Pierce would have departed the next day. He was sure *Island Expedition* was in satisfactory repair and would make the voyage without difficulty. Yet the next few days could be spent in optimizing the seaworthiness of the schooner and topping off stores and fresh water. With his mind on water, he recalled the treatment that Dr. Robertson had made to the casks some months earlier, recalling that as of late the water still in those casks tasted much fresher than could normally be expected.

Aside from the matter of provisions, with which they were already sufficiently stocked to reasonably expect them to reach England, there was the matter of the route home. Smythe had explained many weeks ago that it was not a matter of simply reversing their course through the five plotted positions that had brought them to this world. The way back to the world they remembered also passed through five precise locations, but they were situated differently and required a different route through them. Smythe was still working on the details of that passage. Finally, Smythe completed his calculations. With that information in hand, *Island Expedition* sailed with the morning tide on March 20th. Stone Island was lost to sight by the end of the afternoon watch, and Pierce set course for the first of five positions that they would need to pass through with great precision. As he had on the outward voyage, Pierce insisted that all of the schooner's officers actively involve themselves with navigation. Everyone calculated the daily fix and compared results, the idea being one of checking, re-checking, and cross-checking the others' work. The ultimate goal was to be as accurate as possible and ensure they crossed those sites as precisely as possible.

To him, these spots on the charts were just that: spots over which they had to pass in order to voyage back into the Indian Ocean and eventually to England. He saw it as much the same as navigating a tricky passage amongst the rocks and shoals of any of a number of dangerous coasts. But as they approached the first of the locations, he noticed a great deal of apprehension in many of the crew.

On that particular evening, having reconciled the results of the day's individual navigational efforts, Pierce stood idly at the taffrail, watching the schooner's slightly luminous wake. Hotchkiss joined him, bringing his captain a glass of madeira. "A change from coffee, Edward," he said quietly.

"Thank you. Perhaps I am overdone with that brew. A good bottle, this. If it or its brothers lasts awhile, I'll not be disappointed."

"Nor I. Yet I believe only two more exist in our stores. But we do have several bottles of this world's equivalent. Some of it is quite excellent."

"Of course, Isaac, there is always the stock of rum. It would not be the first time that we have shared that sea-going elixir with the hands."

"Indeed not, sir. And speaking of the hands, have you noticed a certain wariness growing around some as of late?"

"Aye. I've puzzled over it the past few days, wondering at times if I was the only one who noticed it. But, my friend, you have seen it too, and once again proven your worth as first lieutenant."

"I waited until I was certain of it, before bringing it to your attention. I believe that as first lieutenant, it is also my duty to screen such matters, lest they distract you."

"Prudent, Isaac," said Pierce. "Still, I would know the cause of this unease. You haven't an idea of it, I'm sure."

"Not that I could conclusively state...."

"But you do have an idea...."

"Aye."

"Then shall we hear it?"

"Quite honestly, Edward, I've been feeling it as well. You remember on our voyage here, that when we crossed the first point, I became quite upset?"

"Yes."

"Now, I am experiencing much that same feeling. Not to the point of panic, but more as a dread for what we are to experience shortly. We successfully made it through all the points on our voyage here. Were we lucky? Is it as simple and straightforward a process as we make it out to be? What are the limits we must be adhere to as we cross those spots? What if we stray beyond those limits? What then, Edward."

"I don't know, my friend. Let us hope we do not find out. But I thank you for your admission and your insight. Perhaps I am in such all-fired haste to be home that I haven't considered all the perils of the voyage. Many of the hands must be feeling the same apprehension that you are. With another day or so before the first crossing, let us make tomorrow make and mend. Give the hands time to relax and contemplate a little. I will try to say something encouraging."

"Aye, and perhaps an extra ration of grog will bolster their spirits as well," added Hotchkiss. "It has aided me greatly, just to talk of it."

Despite the nervousness felt by Hotchkiss and many of the hands, passing through the particular points was the same as it had been on the outward journey. Pierce again had feelings of timelessness or of belonging to all eternity. Hotchkiss once more witnessed the schooner voyaging amongst the stars. Others envisioned the vessel becalmed and beset by gale force winds at the same time. The helmsman, whoever it happened to be at that particular time, also noticed the compass needle swinging wildly, as if lost and desperately searching for north. In addition, the next day's noon sighting often showed them to have journeyed farther than possible since the last sighting.

Pierce and his officers continually strove to be as accurate as possible in their navigation. As they sailed from point to point, they noticed their track often took them miles inland of the supposed shorelines. Now equipped with maps of both worlds, it appeared that they often passed directly over what should have been dry land in both.

On the 22nd of May, land was sighted, and a noon sighting confirmed their location. The land was determined to be the southwestern corner of New Holland.

Pierce smiled and said, "In a way, Mr. Hotchkiss, we are home!"

"I'm just so damned glad to be back in the real world."

"But which is the real world? Here, where we have lived since birth, or there, where we left Smythe and our friends? It seemed quite substantial to me."

"I suppose, Edward, that both are real. It is more a matter of familiarity. I'd think that the *unreal world* might be the one from which we have just emerged, the world where all is water and we sail directly over lands we know exist. Perhaps the world between the two is what is unreal," Hotchkiss theorized.

"You may be right, friend. It is strange that no matter what our track shows, we have never seen any land between the first and the fifth location. Could that world be nothing but sea?"

"Someday we may find out."

"Perhaps. But now, Mr. Hotchkiss, if you would ask the bo'sun's mate to pipe 'up spirits,' I believe the hands would celebrate our return."

"Aye aye, sir! I would celebrate it as well, Edward!"

Following the extra issue of grog, they stood off to the southeast and gradually altered course to run east before the west winds, and on the last day of the month, rounded the southern end of Tasmania. June 5th found them at Sydney Harbor and Pierce going ashore to meet with the governor.

## Chapter Nineteen
# A Perilous Voyage

**P**ierce sat for a long time in the governor's outer office. Because it was now well into the southern winter, and mild at this latitude, a fire burned on the grate. The room was hot, and sweat trickled down his back and pooled on his abdomen. His full dress uniform was damp, and he felt the carefully prepared crispness of his neckerchief disintegrating as perspiration steadily soaked into it. At long last the governor's secretary rose and nodded. Pierce stepped into the inner office.

Phillip King simply said, "About damn time, Pierce! I was thinking that you had floundered!"

"To the contrary, sir," Pierce answered politely. "As can be seen."

"And the transported convicts?"

"On the island, sir, with Mr. Smythe."

"Oh come, come, my dear, sir. That tale of a legendary island is true? What do you take me for, sir?"

"I was quite skeptical until I saw it, until I was actually there. Indeed, there is more to the world than we see or know."

Captain King, Governor of the Botany Bay Colony, snorted in disbelief. "No doubt you've set them ashore somewhere to fend for themselves. A most callous act, if I do say so. I understood you would make a cursory search for the island to humor Smythe, and then bring the convicts here."

"If such was intended for me to fulfill my commission, sir, it was never passed to me. Quite naturally, I doubted the island's existence. Had we not found it, we would have arrived some two years ago, along with the transported convicts."

"And what's this nonsense, Pierce, here in your report? Combat with a sloop-of-war? Reversed colors in the Union Flag? New nations? New lands?" King gazed steadily at Pierce, his eyes full of amazement as well as condemnation. "Detained? Most improper, sir! And most improper, accepting so-called citizenship from another nation."

"A nation you believe does not exist. But if it does, they offered it as a means of obtaining our liberty. If it exists, and should I find myself there again, I will consider myself a citizen of that nation. Here, I am, as I have always been, a loyal subject of His Britannic Majesty."

"My God, Pierce! Such admissions might be construed as treason. It is due only to particular orders I have regarding your voyage that I do not immediately place you under arrest. Yet I wonder if someone else should command *Island Expedition* upon her return to England."

"I see no need for that, sir." Pierce was now warmer than he had been while waiting.

"Seriously Commander, I wonder about your health. It may be that the strain of command and a long voyage are too much for you."

"It would seem, sir, that the entire ship's company is afflicted as well."

"How so?" Phillip King raised a critical eyebrow.

"Every one of them can and will back what is documented in the report."

"Coerced? Promised something in return, no doubt? You certainly seem a conniving sort."

"Indeed not, sir. What would any of us have to gain, formulating such stories?"

"I would not hazard a guess."

"But I do agree that the story is beyond the bounds of believability."

"You do?"

"With certainty, sir," Pierce answered. "It is only because it is so unbelievable that I insist it is true. Someone in the highest levels of government must have believed even a little of the possibility. Else, why did the mission take place?"

"I would think," King responded, "that perhaps there are some in government whose sensibilities might be questioned. Beyond that, it no doubt proceeded on two levels. In a practical move, the first was to cause the Frogs wasted efforts searching for the island.

Hopefully they would have diverted ships away from European waters, and perhaps would have tipped their hand regarding resumption of the war."

"A possibility I was instructed to watch for."

"Secondly, it was to quietly get rid of Smythe. He was a distraction and a real bother to many in His Majesty's Government. Allowing the voyage satisfied all factions."

"But what of the freedom colony, sir? Other than verifying the island's existence, was that not that the prime reason for the journey? What about the transportation of convicts determined to have been unjustly accused or unfairly convicted?"

"Surely it was to pacify Smythe and his odd sense of justice. It gave him the incentive to leave, and quieted his supporters. No doubt, some in that damned British Island Expedition Organization really believed that aspect of it. Regardless, you ferried over a hundred undesirables out of England. That is the prime thing, and depending upon the situation upon reaching England, you may have a chance to bring off more."

"Perhaps sir, some thusly removed might be those who make ill use of those honestly in the King's Service."

"Now Commander, do not be hasty in your remarks. Pray, sit and have a glass of Madeira. Relax and calm yourself. If it pleases you, all in the King's Service often feel ill-used by our seniors."

"Aye, I'll concede that, sir," sighed Pierce

"While I doubt the details of your report and wonder as to your mental stability, I shall not insist upon relieving you of your command. I will offer you the chance to resign. It would not be a violation of my orders to do so. The schooner, your crew, and you will still be en route to England."

"As you offer me a choice, I must refuse and remain in command. As to water, stores, and other replenishment, sir?"

"We have somewhat limited stores at hand, sir. Do requisition only what is truly needed."

"In that case, sir," said Pierce, "we are well-provisioned. We departed Stone Island only a few weeks ago."

"Damn, Pierce! I was thinking to forget your imaginative tales. Now you mention that damned island again."

"I had thought, sir...."

"Oh, damn my eyes, sir! Remember not to mention those details of your voyage in my hearing!"

"Aye aye, sir!"

Phillips turned his gaze away from Pierce, but did not dismiss him. The governor took a sip at his glass and sat in thought for a moment.

Just before Pierce decided that to ask if that was all, Phillips sat his glass down and faced him again. "You have seen the papers, Commander?"

"A few older ones, sir."

"Then you are aware that the war has resumed?"

"It does not surprise me."

"Then I trust you will be vigilant during your return. With your previous record, Pierce, you will be needed."

"Aye aye, sir."

"And it is because of your previous record, and the trust evidently placed in you by highly placed persons, that you are allowed to continue homeward."

"Indeed, sir!"

"Now I have work to attend to. Pray take your leave before I reconsider allowing you to remain in command of that damned schooner!"

Pierce felt a great a sense of relief when they sailed out of Sydney Harbor a week after arriving. They ran south, broad reaching until they could turn east, put the schooner before the wind, and fly along with the roaring westerly winds. They cleared the southern end of New Zealand and crossed the 180th meridian, halfway around the world from England. They were flying along. All sail that could be carried was set, and Pierce cut the margin of safety to the narrowest, such was the urgency he felt to be home.

Recollection of the heated conversation with the governor brought the color to Pierce's face. He could no longer stand idly and watch the hands at work. He began to pace, which was something he did not normally do. Up and down the small expanse of deck that was his privileged sanctuary, he walked, a set number of strides forward, and a set number of paces aft.

As Pierce and the *Island Expedition* pressed on through the southern Pacific Ocean, he thought about the continuing war with France. It had resumed over two years earlier, and in fact on the very day the expedition had received as its first visitors, Shostolamie and the small Kalish contingent. The war added one more distraction to a successful completion of the voyage. He consoled himself with the knowledge of having a specific and identifiable enemy. Should they meet a French ship, there would be no wondering about hostile intent.

The prospect of disbelief regarding the island and the other world also added to his troubles. Pierce had long ago realized that he might have difficulty in convincing his superiors and those in government that his claims and reports were true. Still, he had been shocked to find Governor King so disbelieving and hostile.

The *Island Expedition* coasted along under minimum sail, riding easily over the white flecked waters of the southern Pacific. Until today, that largest of oceans had not matched its benevolent and calm name. Under reefed mainsail, reefed topsails, and jib, the schooner carried more sail than she had in three weeks. Storm after storm had thrown their fury against her, winds shrieking and seas building into veritable fluid mountains. Sail had been taken in--a little at first, and then nearly all, and at one point they had thought to heave to and ride out nature's fury. But she had been put before the wind, racing with it, staying one step ahead of the giant seas that threatened to crash unrestrained upon the tossed-about craft. Such sailing had been an exercise in diligence and precision. The smallest error could have put the vessel beam-on to the giant swells, or caused her to have been pooped by a following sea. As one storm had weakened and blown itself out, another had taken its place. There had been no respite for the bone-tired crew, the weary captain, nor the battered vessel.

Pierce stood easily on the weather quarterdeck, matching his movements to those of *Island Expedition* and reveling in the comparative calm of this late afternoon. It was calm enough that did he desire it; considerably more sail could be set. But he was tired, and so was the rest of the crew. Battling through storm after storm had exhausted them. They had been cold, wet, hungry, tired, and seasick as the winds had increased, the temperature had dropped, and the rain, bits of ice, and snow had pelted them like musket balls. The galley fires had gone out and had been impossible to relight. What they had managed to eat had been consumed raw and cold. It had never been enough to really satisfy them.

A wisp of smoke curled from Charlie Noble, the galley smokestack. The fires were going! He hoped they would remain in this relative calm weather long enough that a real meal could be prepared for all, and that they would have time to eat it. He wondered briefly what Eubanks and Franklin could be preparing. Then it occurred to him that *what* really didn't matter. *Something* hot and satisfying was being prepared that would put life back into his weary crew.

What Pierce desired more than anything was a cup of hot and fresh coffee. He hoped fervently that the cook and his mate had started some brewing. Momentarily he felt he could forgo the anticipated meal, as long as he had a steaming and delicious mug. With his entire being craving coffee, he thought about sending someone to see if it was brewing, and threatening the cruelest punishment if it wasn't. But Pierce was a kind-hearted soul who abhorred so much of the violence and physical abuse that seemed integral to the Royal Navy. While he may have harbored thoughts of vengeful wrath, his very nature would not allow him to actually order it.

Even as captain, he was only one of sixty-odd souls aboard the schooner. It was imperative that all soon have something warm and filling. His personal cravings would simply have to take a lower priority and await the proper time to be fulfilled. Still, it seemed like forever, and in fact it had been several days since he had last had a cup. With an inward and unnoticed sigh, he committed himself to waiting longer.

Late in the afternoon watch, the weather calmed even more, and the hands could move freely about. While the sea and sky were considerably more benign, a thick overcast still obscured the sun. Pierce hoped fervently that the storms would hold off for another day or two, and that the skies would clear enough to allow noon observations.

The pumps steadily emptied the seawater that had found its way into the schooner's bowels. Some had seeped through the seams as the hull flexed in reaction to the violent seas. Much had cascaded down the one hatchway that had remained open for access below. The carpenter, much to Pierce's disgust, continued to compare the soundness of the hull to the carnal qualities of a young woman. He allowed, upon reporting only eighteen inches of water in the well, that "she was still pretty tight considering how she'd been used as of late!"

"Thank, you, Mr. Cook," replied Pierce, too tired to once again reprimand the warrant officer for his obsession. He was not opposed to discussion of physical pleasures, but he had been trained to regard the quarterdeck as a place of respect. Decorum demanded civility in one's speech, and effectively prohibited discussions of matters of the flesh, even if it was tactfully disguised. After more than two years, nearly all aboard *Island Expedition* had learned that Pierce would not tolerate graphic, profane, or sexually explicit speech on the quarterdeck.

Despite his ongoing insistence on quarterdeck purity, Pierce was no pious "blue-light" captain. At the proper time and place, he enjoyed ribald songs, stories, puns, and jokes. He just wished that others, especially the ship's carpenter, recognized those distinctions. But he knew that seamen the world over could find some sexual connotation in nearly every aspect of life. Often he could enforce and strengthen his point if he could relate it to their favorite subject.

Eight bells marked the end of the afternoon watch. Hotchkiss came on deck via the aft companionway. Tipping his hat slightly to Pierce, he said, "Eubanks remarks that supper is nearly ready, and with your permission, sir, we may pipe hands to supper!"

"Excellent, Mr. Hotchkiss! You and Mr. O'Brien may eat now if you choose. I'll keep the deck and eat later."

"Aye, sir! Thank you, sir!"

Pierce was as hungry as anyone, but felt it his duty that his crew be fed first. The watch had already been changed, and those now on deck would eat in turn. The lessening wind revealed small patches of blue sky. If it continued to clear, he could use the stars to accurately establish their position.

Hotchkiss was on deck, and apparently had been for some time. Pierce had become lost in his thoughts, watching the calm evening fade into darkness. "Sir! Sir! You should go below now for a bite. I've eaten, and will take the deck."

"Hmm? Oh yes! Quite right, Isaac. I am hungry!"

"And you would stand there with that far-off look in your eyes until England, had I not spoke?"

"Or until I turned to dust and blew away."

"Thinking of home, Edward?"

"I am thinking more of the voyage, both in terms of where we've been and where we are going. I find my very loyalties being called to question, it would seem."

"You will find an easier answer with a full belly. Go below now.

Eat, drink, and relax! With luck, this clearing will last and we'll have a respite from the storms."

"Pray we do," said Pierce, turning towards the companionway. "Please ensure that all hands have adequate dinners and that they get sufficient rest. We'll need work from all hands to put this vessel to rights."

"Aye aye, sir! And if you will allow, Mr. Morgan says that his stump indicates fair weather for some time."

"The glass is rising as well," mused Pierce. "It seems Mr. Morgan has gained certain abilities while healing."

"Aye."

"If only his broken and aching heart could be mended as well."

"A seaman's lot, isn't it?" asked Hotchkiss, who did not expect an answer. "There's always the girl left behind. He's no different from you or me, sir, excepting in where he left her. We journey closer to those young ladies we have so long pined for. He sails away farther each day from the one who puts a gleam in his eye and laughter in his heart. Perhaps one day he will sail in the other direction."

"Perhaps." Pierce yawned. "And now my friend, I'll be below awhile."

He descended to the lower deck and made his way aft. At the table running the entire length of the stern cabin, he found a solitary un-used place setting. Next to it was a small pan, its contents kept warm by two spirit lamps. It was just enough, he decided, to make a meal. He momentarily stepped into his sleeping cabin, fetched his mug, and returned. It was the only one left of a set of six. Four had met with mishaps. The fifth he had flung in anger when fresh coffee had not been available one groggy morning. He filled it with beer from the small keg in a rack under the stern windows. Then Pierce spooned the warm concoction onto his plate and began to eat.

As crude as it was, it was a very good meal: a thick stew, chunks of salt pork, salt beef, and assorted vegetables, boiled in the coppers on the galley stove. Crumbled biscuit thickened it, and Eubanks had been generous with pepper. Pierce found it very good, very filling, and he ate heartily.

He wondered if the hands thought it strange that their captain and officers subsisted on the same food that they did. It was generally expected that a captain in his isolated splendor and officers in the more genteel setting of the wardroom would dine as befitted their station. Meals would be prepared from private, jealously guarded stores, served with great formality on the highest quality tableware, by specially trained seamen who were adept at providing for their seniors. Indeed, that was the way of it aboard many ships. Even in vessels smaller than *Island Expedition*, one could expect to find such distinctions between the meals served and dining accommodations of the officers and the hands.

Ever since the schooner's commissioning, Pierce had not appointed a personal steward. Undoubtedly amongst the crew at least one person would be skilled in providing and serving meals to his captain. Nor had members of the wardroom and gunroom sought the services of a steward or servants. Since the single stern cabin served all three entities, the status of host revolving amongst them, they had evolved a certain routine, which was marked by a lack of formality and a great deal of self-service. Normally all the officers, except those on watch, would be there for the evening meal.

Today they had eaten singly, or in small groups, as they found time to break away from their duties. As he finished his generous portion, Pierce wondered if he was the last of the entire ship's company to dine.

His hunger quieted and his thirst eased, Pierce grew sleepy. He nodded in the chair, and slid down into a somewhat reclined position while his chin fell forward onto his chest. His last thought was to turn all hands to at the end of the second dog watch.

Pierce awoke to eight bells announcing that particular time. He sat upright, fighting the urge to slump once more and return to blissful unconsciousness. Intuitively he sensed the movement of the schooner and knew that neither the wind nor the sea had increased during his nap. He got to his feet, grabbed his mug, and headed forward. Finally he would have the coffee he had desired for so long.

On deck he determined that there wasn't sufficient light by which the hands could turn to and begin the repairs required by the recent and ongoing storms. With the promise of fair or decent weather over the next few days, repairs could wait. It was more important that all hands gain a little rest and go at the work with full strength and alertness. None of the damage was so severe that it hampered operation of the schooner. When the forenoon watch began the next morning, repair work would start with hands well-rested.

"How is the leg, Mr. Morgan?" Pierce asked the officer of the watch.

"Quite well, sir, now that the glass is rising. It doesn't ache as it did during the storms."

"Very glad to hear it." Pierce sipped at his coffee. "I suspect that we'll be in a normal night routine. I'd not call on the watch below unless absolutely necessary. We shall be busy enough tomorrow."

"Aye aye, sir!"

As Pierce had hoped, the sky continued to clear. Stars by the millions twinkled in the nearly cloudless sky. He went below and fetched his sextant, a pencil, and a scrap or two of paper. On deck he took sightings of several heavenly bodies, measuring their altitude above the horizon, their bearings from one another, and their bearings in relation to the schooner. He went below, passing by the galley, where he refilled his mug, and then retired into his cabin.

He completed his calculations and upon marking the results upon the chart, found himself pleased with the voyage's progress. They were nearing the eastern edge of the South Pacific Ocean. In a week at the most, they would have to alter course to the south in order to clear Cape Horn. Once past the tip of South America, it would be a matter of sailing to the north, crossing the Tropic of Capricorn, the Equator, and the Tropic of Cancer.

Pierce drained his cup, debated whether he would get another, and eventually decided he had had enough that evening. Much more, he argued, and he would not sleep. Even now he did not feel sleepy. Perhaps a turn on deck would awaken him or allow him to sleep. While he was thusly contemplating, his eyes closed; his head fell forward, cradled in his arms.

He awoke moments later to the sound of his snoring. Apparently not needing a turn on deck, he pulled off his boots, removed his coat, and crawled into his swinging cot.

Pierce momentarily awoke at four bells in the morning watch. The telltale compass in the overhead indicated the schooner's course still towards the east. The easy motion and a glance out the window confirmed that the clear weather held.

The smell of bacon cooking in the galley wafted its way about the deck. Pierce did not normally eat breakfast, not because he didn't care for it, but because if he regularly ate more than one meal a day, he gained weight. Normally he ate enough at dinner to last him the entire day. But the bacon smelled good, and he guessed that Eubanks and Franklin were cooking up double rations. A little bacon, a couple of eggs, if any were to be had, and some oatmeal, burgoo perhaps, would surely hit the spot.

Of course he would have coffee. By now, the cook or his mate would have thrown out the remnants of last evening's pot and would have made fresh for this morning. Failure to do so would risk putting their captain in a nasty mood for the rest of the day. Fortunately for Pierce and the ship's company that would have borne the brunt of his displeasure, freshly made coffee awaited him when he got to the galley. He joined the others for breakfast, and when he mounted to the deck, he was full, awake, and in good spirits. A quick look ensured him that things were as they should be, even considering the strain *Island Expedition* and her crew had been under for the past weeks.

"Mr. Hotchkiss!" he called, once he had been on deck for some time, and after he had cleared his mind of extraneous thoughts.

"Aye, sir?"

"We will commence putting things to rights!"

"Aye, sir." Hotchkiss waited a moment to see just where his captain might want to start.

"We could do with a new main topsail. The current one will surely blow out in any real breeze. We must also fish the fore topgallant mast. Cartney and his mates are to inspect all running rigging. Anything worn or frayed is to be replaced or repaired!"

"Aye aye, sir!"

"And see that Harris checks the breechings of the great guns. We do not want one breaking loose."

"Of course, sir."

Pierce didn't need to detail the work to Hotchkiss. As first lieutenant, his friend could be relied upon to take the appropriate action when needed. Still, Pierce felt more involved and in touch if he initiated some of the required tasks. As eight bells sounded, ending the morning watch, Pierce retreated to the windward quarterdeck and watched with critical aloofness as Hotchkiss got the repair work underway.

*Chapter Twenty*

# Yet So Far to Go

Pierce began to pace. Once repairs were complete, he planned to crack on again, drive the schooner hard through the turbulent waters, around the Horn and back to England. He had faith in the strength and seaworthiness of *Island Expedition* and in the abilities of her crew. If she did not survive to reach England, no vessel would. Weather, the greatest threat, was something ever-present, and should it prove too horrific, there was naught that could be done. The French posed little threat, as most of their ships were bottled up in port, stoppered like an unopened wine bottle by the Royal Navy. Anything they might run across would be no match, even for his relatively small schooner. Should they chance upon a larger French warship, *Island Expedition* would need only to spread sail after sail to the winds and show Johnny Crapaud her heels before disappearing over the horizon.

But it would not hurt to be prepared. If repairs were completed early enough, he would exercise the guns during the late afternoon. If repairs lasted into the afternoon or evening, he would exercise the guns on the morrow. But now, Pierce saw that he was in the way of the repair efforts. Because of his somewhat darkened mood, evidenced by his unusual pacing, no one had respectfully dared ask that he move. But he sensed that they were waiting for him to do so, and with his mind now back aboard and more in the present, he did.

Below, he checked that a proper dinner was being prepared, filled his coffee mug, and retired to his cabin. Working methodically he updated the log and journal, detailing the efforts now being made to set the schooner to rights. That done, he turned to the stack of newspapers and periodicals that he had gained at Sydney. Many were old, but having been gone nearly three years, even the stale news they contained was fresh to him.

He learned, from worn and tattered copies of the *Gazette*, how many of his friends and fellow officers had fared with the war's resumption. John Douglas, once captain of *Acorn*, now commanded *Theadora*. An individual he didn't know was aboard his old ship as first lieutenant, while his old shipmate Small had gained his commission and served as second lieutenant. Sollars, the bane of his existence, was not mentioned anywhere. It was a relief to learn Sollars was not available to make life absolutely miserable for his juniors.

Granville Jackson, his former captain, friend, and mentor now commanded *Doris*, a thirty-eight-gun frigate. Charles Forrest had followed Jackson to the larger frigate and once again complemented that worthy individual as his first lieutenant.

A certain acquaintance, Leonard Rowley, had been promoted to Master and Commander and given command of the ship-sloop *Lightning*. Sent to sea prior to the resumption of hostilities, through seamanship and deception, he had already accounted for a large French corvette. From the reports and letters, the young man was making a name for himself, both as a thorn in the side of the French, and as a hero in Great Britain.

Another item that caught his eye was mention of Rowley's marriage in Portsmouth prior to *Lightning's* sailing. While he had met Rowley only a time or two, an acquaintance's nuptials led Pierce to thoughts of Evangeline. It was strange, but as of late, he had not thought that much about her. That was good, because when he did think of her, he could not sleep. Then the ache of his loneliness returned, he found himself doubting her loyalty, and he would work himself into a fever of self-pity and despair. Perhaps he didn't often think of her because he hadn't seen her in such a long time.

Nor did he think very much about Leona Jackson, in spite of the pleasant diversion she had provided. In Brunswick to meet her husband when he put in for supplies, Pierce had met her at a dinner, and it was quite obvious now that she had seduced him. At sea and without pleasurable female companionship for several months, he had been a willing victim. Even so, because she was another man's wife, he had had to think twice before falling into the sweet trap of her bed. The relationship had been wrong from the very beginning, although he brazenly justified it as vengeance for Captain Lowell Jackson's brutal treatment of his crew.

Once he had surrendered *Island Expedition* to the overwhelming forces of the Kentish Navy's Flying Squadron, he and Isaac Hotchkiss had been transported to Brunswick aboard HRMS *Furious*, commanded by Jackson. During the time spent aboard the frigate, Pierce had come to loathe her captain. Never in ten years of service in the Royal Navy had Pierce seen brutality equal to that with which Jackson disciplined his crew.

During the months spent in Brunswick, he had learned that neither Jackson seemed to take their marriage seriously. The captain conveniently forgot his vows each time he was gone, and she exhibited very little restraint while awaiting his return. Each apparently knew of the other's wanderings. She generally welcomed him back, while he played the jealous and victimized husband. If Jackson did not directly challenge someone suspected of enjoying his wife's company, he resorted to other means to cause the man's ruin.

Eventually Jackson's jealousy had led to his demise.

Now Pierce had left that world behind and was back where he had grown up and had served George the Third for over a decade. He looked forward to England and seeing his parents and brothers once again. He eagerly anticipated the chance to once again be with Evangeline and press his suit for her hand. To him, what had happened in the confines of the Tritonish Consulate had happened, but it had occurred in a different world. There it would stay.

Pierce returned to the deck. Repair work had shifted away from the quarterdeck, and he resumed his place. A quick glance showed that the work was well on its way to completion.

"Mr. Hotchkiss!"

"Sir?"

"Topgallants, if you please! And the reefs out of the topsails!"

"Aye aye, sir!"

"We'll change course to east southeast by east!"

"Aye aye, sir!" answered Hotchkiss. "Close enough to angle for the Horn?"

"Yes. We'll save time doing it gently, rather than closing the South American coast and steering nearly south."

"Aye, sir."

"After dinner, Mr. Hotchkiss, we'll exercise the guns."

"Aye, sir?"

"We are a nation at war, Isaac, and it is prudent that as we near home, we prepare to meet any enemy."

"Of course."

With the change in course and the press of additional sail, *Island Expedition* heeled more to port and leapt more rapidly into the white-capped seas. Without thinking about it, Pierce adjusted his stance and altered his balance to accommodate the different motion.

Six bells had sounded recently. In less than an hour, the forenoon watch would end, and it would be noon. But when would noon actually occur? When would the sun be at its highest point of travel for the day? Traveling east caused the sun's highest point to happen earlier each day. Since it had been several days since their last reliable noon sighting, Pierce realized that today's noon might be much earlier than indicated by his watch. A number of clouds dotted the wind-scoured sky, but they were scattered enough that a noon sighting should be possible. Because the time of actual noon would be advanced, he decided that preparations for it should be made as soon as possible.

"Mr. Dial," he said. "Notify all officers that we shall attempt a noon sighting shortly!"

"Aye aye, sir!"

"And tell them, Mr. Dial, that I desire that all attend to this, as we need a most accurate reading to re-establish our plot."

"Aye aye, sir!"

Pierce went below, grabbed his sextant and some scraps of paper, and returned. Shortly the rest of the officers were on deck, jockeying for a place from which to observe the sun and measure its height above the horizon. Pierce took a preliminary reading. A few moments later, the master took another. The sun still ascended higher in the sky. Seven bells sounded just after Hotchkiss took a sighting and announced his result. Moments after he finished, Morgan, with the base of his wooden leg snug against a ringbolt, took another sighting and told his findings. The two results were nearly the same. The rate of change diminished as the sun reached its zenith.

"I would say it's noon, gentlemen!" said Pierce, upon taking an additional reading.

A murmur went through the group, and in time-honored tradition, O'Brien reported, "Noon, sir!" to the first lieutenant.

"Thank you, Mr. O'Brien," answered Hotchkiss, who in turn, reported the fact to Pierce.

"Very good, Mr. Hotchkiss. Sound eight bells! Pipe 'hands to dinner,' if you would!"

"Aye, sir!" responded Hotchkiss, and the official new day began. They had gained over thirty minutes' easting from the last time they had accurately established noon. However, based on celestial sightings taken the evening before, they were near to where Pierce thought them to be.

After dinner, as he had told Hotchkiss earlier, Pierce set the hands to drill and practice with the guns. Its having been some weeks since the guns had been worked, they ran through the procedure several times without the use of powder or shot. On the next repetition, the guns were actually loaded, and at the command, fired. Pierce was glad he had been able to convince Smythe and the Organization to purchase additional powder and shot, beyond that allotted by the Ordnance Board. He believed that practice where the guns were actually fired, time and time again, was much more effective than simply going through the motions. That philosophy had paid off during battle with HRMS *Hawke*. Now that England was once again at war with France, no one could predict when they might be in battle once again. While prospects were slim, the chance of sighting an enemy vessel in the Southern Pacific could not to be discounted.

Pierce timed the gun crews, observing how long it took them to fire, reload, and fire a second broadside and then a third. The hands completed the drill in a respectable time, but not as quickly as he had seen before. Tomorrow they would drill again, and then every day, if possible, until they reached the rate they had once achieved.

Gun drill the next afternoon produced better results, but they were not yet at the level that Pierce hoped for. As the guns were being secured following the practice, Morgan remarked, "I'll wager the wind is getting up. My stump aches!"

Pierce went below to check the glass and found the barometer falling. Not knowing to what extent the weather would change, Pierce assumed the worst. Well before the winds rose, and well before the seas changed to liquid mountains, sails were taken in, lifelines were rigged about the deck, and hatch covers were stretched and battened down over the gratings. While the galley fires still burned, Eubanks and Franklin boiled up a triple ration of salt pork and salt beef. Hopefully it would be enough that all could have a cooked meal, even if eaten cold while the weather was foul.

By the end of the evening watch, the wind had risen, the seas were rougher, and a cold driving rain beat against the remaining sails, the deck, and those forced by duty to be topside.

No one in the ship's company and no man in the two worlds had been happier than Edward Pierce when *Island Expedition* had made her way out of the harbor at Brunswick, New Guernsey. Now, as the schooner thrashed through the mounting seas, Pierce reflected on those months spent in Vespica.

Compared with the world of Pierce's youth, that new, young nation was most similar to America. Having long admired the United States, Pierce had been dismayed to learn that the Independent Lands had not developed to the same level. They were not only free from Grand Triton, their former colonial masters--but also, it seemed, independent from each other. There was no unity, very little cooperation, and no real status amongst the other nations of that world.

Yet, the Joint Council had acted in united fashion, tentatively annexing Stone Island, where the British Island Expedition Organization's colony had been established. All those on, or from the island, were declared Vespican citizens. Because of that, the Joint Council's demands and orders from his government, the Tritonish Ambassador had reluctantly ordered the release of *Island Expedition*, Pierce, and her crew.

Their captivity, if it could be so called, had not been at all difficult. Remembering the time spent with Leona Jackson, Pierce acknowledged that it had been, in fact, quite pleasurable. Yet he had a distinctly bad feeling regarding the Tritonish. It irritated him that in so many ways they were so close to his own Great Britain. How he could revere one and detest the other when they were so much the same? Did Great Britain have the effect on others that Grand Triton had on him? He hoped that his own beloved land did not affect foreigners that way. While no great hatred raged as he remembered their enforced stay, it was the overall Tritonish attitude that bothered him. Despite a strong urge not to do so, he wondered about his own loyalties.

Now, some four months after departing Sidney, Pierce stood immobile on the deck of *Island Expedition* as she sailed northward through the Atlantic. While others topside thought the schooner's captain watched every move they made, in truth, he was many miles and years away. He was aware of the activity on deck, the motion of the ship, and their general position upon the sea. Yet he was at home, in the little house of his childhood, warm and cheery, along with his parents and brothers. In a strange twist of time and place, he was there as a boy, and yet Evangeline was there with him. They were all in the kitchen, seated at a small plain table, drinking hot cider, eating roasted chestnuts, and telling fanciful tales. There was a lot of laughter, and the warmth that can be found only amongst family and true friends.

That cheerfulness starkly contrasted with the dismal day that surrounded Pierce's physical presence on board *Island Expedition*. He had noted, before his mind journeyed home, that if an artist had painted this particular day, he would have needed only black and white to blend into various shades of dull and depressing gray. Even those parts of the vessel that were normally bright and contrasting could have been depicted in somber and dull tones. The sky was solidly overcast, although at the moment, no precipitation came from it. A limited amount of light reflected off those sullen clouds onto the surface of the choppy sea. There was enough wind to create a flurry of whitecaps upon the water's surface, but even these were seen as hues of gray. Having been away from England for so long, and nearing the end of the long voyage home, he should have been joyful. Yet his mood matched the gloom of that mid-autumn day.

As much as he longed to be home, to have completed this voyage, he also dreaded the return. How would the Admiralty react upon reading his reports? Would they scoff at the idea of finding a legendary island existing in a completely different world? Acknowledgment of that other world, complete with its strange and yet familiar nations, would send his credibility by the boards. He would be laughed at, scorned, and deprived of any further chances of sea-going employment or command. He might even be court-martialed for daring to submit such a report. He would be lucky to return to the village of his youth and live out his days as the young boys pointed at him, mocked him, and identified him as the Royal Navy officer who lost his sanity during his very first command.

So what if the other sixty-odd souls on board had seen and experienced everything and had been everywhere he had? It was a small and ineffectual comfort that they would be able to back him. The Admiralty and other officials might decide that the whole lot was addled. Already he had faced disbelief, sympathetic amazement, scorn, and even hostile belligerency when he had told the true story of the voyage. In Sydney, Governor King had suggested that Pierce should be relieved of his command and brought home as a passenger aboard that very vessel. East India Company officials at St. Helena had not been much kinder when the schooner had stopped there a month and a half ago. Those worthy individuals had tried to hide it, but from time to time he had seen that look on their faces, and had imagined the sounds of pity in their voices when they thought he was out of sight or hearing.

During the three years that he had been away from England, the one thing that had kept Pierce focused was his memory of Evangeline. As precious as it was, for most of the voyage he had functioned best when he had been able not to think of her. When he did, the longing and the loneliness were more than he could bear. As the expedition had stretched into months and then years, he had found himself questioning the relationship. Had she entertained others during his absence? At times he imagined that she had completely forgotten him. Then those supposed betrayals welled up within and brought out all his suppressed self-loathing and self-doubt.

The papers obtained at St. Helena had done nothing to ease his doubts about their relationship. He had found notice of the death of a Lieutenant Carlisle, killed recently in a ship-to-ship duel with a marauding French frigate. The deceased was not a friend or former shipmate, and with all the death notices he had seen, and with all those deaths he had personally witnessed, the passing of an unknown officer had meant very little to him. What had caught his eye was mention of the man's widow, one Evangeline Carlisle. That she had the same name as his beloved preyed insidiously upon his mind. Could it be, he wondered? In a later edition of the paper he had noticed the report of a child born to the late Lieutenant and Evangeline Carlisle.

While nothing indicated that this Evangeline was the young lady he had left nearly three years ago, the fact that she had the same name perturbed him. This fed his growing dread of returning home. While he wanted so much to be with her again, he did not want to find that she and the widowed Evangeline Carlisle were one and the same. Had she tossed him aside and gone on with her life as if he had never existed?

The uncertainties raised by the notices fanned the doubts and fears that already occupied his thoughts of late. Many times he was tempted to 'bout ship and return to the world of Stone Island, Vespica, the Tritonish Empire, and its war with the Gallician Republic.

Had he betrayed her as well? The old adage that no sailor is married at sea eased his guilt somewhat, as did the fact that they were not married. As much as he longed to see her and hold her again, he was very much afraid that she would know of his transgressions, and that she would no longer desire him. He was afraid to be with her once again, only to find that she too had strayed from a true heaven-sent relationship.

While Pierce could be slightly antagonistic at times, after departing St. Helena, his dark mood had been blacker than ever before. He shunned the company of his fellow officers, often eating alone in his cabin, the door shut against the crowd at the table in the great cabin. Conversations, even with Isaac Hotchkiss, had all but ceased, and then concerned only the day-to-day operation of the schooner.

A stronger gust of wind blasted cold against his face. He sipped at his remaining coffee. Cold! Damn! Time to go below for a fresh cup.

He looked around, checking to see that all was normal onboard. In his current state he sincerely wished that he could spot something amiss to rant about, not so much for its being out of line, but to appease the dark anxiety that gnawed at his being.

As he realized that nothing on deck would give him an excuse to verbally flog some hapless individual, and as he determined to fetch more coffee, the lookout hailed.

"Deck there! Sail to starboard!"

"Be more specific, Jones!" shouted Andrews, the officer of the watch.

"Nearly abeam of us, sir! A point, no, two points towards the bow, sir!"

"What do you make of her?"

"Reefed topsails, it looks, sir. Same course as us, sir."

"Very well!" interrupted Pierce. "Mr. Spencer, you may borrow my best glass. To the masthead with you, and see what you can make of her!"

"Aye aye, sir!"

"Friendly, do you think, sir?" The shouted exchange of orders and information had been heard throughout the schooner. Hands and officers, below in the comparative warmth of the 'tween decks, came on deck to see what was about. Hotchkiss joined his friend and captain on the quarterdeck, habit and duty prevailing. Pierce honestly had thought that his friend would likely avoid him, due to his snappish mood of late.

But Hotchkiss didn't act according to his friend's black humor. That pacified Pierce somewhat, and he replied with unusual familiarity. "I would expect so, Isaac. It's either a merchantman or of the blockading squadron. With the weather, they may have stood out from shore and a close blockade. And yet a Frenchie may have managed to slip out."

"Very much my take on it, Edward." Hotchkiss paused momentarily. "I'm sure we'll know shortly."

The first lieutenant's use of his first name, even on the quarterdeck, further lightened Pierce's mood. "Aye, my friend, we will." Normally Pierce was a stickler for formalities while on duty, and would have insisted upon proper forms of address.

"Sir! Sir!" Spencer's voice sounded distant as he hailed from the masthead. The winds worked to blow his words away.

"Yes, Mr. Spencer?" shouted Pierce in reply.

"She's altering course, sir, converging on us now! Setting topgallants as well!"

"Thank you, Mr. Spencer. Watch her!"

"Aye aye, sir."

"It would appear we have been seen, Isaac. I would think it prudent to have our number and the recognition signal ready to run up."

"Aye, sir."

"I believe it would also be prudent to beat to quarters."

"Aye aye, sir!" Hotchkiss acknowledged. He turned to give the necessary orders, but before he could, Pierce stopped him.

"We are in no hurry, Mr. Hotchkiss. Send someone to check on the progress of dinner. If it's close to ready, we will have time for the hands to eat before clearing for action. And we have time yet before she's near enough for signals."

"Aye, sir."

## Chapter Twenty-One

# Obstacles to a Return

Pierce felt fear creep into him. He was cold, colder than he should be, even on such a raw and blustery day. At the same time, the dampness of an unwelcome sweat soaked into his clothing. God, he wished that he wouldn't go through that every time combat loomed. Yet, it had happened so many times in his naval career that he had come to expect it. If he didn't experience those symptoms, and went into battle unperturbed, something would be wrong. Still, Pierce wished he could approach danger with the same ease it seemed everyone else did.

"I shall go below momentarily, Mr. Hotchkiss!" he said as nonchalantly as possible. Fear of possible battle always caused him to think he might need to use the head. However, years of experience told him it would be a wasted trip. Still, he could go below and get some coffee, which he had determined to do when the lookout had hailed. He would simply carry on with his original plan.

When he arrived back on deck, Midshipman Andrews reported Eubanks had allowed that dinner could be served in five minutes.

"Very well, then," said Pierce. "In five minutes you may pipe 'hands to dinner.' You may also pipe 'up spirits,' as well. A warm meal and a splash of grog will warm us all. Depending upon what our friend is up to, it may be our last chance at either for some time."

"Aye aye, sir."

Five minutes later, the bo'sun's pipes squealed, and the majority of the men aboard the schooner ate their dinner an hour and a half early. Pierce went below to join the others of the combined wardroom and gunroom. Today was his turn as host, and the members of those two messes were, in essence, dining at the captain's table at his invitation. As he arrived, they stood. He bade them to be seated and added, "We'll not stand on formalities today, gentlemen. Eat quickly if possible, and return on deck so those with the duty might also dine. I see no great rush at this time to go to action stations. Yet, should our approaching friend prove hostile, we must be ready to flee or fight."

He watched as the others tore into the meal with hearty appetites. They ate as if they had not eaten in weeks, even as they faced the possibility that they would never eat again. Pierce picked at his food, ate a little of this and a little of that, and hopefully made enough progress with his victuals to make it appear he had eaten as well as anyone. He had no appetite, even though the meal was a favorite. In spite of the stores' age, Eubanks had done well in preparing it. Pierce hoped the approaching ship proved friendly, and they would not have to fight. Then he would be able to eat and enjoy supper that evening.

While he picked half-heartedly at his dinner, he enjoyed the company of the others. Did the prospect of conflict drive away some of his dark and brooding melancholy?

On deck, noting that Master's Mate Dial had eaten, Pierce said. "To the masthead with you, sir. Keep an eye on our friend there and allow Mr. Spencer his chance at dinner."

"Aye aye, sir!"

When Spencer descended to the deck, Pierce intercepted him. "Now, lad, what is our friend there up to?"

"She's seen us for sure, sir. When I first went aloft, she was on the same course, or nearly so, maybe a point or two to the north. She's altered sir, more northerly, even a bit to the west. She's closing now, sir."

"As I thought, Mr. Spencer. Go below, have your dinner, and your spirits. Warm up, and perhaps we'll have a warmer time of it during the afternoon watch!"

"Aye aye, sir."

Friend or foe, the ship on the horizon was interested in *Island*

*Expedition.* When first sighted, the two had been on nearly parallel courses. The schooner had been on a broad port reach for the past few days, north northeast by east, with the westerly winds on her port quarter. When sighted, the stranger had been heading the same, perhaps a point or two closer to north. If they continued long enough, and if their speeds stayed the same, they would eventually close with each other, their courses gently converging together.

But upon first sighting, the stranger altered course significantly, swinging her bows to port and heading north northwest. Depending upon their speeds, the meeting point of their routes over the waves would occur much sooner.

It was obvious to all aboard that the strange sail had seen them, and had altered course to intercept. Not knowing the stranger's identity, there was the possibility it was a fellow Royal Navy vessel investigating a strange sail. But it could be a marauding French raider or privateer. A merchant ship would have already turned away and not risked the chance that the unidentified *Island Expedition* was an enemy. It crossed Pierce's mind that perhaps the other's course change had nothing to do with them, and had occurred at that time, purely as a matter of coincidence.

"Mr. Hotchkiss, shake the reefs out of the topsails! Set topgallants as well! We'll see if that has any effect on them."

"Aye, sir."

"And starboard the helm, if you would. Due north should serve!"

"Aye aye, sir!"

The schooner spread more sail to the blustery winds, and turned to the north with the wind on her port beam. With more sail, she heeled farther to starboard, and drove her bows forcefully into the waves. Foam and spray cascaded over her starboard bow as she continuously buried it in the choppy seas.

Pierce sipped at his ever-present cup of coffee and waited for some word from Dial regarding reaction from the strange vessel. He was about to holler aloft to see if the lad was awake, when the master's mate hailed. "She's gone to royals, sir!"

"Changed course?"

"Not that I could see, sir."

"Thank you, Mr. Dial!" Pierce shouted. "Keep an eye on her!"

"Aye aye, sir!"

"Now, Mr. Hotchkiss, let's ease her a bit. Gently! We'll settle back to our original course and see if that gets a reaction."

Moments after *Island Expedition* resumed her original heading, Dial once again hailed the quarterdeck. "She's come more into the wind, sir! Close-hauled on the port tack!"

"Thank you, lad! Mr. Hotchkiss, it is time that we beat to quarters!"

"Aye aye, sir!"

From the strange sail's reactions to their latest moves, Pierce knew the other vessel was interested in them. As he did not yet know the other's identity, he would err on the side of safety and clear for action. Should she prove hostile, it would be better that they were ready to fend off any attack. If the stranger ended up as a friend or ally, they could relax and secure from action stations.

The marine drummer began the frantic beat upon his drum. Hands moved to their places with a measured, hurried purpose. There was no wasted effort. They had done this so many times, at Pierce's insistence, that it was second nature. Decks were wetted and sanded. Bulkheads and canvas screens that delineated the cabins were knocked down and struck below. Boats were hoisted out to be towed astern. Guns were cast loose and run in for loading. Harris the gunner and Simmons his mate descended to the magazine to fill cartridges and pass them to the powder monkeys.

"Load! Do not run out!" shouted Pierce. "Double shot, if you please!" The order was passed along so that all could hear and obey it. Unlike many captains, Pierce did not keep the guns aboard *Island Expedition* loaded. He had found it better to load as the possibility of battle approached, when he could determine just what shot would best serve the current situation. He did note that he almost always ordered the guns double-shotted for that all important first broadside. It was a matter of providing the enemy with a broadside twice the weight of the guns presented.

*Island Expedition* rose to the top of a large sea. Excitedly, Midshipman Townsend announced that the strange vessel had momentarily been visible from deck. Pierce crossed to the lee rail. When the schooner rose atop the next swell, he too caught a brief glimpse of the stranger. It was a quick sighting, a flash of sail, white against the leaden sky and slate-gray sea. But in that brief moment, Pierce saw that their potential antagonist was ship-rigged and carried more sail than he thought prudent, and that it indeed appeared determined to close with them.

Once before, Pierce had watched another vessel close with *Island Expedition* in much the same manner. Then he had allowed the approach because he hoped to converse with her. That ship had proven hostile, and only through a premonition that it might be so had they been ready for the onslaught. Once the battle had commenced, recent gunnery drills aboard *Island Expedition* made the difference, and Pierce and his crew had emerged victorious.

The present situation was similar, although now he did not look to converse with another ship. But this strange vessel was endeavoring to close with them, and by the direct manner employed, Pierce could not think her intent anything but hostile.

He knew that his fast and nimble schooner could stay out of harm's way, or if forced into combat, out sail the other vessel and deliver devastating broadsides with the relatively heavy armament carried. His biggest fear was being boarded. There were enough in the crew to man the guns and to trim sails as needed. Should they be boarded by any sort of force, they would be overwhelmed.

Pierce's first duty was to return to England. He had dispatches and messages to deliver, including his no doubt controversial reports of the voyage to the Admiralty. As well, there was Smythe's accumulated correspondence for the British Island Expedition Organization. Yet as a Royal Navy officer, he was duty bound to engage an enemy ship, should one fall under his guns. But they had been gone for three years, and only weeks away from anchoring in English waters, Pierce did not want even a minute's delay in completing the journey.

He decided not to alter course at present. He would continue on and let the approaching vessel decide what was to be. If she proved friendly, he could exchange pleasantries, perhaps indulge in a brief captain-to-captain visit, and be on his way. If she proved hostile, he would do whatever was required to continue and complete the voyage.

"Deck there!" Mr. Spencer was once again at the masthead, and his voice was all but carried away in the wind.

"Aye, Mr. Spencer?" Morgan answered, now on deck with the crew at action stations.

"I see her colors, sir!"

"Can you make them out?" questioned Pierce.

"Aye! Looks like the Tricolor, sir!"

"Damn!" muttered Pierce. He had suspected, and in all honesty had expected as much, although he had hoped the fast-approaching ship would prove friendly or neutral. With Spencer's announcement, a general murmur of approval and excitement ran through the com-bat- ready crew.

It both pleased and perplexed Pierce that the hands were ready and eager for combat. If combat was inevitable, it was best to have a crew primed and ready for it. But did they think about being sliced in two by flying shot, ripped to shreds by splinters, or hacked to death by a cutlass- and pike-wielding boarding party? Did they think of spending the rest of the war in a French prison, neglected, starved, and mistreated? Did the hands even consider the importance of their return to England?

"She's forereaching on us, sir!" hailed Spencer. At the present rates of travel, the enemy ship would intersect *Island Expedition*'s intended track before the schooner arrived at that point. There, even as now, the stranger could effectively block the schooner's path to England.

It was one of those odd times when it would be advantageous not to have the weather gage as they did now. If he had the lee, as did the approaching ship, he could crack on all sail possible, run before the wind and watch the enemy disappear astern. Or he could alter course, head to the northwest on a port tack, and lie closer into the wind than his antagonist. But that would put him off his intended course, and he had already determined he would not abide any delays in completing his return. "Ease her, just slightly, Mr. O'Brien!" he said. The master was near the helm, his duty station during battle, directing and over-seeing control of the schooner.

"Aye, sir!" He nodded at the helmsmen, who let the schooner fall off a point or two, heading a little more to the east than she had been.

This slight alteration would allow the meeting of the two ships to occur a little sooner. Pierce would avoid battle if possible, but if there was no way around it, he would as soon it commenced and was done with. Should there be any mistakes in handling by the approaching ship, perhaps *Island Expedition* could slip past, gain the lee, and speed away.

The enemy was well up on the horizon now. Her great spread of canvas was visible from deck, and Pierce wondered at the wisdom of so much of it in the current wind. From experience and instinct, he saw she wasn't that much bigger than *Island Expedition*. But as she was still hull down from deck, he had no idea of her armament or hull configuration.

"Mr. Spencer! If you would, lad, can you see what her guns are?" Pierce shouted. He watched the young man peer intently through his glass.

"Can't see all that clear yet, sir! Think she might be a privateer!" Spencer studied the fast approaching vessel another minute. "She's run out her guns. Nine to a side, sir!"

"Thank you, Mr. Spencer. You are welcome to return on deck. Hurry, and perhaps Mr. Gray will spare you a second spirit ration, unless you are already warm enough."

"Aye aye, sir!" The young man descended by way of the backstays and was on deck in an instant.

"Mr. Steadman!" bellowed Pierce. "You may take his place for the while, although I won't promise a chance at a second issue of grog!"

"Quite all right, sir!"

Events now progressed at a more rapid pace, although as he often did at such times, Pierce felt detached and apart from the action. With the potential for action drawing ever nearer, he was amazed that he could think so clearly, as if he were playing a game of chess, or diagramming a battle on the tabletop.

He saw the enemy, hull up, when the schooner topped out on the crest of a large sea. With every moment that passed by, and as the two drew nearer, he had longer uninterrupted views of the approaching foe. She was a trim and fast vessel, and he observed that Spencer had been correct. Eighteen guns: nine-pounders, he imagined. They might be six-pounders; guns still big enough to do considerable damage if *Island Expedition* came under their fire for more than the briefest interval. Pierce had no intention of letting that happen. He did not desire direct combat if it could be avoided. His wanted to get to leeward, crack on more sail, and return to England. But if forced to exchange broadsides with the enemy, he would do it.

"Another two points starboard, Mr. O'Brien!" Pierce said tersely. Perhaps *Island Expedition* could cross the Frenchman's wake. That would give the schooner the lee of the situation, which was precisely what Pierce wanted. He watched the position of the fast-closing enemy change as they completed their alteration in course. She was no longer off the starboard bow, and in a few minutes, Pierce would again alter course slightly. If the other crew was inattentive in the least, it might give him the edge needed.

"She's coming around, sir!" shouted Hotchkiss. "She's going to tack, or back, sure as hell!"

Pierce noticed. There was a good crew aboard the Frenchman. The fact that they had gotten past the strangling British blockade also attested to that. The range was great enough that Pierce wasn't concerned about the hostile broadside facing them. What did worry him was that their slight course change had been seen and acted upon swiftly. While inherent gallantry allowed him to wish for an opponent with skill and ability, practicality demanded an inept bungling fool. His counterpart was not what he hoped for.

As he watched, a flame flared briefly alongside the other ship. Smoke billowed briefly and was dispersed by the wind. The faint report of the discharge reached his ear, and he saw the splash of the shot. It fell a good two hundred yards short, although dead on at the schooner. Was it a ranging shot, or a shot across the bow? While the shot's intention was difficult to ascertain, it did notify all aboard of the Frenchman's hostile intent.

As Pierce watched, the ship completed her swing through the wind and came up on a starboard tack. The two were on opposing courses. If nothing changed, they would pass broadside to broadside.

"Not what we would normally expect, sir," commented Hotchkiss. "We stay this course; she'll pass to windward and have her lee guns in action. We'll end up with the weather guns bearing. She can aim for the hull, and it'll be easier for us to go for the top hamper!"

"Aye, Isaac, the opposite of what it usually is," replied Pierce. The French generally preferred the leeward side, where the heel gave their guns better elevation in order to concentrate on the opponent's rigging. The English normally wanted to be to windward, where the guns of the engaged side pointed directly at the enemy's hull. But Pierce had decided earlier that he wanted the lee in this confrontation. He wanted to sail away, to escape the situation, and the possibility of a prolonged battle.

If the two vessels continued on course, his wish would come true. They would pass port side to port side, exchange broadsides, and *Island Expedition* would slip into the lee. Pierce would be able to refuse battle and continue on to England. Thoughts of such action being less than a full attempt to defeat an enemy crossed his mind. He dismissed them and returned to his original idea, determined when the other ship had first been sighted. The success he hoped for depended upon the action--or rather, the inaction--of the enemy ship. If she did not alter course, the foreseen and hoped-for events would occur.

Pierce had already noted that the French captain and crew were not fools, so he did not expect them to blithely sail directly into a broadside-to-broadside exchange. The Frenchman would make a last-minute maneuver to gain even a moment's advantage. Would she swing south, cross the schooner's bows, and deliver a broadside that could not be immediately returned? Might she head into the wind and bring her guns to bear as she came about onto a port tack? Pierce mentally examined all the possibilities, and formulated maneuvers to counter every action he could predict. Different orders and commands formed in his mind, each ready for instant implementation, depending upon the Frenchman's next move.

The wind gusted momentarily, swirling through the schooner's top hamper and nearly catching the helmsmen off guard. *Island Expedition* staggered at this sudden onslaught of nature. Watching the approaching Frenchman, Pierce noticed her sails shiver and saw the added roll as the gust caught her. Then, other movements aboard the nearing enemy caught his eye. She shortened sail, taking in the vast spread of canvas carried to intercept his vessel. Royals and top gallants were furled, quickly and perhaps a bit sloppily, but that was to be expected of the French. Main and fore courses were clewed up, leaving the ship carrying fighting sail.

*Island Expedition* and the small French corvette were now close enough for Pierce to distinguish the movement of men about her deck. A sudden flurry of activity signaled Pierce that some maneuver was about to begin. He waited, hardly daring to breathe.

Slowly, the Frenchman's bows swung to the south. As her rudder bit into the cold sea, she turned, faster with each heartbeat. The aggressive enemy rapidly turned, progressing from a starboard tack to a broad reach. If Pierce did nothing, the Frenchman would cut directly across the schooner's path and bring her broadside to bear on *Island Expedition*'s vulnerable bow.

"Helm alee!" he shouted. "Stand by the starboard battery!" A turn northward would bring them under the enemy's guns a moment earlier, but they would present a moving target, and not one coming straight on. This move would also present their better-protected side to the enemy's fire and enable a reply at nearly the same instant.

Flame exploded from the side of the Frenchman. Smoke billowed over the ship before the wind whipped it away. The schooner's fore topsail shuddered, and a jagged hole tore through it. With a "twang," a starboard main topmast backstay parted. The slack lower end dropped, and missed O'Brien by less than a foot. The master grinned in relief. Forward, clouds of splinters arose as other enemy shot struck home. More flying shot punched through the sails, and additional lines parted.

"Just like the Frogs not to take advantage of being to windward," murmured Hotchkiss. "Even with it, they're aiming for the rigging!"

"Now lads! Let 'em have it!" Pierce roared. *Island Expedition*'s turn had progressed to where her guns now bore on the corvette.

"As your guns bear! Mind the roll! Fire!" yelled Hotchkiss.

There were a few brief seconds of silence. Gun captains waited until the enemy vessel lined up with their guns and until the schooner's roll placed them at the proper elevation. Then, in ones and twos, the guns fired. They recoiled and hurtled inboard, brought up short by the heavy breeching ropes.

Pierce lost sight of the French ship, his vision blocked by the clouds of smoke spewed forth by *Island Expedition*'s twelve-pounders. When it dispersed, he saw the results. The broadside had struck home with devastating accuracy. The enemy's bulwarks were battered and torn, the hammock netting ripped, and several jagged gaping holes appeared between wind and water. Lines had parted and several dangled, slack and unusable, from the spars.

"Keep her at the turn!" Pierce roared at the helmsmen. "Ready the port battery!" Even as the French fired their own broadside, they reversed their turn, intending to pass across the schooner's vulnerable stern. Pierce gambled that it would take the French a few moments to reload their already discharged starboard guns. Relying upon the nimbleness of his schooner and continuing his turn to port, he would quickly come about and present his unfired and deadly port broadside.

However, the French crew was well-practiced, and the corvette was quicker than he thought. Before *Island Expedition*'s bows passed through the wind, the Frenchmen's guns boomed again. More holes appeared in the canvas overhead, and more lines parted. A cloud of splinters blasted into the air from the port quarter bulwarks. Another shot struck near the starboard aft carronade.

Midshipman Townsend, in the midst of giving orders, stopped in mid-sentence. His mouth moved, but no sound came out. He stood a moment longer and then sank heavily to the deck like a sack of grain. Townsend pitched forward, blood soaking his shoulder. Two hands scooped him up and carried him to the relative safety and gruesome horrors of the cockpit. As Pierce watched the still form being carried below, he knew that Townsend, whom he had always regarded as a younger brother, might not complete their journey.

His original plan had been to fight only if forced to do so. He had earlier thought to dodge around the French presence and continue on to England. Pierce had half abandoned that idea when he continued the port turn and came about to fire a second broadside. But he still had it in mind to break off and continue homeward. With the injuries to Townsend, Pierce completely discarded that plan. He coldly decided to continue and win the battle.

The Frenchman continued turning to starboard and passed through the wind, ending up close-hauled on a port tack. *Island Expedition* had already passed through the wind on her starboard turn, and with the wind now on her starboard bow, found herself across the bows of the French ship.

"Fire!" raged Hotchkiss at the portside gun captains. They were well-trained, and without the reminders earlier passed to the starboards, waited until the alignment and the roll were perfect. Then they fired. Again, the broadside appeared to be ragged and undisciplined, but the shots struck home with great effect. With the guns inboard from firing, crews leapt to reload and ready them for another broadside.

Clouds of splinters, debris, canvas, and body parts erupted at the Frenchman's bows as the schooner's shot struck home. As Pierce watched, her second bower fell from the cathead. "Keep to the turn, Mr. O'Brien!" In spite of the enemy's quickness, the schooner was quicker. Hopefully he could bring the starboard guns to bear on target again before the enemy brought her yet-unfired port guns to bear on him. At this, he was successful, although not by a wide margin. The starboard battery banged and punched more holes in the enemy's port bow, seconds before her port broadside spat fire, smoke, and deadly iron shot.

The two vessels ended up on parallel courses, side by side, heading to the northeast, roughly the same course *Island Expedition* had held before the first exchange of cannon fire. It appeared Pierce would need to forego the style of fighting that he preferred. Side by side as they surged along, it would be a case of dishing out and taking it. The weight of shot, the accuracy of the gunnery, and the rate of fire would be all important. He could not hope to maneuver to escape the enemy's broadsides while he poured round after round of twelve-pounder shot into the adversary. He and the schooner would have to stand and slug it out.

## Chapter Twenty-Two

# Boarders Away

"**C**ome on, lads! Reload!" Pierce exhorted the starboard gun crews as they worked fiendishly to recharge their weapons. Crewmen from the unused port battery helped. "Aim for her mainmast! Aim low, lads!"

"Fire as you bear!" ordered Hotchkiss. The guns went off singularly, or in twos and threes. "Reload! Continue firing!" Now they would see if all the practice Pierce had insisted on would pay off. Could they reload and fire faster than the French? Could they take all the steps needed to ready the guns for another round, even with the enemy's deadly muzzles only yards away? Would *Island Expedition* be able to properly man her guns in the face of the Frenchman's deadly fire? Time--perhaps a very short time--would tell.

The enemy's next broadside crashed out. Shot tore across the schooner's deck. Splinters flew! Men screamed in agony! Great gouges appeared in the deck planking. Blood ran across the once-clean holystoned deck and turned it a dull muddy brown, contrasting with its earlier snowy white appearance.

The efforts to reload and fire the starboard battery never ceased. As soon as the last French gun had recoiled against its breechings, the first of *Island Expedition's* starboard twelve-pounders was run out through its port. When it was hard against the port sill, the gun captain checked the aim, waited for the roll, and pulled the lanyard. The gun roared, bucked, and raced inboard, halted by its breeching rope. By now, the other guns were loaded and run out. They fired as the crew of the first gun began to reload again.

He noted with satisfaction that the first gun was ready to fire once again before the first French guns showed through their ports. Those deadly guns did not fire until the entire battery had been run out. Two of the schooner's starboard guns fired three times during the time it took the French to fire, reload, and fire a second time. At this time, the British had the advantage of larger weapons and a higher rate of fire. Yet to sit alongside the enemy and pound it out was not what Pierce preferred. He would rather maneuver smartly--dart in and out to damage the enemy while avoiding being damaged in return.

Large numbers of men gathered on the Frenchman's deck. The gap between the two vessels narrowed as the corvette swung, imperceptibly at first, to the north. She planned to board.

"Let fly topsail sheets! Mainsail, foresail sheets! Shiver 'em, lads!" Pierce roared. "Get the way off o' her! Let fly the headsail sheets!" With sheets let go, the wind spilled under the topsails and around the foretopmast staysail and jib. The huge mainsail and foresail were hauled by brute force against the wind until they were parallel with it. Suddenly deprived of the wind's pressure against her canvas, *Island Expedition* slowed and the Frenchman surged ahead.

"Now lads! Sheet home! Port your helm! Port battery ready!"

Sails were quickly sheeted home, and *Island Expedition* lunged forward again, turning across the Frenchman's stern. For a brief moment, her unprotected bow would point dead on at the corvette's deadly broadside. The enemy had just fired, and Pierce crossed his fingers and prayed that she could not reload and fire while the British schooner was in this vulnerable position. The seconds passed with agonized slowness. Pierce heard the beat of his heart, racing with the terror of waiting. It boomed in his ears, like the cannon shots he willed not to come.

The French did not fire. Thank God they were not as quick at reloading. Very soon now, the schooner's port battery would bear on the enemy's port quarter and stern.

"Starboard helm, now! Port battery, fire!" The wheel spun, the spokes a blur in the dull light of that somber gray day. Their antagonist maintained her port turn, initially undertaken in order to close and board. With the schooner falling back and attempting to cross her stern, the corvette raced to keep that delicate area beyond the reach of the schooner's guns. Not being as quick and handy, she failed. Island Expedition's port battery crashed and roared. Flames and smoke belched violently from the twelve-pounders, long guns, and carronades alike. Double- shotted, they smashed into the Frenchman's port quarter gallery and stern windows.

Pierce was satisfied for the moment. He had successfully gained a position on the corvette's port quarter. His vessel was located where enemy cannon fire could not bear, yet he could keep up a continuous and devastating cannonade of his own. This was more the way he desired to fight. He had tremendous respect and admiration for Lord Nelson, but did not hold with the Admiral's admonishment to "forget maneuver and go straight at them." Pierce would rather twist and turn, dodge, kick, scratch, and punch if he could. He wanted to deliver punishing blows, fire bulwark-shattering broadsides at his foe, and receive no or very little return fire. His goal was to damage or destroy the enemy vessel, not his own. Having reversed his turn, Pierce kept *Island Expedition* on the Frenchman's port quarter, following her around in a port turn.

The two vessels continued to turn, passing through north and coming closer and closer to a westerly heading. The Frenchman was now on a port tack and nosing closer into the wind with each second that passed. A moment of decision loomed for her captain, and depending upon his choice, Pierce would have a decision to make as well. The corvette eased out of her port turn. *Island Expedition* had just fired another broadside and would not be able to further harm her exposed and vulnerable stern, still under the deadly English guns.

Pierce thought the French would reverse their turn and attempt to bring the English schooner's starboard bow under the guns of her starboard battery. The French apparently did not want to continue to turn into the wind and risk missing stays. While she appeared to be well- handled, perhaps her captain did not trust his crew's sail-handling abilities while in battle.

Pierce had no such lack of confidence in his men. "Mr. O'Brien! Ensure the helm is hard over! Let fly headsail and foresail sheets!" With the pressure of the wind released forward, its force on the huge mainsail accelerated the turn. The schooner's bows pointed directly at the corvette. Then they swung past, and closer and closer into the eye of the wind.

Seeing the opportunity, Hotchkiss roared out, "Starboard battery! Fire as you bear!" Those eight guns, unused for the past several moments, rang out loudly. Once again, splinters flew from the Frenchman's stern.

*Island Expedition* was far enough into the wind that with the yards braced sharply as could be, they could not keep the wind behind them. The topsails backed, the breeze pressing them to the masts. Momentum carried the schooner through the wind's teeth. "Hands to the braces! Bring them around! Shift the headsail sheets! Headsails, foresail, and mainsail! Sheet home!"

Pierce originally planned to go from the starboard tack to a starboard reach, a broad reach, and finally before the wind to close once again with the corvette. But the enemy might expect such a move. As soon as they settled on the starboard tack, he ordered, "'Bout ship! Helm to port!" The bows swung back into the wind.

By the time the schooner had crossed through the wind and the sails were drawing well on the port tack, the starboard battery had been reloaded and was ready to fire again. The distance between the two combatants had increased with the latest maneuvers, but they were still within range. "Fire!" bellowed Hotchkiss. Even with the greater range, many of the twelve-pounders' shot struck home. With a nod of agreement from Pierce, Hotchkiss ordered, "Port battery ready!"

The French ship continued her starboard turn until she headed nearly east. Then she reversed it, turning to port and heading more and more to the north. This time, it would seem, she would continue the turn and come back at the schooner on a starboard tack. Now close-hauled on a port tack, her guns bore directly upon *Island Expedition*. Her port broadside bloomed in deadly flowers of fire and smoke. With the extreme range, only a few of the shot struck home.

The schooner continued her turn to starboard. Soon her port battery had the angle on the Frenchman. Those guns banged again.

"Starboard, you helm!"

"Aye aye, sir!" The wheel spun. Port gun crews worked feverishly to reload. At the instant the schooner passed back to a port tack, and as the corvette settled on a starboard tack, fate placed the English directly across the bows of the French ship.

"Starboard battery! Fire!" All the drill Pierce had insisted upon during the entire voyage paid off. The guns resounded, eight of them as one, and double-shotted, flung nearly 200 pounds of deadly iron projectiles at the nearing Frenchman.

"Starboard turn, Mr. O'Brien! Port the helm! Port battery ready! Train 'em forward, as far as they'll go!"

"Aye aye, sir!"

"Mr. O'Brien! Once we come around and the port battery fires, reverse the turn again! Keep us directly at them! Yaw so alternate batteries can bear!"

"Aye aye, sir!"

"Mr. Hotchkiss, if you please, sir. We'll double load grape after the next broadsides!"

"Aye aye, sir!"

"Sergeant Lincoln! Muster your marines and be ready to board!"

"Aye, sir!"

While Pierce preferred a battle of twists and turns, dealing deadly blows and avoiding those in return, the French captain was a most able opponent. This fight could take forever if it continued as it was. He wanted to avoid being boarded and the resulting hand-to-hand combat because of the relative sizes of the crews. In spite of the confidence he had in his men, he knew they would be outnumbered and more susceptible to defeat. Earlier, he had acted to counter such a move on the enemy's part. Had that given the impression that he would not resort to such tactics? Now, with several well-placed broadsides into her, would the Frenchman's fighting spirit be lowered? A sudden increase in the ferocity of his attack might surprise and demoralize them. With a rapid closing, grappling hooks, and a sudden swarm of British seamen and marines, he might yet take her.

Such success was not without precedent. Lord Cochrane and HMS *Speedy*, a small fourteen-gun brig, had taken *El Gato*, a Spanish thirty-two gun frigate in the Mediterranean prior to the Peace of Amiens. If Cochrane could do it, he could as well, reasoned Pierce.

Being to windward was to his advantage. Rather than feint and spar with the corvette, he would sail directly at her. Bow on be damned! They might receive one or two broadsides as they closed the gap, but the French were not nearly as quick at reloading as the British. With guns trained forward as far as they could be, he could yaw from side to side during a headlong charge and keep up a constant fire at the French. After the next set of broadsides, they would begin firing grape, hopefully clearing the decks of Frenchmen and evening their odds all the more.

*Island Expedition* swung south and crossed the corvette's wake. That vessel had continued her port turn and now headed to the east, running with the wind, trying to gain some distance from her adversary. Another two points to the south and the schooner's portside guns bore directly on the Frenchman. "Fire!" yelled Hotchkiss.

O'Brien nodded at the helmsmen as the guns' thunder echoed over the deck. The wheel spun to port and the curve to starboard halted. The bows pointed north again. Starboard gun crews used handspikes to lever their bulky machines of destruction as far forward as they could. Port gun crews reloaded hurriedly.

It was almost a chase now, the Frenchman to leeward, running before the wind, and *Island Expedition* also before the wind, attempting to close with her.

"I'll have the topgallants, Mr. Hotchkiss!" ordered Pierce. "We need the speed," he explained. "We sail a greater distance as we yaw to bring the guns to bear."

The schooner pressed forward, with additional canvas spread to the wind.

When their bows were dead on to the corvette's stern, that ship began a turn to the north. Perhaps they were attempting to again establish a broadside to broadside duel. If the schooner fired its starboard guns and immediately reversed her turn, the Frenchman might take advantage and rake the Englishman with her port battery.

Pierce foresaw the possibility. "Starboard battery! Once you've fired, lads, reload like you've never done before! Quickly! Quickly as can be!" He turned to the sailing master. "Hold to this turn after the next broadside!"

"Aye aye, sir!"

With the French turning in the same direction, it took longer for the starboard battery to bear. Finally the angle was right, and the guns roared. Even as the sound still reverberated and clouds of smoke rolled away towards the corvette, the gun crews leapt to the task. Supported by individuals from the port gun crews, their guns already loaded and ready, they worked feverishly to reload their deadly iron beasts.

The enemy had slewed her port guns as far aft as possible. Moments after *Island Expedition's* latest broadside, her own rang out. The range had decreased again, and several shot struck home. Splinters flew, lines parted, and more gouges appeared across the once spotless and pristine deck. Pierce felt a sharp stabbing pain in his left calf. He stood, transfixed for a moment, not daring to move, as if complete immobility would prevent the injury from being any worse than it was. Tentatively, he rose on his toes. It pained him, but he could move. He glanced down and saw his trouser leg torn and slowly turning red. Nonetheless, Pierce could stand and move without much difficulty. There would be time later to attend to it.

Through the hail of enemy shot, the starboard gun crews labored mightily to reload. In what seemed like seconds after the French onslaught, the starboard side twelve-pounders were run out again.

"Fire!" Pierce roared, now full of fighting rage. The guns discharged with an angry vengeance and he ordered, "Helm aweather! Hard to starboard! Port guns make ready!"

Momentarily *Island Expedition's* unprotected bows pointed directly at the menacing muzzles of the French warship. Because the French were slower at reloading, those deadly iron tubes were impotent and lifeless. Still, before the schooner swung far enough south for the port battery to fire, the enemy's port broadside boomed again. More shot rampaged over and through the English schooner. It seemed that no one was hurt, but an errant shot or flying splinter knocked Pierce's hat from his head.

Then *Island Expedition's* port guns fired. This time they had been loaded with grape, and even with the distance between the two vessels, Pierce could see the swath of destruction and death that cut through the French.

"Helm hard to starboard! Hard over, lads!"

With her helm hard over, *Island Expedition* described the better part of a half circle before her starboard guns bore. The double loads of grapeshot they spat out swept the length of the Frenchman, ripping, smashing, maiming, and killing from stern to stem.

Any farther into the turn and the schooner would be close-hauled on the port tack. "Helm aweather! Back the fore topsail!" They turned and stopped almost instantaneously. The bows pointed north and then back to the east. "Steady at that, lads! Hands to the braces! Port battery ready!"

The range had narrowed considerably, and as *Island Expedition* charged along a north by northeast track, the French corvette pointed as far into the wind as she could. Would she continue through the wind, and tack? Or would she reverse her turn, and bring the wind aft? Pierce sincerely hoped she would do just that.

"Port guns! Two quick broadsides from you!" The turn continued. The guns bore, spoke, and were reloaded in an impossible flurry of flailing rammers, sponges, cartridges, and stands of grapeshot. The brunt of the broadside caught the Frenchman's stern, smashing and gouging the ornate gingerbread, shattering glass in the stern windows and the starboard quarter gallery.

"Ease your helm, lads! Steer into her! Port guns, when we are alongside, one last broadside into her! Then we board!"

The guns were reloaded, their muzzles pointing dangerously out of the ports. Starboard gun crews hurriedly ensured their weapons were secure, abandoned them, and sought boarding pikes, cutlasses, and pistols. They massed inboard of their portside counterparts, leaving them enough room to work the guns.

The distance closed. The schooner came along the corvette's starboard side, both heading nearly to the north. Campbell and Davis stood by with grappling hooks. Gun captains stood at the ready, the lanyards to the gunlocks tight in their hands.

For a moment, the only sound was of the water alongside, the groan of the hull as it worked in the seas, and the snap and pop of the colors dancing in the cold westerly airs. Pierce watched, judging the speeds of both vessels, mindful of momentum. For a moment his gaze shifted to the Frenchman's quarterdeck. He was taken with the familiarity of one who stood there.

"Now lads!" Pierce yelled. "Fire! Helm alee!" The port guns sang their last planned devastating notes. The bows swung into the wind and into the Frenchman. Because of the mechanics of a ship in a turn, the distance between the vessels increased at the stern. Seconds before

*Island Expedition's* bow smashed into the Frenchman's starboard fore chains, Pierce ordered, "Helm aweather!"

The schooner drew parallel with the Frenchman, while the distance between them rapidly lessened. "Everybody down! Flat on the deck!" roared Pierce. The enemy's starboard battery had not fired in some time. They had plenty of time to reload, and with a target only feet away, they would not waste the chance.

No soon had he given the order and had thrown his own form prone to the deck, did Pierce hear orders shouted aboard the Frenchman. Her guns roared, shot crashing into *Island Expedition*. Flattened against the deck, British casualties were slight, despite the destructive force of the broadside. The two vessels came closer still. Spars and rigging intertwined and tangled, effectively locking them together. Campbell and Davis hurled grappling hooks, which caught in the corvette's rigging. Other seamen grabbed at the foe's rigging and hull, lashing the vessels together.

"Boarders away!" Pierce sang out. The cry was taken up by Lieutenant Hotchkiss and then the other senior people aboard His Majesty's Schooner. Soon all the British were yelling as loudly as could be. The clambered over the rail and leapt onto the enemy's deck, cutlasses swinging, slicing, chopping, and cutting ferociously. Boarding pikes flashed and whirled. Pistols banged and muskets boomed. Relentlessly, the English seamen pressed forward onto the Frenchman. Along the after portion of the port rail, the marines fired one final musket volley into the French. Then they vaulted over, landing aboard the enemy vessel. Pierce followed, sword in hand and a brace of pistols in his belt.

Alighting on the enemy's deck, Pierce felt two unrelated sensations. The deck was slippery, and he had to watch his balance. There was also a sharp stab of pain as weight came suddenly on his left leg. In the turmoil of combat, and the commotion of boarding, he had forgotten about his injury. A small splinter, perhaps a tiny chunk of flying metal, chipped off a gun, had earlier sliced into his calf. He gritted his teeth, silently uttered a blasphemous curse, and charged headlong into the fray.

Pierce drew a pistol from his belt. Already on half cock, he pulled it back into full. A Frenchman, wearing a liberty cap, loomed through the smoke. Pierce fired and tossed the pistol away. He did not have time to reload. He readied his other pistol. Looking aft, he saw the familiar-looking French officer disappearing down the companionway. Pierce fired. Splinters flew from the hatch coaming as his ball grazed it. The flight of the projectile was deflected, and merely knocked the Frenchman's hat off as he disappeared from view.

"Damn!" said Pierce, returning the second pistol to his belt. It was of no use as a firearm, but it would be handy as a club. Possibly he could use it to bluff an opponent. Now, it was blade time. He had never been able to afford a sword of distinction or exquisite and artistic workmanship. His was of standard pattern, plain and undecorated. It was serviceable, strong, flexible, and held a good edge, although Pierce often preferred to use a cutlass.

Their one chance for success lay in sustaining the ferocity of their attack. They had to swarm aboard the Frenchman, charge into them like hornets, and push them rapidly to surrender or into the sea. It needed to be done quickly, before the enemy recovered and realized the thinness of the English ranks. If he had to, he could call back to *Island Expedition* for a second wave of boarders. Perhaps the Frogs would believe, even for a moment, that the schooner harbored seamen who were not yet engaged and awaited their time to board. It had worked for Lord Cochrane, and that battle had been won against much greater odds than those now facing the men of *Island Expedition*.

As he moved savagely aft, he saw the destruction wrought by his vessel's guns. Those twelve-pounders of his, those guns that everyone claimed too big for the schooner, had done their dirty work. Double-shotted for the first few broadsides fired, they had torn the corvette to splinters.

He hobbled a bit as the soreness in his calf manifested itself. He cursed silently again, and for a quick moment thought anxiously about Townsend. Hopefully the midshipman was all right, patched and mended, resting comfortably below deck.

Across the entire upper deck of the French corvette, the English pressed forward. Their ferocious onrush demoralized the French, who fell back, gathering in little groups whose size continued to diminish. Soon these groups of Frenchmen were mere islets in an ocean of British seamen. Near the wheel, a French officer battled ferociously against his attackers. Pierce forced his way to that particular melee.

"Do you strike, sir?" he asked.

There was no immediate reply, only the apparent redoubling of effort by the hard-pressed foe.

"Sir! Do you strike before all your men are killed?" Pierce insisted.

At the sound of Pierce's voice, those engaged in combat with the French officer slowly and warily backed off. Not hard-pressed for the moment, that individual changed his focus from his immediate attackers and looked about the deck. Seeing his crew surrounded by and beset upon by the British, he shrunk noticeably in stature. His fierce demeanor faded.

"Oui, m'sieur. We are over it," he said despondently. Then he sorrowfully shouted out an order to the remainder of his crew. They ceased their efforts to defend their ship, laid down their weapons, and stood meekly under the guns, cutlasses, pikes, and glared at the victorious *Island Expedition* seamen.

## Chapter Twenty-Three

# An Old Acquaintance

"Thank you, sir!" said Pierce to the just-surrendered French officer. "Mr. Hotchkiss, take charge here. Sergeant Lincoln, three
marines and follow me!"

"Aye aye, sir," replied Hotchkiss, who had the experience to handle
a numerically superior but subjugated foe.

"Aye, sir!" responded the marine sergeant. "Duncan! Phillips!
Reading! On me! With the captain!"

Pierce made for the aft companionway where the familiar-looking
enemy officer had disappeared. If that individual was destroying secret
documents, would he arrive in time to prevent their loss? Some minutes had gone by since sighting the officer and the final surrender on
the quarterdeck. He was also spurred on by the haunting familiarity of
the Frenchman. Beyond wanting to prevent the destruction of sensi-
tive papers, he wanted to know who it was beyond any doubt.

"Sergeant! Take two and sweep forward! Roust any Frenchmen
that may be hiding! The other, on me!"

"Aye aye, sir," said Lincoln. He nodded slightly at Reading, indicating
that he would remain with Pierce. The three marines moved forward.

"Right, Reading, let's see what we find aft!"

"Aye aye, sir!"

In the great cabin, nothing was amiss, other than damage caused
by their own broadsides earlier that day. Looking closer, Pierce found
an officer's cocked hat, overweight with gold lace as favored by the
French, lying near an open stern light. The hat was torn, holed as
if struck by a projectile hitting it at head level. Suspecting that the
wearer had gone into the sea through the window, Pierce looked out.

Several yards aft, a uniform coat floated, trapped air keeping it on the surface. There was no sign of the wearer.

"Reading! Grab hold of my feet! Do you drop me in the drink, and your grog will stop until Hell freezes!"

"Aye, sir?" replied the marine, unsure of Pierce's intended actions.

Pierce stuck his head out and looked down, trying to see those portions of the hull under the stern that were normally out of sight.

"Hold on!" Pierce climbed farther out, wanting to see if the elusive Frenchman had hidden himself under the stern, hanging on to the upper pintles and gudgeons. He saw no one, and for the moment thought the person might have gone into the sea and drowned.

"Bring me back in, Reading!"

"Aye aye, sir!" The marine's sinewy strength soon had him back on deck.

"I'll see you get an extra tot for your services. Now let's be off!"

"Aye, sir! Thank you, sir!"

Pierce picked up the discarded hat, tucked it under his arm, and with Reading in tow, descended into the bowels of the French ship.

Forward, along these lower platforms, he heard voices. It puzzled him that they sounded so cheerful, relieved, and English. The corvette must be a commerce raider, and these were prisoners taken from vessels she had captured. The majority of the crews had been left aboard, transported to France as prisoners, while the vessels became prizes of war. Others, ship's masters or important passengers, had been transferred to the corvette. They had been sent below when the French captain decided to intercept a strange sail on the horizon, a sail that had turned out to be *Island Expedition*. The cable tier and hold were amongst the safest locations during a fight at sea.

Sergeant Lincoln and his two marines had found the prisoners, who were most grateful for their release. They crowded forward, pressing Pierce and the marines into a tight mass, wanting to shake their hands.

"Steady now!" said Pierce. "We have taken the ship and will keep it with some effort. When we can, we will bring you aboard, and you may again tread English soil."

"What vessel, may I ask, sir?" asked one newly liberated Englishman.

"His Majesty's Schooner *Island Expedition*, sir!"

"Gone in search of some legendary island?"

"Aye."

"And of whom it has been said, will never return?"

"Such remarks were never made in our presence. We found the island and are near to returning home. That is all I know, sir."

"By God, Pierce, it is you!" The voice, from a more forward location sounded very familiar.

"Mr. Sollars?" asked Pierce.

"Yes, Pierce."

"Where are you?"

"Forward, locked in the bo'sun's locker. Lift the latch, would you, sir?"

It gratified Pierce to have Sollars address him as "sir." He stepped forward and lifted the latch, a simple but effective device that locked whenever the door was shut. It had provisions for a lock, so that items placed inside would be safe from pilferage. A latch string normally led through the door, allowing anyone inside to open it. To secure the prisoner housed there, the string had been removed.

When Sollars first spoke, the other Englishmen set up a clamor. "Some quiet, if you please!" shouted Pierce. "Sergeant, see these people are taken aboard *Island Expedition*. The colonists' berthing should suffice to accommodate them."

"Aye aye, sir! Gentlemen, if you'll come with me."

"Oh thank God you're here, Pierce!" Sollars stepped out of the bo'sun's locker and stood near Pierce. "It looked like I'd be aboard this damned Frenchman until the second coming."

"You may go with the others, Mr. Sollars. I've got work enough, ensuring this vessel is secure."

"Yes, quite. But! Well, you see, Pierce--I do not get along so well with some of my fellows. Business, you know."

"Indeed?"

"As you may notice, Pierce," Sollars said with a condescending tone, one reminiscent of their days aboard *Theadora*. "I am no longer a King's Officer. I'm a merchant. Owned and captained my own vessel, until this damn Frenchman came along!"

"Your troubles with your companions?"

"Oh, I underbid someone on a shipment. The others are friends, good friends, and I am the outsider who bested one of their own. Had to beg the Frogs not to lock me up with them when going into action!" Sollars rubbed the top of his head and grimaced slightly.

Pierce looked at him questionably. "Injured, Mr. Sollars?"

"Of all the fool things! With the time I've had at sea, I hit my head on a deck beam. Damn near laid me out. Still quite sore."

"I see," said Pierce. "But we should go topside and see you safe aboard *Island Expedition*."

"Yes, quite."

"I thought to provide you a place in passenger berthing amongst your companions. But as you have difficulties with them, I shall be required to turn Mr. Hotchkiss out of his cabin and provide you with his."

"Most generous of you, Pierce. Mr. Hotchkiss as well, I should think."

In the better light of the upper deck, Pierce noticed that while Sollars was not wearing a hat, the dent caused by one was evident in his hair. "Your hat, sir? Did you misplace it?"

"Damn! I must have left it below. I shouldn't worry about it. It was old, and I have another."

"Quite right, I suppose," said Pierce. A question arose in his mind. It remained there and gently gnawed at him. For the moment however, as he had more pressing matters to attend to.

"Mr. Hotchkiss--status, if you please?"

"Aye, sir," replied the first lieutenant. "All French secured and under guard. We tore her up some, but she's seaworthy. Some knotting and splicing, plug a few shot holes, and she'll do. A good pumping-out as well, I should think."

"About the prisoners?"

"Over a hundred on board, sir. Under guard on the fo'c'sle, and officers by the mainmast. Appears we beat two to one odds."

"Indeed, Mr. Hotchkiss," said Pierce.

"Aye, sir. But one thing more."

"Yes?"

"Their captain is unaccounted-for!"

"Wounded? Killed?"

"If so, we haven't found him, whether as a body or a victim below decks. I speak a little French, but haven't managed to get anyone to tell of his whereabouts."

"Strange, Isaac, but I'm sure he will turn up. Their butcher's bill?"

"As we have it, twenty killed and another thirty-five wounded," responded Hotchkiss. "We have three killed, and seventeen wounded."

"Dreadful, the loss of any life, whether theirs or ours."

"Aye."

"And our condition, Mr. Hotchkiss?"

"We need some work as well. Knotting and splicing for the most part. Not a lot of hull damage. Chips reports no shot holes below the water line."

"Then we shall keep the hands at it. Detail the marines to guard the prisoners."

"Aye aye, sir."

Pierce went below and back into the corvette's stern cabin. Even now he did not know the name of the vessel they had just defeated. In contrast to the common practice of painting a ship's name on her stern, this vessel had none in that spot. Perhaps by looking through the ship's papers, those official records that had not been destroyed, he might find it.

He rummaged through the cabin, going rapidly through desk and bureau drawers. He found a letter of marque, authorization from the French government to prey upon British shipping. In the logbook, Pierce picked out names of the vessels and persons taken. He distinguished names of certain crewmembers. However, he noted, the captain was never referred to by name, but only as *Capitaine X*.

Progressing through the papers, Pierce thought some of the handwriting looked familiar. Where he had seen that hand before? He laid the sheaf of papers on the desk, closed his eyes, and revisited the last few moments of the fight.

Closing with the corvette, he had spotted a familiar-looking individual on her quarterdeck. After boarding, he had fired at what he thought was that same person hastily descending below. The ball had been deflected by the hatch coaming, but had knocked the Frenchman's hat off. Pierce had found the hat, and aft of the ship a uniform coat floating on the sea. Had that man gone into the sea rather than risk capture? Or was that what he was supposed to believe?

He had found his former shipmate, nemesis, and antagonist locked in the bo'sun's locker. Had Sollars been in the locker for the duration of the battle? The door could be opened any time from outside, although once inside with the door shut and latched, there was no way out without assistance. Sollars was hatless, had a slight head wound that matched the hole in the discarded hat. From the marks in his hair, Sollars had recently worn a hat.

Could John Sollars be the missing captain, the familiar-looking officer Pierce had seen on the corvette's deck? Had Sollars, desiring that Pierce think a French officer overboard and drowned, simply tossed the uniform out the stern window? Was that why the handwriting looked familiar? He had seen Sollars' entries in *Theadora's* deck log often enough. But as much as the evidence pointed to Sollars' complicity with the French, Pierce could not bring himself to believe it. He could not announce, even to himself, that his former shipmate now worked for the enemy. Even if John Sollars was not a dear friend, Pierce could not believe that he was a traitor to King and Country.

Pierce gathered up the papers and took them, along with the hat, back aboard *Island Expedition*. "Mr. Hotchkiss! Leave the deck to Mr. Morgan and join me below!"

"Aye, sir!"

In Pierce's cabin, still devoid of furniture following the battle, the two sat, each with a mug of grog. "Up spirits" had been piped to reward the hands for success in battle, and the two had each obtained a share.

"It pleases me that we've prevailed and taken her, Isaac. But that we have causes complications," remarked Pierce.

"Quite so?"

"We now have two ships to man and prisoners to guard. That will stretch us thin, I'm thinking."

"Aye, Edward," replied Hotchkiss. He would have used the more formal "sir," except that moments earlier Pierce had relaxed into the first name familiarity of their youth. Hotchkiss continued. "As I know you, you have a design for this situation."

"I do at that. We will remain as we are for the night. Darkness is fast approaching, and much more needs to be done. Tomorrow, you will take command of the Frenchman. I'll give you Mr. Andrews, Mr. Dial, and Mr. Steadman. You may choose either the port or starboard watch, or any hands from the other that you would prefer. You will have the marines to guard the prisoners."

"That will leave you short, sir!"

"Yes, but this vessel can be sailed with a smaller crew because of her rig. And we won't have prisoners aboard to worry us. In the extreme, we do have the released merchant masters. As seamen, their help would be most welcome."

"True!"

"And I'm afraid, Isaac, that I've promised your cabin to the former Lieutenant Sollars. He and the other Englishmen we rescued apparently do not get along."

"From what you have told me of him, I do not doubt it. With the work involved, I'll not need my cabin much this night."

"Nor will I need mine."

Pierce paused for a moment, thinking. Then with his voice lowered to a conspiratorial whisper he said. "Mr. Sollars may not be what he claims."

"Indeed?"

"Aye. Several things don't fit, as if one is wearing clothing not made for that individual. They fit, but not perfectly. The little things add up, and honestly I don't like the answer. Despite my personal dislike of the man, I hate to suspect a former shipmate and King's Officer. Yet he could be our missing captain."

"Possibly," remarked Hotchkiss when Pierce had voiced the details of his suspicions. "But dare we arrest him on those suspicions alone?"

"I think not. We will watch him closely. Does he exhibit behavior or action that would prove it, then we shall have him."

"Aye."

Following his conversation with Hotchkiss, Pierce went below and had Doctor Matheson tend to his wounded leg. It was relatively minor, and he had carried on for hours after sustaining the injury. Yet it was sore, and having experienced similar injuries in the past, Pierce knew it would bother him for some time to come.

He also checked on Townsend. Had the young gentleman not fallen in the opening moments of the fray, Pierce would have avoided battle and been a day closer to England. But because Townsend had fallen, Pierce had changed his mind and had pressed the attack. He was most gratified to find Townsend a survivor and resting comfortably.

Pierce and the others aboard *Island Expedition* had been extremely fortunate. None of the wounded were in danger of succumbing to their injuries. The three killed had died instantly and had not suffered. But of those three, he deeply mourned their loss.

Dawn the next day found the two vessels still lashed together. Repairs were nearly complete to both. *Island Expedition's* crew was exhausted, having fought desperately the day before, and having labored through the night to make repairs. Pierce had finally crawled into his cot in the wee hours of the morning, but had been up for most of the night.

Eubanks and Franklin had gotten the galley fires going soon after the combat ended the afternoon before. They had quite liberally borrowed from the fresher stores on the corvette, and had prepared a most welcome supper. Some hands objected, but Pierce had ensured the meal was shared with the French prisoners, now guarded and detained aboard their own ship. This morning, the coffee was fresh and hot. It warmed him and pushed his fatigue further into the background.

Pierce carried his steaming mug as he strode about the deck, checking details and ensuring all was going as planned. He paused every few moments to gulp the hot and restorative brew. With each sip, he felt life returning to his tired and aching person.

An English ship's master came on deck. He yawned and looked about, somewhat confused. He spotted Pierce and made his way towards the schooner's captain.

"Damn glad you happened along, Captain!" he said. "I was thinking we'd be aboard that dammed corvette until the war ended. Damn fine timing, sir!"

"Should you say so, Mr.... Mr.?" remarked Pierce quite noncommittally. "I'm sorry, but I do not remember your name. A long day and a long night, you see."

"Understandable, Captain. I'm Howell, master of *Ellen May*. Or I was, until that damned corvette came alongside in the middle of the night. Boarded and captured, nearly in our hammocks. Never fired a shot! Damn, but they were aboard afore we knew!"

Pierce nodded in commiseration. "A sly dog, to be sure. Even going through the papers we found, we haven't yet determined her name."

"Because she has none, Captain. Do you check her stern, you will find none painted or carved there."

"That was noticed, sir, even during the fight."

"But if you check closely, you will find bolts in the area where a ship's name would go. Somewhere aboard you will find a selection of names, carved and painted, each on its own plank that can be quickly affixed to the stern."

"Then she'll be seen as different ships at different times."

"Aye, and she carries canvas screens fitted to alter her appearance. The damn Frogs can change the color of the gun port stripe, or eliminate it. The bastards have one set that'll make it look like she's got more gun ports than she does, and another that'll make you swear she's got two less."

"A most clever man, their captain," said Pierce. "I am sorry he was never found."

"But you are not looking in the right place, Captain."

"And where should I look, Mr. Howell?"

"Damn, Pierce, must the captain of a French privateer be French?"

"No, I suppose he might not be."

"Then look to your friend, Captain! Like hell he was locked in the bo'sun's locker all the while! He came running below as you boarded. Headed aft and then came forward, putting on that shabby civilian coat of his. Let himself into the locker, moments before the marines arrived! Surely you've noticed yourself the ease with which it opens from outside?"

"I did at that."

"Mother of God, Pierce! That fool is her captain, not a prisoner as we were!"

"He has implied that your party might level such accusations against him. 'The business end of it,' he said," replied Pierce.

"Damn him, sir! He's lying to you! Do you not see it? I'm sure he feels old shipmates and fellow officers will take him at his word! Do that, sir, and it will be an error you will regret. I'll bring charges once we're in England. Against him! Against you, if I must!"

"Calm yourself, Mr. Howell. It is true he was a Royal Navy lieutenant and a former shipmate. But he is not now deserving of protection from any brotherhood of officers. I came to the same conclusion last evening, even while you and your friends rested."

"And you did not arrest him?"

"It would be far better that we find something, or that he does something to give us definite proof. Now we have only my suspicions and your accusations. He remains in the first lieutenant's cabin, both to hide from your friends and to avoid members of this crew. Many have sailed with him before and would gladly see him done for."

"Damnation, Pierce! Watch him, or he'll ruin you!"

"Rest easy, Mr. Howell," sighed Pierce, quickly taking a sip of coffee. "I will watch him closely, as will others of the crew!"

"Mark my word, Captain! That man! That friend of yours is her captain!"

*Chapter Twenty-Four*

# HMS *Pickle*

T he day, which had promised to be fair at dawn, continued as such. Repairs to the corvette were complete, or defects were jury-rigged and would serve for the short run to England. Even with over half the schooner's complement manning the prize, Pierce worried that they would not be able to adequately handle her. A full-rigged ship, the Frenchman required a larger crew to sail her than did *Island Expedition*. There was also the complication of prisoners very well-determined to retake their ship. Such a combination might prove disastrous for Hotchkiss and his prize crew, unless something could be done to even the odds.

"Mr. O'Brien!"

"Sir?"

"Do you go aboard and see her royal and topgallant yards struck on deck. Likewise, send down her topgallant masts."

"Aye, sir."

"You may put the prisoners to the task, does it please you. Can it be done, those spars and canvas to be sent aboard this vessel. If not, overboard with them."

"Aye aye, sir," the master acknowledged, even as he looked quizzically at Pierce.

Pierce, seeing the look, explained. "It will ease the work for the prize crew. Nor will the Frogs have the option of sailing away from us, should they retake her."

"Aye, sir. Understood."

Pierce yawned. Up most of the night, overseeing repairs, he had slept for a couple of hours as the darkness had faded into day. His eyes burned and watered from fatigue, as well as the icy breeze that blew across the deck.

Hotchkiss appeared bearing two steaming mugs of coffee. "I thought you could use another, Edward. Lord, I could drain the pot and still not be awake."

"An appreciated gesture, my friend." Pierce sipped enthusiastically at the hot beverage. "As tired as I am, I believe I've come upon a stroke of genius, although you might disapprove that I deprive you of your loftily sparred and fast-sailing corvette."

"Indeed, sir, I do not. I can readily see that Mr. O'Brien and friends labor to lessen her top hamper. I do understand the reasoning and am grateful for it."

"I did not doubt you would be. But tell me, did you convince any prisoners to sign on?"

"Eight, sir."

"Good! They are, of course, on board? It wouldn't do for them to be assigned as prize crew with their former shipmates as prisoners."

"Campbell is seeing them accommodated, even at present, sir. Yet of those that did not enlist, I seemed to have heard English voices. Three, I believe they were."

"For my own clarification, Mr. Hotchkiss, might they be amongst those Mr. O'Brien has enlisted to help reduce the corvette's top hamper? A couple of those fellows look very familiar."

Hotchkiss studied the activity on the Frenchman's deck. "Yes, there, at the main topgallant halyard, sir. Two of them, I believe."

"Yes, they're the two I noticed. My God, but they look familiar!" said Pierce. Were they deserters, men he had sailed with earlier in his naval career? No! That didn't seem to be it. Pierce stared hard at the two for a while longer.

Then he exclaimed: "I do recognize them. They are two of the brigands that waylaid Evangeline and me on the Isle of Wight!"

"Four, all told, were there not?"

"Aye, and at our commissioning, Jackson confided to me that rumor mentioned that Sollars may have had a hand in that incident. With some of the perpetrators found aboard the same vessel as Sollars, my suspicions mount to new heights."

"Mine as well, sir," added Hotchkiss.

After some moments of thought, Pierce asked, "Will you be better served to have additional English sailors aboard in place of those who have joined us?"

"Indeed I would, sir. And might I also have the services of either Eubanks or Franklin?"

"Eubanks or Franklin?"

"If I'd not noted it previously, their cook was amongst those killed, sir. Someone knowing his way around a galley stove would be welcome to all aboard, prisoners and prize crew alike."

"A shame you are deprived of French cuisine, even that provided by a ship's cook. I would suggest Eubanks accompany you. He is the more experienced and will have a larger number to feed. With only a half crew aboard, we can make do with Franklin's sometimes limited abilities. You may inform him at your convenience. Additionally, you may choose the extra hands you wish to go with you."

"Thank you!"

Hotchkiss departed to attend to his myriad duties. Pierce remained for a few moments, watching the activity aboard both vessels. Satisfied that all was in order, he went below.

"Mr. Hotchkiss, your orders," said Pierce as he handed over a sealed packet.

"It's simple enough, I believe," that individual replied. "Sail an unfamiliar ship with a partial crew, seriously outnumbered by our French prisoners."

"It's been done before, Isaac, and you will benefit in having Sergeant

Lincoln's marines to watch the Frogs. Thus, you may concentrate on seamanship and navigation."

"That does ease the task greatly, Edward. The marines even the odds."

"While you didn't ask, Isaac, I know you wonder about the written orders. Truth of it is, we've both sailed captured prizes only with our captain's verbal 'Make for any English port' ringing in our ears. Yet I believe they will serve us well, should things go amiss."

"I pray they do not."

"As do I. Now as we get underway, you will stay in our lee. Then we may close rapidly to deal with any situation that might arise."

"Aye aye, sir!"

The two spread canvas to the wind, and headed north. Pierce would have set all possible sail, but he was constrained by the maximum speed of the prize, now limited by the recent reduction of her top hamper.

Aboard *Theadora*, Pierce had learned the advantages of having a well-rested crew. Captain Jackson had always tried to ensure that all hands got adequate rest when it did not interfere with the frigate's safety or mission. With these lessons in mind, Pierce always tried to see that *Island Expedition's* hands were well-rested. On the outward voyage, and with additional crewmen from amongst the passengers, he had made the schooner into a three-watch ship. On the return journey, with the smaller regular crew further depleted by two vicious battles, he had been obligated to return to a normal two-watch system. Now, with over half of the ship's complement gone as prize crew aboard the Frenchman, Pierce had to keep the remaining hands on nearly constant watch. Fortunately, the weather was mild for the first days after the battle, and those hands not performing an immediate duty could often curl up on deck to grab a quick caulk. When he could, he let less essential personnel retreat to bunks or hammocks for a more complete rest.

Pierce now stood duty on a watch and watch basis. If he wasn't on deck, Midshipman Morgan, acting as first lieutenant, was. O'Brien and Spencer spelled each other, serving as both navigator and midshipman of the watch. Pierce was pleased to see that they and all hands adapted willingly to the longer hours and demands of the current situation.

With Morgan, Pierce evolved a routine in which one remained on deck and on duty as long as possible. When fatigue won out, the other was called for relief. Then the relieved individual went below and crawled fully clothed into his cot for a little sleep.

Because of the new routine carried out by the short-handed crew, hands were not piped to meals. Each day Franklin cooked what he could and kept it warm for as long as possible. Hands ate when they could be spared, or when meals were available. Pierce and the remaining officers followed suit in much the same way. Occasionally they managed more formal meals, primarily so they could offer some reluctant hospitality to the recently freed English prisoners.

That group largely remained in the former passenger berthing area, where they talked, argued, and drank. They had not volunteered to help work the schooner, and thusly Pierce preferred them to remain out of his sight and clear of the short-handed crew. While he and all aboard would have welcomed their help, it was not in Pierce's nature to press them into service.

Sollars spent most of his time below as well, voluntarily locked in the after most starboard sleeping cuddy. From his condition when he did venture out, Pierce could tell that he also kept constant company with the bottle. That did not surprise him, having served in *Theadora* with Sollars. That individual did not come out of what had been Hotchkiss' cabin unless necessity required he do so. Bad blood existed between him and the other liberated Englishmen. Whether the hostility existed because of a business coup, as Sollars claimed, or because of any treasonous acts on that individual's part didn't matter to Pierce. What did matter was that for the most part Sollars kept out of his way.

Pierce soon dreaded those times when Sollars did leave the cabin. Then he sought Pierce's company and seemed to look to Pierce for protection from the other rescued Englishmen. He dogged Pierce's shadow, almost as if he were afraid to be alone. He apparently respected Pierce's rank and position, but at times his old five-month seniority as a lieutenant came through, and he criticized everything done aboard the schooner.

On the third day after the battle, the clear pleasant weather disappeared. In its place came the more usual late-October rain, mist, squalls, and a cold blustery wind.

"Mr. O'Brien!" hollered Pierce over the wind. "Do you signal Mr. Hotchkiss, that he may shorten sail as is appropriate! We will follow suit to remain on station." Raindrops beat a rapid and thunderous tattoo against the taut mainsail.

"Aye aye, sir!" The master wiped the rain and salt spray from his eyes. "Mr. Hadley! Mr. Hadley! Signal the prize! 'Shorten sail! Your discretion!' Hurry now!"

"Aye aye, sir."

"This'll be a good blow, sir," remarked O'Brien. "I feel it in my bones. Mr. Morgan said his stump ached terribly just before you relieved him."

"I sense it, too," said Pierce. "I pray we can keep the galley fires going. I don't desire to dine on cold salt pork. And we'll need the warmth and the effects of coffee as well."

"Aye. Might I suggest, sir, a gun to call Mr. Hotchkiss's attention to the signal? In this rain and wind, perhaps they don't see it." As the master spoke, no move to shorten sail had yet taken place aboard the corvette.

"We'll give them a bit more time, Mr. O'Brien. They are shorthanded as well. But you may send for Simmons to prepare a signal gun."

"Aye, sir."

Simmons came on deck some moments later, grousing at having been aroused from his sleep. Under more normal circumstances Pierce would have rebuked him for his disgruntled attitude. But with all hands grabbing what sleep they could, when they could, and finding his own rest in short supply, Pierce let the gunner's mate grumble. Simmons shot reproachful looks at the weather, occasionally at the small knot of officers to windward, and even at the aftermost starboard twelve-pounder carronade as he readied it to be fired.

As he watched, Pierce wondered if his insistence that the guns not be kept in a loaded condition was in error. Had this particular weapon, or any of the others arranged about the deck been loaded, it would have been a simple thing to round up a minimum crew, run it out, and fire the signal.

"Carronade's ready, sir!" pronounced Simmons. "I'll put a crew together what to cast off, fire, and reload, sir."

"Very well, Simmons," answered Pierce.

"But a shot will not be necessary, sir," said Hadley over the wind. "She's reefing topsails now, sir!"

"Thank you, Mr. Hadley! You may stand down, Simmons. We will not need a gun to attract their attention."

"Get the damn thing ready and it's not needed! Which now I'll have to draw the damn charge! All for fucking nothing, and in the middle of my damned caulk!"

"Simmons, watch your tongue! I do thank you for your efforts and do not require you to draw the gun. We may need it later."

"Aye aye, sir." The acting gunner wandered off, murmuring disgruntled profanities under his breath.

"Mr. O'Brien! All hands to shorten sail!"

"Aye aye, sir! Campbell! All hands! Shorten sail!" Then with a grin he said to Pierce. "Simmons wouldn't have gotten much more of a caulk as it is."

"True. If this weather comes on, none of us may see much rest."

"Aye."

Campbell's pipe shrilled loudly, calling those crewmen who had managed to find a place to fall asleep. As they rushed for the upper deck and their stations for shortening sail, Pierce watched the similar effort aboard the corvette. With courses already furled, her topsails were being double reefed. As well, the jib came down and a reef was taken in her driver. Hotchkiss wasn't taking any chances. Did he know more about the coming weather, or was he merely being cautious? Aboard the schooner Pierce calculated what they would need to take in to maintain pace with the corvette.

"Mr. O'Brien!" yelled Pierce when the last man reached his station. "Furl topgallants! Double reef topsails! Double reef fore and main!"

"Aye aye, sir!" He turned to give the necessary orders.

"And get the flying jib in!"

"Aye aye, sir!"

"At the helm, there," said Pierce. "Ease off two points! When we are well clear of a direct run at her, come back to the current course!"

"Aye, sir! Ease off two points!"

"Do you find we are closing, you may vary your course to maintain this distance!" Being to windward, there was the possibility that Island Expedition could close the distance and collide with her prize. Mindful of that, it occurred to Pierce that should the weather get really bad, he would have to abandon his close watch over that ship and allow each more sea room.

Morgan, who had come on deck when all hands had been called, now stood nearby. He flexed his knee and repeatedly stamped the tip of his wooden leg into the deck. He grimaced slightly.

"Aches, does it, Mr. Morgan?" chided Pierce.

"Aye, for sure. Hasn't pained me like this since the Pacific. God, but I think we are in for it!"

"Mr. O'Brien said earlier you thought it would be a bad blow. My experience tells me the same."

"Perhaps some of the nasty gales we remember from *Theadora*, sir."

"Aye. I believe the wind still rises. We shall need to take in sail again before long."

Morgan gritted his teeth momentarily and did not reply. After a minute he said. "Sir, before we are required to do so, perhaps a bit of rest? I'll keep the deck, should you desire a quick caulk."

Pierce accepted the offer, having every confidence in Tom Morgan, and went below. He slipped into a chair at the table. He did not want to crawl into his cot. He was too tired already and knew that if he got too comfortable, he would have a devilish hard time waking if needed. When he awoke, quite on his own, he sensed the increased movement of the schooner, an indication that the wind had risen even more and that the seas were more agitated. He came on deck as Morgan called all hands to once again shorten sail.

Darkness fell, and still the storm's fury increased. During the second dog watch, both the schooner and the corvette shortened sail for a third time. Pierce increased the distance between the two, even though it made sighting the other a thing more of chance than of certainty.

Sometime in the mid watch the wind eased slightly, and the rain stopped. Pierce was still on deck, having refused another offer by Morgan to get additional rest. Instead he had insisted that that individual go below to get what sleep he could. Huddled in the dubious shelter of the windward rail, Pierce wondered if he'd erred in staying on deck. His eyes burned and he yawned at increasingly frequent intervals. The galley fires had gone out during the evening watch, meaning there was no coffee to keep him awake.

Off the schooner's lee, he made out the prize as it rode laboriously under a storm jib, triple-reefed main topsail, and fully reefed spanker. With the wind blowing less fiercely now, neither vessel strained as they had earlier. But with the wind easing, the seas it pressed flat roiled up and increased in size and power. *Island Expedition* tossed wildly amongst the gargantuan waves.

Eight bells struck, marking the end of the morning watch. As the wind slackened, the air grew colder. Pierce, already soaked through and cold, thought to go below for warmer and drier garments. The addition of his boat cloak might serve to ward of the chill he felt.

"Mr. Spencer," he said. "I shall go below to fetch something against cold. May I retrieve anything for you?"

"Why I thank you, sir. But I am quite comfortable at present. Should I desire something later, I believe you would permit me a quick dash to fetch it."

"Of course, lad. You know me too well. I'll be back momentarily."

Below, Pierce saw that the door to Hotchkiss's cabin, now used by Sollars, was open. That was odd, he thought, because Sollars had not been on deck since the previous afternoon. With the hostility existing between him and the merchant captains, Sollars would not have left the door unlocked and open. Pierce's shoes were well-worn and the soles softened by constant exposure to the elements. He moved silently to his own cabin, puzzled, but not concerned that anything might be amiss. He intended to change into dry clothing, fetch his cloak, and return to the deck. He noticed that the door to his cabin was ajar and became more wary. Normally he didn't lock it, but always made a point to fully close and latch it. As he approached, Pierce detected a faint glow of light from within and heard rustling papers.

Alert and suspicious, Pierce grabbed for the sword he was not wearing. Damn! He swore silently to himself.

He opened the door. "May I help you, Mr. Sollars?" he asked, quite civilly. John Sollars sat on the deck, engrossed in the paperwork, charts, and maps that were spread haphazardly before him. From the much-folded appearance of much of it, Pierce's one-time shipmate had found the important documents so carefully hidden beneath the deck planks.

"Ah, Pierce, what's this?" Sollars slurred. "No privacy afforded a former shipmate? No knock? No, 'By your leave, sir?' No respect for a former prisoner? Do you forget that I was once senior?"

"Stow it, Sollars!" glared Pierce. "What are you doing in my cabin?"

"Your cabin?" asked Sollars with feigned surprise. "But this one is mine, sir. Did I choose wrong upon returning?"

"You are enough a seaman to know port from starboard, even when dead drunk! You are in my cabin, not because of a sot's error, but for other reasons. That you are is enough. Get out! Get out, now!" Pierce moved towards Sollars.

As Pierce stepped into the cabin he shouted, knowing his voice would carry up the aft companionway. "Mr. Spencer! You and two hands to the great cabin! Now, sir!"

He heard the clatter of feet overhead as the master's mate jumped into action. Sollars sprang to his feet, one of Pierce's pistols in his hand. He pulled it to full cock, pointing it menacingly at Pierce.

"Damn you, Pierce! You've always won! At everything! You've always won!"

"But we were never in competition, sir!" said Pierce, wary of the pistol.

"You had Jackson's ear, even as junior lieutenant in *Theadora*. Damn! He listened to you and all your foolish and idiotic ideas. He liked you! Hell, even the hands liked you! They'd 'ave followed you or him to the ends of the damn earth!" Sollars waved the pistol and pressed it closer to Pierce's torso.

"Well-trained and disciplined men will do as they are told, Sollars," Pierce said quietly and evenly, ominously aware of the weapon.

"So you say, Pierce. But did Jackson listen to me? Seek out my counsel? Would the hands act at my mere suggestion? Would they do the simplest thing without an order and promise of a flogging?"

"I understand your vexation, Mr. Sollars."

"Bloody hell, you do, Pierce!"

"But is your discontent enough that you go over to Bonaparte?"

"To hell with that stunted Corsican scrub! There is more to the war than Frogs or Tom Roast Beef! There are powers that most do not know about. But I do! They will be victorious, rule in the end, and I will be greatly rewarded for my services."

"I doubt it."

"Because you take my ship? It matters little. I am quite hipped about it, Pierce, but it doesn't alter what will be. The *seekers* of a long-forgotten knowledge shall find it and reign supreme over this and other worlds. And I shall share in that rule!"

"My God, have you gone mad? You serve the French and yet deny it! You spout drivel about unknown powers, lost knowledge, and other worlds! These are things no sane man would dare utter!" But even as he said it, Pierce realized he lied. He knew of at least one other world, having recently been there. As his mind raced, he recalled Captain Cooper's recounting of Professor Parks' theory and the apparent Gallician attempt to take *Island Expedition*. How much did John Sollars and others in this world know?"

"I'm no more insane than you, Pierce, if your papers are to be believed. I see you found the island you went looking for. Knowledge of that, my old friend, shall set me in good stead with the *seekers*."

Sollars was quiet for a moment. The pistol shook in his hand, and he gestured threateningly at Pierce again. "No sudden moves, Pierce. I'll put a ball in your belly as sure as I stand here! Now back out slowly!" He advanced towards the door and Pierce sensibly backed away from the pistol.

In the great cabin Pierce stopped and looked cautiously about. Spencer and two hands, Hopkins and Mitchell, were there. They came to a complete halt, nearly paralyzed as they saw the pistol pointed at Pierce's gut. Watching Sollars' eye, Pierce saw he had noted their presence. "No mistakes, lads," Sollars said. "I'll splatter him all over this cabin. Mark my words!"

Suddenly Sollars reached out with his free hand, trying to grab

Pierce's arm to turn him about and gain a more advantageous position behind him. While Sollars moved quickly, Pierce moved faster. He stepped quickly to his left, away from Sollars' grasping hand. At the same time he kicked at Sollars' hand holding the weapon.

The suddenness of it delayed Sollars' reaction for a brief second. He fired! Pierce's kick deflected the muzzle enough that the shot just missed him. Even so, he felt the heat of the blast, scorching hot at close range, and the sting of unburned powder grains that erupted from the muzzle to embed in his skin.

Angry now, and before Sollars could do anything else, Pierce swung his closed right fist and caught Sollars full in the face. He staggered drunkenly, both from the effects of drink and the blow, but he did not go down. Pierce swung at him again and grimaced as his knuckles scraped across Sollars' bony unshaven chin.

Seeing an opening, Hopkins and Mitchell seized Sollars' arms. Roughly they twisted his arms behind him, and Spencer tied his hands. Pierce drew a full breath for the first time in what seemed to be ages, and shuddered with pain. Sollars had indeed shot him!

The wound was not serious--a mere scratch, as he saw it, and the end of the afternoon watch saw Pierce on deck again. Morgan had insisted that his captain get some rest, and after treating the wound himself, Dr. Matheson being aboard the prize, had stood duty until Pierce awoke.

"Where's Sollars?" Pierce asked, half hoping the hands had pitched the bastard into the sea.

"Below, sir. In chains and well-guarded." Morgan flexed his knees slightly. "A little roughed up, I'm afraid. There were a great many volunteers to see him below."

Pierce nodded. Several of the crew had served with Sollars in *Theadora* and couldn't resist a chance to settle with their former second lieutenant. "No doubt he fell down the ladder?"

"Three times," said Morgan, with a knowing and barely perceptible smile. "I think the weather eases some. It doesn't pain me as it did."

"The prize?"

"As before, sir. Minimum sail, and in sight to leeward."

Pierce turned to look for the corvette, forgetting the wound Sollars had inflicted with his own pistol. "Damn!" he exclaimed painfully.

Before he could draw a breath and recover, the foremast lookout hollered. "Sail off the port quarter!"

"Details, man, details!" yelled Morgan.

"A schooner, sir! Driving hard, and coming up fast. Too much sail in this weather, I think, sir!"

"A Frog, sir?" asked Morgan.

"I wouldn't have the foggiest, Tom," replied Pierce. "Should it be, do we attempt a second prize?"

"I shouldn't advise it, sir. We are undermanned and stretched to the limits as it is, now."

"My thought as well. But do have our colors hoisted, and signal Mr. Hotchkiss as well. Add that he may set additional sail as the weather eases."

"Aye aye, sir."

A few moments after the blue ensign broke out in the wind aboard *Island Expedition* and the captured corvette, the lookout hailed again. "The white ensign, sir, and driving like mad!"

"Mr. Hadley, aloft with you, sir!" said Pierce. "My best glass, if you wish, and see if you can make her number!"

Moments later the midshipman hollered down the approaching schooner's recognition number. Pierce couldn't relate it to a particular craft, and went below to consult the code book. Back on deck, he said to all who waited anxiously for an identity to be placed on the fast approaching vessel, "His Majesty's Schooner *Pickle*, I believe, gentlemen, Lieutenant John Lapenotiere."

"*Pickle*, sir? Why I believe she's an advice schooner attached to Nelson."

"With the way she cracks on, she must have dispatches of some importance!" stated O'Brien.

The vessel was now observable from deck, and even in the lessening wind, Pierce thought she carried too much sail. She was a small schooner, rigged in the traditional topsail schooner fashion. Had she been a foe, *Island Expedition* would have been more than a match for her. On her present hard-driving course, she would soon pass close by the larger schooner and her prize.

"Mr. Morgan, do see that our recognition signal is out, sir!" ordered Pierce.

"Aye aye, sir."

As the second dog watch began, the smaller schooner neared to hailing range. "What news, sir, if I may?" hollered Pierce with the aid of a speaking trumpet.

"A great victory at Trafalgar, sir!" came the reply. "Alas, poor Nelson was done in."

"We rejoice in the victory and mourn England's great loss!" shouted Pierce in response. "Mr. Morgan, a moment of silence about the deck!" When the moment had passed, Pierce continued. "And now lads, a cheer for His Majesty's Schooner *Pickle!*"

When the "huzzahs" and the "hurrahs" died away, Pierce turned to Morgan. "Do allow us to close with the prize, that we may inform Mr. Hotchkiss of the news."

"Aye aye, sir!"

When the evening watch was set, all that could be seen of the small schooner were her lights as she raced towards England with her triumphant yet sobering news.

## Chapter Twenty-Five
# An Unnoticed Return

Pierce kept the deck until seven bells in the evening watch as *Island Expedition* eased through the lessening seas. Many of the hands had served with Nelson in the past. A feeling of sadness clung to the schooner, not to be dissipated by the ever-present wind. He felt it too, having been in *Orion* when Nelson had won his great victory at the Nile. Pierce had even dined with the great man at one point, although he could not remember ever having spoken with him.

Morgan came on deck following his rest. He carried a cup of grog and one for Pierce. "Do you think, sir, we should drink to Nelson?"

"Aye, thank you, Tom," said Pierce.

"I never served under him, sir, but I feel that England has lost her greatest protector. No matter the threat, Lord Nelson was sure to prevail and guard us all."

"If his victory was complete, perhaps he has done that, even in passing."

"Perhaps?" said Morgan. "Lord Nelson and his memory!"

"To Nelson," echoed Pierce. He lifted his cup in salute and quickly drained it.

"And now sir, might I insist you go for a rest? I know you're tired."

Morgan was right, Pierce agreed silently. He nodded and went below.

It was ten days into November of 1805 when *Island Expedition* approached the anchorage at Spithead. In consort with her prize, a nameless French corvette, she saluted the port admiral. The answering cannonade echoed across the wind-whipped, rain-laden waters.

"Make ready!" bellowed Pierce.

"Aye aye, sir! Starboard bower ready!"

"Helm, ease into the wind!"

"Aye, sir. Ease into the wind."

"Back the topsails! Strike the headsails!

The schooner rounded into the wind, slowed, and for all intents, stopped.

"Let go!" The starboard bower dropped with a splash into the sea, the hawser following out the hawse pipe. A trace of smoke arose from the friction of its passage.

"Clew up, there, Mr. O'Brien! And the mainsail in as well!"

"Aye aye, sir!"

"Mr. Morgan!" said Pierce. "Signals to the port admiral and senior captain present. 'Standing by to report. Prize has prisoners to be off-loaded. Require return of prize crew aboard.'"

"Aye aye, sir."

"And Tom, call away my gig! I shall be below momentarily, readying my reports."

"Aye aye, sir."

Before going below, Pierce watched the prize round to and drop her hook into the slate-gray water. Hotchkiss and his prize crew put on a fine display of seamanship, even as short-handed and fatigued as they were.

In his cabin, Pierce looked through his reports once more to ensure that nothing was amiss. Luckily he had kept them up to date during the course of the voyage and had only to add the accounts of encountering the corvette and the last leg of the journey to finish them. He checked over them again, knowing they were as complete, accurate, and truthful as they could possibly be. But because of the truth that was in them, a truth he knew his superiors would not easily believe, Pierce was reluctant to sign, seal, and wrap them in their protective canvas covers. There was enough evidence in those documents, he reasoned, that charges could be brought against him, as well as provide ample evidence of his guilt. Over the last weeks of the voyage he had tried not to think of the furor he knew his reports would cause, but now, faced with the realization that they would soon be in official hands, the fear of their pending disbelief came to the fore.

Nevertheless, the reports had to be handed on. He signed, sealed, gathered them together and returned on deck. By now, O'Brien had all sails tightly furled, yards set square, and falls flemished, faked, or coiled neatly. Morgan had gotten the gig into the water and had scraped together a crew. Lofton was in the prize crew aboard the corvette, so Jones was at the helm as the gig rode easily alongside the entry port.

"No replies yet, sir," said Spencer, now acting as signal midshipman.

"Damn!" commented Pierce. He had estimated that by the time he had returned to deck, signals would have been seen demanding why he hadn't already reported. Others would inquire as to how many prisoners, and that a relief for the prize crew could not be arranged. Yet, the only flags that flew were those from *Island Expedition's* own signal halyards. Should he wait for acknowledgment and orders to report? Or should he go ashore, report, and deliver his documents unbidden? "This is most unusual!" he added.

"Aye," said O'Brien.

"A boat's putting off from the hard!" hailed Thomas from aloft.

Pierce gazed shoreward, and certainly a boat, possibly a captain's barge, crept into the anchorage. No doubt it conveyed a captain returning aboard after business, official or personal, ashore. Confused and slightly irate at the lack of communications, he watched the boat's progress. Amazed, Pierce saw that it headed directly for the schooner. "Gentlemen, it appears we will have company. Fetch Campbell directly, and muster side boys!"

"Aye aye, sir!"

As the boat neared, Spencer hailed, "Ahoy the boat?"

The coxswain answered. "*Doris*," and held up four fingers.

Jackson? Granville Jackson was coming aboard? Pierce joyfully awaited the arrival of his old captain, friend, and mentor. But his gig awaited him alongside and would block the approaching barge's access to the schooner's side. "Jones! Take my gig to the port side. Clear a spot for Captain Jackson!"

"Aye aye, sir."

Granville Jackson's hat appeared at the edge of the deck. As he mounted the steps affixed to the schooner's side, Campbell started piping and the side boys raised their hats some six inches over their heads. Pierce and the other officers did the same. Jackson reached the deck, lifted his hat in salute and the shrill echo of the bo'sun's call faded.

"Welcome aboard, sir!" said Pierce warmly as he extended his hand.

"And welcome back, young sir!" replied Jackson just as warmly. "You are here, with a prize in tow. Indications, I trust, of a successful voyage?"

"Indeed, sir. Very much indeed!"

"When there is time, you must tell me about it. But I see you have more pressing matters just now."

"Aye, sir. I'm dismayed to have not had a response from shore yet."

"Most unusual, yes. But we are all aback with the news of Nelson's great victory. Or have you heard, Edward?"

"We were overtaken by *Pickle* a fortnight ago, sir. No details, as it was: only that Nelson had died victoriously."

"Rest his soul, he did. Off the Cape of Trafalgar. Word reached here only recently." Jackson replied with a touch of sadness in his voice. He too had once served under Nelson. "Now Commander, the port admiral will call for your reports, written and in person, in good time. Until then, what do you require? Perhaps I have enough weight upon my shoulders," Jackson said, indicating his two epaulettes, "that I can move things along. Two swabs are better than one."

"Aye, sir. There are prisoners aboard the prize to be taken off."

"Yes. Anything else?"

"I would hope to turn the prize over at the earliest instance and have my prize crew back aboard, sir."

"Understandable. I'm owed a favor. Prisoners should be taken care off by sundown. I cannot promise relief of the prize crew, but should you wish it, I will send hands in their stead."

"Very kind of you, sir."

"My pleasure, Commander Pierce," Jackson said. "If you will notice, the port admiral has seen fit to answer your hail."

Pierce turned. "Indeed he has. Then I must go and deliver my reports. I'm most grateful to have seen you again, sir."

"I as well. I must return aboard and see what can be done for you. I trust you and your officers will join me for dinner tomorrow?"

"With pleasure, sir!"

Ashore at the port admiral's official residence, things progressed much as Pierce had dismally expected they would. He was kept waiting for over an hour in the outer rooms while the flag officer read the reports. Then he was called in, made to stand tall and explain how he could possibly submit such incredulous and imaginary reports. There were threats of relief of command, arrest, and court-martial, much the same as he had experienced in Sydney from Governor King.

Finally the admiral relented slightly. "Damn, Pierce, you know if it were my choice you'd be under arrest, even as we speak. But I have orders concerning you--orders telling me that regardless of how incredible your documents might seem, I am to extend you every courtesy and aid."

"Aye, sir," Pierce said.

"As we speak, arrangements are being made to unload the prisoners from the prize. I understand Captain Jackson has arranged that your prize crew might return aboard *Island Expedition*?"

"Yes, sir."

"Now Pierce, my orders require me to send notice of your return to London, and to have you remain until word is received back. You may of course go ashore in the local area as you see fit. Your crew may be allowed ashore at your discretion, although I do not advise it. You'll lose the lot of them, mark my word!"

"Sollars?"

"Oh yes, that damned scrub!" the admiral spat. "He is officially re-signed from the service. Can't be court-martialed, you know. He'll be taken to London and stand trial as a civilian. A damned good solicitor and the bastard might survive it. He's aboard the schooner?"

"Aye, sir."

"I'll send a boat to fetch him ashore and turn him over to the civil authorities."

"Thank you, sir."

By the next afternoon, a midshipman and several seamen from HMS *Doris* had gone aboard the captured corvette. Their presence allowed had allowed Hotchkiss and the prize crew to return aboard *Island Expedition*. "Mr. O'Brien," said Pierce. "Make and mend for the remainder of the day. Tomorrow as well, I believe. Starboard watch to have liberty after eight bells."

"Aye, sir."

"All hands aboard prior to tomorrow's forenoon watch. Port watch to have liberty as the first dog watch commences." Pierce made this last remark, not so much to instruct the master, but so hands within hearing would know when they could expect to go ashore. He was departing, going aboard *Doris* for dinner with Captain Jackson, but would return in a few hours.

"Aye, sir."

"Now gentlemen, are we set? Good! Now into the boat with you!" said Pierce. "We do not want to keep Jackson waiting."

Granville Jackson had invited not only Pierce to dine, but the schooner's entire cadre of officers as well. There had been a flurry of activity on board that morning as all going made an effort to be presentable. Over the past weeks, with half the crew being aboard the prize, matters of personal appearance and neatness had taken lower priority. In fact, upon hearing of the invitation, Hotchkiss had remarked that he would "much rather catch a good long caulk. But as it is Jackson who entertains us, I will bear up."

Alongside *Doris*, as Pierce climbed aboard, he was momentarily surprised to hear the bo'sun's pipes and drum rolls welcoming him aboard. For the first time in his life, he was being piped aboard another vessel. It was a most welcome consideration, he thought. Jackson and Forrest, the first lieutenant, and a former shipmate as well, met him warmly and then turned to great the remainder of the party from *Island Expedition*.

"Mr. Hotchkiss, sir. I'm pleased to see you again," said Jackson. "Welcome aboard!"

"Thank you, sir." Hotchkiss shook the proffered hand.

"And Mr. Morgan, and Mr. Andrews! You are not the squeakers you were when first aboard *Theadora*!"

"I should hope not, sir," Andrews said with a smile.

"But I see you have been hurt, Mr. Morgan. I trust you have mended well." Forrest noticed the wooden substitute for Morgan's lower right leg.

"I was fortunate to have most excellent medical care, sir."

"Hadley--how you've grown, lad!"

"Yes, sir."

When all those from *Island Expedition* had come aboard and been warmly greeted, Jackson introduced the officers serving in *Doris*. Then he suggested that all proceed below to where dinner awaited in the great cabin.

True to what Pierce remembered of serving with Jackson in *Theadora*, the meal was not fancy. Like Pierce, Jackson came from rather humble surroundings and much preferred common everyday dishes to the exotic and rare. Much of what was presented to them could be found forward in the crew's mess, but aft, it was prepared with extra care. While several wines and brandies were available, Jackson also provided ship's beer and grog for his guests to wash down their victuals.

Rather impolitely, although apparently not noticed nor complained about by those of the frigate, Pierce and his group dominated the conversation. That had come about simply because Jackson had said, "Now Pierce, you must tell us about your voyage. Should any of you wish to add, feel free to do so. You may recall that at my table, a junior need not wait until addressed in order to speak."

Somewhat reluctantly at first, Pierce began the account of the voyage. The first part was easy to tell, but relating those circumstances occurring after Cape Town was difficult. How would Jackson, Forrest, and other old shipmates receive the tales of having found a completely different world? By this time, the meal had gone on for some time, and most had imbibed considerable amounts of wine and spirits. The younger members of the schooner's contingent weren't quite so shy about describing this aspect of the voyage. To Pierce's partial relief, they spoke up and described those portions of the journey. He spoke only to confirm what the others said, or to clarify some point brought forth by Jackson or others of *Doris*. Pierce closely watched his former captain and the frigate's officers for signs of disbelief.

Seeing none, and upon hearing no remarks as to his sanity, Pierce wondered if they really believed it. He was just at the point of daring to comment on the fact, when Jackson remarked, "I do find some aspects--no, many aspects--of this tale very hard to believe. But I know you, Commander Pierce. I've served with you and many of the others as well. I know that none of you, separately or together, would concoct such a story. If you say it is true, then it must be."

"I am greatly relieved by your confidence, sir," said Pierce.

"I'm not sure but what Admiral Tompkins and the British Island Expedition Organization might have suspected such all along."

"I wasn't aware he was a part of the Organization, sir."

"Not directly. His involvement was why he told you of the voyage that day aboard *Bristol*. If he were not in the West Indies, he would be most anxious to hear of your expedition."

"Aye, sir."

"But Pierce, be prepared for most not to believe you. You must be prepared for doubts or questions of your sanity. For the rest as well, gentlemen, there will be rough sailing ahead."

"Much as I've already experienced, sir. I believe I mentioned the reaction in Sydney. It was much the same at St. Helena, and again with the port admiral yesterday."

"My point, sir," continued Jackson. "But others in higher places have confidence in you. Hence you are still in command and not facing court-martial."

"To my great relief."

They ate in silence for a while. "It's a shame that Mr. Townsend couldn't join us," remarked Forrest as the meal approached its end. "I remember he often would say the wrong thing at the wrong time, quite often to our amusement."

"A little to drink, sir, and he still does," commented Pierce. "I've tried to correct him, but seemed to have failed. But I do miss his presence at the table."

"In another week, perhaps, gentlemen," said Dr. Matheson. "He is healing well. However it is just too soon for him to be up and about."

"I too will look forward to seeing him again," said Jackson. "I must say, you all have had quite an adventure."

"Beg your pardon, sir," said Hadley. "But for all the adventure, and the taking of that corvette, it seems our return has gone quite unnoticed."

"Had you returned even two weeks ago, a bigger ado would have been made of it. Unfortunately you have arrived upon the heels of news concerning Lord Nelson's victory and death. All of Portsmouth, indeed all England is consumed with it. At this time we know so little of the battle, that speculation and rumor run rampant.

"But gentlemen; your capturing that French corvette will not go unnoticed for long. It has bedeviled us for the past two years."

"And Sollars in command of her!" said Forrest with disgust. "I wish I had followed my instincts aboard *Theadora*."

"I as well," said Jackson.

"Still," added Pierce, "I was quite surprised at his fighting ability. I never expected him to be quite so accomplished. He proved to be a most worthy adversary."

"Perhaps he learned more in *Theadora* than we imagined," said Forrest.

"Aye, perhaps he did," said Jackson. "Now shall we go on deck for some air?"

Nearly a week later, Pierce was on deck, idle, as he watched a boat pull away from the hard. Bored, he kept watch on it, trying to determine where it was headed. Soon it became apparent that the craft was making its way towards the schooner. It approached the side, and the bow hook caught hold of the main chains. A young lieutenant, splendid in a newly tailored full dress uniform, came up the side. "Come aboard, sir?" he said crisply.

"Aye aye, sir," replied Andrews, who served as officer of the watch. "May I help you, sir?"

The lieutenant eyed Andrews' worn and somewhat stained uniform, the scarred, beaten deck, the worn rigging, and tattered sails. Apparently finding it all unsatisfactory to his impractically squared-away mind, he sniffed. "I have orders for Master and Commander Edward Pierce."

"Aye, sir. I will see he gets them."

"I am to deliver them directly into his hand."

"Very well sir. If you will come this way?" Andrews led the lieutenant from the entry port to the taffrail, where Pierce waited and watched. Making the introductions, Andrews returned to his duties. Even then, face to face with Pierce, the lieutenant seemed reluctant to hand over the packet of orders. Perhaps it was because Pierce, bundled against the cold and not expecting visitors, wore an old pea jacket with no epaulette on the left shoulder.

Pierce glowered at him and finally said, "Damn it, man! Must we all be dressed for Sunday inspection?"

"Indeed not, sir. My apologies. If you will sign here, so the admiral will know you received them?"

"Of course. He would not take your word for it?"

"He would, sir, but he has orders for your signed receipt as well."

Pierce watched the sharply dressed lieutenant climb down the side and order the boat's crew to "shove off." On such a cold and blustery day, he should have invited the messenger below for a cup of coffee, a warming glass of brandy, or at the very least, the chance to be out of the wind for a few moments. But Pierce had seen the disdain in the man's eyes and had caught the aura of supposed superiority in his manner. Let the pompous fellow provide his own refreshment. No doubt he was an excellent seaman who could keep yards squared, decks holystoned, and bright work shined. But could he fathom the tremendous effort that had been made to bring *Island Expedition* to the state she now exhibited? Could he understand that this vessel had just completed a circumnavigation of the globe, with much of the final portions of the voyage through heavy seas and high winds? Could he appreciate the damage and destruction that had recently been wrought by the French corvette's guns? If not, then the fool could provide for himself.

Pierce tapped the packet of orders against his hand, but made no move to open them. He contemplated reading them on the windswept deck, but thought the better of it. They could get wet, be smudged beyond legibility, or worse yet, blow away and become lost. He went below, entered his cabin, and closed the door.

With his penknife he cut the cord and broke the seal. A note written by the port admiral's secretary was on top. It merely said that for Pierce's convenience in carrying out the enclosed orders, a carriage would wait on the hard at morning's first light. Under that lay another packet, this one secured with an Admiralty seal. He opened that as well and read rapidly through the document. Then he reread it, slower this time, pausing to ensure he understood its content.

Pierce opened his door and looked about the common central portion of the great cabin. At the cabin's forward door he said, loudly enough to be heard on the other side, "Pass the word for Mr. Hotchkiss there!"

"Aye aye, sir! Mr. Hotchkiss to the cabin! Mr. Hotchkiss to the great cabin!" The call was passed along, and within a few moments that individual appeared.

"Yes, sir?" he said, somewhat breathless. "My pardon! I was aloft, checking that shot strike on the fore topgallant mast."

"No cause for concern, I trust?"

"No, sir, none." Hotchkiss poured himself a cup of coffee, and at Pierce's non-verbal invitation, sat down. "You've received orders?"

"Aye. But one might say that we've received orders."

"I as well?"

"I am to go to London, to Whitehall. You are to accompany me."

"Then we do not sail."

"No, there will be a carriage in the morning. Mr. Morgan will have temporary command. And I would advise you to pack well. There is a chance we will stop at home on our return, and it is my intention to let you remain for some short time. I am to return aboard with reasonable dispatch."

"Aye," said Hotchkiss. He smiled.

The trip north was a thoroughly miserable undertaking. It rained steadily, and the road soon became a vast sea of mud. Traveling in second best editions of full dress uniforms, Pierce and Hotchkiss attempted to stay clean and dry. They planned to obtain a room upon arrival and shift to their carefully packed best uniforms before reporting. But several times the carriage became hopelessly mired and both got out to help push. Two days later they were mud caked, mud spattered, and soaked through as the carriage entered the outskirts of London.

Teeth chattering, Pierce hollered at the driver. "Any decent inn near Whitehall will do, if you please!"

"Aye, sir, but I've got orders to see you straight to the Admiralty."

"Damn!" said Pierce. Hotchkiss nodded in agreement. What a spectacle they would make, dripping muck all over the cold stone floors of Britain's naval headquarters. Pierce steeled himself against the expected glances of disapproval. On a day such as this, many with business at the Admiralty would be wet from the rain, but they would be in their best and not wearing half of Southern England on their persons.

Unexpectedly, they did not pull up to the front entrance. Instead, the carriage went around to the back. The footman dismounted, and tapped solidly on a nondescript door. It opened a moment later and a thin middle-aged man in civilian attire hurried to the carriage.

"Commander Pierce? Lieutenant Hotchkiss? I am Mr. Clemens, secretary to the Head of Special Projects. Won't you please come in?"

Through the nondescript portal, Pierce and Hotchkiss found themselves in a small but comfortably furnished room. A fire burned on the hearth, and both were drawn to its warmth. Two desks, a large table, several cabinets, and many comfortable chairs filled the space. The driver and footman brought in their baggage, which they set quietly along the far wall. Mr. Clemens handed each of the carriage men two shillings, thanked them, and suggested that they as well find a warm place out of the rain.

"Here, gentlemen," he said, turning to the officers. "You may warm yourselves and then clean as you wish and shift to more presentable clothing." He indicated a doorway. "Through here you will find water--hopefully hot--soap, towels, and so on. I will see that a small meal is delivered shortly. Please rest and refresh yourselves."

"Our duty in reporting, sir?" asked Pierce.

"I shall be on my way to inform his lordship of your arrival. He may not be ready to receive you at the moment, so do take advantage and recover from your journey."

"A practical idea, sir," said Hotchkiss.

"Yes, I suppose it is," added Pierce. "Might I ask, sir, if there is someone who could engage us a room nearby for the night? A night's sleep would be most welcome prior to returning to Portsmouth."

"Oh, there is no need for that, Commander. Through the other door are accommodations you may use as required."

"Very kind, sir."

"And now if you will excuse me, I will see your dinner delivered and the First Lord informed of your arrival. Later this evening, per-haps tomorrow, there is a gentleman who wishes to meet you. When he is ready, I will take you to him. In the meantime, gentlemen, I urge you to rest and refresh yourselves."

"Most certainly, sir," said Pierce. He was quite warm now, and moved farther away from the fire.

Late that afternoon, having washed, shaved, dressed, and having eaten heartily of the meal brought to them, Pierce and Hotchkiss were led through a series of corridors and back rooms to the First Lord's chambers. Charles Middleton, Lord Barham, welcomed them warmly, and begged them to be seated.

"Oh, to have sailed on such an excursion, gentlemen! Magnificent! Truly magnificent! It is a shame Nelson's great victory and lamented passing overshadows your own glorious accomplishments."

"We are most grateful, milord, that you so readily accept all that is accounted-for in the reports."

"It is not that I accept your reports at full value, Commander. However, there are others, some in positions of power greater than mine, who do. Their belief and recommendation are enough for me."

Pierce glanced at Hotchkiss, who looked back with the same inquiring expression. "I'm not sure we understand, milord," said Pierce.

"In all honesty, I'm not sure I do either. I do understand that you will be meeting one of the gentlemen concerned this evening."

"Yes, milord?" answered Hotchkiss.

"Perhaps he will be able to better explain it. Now, do you excuse me, I've other matters to attend to. And might I offer my congratulations on the successful completion of a most arduous voyage."

That evening, Mr. Clemens invited them to dine at his club. When the meal was finished, he said, "If you will come with me, there is someone desiring to meet you." He escorted them to the top floor of the building. At a door at the far end of the hall, he knocked, the door opened and all three stepped inside.

The room was quite dim and it took Pierce a few moments to accustom himself to the darkness. In the far corner, a single candle burned on a small table. From out of the nearby shadows, a frail voice welcomed them. "Come closer and sit with me!"

Two chairs sat on opposite sides of the table. Pierce headed to his left. "Do we not need a third seat, sir, for Mr. Clemens?"

"I think not," said the voice. "He has accomplished his mission in bringing you here. Now he has other tasks to attend to."

"I see," Pierce replied. "Do we introduce ourselves?"

"I know who you are, lads. As a matter of safety, mine and yours, it is best you do not know who I am, thus the lighting theatricals. But pray, do sit down."

"Aye, sir." As he sat, Pierce spotted a shadowy figure at the end of the table. The light was sufficient enough that the man's form could be made out, but the distinguishing features of his face, further concealed beneath a cowl, could not be seen.

"I must congratulate you on the success of your voyage," he said. "Your reports confirm what we have long believed. Your recent encounter with that unnamed French corvette also confirms our worst fears."

"Sir?" asked Hotchkiss.

"There is an international consortium that has always believed this other world exists. Feeling Harold Smythe had a good chance to find it, those of us in Britain helped found the British Island Expedition Organization."

"You're not only British?"

"Indeed no. We have associates throughout Europe, the Americas, Asia, and Africa. At one time we had power beyond your imagining, influencing and guiding kings, emperors, and even religious leaders. We never sought it for our sake, but rather to accomplish our primary task. Over the past century or so, we have become a society of old men, exchanging letters and theories about the supposed existence of that world. Still, many of us have great wealth, and with that there is always influence of some kind. Smythe brought us out of our libraries and into the real world again. Now you have proved that that world and the island exist, we must again press on with our true mission."

"May I ask, sir?" inquired Pierce.

"Somewhere in that world, somewhere on that island you have found, we believe there is a great store of knowledge. If it is found by those truly deserving, it will be of great help to all mankind. However, if discovered by others, it may well lead to the total destruction of civilization."

"The Ancient Ones?" asked Hotchkiss, looking at Pierce.

"Perhaps," that individual replied.

The shadowy figure continued. "There are others, gentlemen,

desiring that knowledge. They wish to use it to further their own ambition and quest for power. While we hope to access it someday, it is much more important is that the *seekers* be denied its use."

"Professor Parks?" remarked Hotchkiss.

"And some of what Sollars said as well," added Pierce. "We have heard the term *seekers*, before."

"Yes, they are all around us, and seem to have a great deal of influence with Napoleon and the French. They offer great things to the greedy, and those hungry for power."

"Sollars," said Pierce. "Fits that profile nicely."

"Yes," said the unidentifiable presence. "It was his debt and a willingness to do anything to pay it that led to his recruitment. On the other hand, Commander, you accepted command of the schooner with no question of pay at all. If I understand correctly, Smythe had to insist that you even discuss it with him."

"I suppose that's true, sir."

"That was the biggest factor in granting our approval for him to hire you. The arrangements with the Navy were a matter of convenience for all of us."

"But what now, sir? What do we do?"

"You may do as you wish, Commander. If it is in your destiny to continue in service to the *guardians*, you will. We will never insist or ask you to turn your back on your country or friends."

The conversation continued for some time after that remark. At long last the old man, for there was something in his very presence that suggested antiquity, rang a bell. In a few minutes, there was a knock at the door. It opened, revealing Mr. Clemens, who escorted Pierce and Hotchkiss through the club and back to the small suite of rooms at the Admiralty.

For a long time upon their return, neither Pierce nor Hotchkiss said much. As neither made any preparations to sleep, it was obvious that the day's conversations continued to influence their thoughts and actions. At last, over a second glass of fine Madeira, Pierce said, "Isaac, did you notice the gentleman's ring?"

"Why no, I didn't."

"Perhaps there was not enough light from your seat, but a time or two he extended his hands out of the shadows. Old hands, gnarled and wrinkled, bent and broken with the rheumatism, but on one he wore an exquisitely fashioned ring."

"Not improbable for one reportedly having great wealth, Edward."

"No, the ring itself did not amaze me, but the figure under the translucent blue stone did."

"May I ask what it was, Edward?"

"Of course. It was a white, or lighter blue, four-pointed star."

"The same as the Unity Congress symbol?"

"Aye! Exactly the same!"

## Chapter Twenty-Six

# Reunion

The return to Portsmouth was more leisurely than the trip to London had been some days earlier. They stopped each night, rather than changing horses and pressing on. As the second day ended, they found themselves nearing Petersfield. Home was nearby, and they urged the driver to go the extra distance prior to stopping for the night.

Pierce stayed two days, visiting with family and friends. Sadly, his older brothers were not there. Rather than risking press gangs again, they had volunteered for service when the war resumed. At last word they had been serving in HMS *Conqueror*, a vessel that had taken part in the recent triumph off Cape Trafalgar. As of yet, there had been no word of their fate. While he would have liked to have stayed and supported his family during this time of uncertainty, he had orders to return aboard *Island Expedition* as soon as was reasonably possible. Therefore, he bid farewell and set out for Portsmouth. Having been promised a longer stay, Hotchkiss remained, agreeing to return the next week.

Tuesday the 3rd of December, 1805 found *Island Expedition* still at anchor off Spithead. It was a cold gray rainy evening, typical for that time of year. The cold wind whistled through the rigging and tugged at the ensign and jack that flew from their respective staffs. It flung spatters of rain with spiteful venom into the faces of those unfortunate few on deck. The wind stirred the sea into motion, so that even in the sheltered waters, the schooner moved noticeably to the surges of the icy brine.

As Pierce sat in his cabin that stormy December night, he felt like an old worn-out gun, charged with too much powder and trying desperately not to burst from the force of the explosion. He was drinking rum, straight, and not watered into grog, rather than his usual coffee, which told of the strain he felt.

While the trip to London had been enlightening and had brought relief in the knowledge that he would not be court-martialed, Pierce grew tired of the continuous waiting. The port admiral had no duties for him. Letters and reports to the British Island Expedition Organization, or to those whom he thought were the Organization, yielded no response. Immediately upon arrival he had seen his long continuing letter to Evangeline posted. He had had no reply, either to that large packet or to the shorter missives he'd sent since.

Having not yet heard from Evangeline tore at him like a hurricane-force wind shredding worn and ragged topsails. Had she completely forgotten him over the three years of the voyage? Could he have somehow so angered her that she refused even to acknowledge his presence in England? Had she been so in love with this Lieutenant Carlisle, and was she devoted so completely to his memory, that she could not accommodate even a short letter to him?

He heard voices on deck, the clatter of feet on the companionway, and then a knock at the door. "Yes?" he said, struggling to sound civil and relaxed, when his temper desired he answer with angry tones and vile words.

"A letter for you sir, brought out by shore boat."

"A letter? Come in, Mr. Dial."

"Aye, sir," said Dial as he stepped into the cabin. "Here, sir. And the boatmen said they were promised sixpence each should they reach us, sir."

Surely whoever hired them meant that they should collect that payment when back on the hard. Obviously the boatmen were trying to collect a double fee for their service, being paid both by those on shore and those aboard the schooner. He was about to have Dial to tell them to shove off and collect their sixpence each from shore, but he glanced at the letter, recognized the handwriting, and softened. With the weather as it was, he knew they had struggled to bring the letter out to him.

"Two of them?" he asked, pawing through the loose coins in the top desk drawer.

"Aye, sir."

"Well, then, Mr. Dial, they shall need to share this, as I do not have the proper coinage to give them each." He handed a shilling to Dial. Then he softened a bit more. "No, Mr. Dial, we'll reward them double. A shilling to each." He handed Dial an additional coin. "You may offer them coffee, if that will warm them."

"Aye aye, sir." Dial left to pay the boatmen, see them off, and resume his duties.

For some time Pierce sat at his table, the letter before him. He wanted to tear it open and to read the words she had written. Yet he was very much afraid of what truth might be revealed once it was unsealed and the words, written with her own hand, were revealed. Absently he reached for his glass. The pungent odor of rum tickled his nose, and as the rim reached his lips, he thought otherwise and set it down.

He pushed the glass, half full of rum, to the back edge of the table. Then he dug out his one remaining mug and departed the cabin. He hoped that there was coffee, hot and fresh, on the galley stove. He suddenly and desperately wanted a cup of the hot restorative beverage. As he made his way forward, he reminded himself to not vent his anger, frustration, or disappointment on the cook should no coffee be ready.

Back in the cabin, Pierce took a long sip from the cup of coffee. It was hot and relatively fresh. He broke the seal, unfolded the paper and read:

"Edward,

I have received your letters written during the voyage, and indeed a few written as you are anchored at Spithead. I humbly apologize for not replying with more haste.

During your absence, things occurred that I did not plan for, and because of them, things between us are not as they were. I do not want to leave things between us unresolved, so I have journeyed to Portsmouth and have obtained rooms at the George. Please do not be so angry that you would refuse to call upon me for dinner tomorrow. Evangeline."

He read it through again. It was rather cool, he thought, not full of the passion that she had once held for him. Still it was not as cold and dismissive as it could have been, and she did want to see him one more time. Although he was quite disappointed with the current state of their relationship, he certainly would not refuse a chance to see her once more.

He was awakened the next morning by the sounds of the returning liberty party. Pierce did not fear his men would run at the first opportunity. To a man, they were as loyal and honorable, in the British seaman's unique way, as any group of underpaid, overworked, and often harshly disciplined men could be. He had worked to ensure that loyalty by tempering the usual brutal Royal Navy discipline with a touch of common sense, a little kindness, and a spirit of trust. They had been recently paid the three years' wages earned during the voyage. Besides the rather paltry sums that had accumulated on the Royal Navy's books, they had collected from the British Island Expedition Organization. It would have run counter to his nature and lessened their continued support had he kept them onboard and denied them a run ashore.

From the sounds that reached his ears, the chance had been worth it. He heard laughter, shouts, merry voices, and the clatter of shoes on the deck. He also heard Hotchkiss, who had returned aboard the day before, admonishing a few not to be sick on deck. He also detected the groans of those who had drunk too much.

Lying in his suspended cot, Pierce's head ached, his stomach churned, and his pulse throbbed loudly in his ears. He was glad all had returned, although he based that on the volume of noise overhead. Apparently all had an enjoyable time, again judging from the sounds intruding into his cabin. Perhaps some of them had gotten lucky the past evening, and with a little more luck, they would have had their enjoyment and not contracted the pox.

But God, did they have to make so damn much noise? Did Hotchkiss have to yell so damn loud in his efforts to quiet them down? Pierce felt nauseous and discovered that he was wet with sweat. That confirmed it. He also had drunk too much the previous evening. Perhaps if he went back to sleep?

But even as the din on deck died down, he found that he could not resume his slumber. He needed coffee! He needed cup after cup of scalding hot fresh coffee! He also wanted or needed, the question of which was not clear in his mind, a bath. With those realizations, he got up and started the day.

Later, having bathed the best he could manage, using basins of hot fresh water from the galley stove, and having finished his fourth cup of decently hot and fresh coffee, Pierce decided that he might live after all. He sat at the table in the great cabin, nursing his fifth cup of hot beverage and eating a rare breakfast. He mopped up the remnants of three eggs with a slice of wonderfully fresh soft bread, slathered with half-melted fresh butter. He ate with care, almost delicately, as he was in his full dress uniform, ready to go ashore on both official and personal business. Hotchkiss sat with him, enjoying his own breakfast of burgoo, toast, and coffee.

"To be sure, Edward," said Hotchkiss, "a run ashore does the hands good. That any would run outweighs the dangers of a ship out of discipline, with women and peddlers aboard."

"Aye," replied Pierce. "Better, I believe, to have a crew one can trust, than to imprison them aboard, even if all conveniences of shore are provided."

"None are missing from last night's liberty party, although a few are in a bad way. No broken bones, but there are numerous bruises and many nasty hangovers."

"That's to be expected. I would tend to put my own person into that category as well," continued Pierce, feeling momentarily dizzy. "I was in the bottle last night, so it is right that I feel as I do today."

"But you are feeling well today, sir, even with your head pounding."

Pierce assumed a quizzical look.

"Why to be sure, Edward, you are more open and of better conversation today than you have been for weeks. I was told a letter came for you late last evening?"

"Aye, one did."

"From Evangeline?'

"Aye."

"And you are to see her?"

"In the afternoon, once I have completed with the admiral."

"Would you say 'hello' for me, Edward? And do extend both my condolences and my congratulations as well."

"Condolences and congratulations, sir?"

"I've read the papers as well, friend, both those we gained at St. Helena, and the ones received after our arrival here. The possibility of her being Carlisle's wife and widow has preyed upon my mind as well. That newer evidence points to it as a fact is not lost upon me, either. Honestly, I would be most nervous to see her again, were I you."

"That you are not does not detract from your accurate assessment. I am most anxious to see her again, and yet I dread it terribly. I fear this will be the last time I shall see her."

"But you will see her! That is the prime thing!"

"You are right, of course, Isaac."

"Aye," said Hotchkiss, taking another sip from his cup.

At that moment, there was a knock at the cabin door. "Yes?" said Pierce.

"Mr. Morgan's compliments, sir," replied Hadley. "I'm to tell you that *Victory* has been sighted, entering the roadstead."

"Thank you, Mr. Hadley. My thanks to Mr. Morgan." Pierce finished his current cup of coffee and then said, "Isaac, shall we go on deck? I would feel strange not witnessing Nelson's return."

"Indeed. I assume his remains are on board." Both of them grabbed greatcoats and hats before going on deck. The day cold but clear, with numerous clouds scudding across a bright blue sky.

Quite far away yet, off the schooner's port quarter, Nelson's flagship, HMS *Victory*, slowly proceeded to her anchorage. The huge 100-gun first rate moved closer, her colors lowered as a sign of mourning. As she passed other vessels, they lowered theirs in a sign of respect and sorrow.

"Mr. Hotchkiss, we would do well to man the rail as she passes."

"Aye. The watch below, sir?"

"No. Let them recover from their escapades. But do see that all in a duty status are present."

"Aye aye, sir!" Hotchkiss glanced at Morgan, who in turn spoke briefly to Hadley. That individual darted forward to ensure that all required hands were on deck. As the liner approached, the on-deck watch manned the port rail. Everyone on the schooner watched silently as the great ship-of-the-line neared.

At what seemed the proper moment, Pierce nodded. "Attention to port!" ordered Hotchkiss. "Off hats! Lower the colors!" Hands stood bareheaded and quiet as the ship passed by. Pierce and the other officers uncovered and stood in respectful silence. As *Victory's* quarterdeck drew abreast, Pierce saw a small movement, an acknowledgement of their subdued salute to a fallen leader.

When the ship had passed, Hotchkiss waited a respectful period of time and then dismissed the hands.

"God, she took a beating!" said Pierce. "She's jury-rigged seven ways to Sunday. And did you see, Isaac, the pumps are still going."

"Aye, it must have been a terribly great battle! I believe we have all been sailing dangerous waters."

Just after six bells in the afternoon watch, *Island Expedition*'s captain's gig came alongside the landing stage at the Portsmouth waterfront. "You lads need not remain. Return to what duties Mr. Hotchkiss or Mr. Andrews may have for you. I shall signal should I require a return trip. Else, I will hire a boat."

"Aye, sir! And the luck be with you, sir."

Pierce had not discussed this excursion ashore with his gig's crew, but it was evident they knew of his impending meeting with Evangeline. They had all met her prior to the voyage, when they were all busy stowing supplies and stores aboard, and when she in her honest and unassuming way had often joined in to help.

The weather had cleared since the previous day. The drizzling rain was gone, and the cobblestones were nearly dry. The sky had layers of broken clouds, each moving with the winds that differed in strength and direction at its particular altitude. Small patches of blue showed through from time to time. An artist's sky, thought Pierce, full of shades and colors and dynamic movement. It would challenge a painter of lesser talent, and yet with the brushstrokes and pigments of a master, become a lovely accent to a seascape or battle scene. But the air was cold, and the wind blew sharply. Pierce shivered as he stepped ashore and headed briskly towards the George.

The walk got his blood flowing and the exertion warmed him, and when he arrived he had stopped shivering. As he stepped inside the welcoming warmth of the establishment, his nose began to run. He reached for his handkerchief.

"May I be of assistance, sir?"

"Indeed. I am calling on Miss... no... Mrs. Carlisle. I believe she is expecting me."

"Ah yes. Captain Pierce, is it?"

"Quite!"

"This way, sir. If you please, sir. The lady has asked that you join her at her accommodations. She has ordered a dinner that is to be served there."

Would this not cause talk amongst those always seeking tantalizing bits of gossip? Was it proper for a widow in mourning to receive a gentleman in her rooms? But it might be better that they met privately, away from the inquisitive eyes that would be on them in the public dining rooms. He followed the servant, wondering how such short legs could carry such a large body so rapidly.

At her door, the servant knocked softly.

"Yes?" Pierce heard her voice from within. He remembered its rich fullness, and his pulse quickened ever so slightly upon hearing her.

"Captain Pierce is here, ma'am," said the man with him.

"Please, do come in!" she said.

The servant opened the door and stood aside. Pierce dug a coin from his pocket, tossed it and said, "Thank you! You've been most helpful!"

"Oh, you're most welcome, sir!"

"Edward! Edward! Do come in!" She had not taken a single room, but an entire suite. It surprised him that she could afford to do so, although he had long suspected that her father possessed greater wealth than he exhibited. As well, Pierce knew nothing of her late husband, whether they had existed on his lieutenant's pay, whether he had collected prize monies, or whether he had left her anything of a personal fortune.

She was lovelier than he remembered, thinner than when he had last seen her, but that could be the effect of what she wore. Once she had been content to wear the most basic things, and at times had been mistaken for a servant.

Now she dressed as befitted the wife of a Royal Navy Lieutenant. Her garments were dark and somber, relieved by the sparkle of small gold or silver buttons and the contrast of white lace along certain edges. The clothing fit her well, and while not particularly revealing, made no attempt to hide her figure. The deep maroons and dark grays of her attire contrasted with and complemented the tone of her clear and unblemished skin. Her luxurious dark hair had been put up neatly and was topped by a small hat that matched the dress itself.

"I am so glad that you have returned, Edward," she said, extending both hands.

He took them gently but firmly and lifted them to his lips. He kissed them in succession, and drew her nearer. The blood raced through his veins with such vigor that it pounded in his temples. All the loneliness of the past three years was at an end! In the next instant, she would be in his arms. He would once again taste her intoxicatingly sweet lips and revel in the closeness of her perfect body.

As he drew her closer, she stiffened. She turned her head and tilted a cheek to his eager lips. Slightly put off, Pierce kissed the proffered cheek. What had once been between them apparently no longer existed. Could it ever be rekindled?

"My dear, I have thought of this very moment for three long years, ever since we sailed that last time from Cowes. As promised, I have returned, and you are here that I may do so."

"Indeed you have, Edward! But over time, things neither of us could have foreseen occurred. But come, let us dine, and talk of other things."

"I do have an edge to my appetite. Perhaps it is the weather?"

"You always, did," she smiled, "regardless of climatic conditions."

She led the way into the dining table, and pulled a bell rope. "It will be up shortly," she said. "I'll sit here, and you may sit across."

"Certainly, my dear." He pulled out her chair for her.

"How is Papa?" she asked, sipping her glass of wine.

Pierce tasted his as well. "He is excellent, both in health, and joyful in realizing his life's ambition. And while he will not admit it, I believe his heart has been stolen as well."

"Oh my! Papa in love? Who is she, Edward?"

"Vera Packingham, a widow from Vespica. She serves as his house-keeper and hostess." Evangeline's countenance clouded. "My dear," continued Pierce. "I'm so sorry to bring up any remembrance of your situation. Perhaps I should not have mentioned it."

"That Papa has personal interests or that she is also widowed? No, it was quite all right that you did so. I'm happy for him. And I know she must be quite wonderful."

"She is very pleasant, to be sure."

"But tell me more of the island and the voyage. The papers have not said much, only that you found the island. They have not provided any details, neither of the voyage nor the island."

"There are those that might withhold such information from the public at large. But have you not seen the reports to the Organization? And I'm sure I included quite detailed accounts in my letters."

"Oh, I recall some from your letters, but I have seen nothing of reports to the Organization, whether yours or Papa's."

"But are you not directly involved? I understood you to be a central and decisive part of it."

"In a word, the Organization, that part with which we were familiar, has become quite disorganized. It has split into factions that spend more time quarreling than doing anything else. Actual control belongs to a group of rather mysterious strangers. While I do not doubt their sincerity, they no longer deal directly with us. Perhaps, had my life not turned as it did, I would know more of what happens."

"The *guardians?*" Pierce suggested. She cocked her head and raised an eyebrow inquisitively. He continued. "I was only recently made aware of them myself. They must be the hidden backers of the

Organization. I believe they have reasons to protect what might be found on the island."

"I see," she said, although from her expression it was clear that she did not. "Could they not have informed the Organization as it existed, rather than allowing it to dissolve into constant discord?"

"Apparently they value their anonymity. But your description of the original Organization reminds me of the Vespican Joint Council."

"The…?"

"I'm quite sure I mentioned it in my letters, but it is the governing body of the Independent Lands of Vespica. The members almost never agree on anything. However, they did concur once, which is why I am here now."

"I do recollect some from your letters. But I confess that with everything else, I have not read them as thoroughly as I should have."

"Understandable."

Conversation halted when someone knocked at the door. The staff quickly and expertly placed dishes on the table, and spooned well-portioned servings onto their plates. Pierce lowered his spoon into the soup, a clam chowder, although thicker and creamier than he would have thought. It was well-warmed, nearly hot, and the unusual thickness caused it to slow and adhere on the way down, warming him, an event for which he was grateful. The delicious flavor lingered on his tongue. On each of their plates were ample servings of halibut. An anchovy sauce would have been the perfect accompaniment, but that none was provided did not bother Pierce in the slightest. In addition there was bread, wonderful soft bread that fell apart from the weight of the butter spread upon it.

"I asked that we not be disturbed by the staff returning and tending to removes, Edward. Therefore, all is available as you see and could want."

"Over the course of the voyage, I've learned to eat as it is presented. I have not become accustomed to, nor am I obsessed with any set dining protocol."

Having finished his soup and a second serving of halibut, Pierce served himself a generous portion of veal and ham pie. "Would you care for some, my dear?" he asked, with a generous portion en route to her plate.

"Oh yes. But please, not so much!" she answered. He lessened the portion and placed it on her plate.

There was also a leg of mutton, and as he started on that, their conversation, which had eased with the arrival of the meal, regained its intensity.

"It would seem, my dear, that many details of the voyage are withheld from the public, because they are too fantastic to be believed. In fact, my reports have caused some to question my sanity and ability to command."

"They would dare question that?" she said indignantly. "You did successfully complete a truly monumental voyage!"

"But I do not blame them. For those who did not experience it, it must seem that I have gone mad." Pierce took another bite of lamb. "I truly dreaded the reception I would receive, knowing how such reports and information would be perceived. While many scoffed at the truth revealed, I fortunately have the support of those who have the real power. I still command *Island Expedition*. Isaac, Andrews, Morgan, and all the rest can attest to the incredible details in my reports. Every man jack aboard can swear to the truthfulness of the reports."

"Thank God nearly all returned. It would prove more difficult if you had been the only one to come back."

"How very true. I might be awaiting court-martial."

"Should I ever meet any of them, I will remember to thank them on your behalf."

"Certainly," said Pierce. "And while this pursues a different course, I am to remember you to Isaac."

"And do remember me to him as well, Edward."

"I am also to pass along his congratulations, and his condolences."

She tensed slightly, caught her breath, and lowered her fork, the bite of lamb untasted. "Edward! My dear Edward," she said with a look of melancholy to her lovely features. "As distressing as it is, I hoped I would be first to tell you of what befell me during your voyage. You should not learn of it from the papers or those who do not know either of us."

Suddenly Pierce did not feel hungry and laid his fork down as well. "But I did learn of it. And I confess it has caused me a great amount of anxiety."

"I'm so sorry to have hurt you, Edward."

He saw the shimmer of tears in her eyes. "But does it matter, now that I am here?"

She sniffled. "Of course it matters. You will never trust me again. You will always know I could not wait for you. If you are at sea, you will always wonder if I am alone, pining for you, waiting for you, or if I have already taken up with the next handsome lad that passes by."

"It would be a lie if a man apart from his love didn't wonder such things. But doesn't she wonder the same about him?"

"Oh yes! But it is expected that a man take what he needs when he can."

"That does not excuse it." *And I am so guilty*, he thought.

"No." She sat silently for a moment and then asked, "Do I ring and have it removed?"

"I may regain my hunger. Wait awhile."

She swallowed. "I really meant to wait. I really did. I longed for us to be reunited, but I was not going to lock myself away."

"I would not have expected you to," Pierce said gently.

"I tried to keep busy. I helped Henry Dawes with the Organization. As Harold Smythe's daughter, I attended many balls, dinners, and parties, most of which were for the other more unseen parts of the Organization. Once I was partnered with a young lieutenant. We got along very well. I saw him at various functions and we always had an enjoyable time. But things happened so fast and I couldn't stop them. When I was discovered to be with child, Kenneth did the honorable thing and took me as his wife."

"I do not expect to be fond of his memory, but he did all duty and honor required."

"Yes. He was an honorable man. He would do what was correct, even if to atone for having done wrong. A month after we wed, his ship sailed, and I never saw him again."

"I grieve for you and your loss," said Pierce, meaning it. He arose and moved around the table to her. She looked at him with her eyes brimming full. He held out his arms to her, so that she could seek shelter and comfort. If need be, his shoulder was available to absorb her tears and misery. Her throat worked as her lips trembled. She stood and moved into his embrace.

Then her tears came, soaking hot onto his unadorned right shoulder, dampening and soaking through to his shirt and his flesh beneath. Between sobs he made out her muffled words. "I always loved you, Edward. Always! I never stopped loving you! Believe me! I never meant to hurt you!" With each admission and each self-admonishment the sobs renewed and she shook with their force.

Pierce gently steered her to a small settee. He sat and drew her down so she sat on his lap like a small child. He comforted her, stroking her hair gently, while with his other hand he wiped away the tears streaming down her face.

When the tears subsided, she plucked a kerchief from her sleeve and dabbed at her eyes and nose. She fidgeted with her hair and mopped ineffectively at the wetness on his shoulder. "I am so sorry, Edward. Even if you are back, even if you have returned, you will not want me! What man of honor would want a widow who is mother to a child of another man?" She sobbed and the tears came into her eyes once more.

Pierce's throat constricted, and tears began to pool in his own eyes. "Truly I am hurt by what has occurred. Yet that pain is so much less than what I felt being away from you. You ask who would want you? I tell you now, upon my sacred oath, that I would. I would!"

She cried once more, the great sobs violently shaking her. Tears spilled forth and her nose ran. Then her arms were about him, grasping, clinging, and holding him tightly to her. He cried too--quietly, less demonstratively, but still he cried. Stiff upper lip be damned! He cried!

Then they were not crying with sadness and despair, but rather from joy and happiness. His lips sought hers, and they kissed. They tasted each other for the first time in many years, that first taste seasoned with the salt and quenched by the moisture of the other's tears.

CPSIA information can be obtained at www.ICGtesting.com
Printed in the USA
BVOW03s1802170114

342095BV00001B/1/P

9 781478 721895